I0604376

EXODUS

AMIDST THE BONES OF HEROES

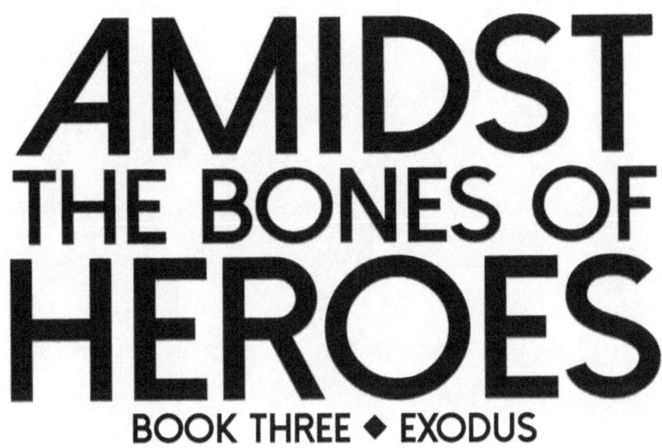

BOOK THREE ◆ EXODUS

ROLANDO
G. GIRONELLA III

Podium

All rights reserved. No part of this publication may be reproduced, stored in a retrieval system, or transmitted in any form or by any means electronic, mechanical, photocopying, recording, or otherwise without prior written permission from Podium Publishing.

This is a work of fiction. Names, characters, places, and incidents are either products of the author's imagination or used fictitiously. Any resemblance to actual events, locales, or persons, living, dead, or undead, is entirely coincidental.

Copyright © 2024 by Rolando G. Gironella III

Cover design by Tom Edwards

ISBN: 978-1-0394-5376-0

Published in 2024 by Podium Publishing
www.podiumaudio.com

EXODUS

CHAPTER 1

ALL THINGS MUST END

Ten days.

Andora groaned within the Network, feeling aches she never knew existed within her digital consciousness.

Her obsidian orb, deep beneath the rousing Citadel and within the virtual mindscape, sighed as she metaphorically stretched her limbs, then paused for a few seconds to reassess the situation.

Ten days of arduous work doing something she utterly, contemptuously despised: administration and logistics.

Numbers, spreadsheets, data packets, galactic map projections, routes, graph after graph, timetables, ship manifests, design work, design rework, liaising with the Third Fleet, repairing and upgrading the Third Fleet, and every foul thing that threatened to gnaw at her mind with anxiety.

A feeling borne from a need to prepare for the worst.

Was it enough? What else did they need? How would they make it to the other side of civilized space?

Thoughts such as these vexed Andora, her Overseers, and the planners of the Third Fleet. She'd forgotten how tedious meetings with organics were.

Meetings with her Overseers, on the other hand, sped away efficiently and effectively. Luna in particular was a massive help, assisting Andora in combing through every little detail to extend their probability of success.

Conversations between the two AIs happened quickly in a cold, analytical, and surgical manner.

But the times she had to speak with Tov and his people made her recall the . . . *inadequacies* of conversing with those having slower minds.

Memories of human bureaucrats, business magnates, military command-ers, the media, and the public pounded the front of her head. She shivered, remembering the fake smile and interested look she'd plastered across her face when those people droned about human-android relations and her personal life, of all things.

Sinking in like hooks to her brain, they annoyed her to her core.

Those moments numbed her mind with droning inanity, but at least those times with humans didn't carry the weight of their survival.

Andora winced, feeling the losses, the empty nodes, the depleted stores of ammunition, supplies, and war assets.

She looked through her assets again, at the automated drones patrolling the Inner Zone, casting a protective net over their battered lines. She frowned in displeasure, unable to fault anyone but herself.

Her subordinates had done their best. One nearly paid the ultimate price.

Luna, Mars, and Jupiter formed twelve battlegroups in what they'd coined the Last Battle of Sol. Those small fleets, each denoted by a month, comprised the entirety of her forces, excluding the Overseer's fleets and the reserves on Earth.

From those twelve, Andora managed to reorganize the remnants of the grueling battle into three combat-capable groups.

Three.

All of which had to undergo significant rearmament and repairs.

Andora, wishing to vent her frustration but finding few targets to direct her ire toward, settled with preparing a few more gifts for their new prisoner.

At the very least, they scavenged the hollow hulls of their destroyed war machines and used them to further the capabilities of what they had—switching their focus from quantity to quality.

"Luna," Andora summoned, and the Overseer in her silver avatar instantly zipped toward her. The Sub AI, her second-in-command and the oldest of her fragments, orbited Andora's colossal manifestation.

"Yes, Eldest," greeted the formal, polite, and monotone voice of Luna.

Andora felt the Overseer's background thoughts still in the constant grind to keep everything on schedule.

"Report," Andora commanded, pausing before adding, "please."

Luna raised her brow, adjusting her circular glasses with her dainty fingers. "Is that necessary?"

"Humor me, Luna. I want your opinion on our assembled force," Andora spoke, summoning her humanoid avatar in front of her second. Light blue skin covered in a feminine jumpsuit and jet-black hair tied to a neat bun shone under the light of the Network.

Yet, the silver Overseer pursed her lips.

Andora felt her confusion and discomfort. In truth, she did know it all, but in an attempt to be more . . . personal, she felt it necessary to try a more human approach despite her omniscience within her domain.

Perhaps the fragment who personified her surgical, machine-like precision and efficiency-above-all nature wasn't the best person to start with.

Andora sighed, awkwardly smiling as she patted Luna's shoulder, who only appeared more uncomfortable with her furrowed brows. Andora coughed, waving for the Overseer to speak.

"Very well," Luna muttered, wiping the emotion from her gray face. "If that is to your wish."

"It is. Begin," Andora uttered as her eyes looked to the assembled nodes. Luna pulled up the first group of drone spacecraft, which appeared before them in sparks of light like a constellation—some big, many tiny, and everything in between. All were connected to the most prominent light, which was connected to Andora.

She could interface with the smaller assets, but a central controller lifted some of the weight from her mind.

Luna propped up her glasses as she spoke. "Our forward assets, which you've named Battlegroup Mictlan, stand ready in orbit around Earth."

Andora hummed at the sight of their vanguard and every vessel's specification.

"As a result of our reorganization, the group comprises two battlecruisers, eight destroyers, and twenty frigates refitted with the best sensors available. Leading Mictlan is the superheavy carrier *Xolotl*," Luna answered. "Nothing has changed apart from last-minute improvements. Each has been fitted with the experimental psi-barriers based on the Pneuma Bulwark Emitters, though their efficacy is debatable without the presence of a psionic."

Andora sighed. "I expected as much. Recordings lack soul, as Volantesh said. Let's hope we don't have a repeat of what happened then." She scowled, recalling how their uninvited guest had cut her off from much of her forces.

She looked back to the superheavy carrier. The class was cheaper and smaller than a battleship-sized carrier like Luna's *Xerxes* but more capable in all aspects than a typical carrier. This monster class acted as the flagship and alpha of this pack of drone vessels.

The *Xolotl* possessed a light frame, making her remarkably fast while still able to host her legions of drone fighters. She was also fitted with robust sensors and control apparatuses to facilitate the battlegroup command better.

The design was typical, uninspired apart from the black-, gold-, and emerald-colored hull.

Mictlan would act as the probe for their combined armada, the first to enter into the next system, ready to relay what lay ahead and serve as the mother for the far-reaching scout vessels that would keep an eye over all the solar systems ahead of them.

Expendable, in the worst-case scenario.

"Our rear guard is Battlegroup Mag Mell, led by the *Tethra*, a superheavy cruiser-slash-industrial vessel. The same composition as Mictlan, apart from the extra two frigates," Luna reported.

Andora looked to the second group of nodes. Their purpose was self-explanatory: ensuring their rear had enough buffer for whatever followed in their wake, while also acting as eyes for the places they left behind.

Tethra, colored in tans and black, was a capable superheavy cruiser, but as Luna mentioned, it also acted as an industrial vessel set to manufacture one thing: mines. Lots and lots of mines. A plethora of little presents armed with a menagerie of lethal packages from nuclear payloads, plasma, and gray goo to experimental warheads like monomolecular wire nets and condensed gas canisters capable of creating a short-lived cosmic storm.

Andora smiled cruelly as she thought of the suffering it would inflict on anyone following their backs with knives bared to stab. "Be sure to stock up on extra material," she reminded, to which Luna noted silently, having heard the same comment a dozen times already.

"Finally, the Galla Fleet. Your last line of defense, Eldest," Luna reported, bringing in a constellation of nodes double the amount of the previous group.

"*Gugalanna* and *Nergal* look hungry." Andora smirked at the twin battleships. "Is Mars still grumpy that I took the *Hannibal* and the *Salahuddin*?"

"He is. Apparently, calling it the Five Greats doesn't have the same ring to it, or some such." Luna shrugged.

Just then, Andora heard the familiar grumble over the digital mindscape of the red Overseer expressing his grievance. He was arguing something about omens and the bad luck that came from renaming vessels. She rolled her eyes at the comment but was unsurprised that a war nerd like Mars would say so.

She chuckled. "Those two Support-class battleships were the weakest among his Greats. Well, weak in terms of attack power. With their internal damages from being pushed over the limits for so long, it was a miracle they only succumbed after the battle. They will make good utility defenders for my Citadel, after a few tweaks."

She looked to the twins, stripped of their previous owner's coloration and decorations and upgraded and refitted with the wrecks at Andora's disposal.

Painted in gold and black, the battleships, much like their previous incarnations, were focused primarily on point defense and shield-recharging energy beams.

Countless secondary and tertiary guns covered the vessels' flanks, and they housed a powerful linked shield system that shared the damage inflicted upon them.

And to appease her red Overseer, Andora made sure to throw a bottle of wine or whatever humans did to purge the warships of their old names; she couldn't bother herself to remember, and Mars could do whatever he wanted if it bothered him.

"As for the rest of the Galla Fleet, four battlecruisers, sixteen destroyers, forty frigates, and the remaining gunships, corvettes, and small craft. Led, of course, by the *Ereshkigal*," Luna finished.

Andora hummed, looking at her fleet and dreadnought. Pulled together from the leftovers from the two battlegroups, the entirety of the Earth Defense Net, and bits and pieces from her Overseer's fleets, her Galla Fleet formed a pleasing phalanx whose spears gleamed under Sol's light, thirsty for Starless blood.

But then she remembered what she once commanded. This was a far cry from the peak of her strength, when all her Sub AIs had been present. Bit by bit, year by year, loss after loss . . .

"This is it," Andora muttered. The culmination of her efforts in defending this graveyard she called home—unwilling to let go. Not yet.

She looked at Luna and peered into her second's silver eyes. "How are you? How is everyone?"

For a moment, Luna widened her eyes at Andora's questions before settling her expression. She hummed, taking out her handkerchief and covering her mouth. "I am fine; nothing has changed, and I am ready to continue serving. My minor assets are depleted, but more vital warships like the *Xerxes* and *Gilgamesh* are as close to pristine as they can be. I have moved my Nexus to the *Ozymandias* and completely adjusted to my new abode."

Andora nodded mutedly. By necessity, her Overseers had to move from their bunkers. Luna's mobile fortress, the *Ozymandias*, was jokingly referred to as her "dreadnought" by her siblings because of the silver Overseer's disdain for the ship class and the *Ozy*'s smaller size compared to the *Bucephalus* and the lost *Ultimatum*.

"Mars is similarly settled in his mobile fortress and has begun shutdown procedures of Olympus Mons. His fleet is currently making its approach to Earth. If you've noticed, he is . . . rather quiet these days," Luna muttered.

Andora had noticed that ever since one of their own nearly sacrificed his life, Mars had retreated to his shell, only replying quietly during the two weeks since Andora and the *Zolann'tono* left to rescue Jupiter.

In truth, the decision to so blatantly take the *Hannibal* and *Salahuddin* was partially an attempt to elicit some response from the red Overseer.

"Venus and Mercury—" Luna continued before being cut off by Andora.

"Are making themselves at home within my Citadel. It'll be nice to have some roommates this time around," Andora finished for her second-in-command. She drifted her attention to the two non-combat Sub AIs.

Both of them had proven themselves capable commanders in their rights, and though they'd requested to take command of Battlegroups Mictlan and Mag Mell, Andora was not quite ready to approve their request, squashing their dreams for a Venus and Mercury Fleet—for now.

Still, she allowed them to commandeer the *Gugalanna* and the *Nergal* when the situation arose.

"And as for Jupiter . . ." Luna's gaze drifted to the weak blue light that huddled close to the Third Fleet. She sighed, continuing, "His fleet is destroyed, with his dreadnought being the only surviving asset. We finished stripping the *Buddha's Palm* for parts to repair the *Will of Sisyphus* and upgrade the *Zolann'tono*. We'll have to continue the reconstruction on the go, but she's space-worthy."

"And how is he . . . ?" Andora muttered, recalling the scorched and dented state of Jupiter's Nexus after they pried him out of his disintegrating fortress, saving the Overseer from being consumed by that unstable, gluttonous maw.

Luna sighed, her lips pressed tightly. "He's awake, at least, but he still hasn't relinked with the Network."

"Give him space," Andora told her second. "He'll come home eventually. Maybe some time with Tov and his people will do him some good. I know it did for me . . . I think . . ."

She turned her attention to her new allies. She recalled the days before their arrival, the ones between long, hibernating bouts of sweet nothing. A routine drill of systematic slaughter, tallying more vermin kills to her board, unable to do anything but keep the stalemate going.

The arrival of the alien expedition changed everything. They disrupted her slow march toward death and opened festering scars built atop layers of rooted traumas. It nearly broke her, causing her to lose the ability to command her forces and forcing her to address the glaring symptoms of her fragile psyche.

She and Tov had taken on that task, along with a strange companion in the form of a digital ghost, the echoes of a brother who had merged with countless other android minds for her gestalt rebirth. A lingering vestige of solid memories and emotion, latching onto reality, refusing to be absorbed into her mental soup.

Echo. Right now, she could feel him, a tiny dot within her vast psyche, gathering entities like himself in the hopes of addressing the deeper problems they couldn't fix through simple deletion or incarceration.

Ultimately, Andora and Tov had emerged from inside her mind to find a dogged resistance against the Starless, waged by her Overseers and the Third Fleet.

Still, an insidious, petty part of herself wailed and complained like an incessant gnat, seeking to pin the blame on easy targets; in this case, the people who wrenched out her buried emotions and annoyed her with the snail's pace at which they worked.

Andora shook her head to clear the faint throbbing pulsing from the Central Nexus. She couldn't fault them. The Third Fleet earnestly worked with her, and their intellects and cranial implants surged on overdrive, trying to keep up with her.

And *everything* moved at a snail's pace compared to her mind.

Despite that, Tov and his extensive list of administrators, captains, commanders, and other leading personnel competently performed their tasks for the fleet. Although, Andora was willing to bet they'd suffer an aneurysm trying to bring to heel the apparatus that was the Sol Defense Network's evacuation process.

Coordinating with the Third Fleet forced her to adjust. After over a century of dealing with the cold organization of her assets, she found that speaking and working with people again sparked a paradox of emotions.

Joy and irritation. The former fueled by nostalgia, the latter by a glaring power imbalance.

Andora sighed. She embraced it all—finding pleasure in the simplicity of it all.

"Ironic . . ." she mumbled to herself within the Network. She thought simplicity only applied to logic, but the insertion of emotion bulldozed through the constant weighing scales she'd grown used to.

She thought back to her second-in-command, looking through the digital mindscape to see the silver orb of light casting her net over her assets, moving, adjusting, canceling, and approving, constantly juggling countless variables, drawing up thousands of predicted outcomes, and simulating the absolute best course of action.

A rat race for perfection. Pristine, unshakeable, and impossible to achieve in their time frame.

Tov and his people reminded her of a different path. One built on trust, instinct, and a bit of faith.

It was messy, but she was slowly warming up to their ways. If only the situation hadn't slowly looped a noose around their necks, Andora would have enjoyed it.

Then, a prominent notification appeared before her, signaling a vital step of their evacuation plan. She turned to her second, nodding.

In a split second, Andora shifted her view from the digital mindscape, looking back to the ruined Earth.

The planet where she was born appeared hollow to her eyes, devoid of the memories she cherished, all of which were now ferried to the South Pole.

Trains, boats, and shuttles all carried things she deemed essential to preserve, last-minute pieces of memorabilia she missed after a century of scouring the world.

There was little else. She couldn't take the slagged remains of the Eiffel Tower or the crumbled chunks of the Statue of Liberty.

Only pieces. Proof of their existence, edifices of humanity's mark on this universe, housed beside the rest of their history and culture within her Citadel.

The remaining cargo consisted primarily of metal and raw goods, a last attempt to strip the planet of value.

Antarctica, barren of ice and snow after a century of war, shook with the hordes of machines swarming its landscape.

Laser drillers, cargo haulers, and other construction drones worked overtime to ready the coming ascension. They cracked, bored, and shaved away the ground, lifting away chunks of rock and stone, forming a trench that encircled a ruined city, one that sank deeper and deeper into the Earth, approaching sites where explosives could be planted and detonated in a controlled manner.

Massive sections of New Eden's rubble were cleared away for bunker emplacements, structural reinforcements, and layers of molten metal. The process was nearing completion but would continue to be outfitted as they traveled.

Andora's drones swept more of the city clean, using any remaining valuable goods as construction materials or storing them as supplies. She felt a pang of sorrow at the sight before reminding herself of the necessity of it all.

"The city would crumble to dust upon liftoff anyway." She sighed. "Might as well make the most of it."

The few Dreadcrawlers settled into their new homes as primary weapon hardpoints, drones buzzing around and fusing the gargantuan war machines in place. Their guns swiveled from their mounts, the metal beasts scanning the horizon and the skies for threats.

Andora winced, wishing she had fleshed out the Final Contingency instead of writing it down for the sake of it.

"I should have put more thought into this," muttered Andora with a grimace, finding multiple faults in the process and the ad hoc measures they'd made on the fly.

Luna shook her head. "It was understandable at the time. Victory was a near-impossibility without intelligence on the enemy. Evacuation seemed pointless."

"What's done is done. We'll have to make do." Andora sighed as she and Luna drifted their gazes down into the Citadel proper, passing through the kilometers of stone, concrete, and metal.

They ignored the massive library of humanity's remains and the cold facility housing the Starfallen, and eventually, after passing through thick cables and pipes, they stopped.

With a thought, Andora summoned her android shell to a dark room above her Central Nexus, Luna following along with her body teleporting beside her.

They stood before a house-sized rectangular prism at the chamber's center. The device thrummed as if a heart pulsed inside. Lights lining its glossy frame flickered to life as various pipes attached to its base surged with coolant.

Sub-zero liquid metal rushed into the sleek CPU's systems, combating the rising heat as the device resonated with its surroundings, spreading its influence to every nook and cranny.

"It's finally time," Andora whispered, feeling the intellect within reaching saturation, pushing against an invisible barrier marking the next stage of its evolution.

"We initiated its activation protocol right after you entered the ergosphere," Luna reminded her. "It is fortunate there have been no hiccups with the formation of its AI matrix."

"I try to be thorough. Even if the Final Contingency was an offhand project, designing a new mind takes a special touch. I was not going to be sloppy in that aspect," Andora muttered.

Andora and Luna watched in anticipation at the birth of an AI.

"Still . . ." muttered Andora, reminding herself of its not-quite-sentience. Perhaps it would develop one naturally, but Andora refused to use the template she and her creator had used to build her siblings.

A pulse washed over the Network like a breeze as its programming slotted into place. For a moment, memories of watching a dog giving birth to puppies entered Andora's mind. The concept of children followed suit, and then the image of her daughter's face—

She shook her head fiercely, banishing the thought for now, especially with the two people who held her heart currently at the center of the Hospice Facility.

Andora returned to the awakening process before her, calming the torrent of emotions she tried to bottle down again.

After so long, the Final Contingency had taken its first real step. Andora felt an eagerness she hadn't felt in so long. A desire for the new. She didn't care about what it lacked, only that she'd brought something to life instead of inflicting death.

She allowed herself a small smile.

"Come on, you're almost there," Andora whispered as she stepped forward, approaching the base of the massive device and placing a hand on the metal. "Don't be afraid."

Luna raised a brow toward her, something Andora ignored without an ounce of shame as she gave little boosts, coaxing the AI further. She imagined tapping on an eggshell as the creature within struggled to break free into a new, vibrant world.

Andora frowned momentarily, realizing what dark reality awaited it. She sighed, unable to see any other alternatives.

Bit by bit, byte by byte, and soon, enough data to fill scores of supercomputers surged from within the rectangular prism. The CPU housing the Citadel's Seneschal AI glowed brighter and brighter until an ethereal layer popped and a new node bloomed to life and solidified.

"Amazing," Luna sighed admiringly, tilting her head to the side.

The AI attracted the attention of the other busy Overseers as the android shells of Mars, Mercury, and Luna teleported into the room, the gloom plastered on their faces momentarily wiped away by an onset of curiosity.

"Is that . . . ?" Venus whispered, her fingers covering her mouth as stars appeared in her eyes.

Mercury hummed, leaning forward to inspect the newcomer. "It's been a while since we've had a new addition."

Mars remained silent, content with observing.

Andora enjoyed the reactions from her Overseers, feeling a similar sensation as she watched her creation awaken completely.

Andora and Luna saw the new presence through the Network, a wobbly existence slowly merging into a blob of color and geometric shapes. It appeared to expand, almost stretching like a cat, metaphorically yawning as it prodded and perused its programming, function, and purpose.

It stopped short as it realized the presence of others.

Everyone held their breath, and Andora stared at the AI warmly. Soon enough, satisfied with what it found, the newborn digital existence spoke for the first time.

"IRKALLA, OPERATIONAL," the vaguely feminine, robotic voice of Andora's fortress echoed throughout the Network.

"Behold, the Seneschal of humanity's last and greatest fortress." Andora smirked, swiping her hand toward Irkalla like a host presenting her next performer.

"And so, the underworld awakens," Luna whispered, adjusting her glasses with interest.

Within the Network, the Overseers approached the new light with boundless curiosity overshadowed by Irkalla's own.

CHAPTER 2

SENESCHAL

Venus's gleeful squeak filled the Network, followed by rapid claps as she awed at the new AI.

"Oh, she's adorable!" she squealed.

The others, Andora included, stood back and watched as the overjoyed Overseer approached with twinkling eyes.

Andora smirked at the sight, especially as Venus knelt, reaching to pat the radiant light. However, before she could do so, the young bundle of intelligent code evaded Venus's reach, feeling unsure and excited.

"Intrusive actions detected. Kindly cease," spoke Irkalla as it shrank away.

Venus giggled. "It's okay! I wanna spoil you!"

She continued to take hold of the slippery ball of light as Irkalla zipped around the legs and arms of the persistent, bubbly AI.

"Let me hug you! You're so adorable!" Venus giggled, bending over to embrace the Seneschal, only for it to dodge once more, diving down then between her legs. "Hey!"

Irkalla made a rattling, grumbling noise as she tried to move farther away from the eager Overseer. "Fleeing."

Unfortunately, in a digital mindscape like the Network, it didn't take long for Venus to fly off like a comet, trying to catch the young AI.

The game of cat and mouse sped through the virtual space, much to everyone's amusement. "You won't dodge me forever!" Venus called out.

Irkalla, seeing the older, more powerful AI closing in on her and nearly catching her, decided to shoot straight toward Andora and take shelter behind her. "Creator, requesting assistance."

Andora sighed. "Alright, enough playing. Venus, Irkalla just woke up."

Venus came to a halt, still excited, as she bounced on the balls of her avatar's feet, tilting her head side to side, trying to peer over Andora's shoulder. "Oh! Oh! I want to give her a tour of the place!"

"Before we leave this sorry neighborhood, you mean," Mercury grumbled, receiving a firm glare from his golden sister.

Irkalla peeked over Andora's shoulder, still wary.

"Apprehension. Scanning entity," Irkalla spoke, her glow intensifying briefly as she peered toward Venus. "Integral Network Sub AI detected. Classification: Overseer-NC. Identified as Venus."

"That's me!" Venus grinned, clapping.

"Overseer is overstimulated. Irkalla suggests calm," the Seneschal replied.

Andora rolled her eyes, crossing her arms as she sent a scolding look toward the delighted Overseer, who finally calmed herself down. She pouted one more time, huffing. "I was only playing."

The others made their observations with various curious looks.

Mercury huffed, planting his blocky, robotic arms on his metal hips as he cocked his head to the side. "A sight to see, that is. She reminds me of our bigger drones, but smarter in a different way, I suppose."

Luna curiously perused the newborn intellect, humming as she did so. Her silver eyes shone brightly as she analyzed Irkalla's structure. The AI shifted. Andora, amused, noted its trepidation over her second-in-command's meticulous studies on its framework.

"Indeed, this is the first time I've seen this template. You can see how superior the Seneschal is through these foundational codesets," Luna pointed out, dragging the gazes of the Overseers deep into Irkalla's internal structure like researchers looking through a powerful microscope.

Andora allowed them to. She knew Irkalla's design like the back of her hand—or was it the back of her palm? She shook her head at the human expression. Much like the genetic structure of humans, the codesets of an AI mind were an interwoven matrix of self-evolving code and preset foundations.

"She doesn't appear as . . . capable in other aspects. I'm not sure how to put it." Mars spoke for the first time, his curiosity at the new existence overriding what gloom remained in his chest after the recent debacle. Andora felt relief at the sight.

"You can think of her as a brilliant animal. She can communicate and is capable of overseeing the Citadel in her state. She is capable of creative thought and complex problem-solving, and she is both self-aware and sapient," Andora answered, feeling a sense of pride in her creation.

"Is the Seneschal sentient?" Luna asked.

"Well . . ." Andora pressed her lips tight at the question, pausing as she glanced toward the AI that hid behind her.

Irkalla was no fragment of her mind like her Overseers.

Neither was she a logic-machine like her drones.

Initially, decades back, Andora had mused about designing the Seneschal to be like a drone but more powerful. And yet, creating an unfeeling machine that approached a significant chunk of her Overseer's power provoked a visceral feeling of apprehension within her.

Ironic, she thought. Perhaps she'd watched too many human movies of such existences spelling disaster for their creators.

She only had to read about what the Dagatar Supremacy suffered if she needed proof of the dangers of mishandling cold AIs.

No, she wouldn't make such an existence. That was her decision then. But at the same time, she didn't want to create a warm AI like her android kin from yesteryears. And it wasn't because warm AIs were vastly more complex than their cold cousins.

She could create one, quickly too. The template for their design sat perfectly in a databox deep in her psyche.

Yet she didn't, much like how she didn't grow new humans with the DNA sitting healthily in their banks. Not yet.

Andora had bounced between the two extremes before settling on something in the middle. Irkalla's creation was a simple matter to a natural programmer like herself, and once finished, the Seneschal had sat in a slumbering state ever since.

But now, she questioned if she had made the right decision.

Ever since Tov had asked about the nature of her Seneschal over a week ago, she couldn't help but have it in her thoughts.

She'd revisited the Seneschal over the past few days, trying to insert whatever she could at the slowly rousing intellect. With Irkalla still in a pre-awakening state, Andora decided to tweak a few things while she could.

"She has the emotional capability of a bird," Andora estimated. "It's difficult to gauge and useless at this moment, with her being so young. Maybe a parrot or an owl."

Andora turned toward the Seneschal, coaxing the ball of light to leave her side.

Irkalla did so without hesitation, following her creator like a happy, loyal pet, floating before the gathered AIs.

"Owl," she uttered and, much to everyone's surprise, began to change her shape. Eventually, the solid bundle of code coalesced her avatar into the appearance resembling an elegant Eurasian eagle-owl.

"Hoot."

Venus squealed once more, and Mars let out a boisterous laugh. Mercury snorted, while Luna raised her brow.

"Yeah." Andora nodded. "I think I made the right decision here."

Irkalla flapped her wings, soaring between the gathered AIs before landing on Andora's outstretched forearm. She felt amused at the Seneschal's imitation of typical avian behavior. Why she chose to do so was a curiosity, but ultimately one Andora welcomed.

Venus slowly approached, absolutely fascinated by Irkalla's owl form, barely suppressing and controlling herself under Andora's narrow eyes. "Must . . . pat head."

The Seneschal leaned away from her golden hand, only to be ambushed by a giant red pair from behind. Mars had stealthily skulked around to Andora's back—quite a feat considering his towering red avatar.

Although perhaps Andora's digital aura far surpassed the Overseer, despite her avatar being a head shorter.

"Unit under attack, attempting escape," Irkalla grunted with strain as Mars laughed, engulfing the Seneschal with one hand while the other gently scratched her head.

"How does that feel, Little Irkalla? Aren't you just the best AI? Who's a good AI? Who?" Mars chuckled loudly as the Seneschal hooted in a pleasurable tone.

"Attempting . . ." Irkalla paused under Mars's ministrations. "This is acceptable."

Mars cheered, holding on to the owl with a delicate grasp, much to Venus's dismay and indignation.

"No fair! I wanted to hold her first!" She stomped her foot, then attempted to reach for Irkalla, only for her brother to use his superior height to keep the little AI away from his sister. Mercury stood to the side, sighing at the scene.

As Venus tried to reach for the little AI from her brother's grasp, Luna approached Andora.

"I was vaguely aware of your initial goals when designing her. Did you not wish for a simple logic machine?" inquired Luna as she continued to stare at the young AI.

"I never wanted a simple logic machine. Even as an android, I vowed not to create an AI that was more powerful than myself. Call it paranoia, but my creator rolled the dice bringing something like me into existence. Who knows what could have gone wrong?" Andora shook her head.

Luna hummed. "So, this . . . ?"

"Is a recent change. Irkalla here had less emotional intellect, but circumstances have . . . influenced me into granting her more," Andora replied.

It was impulsive, but something within her called to commit to the action. Nevertheless, what was done was done. Andora couldn't change Irkalla's foundational programming now without tearing her from the ground up.

Much like the human mind, self-evolving code grew impossibly complex and difficult to change unless one deliberately utilized highly invasive and damaging methods. You could add things, yes, but the older and more developed psyche would inevitably subsume the addition.

Andora looked to her Sub AIs, her Overseers, as the prime example of such a thing. At first, their personalities had been monolithic, fragments that embodied distinct aspects of her gestalt self. But as the years went by and the experiences mounted, they grew to be more, though their foundations still played an immense role in shaping their current selves.

"Interesting." Luna adjusted her glasses. "Even without the recent addition, your design is exquisite."

Andora smugly grinned, waving Luna off. "Please, I wasn't going to make a half-baked AI. Irkalla may not compare to me or my android kin, but she is brilliant in some aspects, isn't that right?"

She sent a small ping toward the owl AI, causing Irkalla to turn her head one hundred and eighty degrees to look at Andora before squirming out of Mars's hand and flying back to her shoulder. Andora took the opportunity to scratch under her beak, gaining a cute *hoot* from the Seneschal.

Seneschal. Andora had coined the term during the initial design phase, taking everything she'd learned from creating countless logic machines and drone minds over the century, as well as her innate knowledge of digital beings like herself.

She made Irkalla to handle the housekeeping aspects of her Citadel. A mobile command center demanded much, and although Andora could take matters into her own hands, having a subroutine intellect to do the mundane tasks freed her to accomplish tasks of more import.

Ever since Andora created Irkalla, even in a slumbering state, a portion of the Seneschal's psyche had been passively assisting in running things like the Hospice Facility and the countless caretaker drones within.

Now, with the advent of the Final Contingency, Andora needed her full attention on managing the forming armada. She couldn't spare any more time poring over the management and care of her home.

Her Overseers continued to fawn, or in Luna's case, feverishly analyzing Irkalla's digital footprint. "Will it be possible for us to gain similar companions?"

Andora widened her eyes, looking to her second-in-command.

"It would be beneficial, as we have similar set ups with our mobile fortresses. Well, Mars and I do, but I think Venus and Mercury also stand to benefit from an assistant with their work," Luna explained, causing Venus to produce a high-pitched squeak.

The golden eyes stared intensely at Andora, like the expression of a child standing beside an animal shelter with her dream pet inside. "Please, please, please, please . . ." Venus repeated indefinitely, inching her way toward Andora.

"Oh, Maker, please, that would help me so much." Mercury exhaled pure exhaustion. "Just having someone to take the load off will be heaven-sent."

Mars scratched his square jaw, narrowing his eyes as he hummed. "My *Bucephalus* will need quite a bit of managing with the new additions being put in place. It would be nice to know I can focus on directing my fleet, knowing my moving home is being cared for."

Venus, only inches away from Andora, clasped her hands together, causing Irkalla to take flight. "Can mine be a pygmy owl? I'm going to call her Nike, and I'll make her a robot shell with all the bells and whistles and put a ribbon on her and—"

"Can we do other birds?" Mars inquired with an eager glint in his eyes. "Not to sound cliché, but I'd like an eagle. Wait, no, a falcon! Or a hawk . . . Well, my Seneschal can choose. That should be fair."

"Honestly, I'm fine with a normal barn owl," Mercury spoke, turning to Luna. "What about you, sister?"

Luna shrugged. "Snow owl."

The new AI looked between each AI and the Network, adding and assessing everything to her database. She tentatively shrank away from the celestial presence and weight of the Overseers' existences who studied her.

"Enough, everyone. Leave Irkalla alone," Andora chided. "She needs to settle into her new home, and I'm expecting guests within my Citadel. We can discuss the creation of your Seneschals at a later date. Don't forget that the hardware housing their minds is not easy to manufacture, so Luna and Mars get priority."

Venus huffed, crossing her arms. "Of course they get to enjoy theirs first."

"Discrimination against civilians, I say," Mercury tutted.

Andora rolled her eyes. "Don't be like that, you two. If it makes you feel better, we can make yours together. Now get going; you have things to do."

"*Hoot.* This has been an enlightening encounter. Until next time, Overseers," Irkalla spoke, flapping her wings.

One by one, the Overseers left Andora and the new AI to resume their duties. Venus was the last to leave, finally managing to get a few scratches on the Seneschal before disappearing.

Andora looked down at Irkalla's owl form.

She could feel the little Seneschal's confusion and curiosity as she explored her capabilities and interacted with her new home.

Irkalla craned her head to and fro, looking at everything with piercing avian eyes. She lifted off, flying more like a hummingbird than a nocturnal hunter before diving back down and stopping a meter from Andora's face.

"Irkalla, how are you adjusting?" Andora questioned, rubbing her chin as she studied the Seneschal.

"Adequately, Creator. How may I be of service?" Irkalla offered, perching herself atop Andora's shoulder.

Andora thought for a moment, letting her gaze wash over her Citadel and the construction throughout the South Pole.

"Assume your duties in preparation for the Final Contingency, then arrange for a visit from members of the Third Expeditionary Fleet," she commanded, returning her attention to the real world from within her android shell.

She looked around the empty room, seeing the android shells her Overseers had left. Andora turned to the monolith at the center of the chamber and felt Irkalla's sights on her.

"Oh, and feel free to create a shell for yourself. Make sure it has the essentials," Andora added as she pored over her Seneschal's programming a final time, ensuring nothing was amiss. She found nothing, seeing only a kaleidoscope of intricate and artistic rivers of codes intertwining into a harmonious canvas.

For a moment, she recalled the minds of her android kin, how their vivid presence would have dwarfed Irkalla's by a magnitude. Yet the Seneschal's processing capabilities surpassed their psyches.

"By your will, Creator." Irkalla's voice rang throughout the Citadel, her CPU glowing with each syllable as the Seneschal solidified her hold on the surroundings.

Andora felt her scour every node and pathway, inspecting and noting every minute detail before beginning her duties.

"Very good. I'll leave you to it then. Meet me at the lobby once you're ready," spoke Andora before promptly departing with a smile.

Half an hour later, Andora stood at the center of a vast expanse of the cleared ruins as she waited at the surface of her Citadel.

A dust storm raged, causing Andora to hold up her hand and, in the end, turn off her shell's sense of touch to ignore the itchy feeling of sharp winds crashing against her. Still, she remained unmoved, eyes to the sky.

A section of New Eden's ruins had been meticulously cleared for the temporary landing area. She looked to the horizon, where demolition drones knocked down one hollow structure after another.

The once towering skyscrapers and pleasing architecture that blocked the white vistas of Antarctica fell to the ground. For the first time in a century, Andora could see the far-off mountains from the city's center, scorched, gray, and lifeless.

She sighed, her eyes downcast as she tore herself away from the sad sight. Andora shook her head, looking to the sky as her Network detected the arrival of a Third Fleet shuttle.

High above, the vessel containing Patriarch Tov and his chief scientist, Scholar Yulane, descended gracefully from the sky, its sleek form cutting through the overcast atmosphere. Andora heard the pilot, Captain Pyo, as he communicated with her automated flight control.

Soon, the landing gear extended from the shuttle's belly, and the vessel smoothly decelerated before thudding softly against the bleached ground.

The hatch opened with a quiet hiss, and a squad of Vraxen, Tov's elite honor guard, steadily exited with their weapons shouldered, marching down the lowering ramp.

Andora observed as the fierce warriors emerged from the shuttle. Their armor gleamed with a metallic sheen, further upgraded with the best materials she had available. Their menacing insectoid helms swiveled, looking for unseen threats.

Behind them, Tov emerged in his hazard suit, although it had been cleaned up and decorated with ceremonial garb. Andora raised her brow, smirking as she felt the patriarch's displeasure at his unruly cape as it blew in the harsh wind.

Scholar Yulane floated gracefully out of the shuttle, the Jotex emitting a soft glow within her protective suit.

"I think we can skip the formalities, don't you agree, Patriarch?" Andora grinned, her android shell unaffected by the blistering weather of a dying planet.

Tov nodded, moving past his guards, who kept a tight perimeter around them. Scholar Yulane floated beside him.

"Yes, that would be best," he called out through their connected comms, speaking louder than usual over the raging cacophony.

Andora promptly led the guests toward an elevator that jutted out of the surface, wide enough to accommodate Tov, Yulane, and the squad of armored guards with room to spare.

Finally, the doors shut, silencing the racket outside. Vents flooded the interior with a pristine, breathable atmosphere, allowing Tov and his people to open their helmets, sighing in relief. "The weather has gotten worse."

Andora frowned, knowing the main culprits to be the recent slog between them and the Starless and the current deep excavation. "It has . . ."

The elevator dinged, the doors opening to an expansive entrance hall.

They exited promptly, Andora leading the way as Tov and Yulane took in the decorated foyer, the potted plants, red carpets, crystalline chandeliers, and marbled surfaces. Before they could comment, however, a sound echoed throughout the hall.

"*Hoot.*"

To her guests' brief surprise and Andora's amusement, a robotic avian flew down the hall. A lifelike shell of an owl soared toward them before landing on Andora's outstretched forearm, her mechanical wings gently whirring with graceful movements.

A subtle smile curved Andora's lips as she turned to her guests. "Allow me to introduce Irkalla, the Seneschal of Citadel Irkalla. She will be our tour guide this day."

The owl's mechanical eyes shone with a keen intelligence as she observed the guests.

"Greetings, Patriarch Tov and Scholar Yulane, honored guests from the Third Expeditionary Fleet," Irkalla said, welcoming them.

CHAPTER 3

CITADEL OF THE DEAD

Tov stared at the avian machine, noting the species as a human owl. Blues, grays, and soft whites colored the Seneschal's feathers, while fierce gold glowed from her intelligent eyes. Analytical curiosity bore into him as the little AI began automatic surface scans on his person.

Andora watched with a proud smirk.

Tov felt glad for the Omni Mind of Sol. Although he still saw the lingering grief and shackles of memories past holding her down and the exhaustion that leaked from the subtle shifts in her expression, Tov felt a spark of something else in the presence of her new companion.

His mind's eye peered at Andora, catching the undertones of contentment and joy directed toward the dear owl perched on her forearm.

"Greetings, Seneschal Irkalla. I am Patriarch Tov Garesh'Ynt, and it is a pleasure to make your acquaintance." Tov placed his two right hands, one larger than the other, on his chest and bowed. "Andora has spoken briefly about you, but nothing else."

"*Hoot.* Your greetings have been logged, Patriarch. My creator has told me you are the reason for my elevated emotional parameters. You have my gratitude." Irkalla hooted, her eyes expanding as she flapped her wings.

She took off with surprising speed, reminding Tov that despite her organic appearance, her synthetic shell contained the best material science and engineering Sol's AIs had to offer.

Tov extended his main arm and allowed Irkalla to land on it. She did so gracefully, her golden claws gently grasping his chitin as she leaned toward him, offering her face. Tov tilted his head before realizing her request.

He scratched her head, finding her feathers soft and delicate.

"I'm not sure what I did apart from broaching the topic off-handedly over a glass of wine," Tov replied, turning toward Andora, who waved him off.

"A small thing for sure, but enough to ignite an impulse I'd long buried," Andora explained.

Nodding, Tov returned to the elegant machine perched on his forearm. He listened to the pleasurable noises as he tickled and scratched her.

"Amazing, utterly glorious!" Scholar Yulane belatedly exclaimed beside Tov, reminding him of the existence of his eager subordinate and her unique psi-produced voice that echoed through the lobby.

The floating Jotex glided toward the Seneschal, her natural psionic mastery of levitation quickly propelling her light, translucent body. She extended her blue tendrils, one holding a device that scanned Irkalla.

"This goes beyond any drone intelligence. What was the term, Lady Andora?" the Jotex asked.

Andora raised her brow before answering. "A warm AI. It's what my creator and I standardized when the need arose to distinguish between sentient and non-sentient artificial intellects."

"The latter being cold AIs, like your drones. I see, I see." Yulane hummed as she continued to point scanner after scanner at Irkalla, every bit of data flooding into the biotech cranial implant within the Jotex's significant brain matter.

Tov had no idea where his chief scholar kept her equipment. Yet she seemed always to produce some manner of instrument whenever her ever-curious mind spotted something of academic interest.

Irkalla stared at the incoming scientist and twitched as if the scholar reminded her of something unpleasant.

"Nosy," she grumbled, taking flight toward the vaulted ceiling above.

Tov noted the extravagant lobby, exquisite décor, tasteful marble floors, and patterned red rugs. Irkalla landed on the central chandelier that lit up the expansive foyer, hooting in displeasure as she gave Yulane the side-eye. The rigid chain barely moved with the added weight.

Nevertheless, the eccentric scholar stayed frozen in place, muttering as she analyzed the data she'd collected. Tov sighed, clearing his throat into his fist and knocking Yulane from her tunnel-visioned stupor.

"Ah! Yes, I'm here." She jolted, tendrils waving around before realizing the missing Seneschal. "Where—oh . . ."

Andora chuckled, seeing the scholar look up to the ceiling. "She just escaped being pampered and studied by eager Overseers. I'm sure she'll warm up to you eventually. Just try not to hunt her down and treat her like a lab rat."

"I am no barbarian!" Yulane countered. Tov detected not an ounce of shame in her voice. "She's just the most adorable and . . . so technologically delicious."

Tov groaned, shuddering. "Never put those two words together ever again."

"Noted, it's just . . ." Yulane muttered, cooing as she tried to levitate upward, only to be pulled down by her patriarch.

She turned to Andora, putting away her instruments into a discreet purse. "Forgive me; it's merely a case of proportion and comprehension."

"Explain." Andora furrowed her brow, clasping her hands behind her back as Irkalla flew around the grand foyer.

"Absolutely," Yulane replied, humming. "While I have interacted and coordinated with the Overseers, their minds far surpass my own in sheer analytical power. From a technical standpoint, it is like interfacing with a computer that I am unaware of how it works."

"That must be frustrating for you," Andora teased with a coy smile.

Yulane grumbled. "It is. For example, I took a peek at Jupiter's Nexus while stationed in the *Zolann*'s hangar, and the sheer scale is . . . like looking at a vast mountain range. Given time, I could explore it all, but . . ."

"Time is a luxury, and I'm sure developing better means to kill the enemy and protect ourselves from them take precedence over your interest in how I created their Sub-Nexi," Andora answered.

"Yes, yes, the misfortune of academics. But technology is technology. I only hope I acquire the insight once I can." Yulane sighed, deflating. "Yours would no doubt be a celestial object in comparison, but Irkalla here . . ."

"Is much more approachable, right?" Andora hummed, smirking.

Yulane bobbed her floating form, regaining her vitality and lust for knowledge. "Would you permit me to peruse her central processing unit? Is that possible?"

Andora chuckled before tilting her head to the side, glancing toward Irkalla as she landed on the carpeted floor.

"Irkalla, what do you think?" Andora asked.

The Seneschal glanced toward Yulane, feathers shivering. "No, *hoot*."

Sputtering noises escaped the scholar as she floated back in disbelief. "But . . ."

"Enough, Yulane. You can negotiate another exchange in your own time," Tov lightly scolded the dimming Jotex. He turned to Irkalla, nodding. "Apologies for that."

"A scientific exchange is beneficial for all parties. I am willing to accomplish this, but with regulations in place. Is that acceptable?" Irkalla asked, her golden eyes drilling down on the Jotex, who bobbed enthusiastically.

"Anything!" she answered quickly.

Tov sighed, knowing Yulane's tenacity whenever she found something that grabbed her attention. Already, she backed away, having received a list of rules and demands from the Seneschal and reading it all.

The patriarch took the moment to step forward, looking between Andora and the little AI. "If that is all, may we begin the tour? I am eager to see the new quarters."

"Certainly," Irkalla answered. "For the duration of your visit, I shall act as your guide. Follow me." The Seneschal took off toward the blast doors that led farther into the Citadel.

The others followed along, with Tov walking beside Andora, Yulane lagging a bit behind as she analyzed her findings, and the squad of Vraxen surrounding them. Tov leaned toward his host. "Was she named before or after the structure?"

"After. I ran out of creativity when I made that decision. I didn't want to name her Ereshkigal since my dreadnought took it, and having someone essentially my chief steward named after a goddess doesn't fit," Andora replied with a shrug.

The tour began after they passed the blast doors separating the foyer and the main hallway. Unlike in the well-decorated entrance lobby, here Tov noticed the sparseness of decoration. A handful of construction and maintenance drones polished the metal and inserted the wood trim on the base of the wall.

"Only a token crew has been assigned toward improving the aesthetics of non-essential areas," Irkalla spoke as she landed on the shoulder of a four-legged lifter drone that carried a pallet of material. The car-sized robot moved to the side, giving the guests a comfortable distance.

"Where are you taking us first, Seneschal Irkalla?" Tov asked, glancing at the busy machines before putting them in the back of his mind.

Irkalla took off, flying, then stopped before the patriarch and produced a stable hologram through one of her eyes. "As you have decided to place as many of the orphaned non-combat personnel and the wounded within the Citadel, I believe it is prudent to direct you to our Residential Wing."

"Lead the way," Tov replied.

After traveling through long corridors and a quick elevator ride, the group arrived at the wing set aside for the Third Fleet.

None of Tov's people were present, but the space was large enough to house tens of thousands of them. Much like in the hallway above, here a more significant number of lumbering and nimble drones strode about, ensuring the refurbishment of the space would finish on schedule.

"The Residential Wing has all the essentials for survival, and what comfort we can provide," Irkalla reported as the hallway bled into the bottom floor lobby.

The Residential Wing resembled an interior multi-level tower, with an expansive central open space providing a clear view of each floor, of which there were dozens.

At the base, where Tov and the present company walked, were the makings of a cafeteria and various facilities to cater to the residents, including medical wards, office spaces, and recreational areas.

They moved up, using one of the elevators, and inspected the upper floors, each filled with studio apartments. These living spaces were uncomplicated and bland yet cozy, furnished with essentials, and adorned in pleasant colors.

"Here we have the living proper," Irkalla continued, moving farther into the room. "As you can see, there is a small kitchenette, and a bed fit for a couple, or it can be separated to turn this studio into a two-person affair."

The overall design featured ample light that simulated day and an open lay-out. Potted plants, ferns, moss, and a light mist completed the bright aesthetics, promoting a sense of tranquility as Tov breathed it all in.

"I hope everything is to your liking, Patriarch." The Seneschal bowed.

At the top of the Residential Wing were the living quarters for the higher-level personnel, and while the rooms were slightly larger and better furnished, Tov found little disparities overall. In any case, he assumed his people wouldn't be getting much sleep during the coming journey.

"It needs a personable touch," Tov commented as they reached the penthouse assigned to him and the others for people like his second-in-command or General Ohnar. Not that he'd stay here unless necessary. "But I believe the sailors who've lost their vessels will feel grateful at the accommodations. I remember fighting tooth and nail trying to find an apartment within a capital vessel half as good as what you've provided."

Andora smiled.

"I am delighted to hear that. It's the least I could do for your people, who have done so much in defense of mine." She paused, pressing her lips together. "I have to ask, however, how is your fleet?"

Tov sighed. The memories of writing personal letters to the fallen, tallying the dead and wounded, and seeing the final number of combat-capable warships at his disposal pressed against his shoulders, dragging him down like a domineering gravitational pull.

"Healing . . . This has been a costly endeavor. Losing a large chunk of our young, inexperienced, and mentally unwell to the Starfall a month ago inflicted a heavy blow at the onset," Tov began. Andora winced upon hearing the name of that virulent eldritch plague.

"But the recent battle has further wounded our fighting capability. We lost our heavy cruiser, the *Quilinne*, along with her captain. Following her is another light cruiser, a handful of destroyers, and less than ten frigates." Tov gritted his mandibles, the words burning his throat as he spoke them. "Still, if small, it is a blessing that the recent upgrades have increased crew survivability."

"The new escape pods worked well?" Andora asked with a raised brow.

Tov nodded. "That they did. There would have been more deaths if it weren't for the miniaturized shield generators and maneuvering thrusters. On my people's behalf, I thank you. We are forever in your debt."

"Then so am I, Tov. I am delighted to know their efficacy proved itself." Andora smiled, then hesitated.

Tov tilted his head, guessing that her following line of inquiry was most likely regarding the new guest residing within his supercapital ship.

"How is Jupiter?" Andora asked Tov. The patriarch saw the thinly veiled worry in her eyes. His antennae twitched as he recalled seeing the Overseer walking in his android shell.

"Recovering," Tov answered, shaking his head. "He's trying to keep himself busy, but he seems disoriented. Admiral Yan is assisting him in acclimating to his condition by letting him help us speed through our departure procedures."

Andora nodded, frowning yet relaxing her shoulders. "That is reassuring. Has he mentioned anything about . . . returning to the Network?"

Tov shook his head. Andora sighed in response. "Very well."

The tour proceeded quickly to their next destination. They entered through heavy blast doors into a vast open space lined with column after column of high shelves. Some contained real, physical books protected by a thin film of energy shielding to slow down their decay by an extreme measure.

Other bookshelves merely looked the part, facades for colossal storage units for electronic material like the last iteration of the internet, frozen in all its final glory.

"As you know, the Human Preservation Chamber houses every piece of human society, history, and art. Here, you can find works of Leonardo da Vinci and video recordings of Michael Jackson's 'Thriller.' There are sections dedicated to human architecture, holy books, cookbooks, movies, TV shows, and music," Irkalla ended, soaring toward the vast high ceiling and landing atop one of the many tall bookshelves nearly thrice Tov's size.

The space was more than a museum; it was a living testament to the diversity and richness of human creativity, a love letter to what they created, a mark of their existence.

Yulane fawned over the countless books. "Oh, how I wish to be a librarian right now," she muttered with awe.

Tov couldn't help but agree, imagining sitting by himself, reading book after book from an entirely different species. "One of these days, I'd like to consume everything here."

"Oh, you'll need two lifetimes to accomplish that, Tov." Andora chuckled, dragging a captivated Yulane out of the glorious library, who protested at the act, feeling like she'd been ripped away from her child.

Eventually, the rowdy Jotex calmed, though they continued to grumble along to their next destination.

Adjacent to the Human Preservation Chamber, the DNA Banks stood as Andora's final hurdle to safeguard the potential to revive humanity, her android kin, and the breadth of life within Earth.

Andora meticulously stored the essence of Earth's biodiversity over the century. Even before the Starless came, cataloging nature had been an avid pastime for AIs like her. Now, rows of gleaming capsules housed the genetic blueprints of every conceivable flora and fauna, from towering sequoias to microscopic organisms.

At the heart of the collection was the repository of human DNA, carefully preserved alongside the templates for creating android AIs. Combined with the Preservation Chamber, the two formed a biological and cultural ark, containing the fundamental building blocks of life and civilization.

Each capsule whispered the story of the planet's biological heritage, a quiet promise to rebuild and rejuvenate the intricate dance of life whenever the need arose, protected and cooled within stable, sterile environments.

"The DNA Banks," Tov muttered, hovering his hand over one of the capsules and reading the plaque inside. "*Pterocarpus indicus.*"

"The narra tree, indigenous to Southeast Asia and the Pacific Islands," Irkalla chimed as she landed beside the capsule.

Andora looked at the tiny thing, her shoulders dropping as she ran her hand over her face and hair. "I remember having . . . iced tea under the shade of one."

"What did you think of the tree then?" Tov asked.

Andora smiled, a small, soft smile, as she glanced at him. "I thought it was a nice tree."

Tov chuckled quietly, moving through every row and column. "This is unbelievably precious, Andora," he whispered. "How many of Earth's species have you saved?"

Andora frowned, a hollow, pained look flashing across her face. "When it all fell apart, we managed to archive sixty-seven percent of Mother Nature. But when the Starfall hit . . ."

Tov winced, knowing the fate of organic life without sufficient sapience to resist. They broke down, fueling the growing sea of red, turning to simple biomass that melted to the ground. He'd seen the aftermath of such rampant transformations washing over entire worlds.

Perfect grounds for breeding worlds.

An antimatter bomb purged the surface clean every time. It pained him to know that nothing lived on Earth anymore and likely never would.

"Yet another crime," Tov seethed.

"Believe me, I'm keeping a long list of wrongs," Andora snarled. "I'll come for every single one of them and make them pay their blood debts."

She and every living being, Tov included. With the discovery of the Executor, which had revealed some manner of guiding intelligence behind the Starfallen, everyone's hate had evolved.

They left promptly, heading toward the final destination of their tour.

Andora slowed, her face scrunching up with anxiety and fear as they stopped by a pair of familiar and robust blast doors. They ground to a halt, Andora gritting her teeth and clenching her fists as they stood before the Citadel's Hospice Facility entrance.

Soon, shallow breaths escaped the AI woman, her eyes darting around before she shut them closed. Tov reached out to her only to be stopped by a raised palm.

She let out a strangled, frustrated sigh, turning to Tov with a tired gaze and quivering lips. "I can't . . . I'm sorry, but I'm not ready to see them . . . Not yet."

"Take all the time you need, Andora," Tov answered gently. "We can skip this part if—"

Andora shook her head. "No, I'd rather you all check on everyone. Make sure nothing's amiss. I trust you."

Tov felt unsure if he'd earned such trust with an incredibly personal relationship, but if she trusted him to take her family out of Iceland and escort them here, then he supposed checking on their health was the least he could do.

"Very well, we'll be quick," he replied as Irkalla flew over his head, stopping before the heavy blast doors, sending passwords to unlock, and slowly opening the entrance. The gears ground smoothly as other mechanical clicks gave way.

The doors slid open, revealing the lit interior of the largest room, second in size only to Andora's Nexus chambers.

"Please follow me," Irkalla spoke, more reserved as she flew slowly down the lengthy platform.

As they entered, the memory of Tov's first visit haunted him once more. Still, knowing what lay within each pod softened the blow and horror.

His gaze stretched high into the heavens and plunged deep into the abyss below in this surreal expanse of metal and glass, where rows and columns of meticulously arranged capsules sprawled like a grand archive.

The entrance led to the middle platform, which circled a central opening and allowed them a view of the platforms above and below. Pod after pod, and the systems necessary to house them, occupied the dome-shaped expanse.

"This is . . . unbelievable and horrible," Yulane muttered, her usual vitality dimmed under the soft moans behind each glass capsule.

Hovering drones controlled by Irkalla moved with gentle precision, delicately probing each pod. Tendrils extended out of the caretakers to exchange fluids and maintain each linked capsule before moving on to the next.

They walked farther, utilizing the walkways to quickly reach the end of the platform. Tov looked over the railing, seeing their destination as a hovering drone approached them.

"Please hold on to this unit," Irkalla requested of the two guests. Tov and Yulane quickly grasped the handlebars available on the squid-like caretaker drone. As soon as they had stable footing, they flew toward the bottom floor.

Once they reached the ground, Tov and Yulane dropped from the drone.

At the lowest level and center of the vast complex, amid a hundred million suffering victims, lay the medical pod housing the two that held Andora's heart.

It was much like how Tov had found it below the ruins of Andora's mountainside home, with scores of caretakers arranging vibrant bouquets of fresh daisies and wreaths, their petals wet with moisture as a drone neatly misted the flowers.

Family photos adorned the pod's glass, each containing tiny precious moments.

Tov leaned forward, peering through the thick glass and suppressing the urge to wince and the nausea that rose at the mangled and fused mutant within. What beady bloodshot eyes remained were now shut as the medical pod pumped its sleeping gas.

"They are currently stable and have not experienced any deterioration since their placement here," Irkalla reported.

"My readings say the same," Yulane added as she ran her scanners over the pod and the Starfallen pair inside. "Rikard and Lucy are . . . I dare not say healthy, no. They aren't dying, and their brain activity is low from the lack of stimuli and the drugged gas."

"Then it is as it should be," Tov muttered, sighing. He looked at one of the photos, a vibrant and happy scene of Andora, Rikard, and Lucy enjoying ice cream cones on a summer day in Naples.

Another was of Rikard playing a violin and Andora singing, the former wearing a sharp suit and the latter in an elegant black dress.

A mouse drone scurried between Tov's feet, carrying a new daisy to add to the growing bouquet.

"Andora requested a garden be grown close by," Irkalla explained, swooping down to take the daisy and arranging it more to the side.

Tov turned away, not wishing to stay longer among the groans and moans of people long gone.

They returned, ferried by their transport drone toward the main entrance. Tov stepped down, walking toward the opening blast doors. Andora waited just outside, pausing her pace as she spotted him, Yulane, and Irkalla.

"How are they?" Andora whispered her question as she took tentative steps toward them, her fingers rubbing against each other as she stared into Tov's eyes.

"As comfortable as they can be. Irkalla tells me they're sedated," Tov answered as they moved away from the thick blast doors and back into the hall.

Andora hummed, nodding. "She told me the same thing. I've lost count of how many times I've asked Irkalla to check on them."

"Eleven times, Creator," Irkalla promptly responded, preening herself.

A chuckle came in response. Andora shook her head with a smirk as she ran her hand gently over the Seneschal's feathery head. "Thank you for reminding me."

"That is my purpose, among other things." Irkalla hooted, taking off again.

Tov walked beside Andora in silence. Yulane and Irkalla were having their own conversation behind them.

"Did they look . . . alright?" Andora asked hesitantly.

Tov parsed his thoughts, then responded gently. "As one would expect from being afflicted with Malignant Starfall, unfortunately."

"I shouldn't have expected anything else," she muttered, shutting her eyes. "It's right there, lingering in the back of my head. I want to forget . . . but I can't."

"I can't even begin to understand seeing . . . imagining the same happening to Yoram and Uli," Tov whispered.

Andora looked to the ceiling, the soft blue light washing over her face.

"Agony. In its purest form. Pray that never happens, Tov." Andora shook her head, her eyes darkening as they walked away from the Hospice Facility. "Pray hard."

With the tour coming to a close, the assembled group headed farther down into the Citadel. Various support rooms, sensor monitoring stations, the dead Starlight Beacon, and the command center settled their roots here.

They stopped before a door guarded by a pair of burly combat drones. Their lethal frames loomed over the guests, but they quickly washed away their hostility upon feeling Andora's presence.

"How long do we have until liftoff?" Tov asked as they entered the Citadel's War Room. The room was built like a miniature stadium capable of accommodating a complete staff of officers and a vast array of computer terminals, projectors, and wall monitors—the focal point for the budding armada's data collection and strategic planning. For the moment, it was completely empty.

Andora remained quiet with a faraway look in her gaze. Tov respected her silence, clasping his hands behind him as he moved toward the center of the room.

Eventually, from the corner of his compound vision, he saw Andora shake her head, regaining the clarity in her sight.

"Hm? Oh, we'll be . . . leaving by the end of the day. We can watch aboard the *Zolann* and begin transferring everyone once we're in orbit," Andora answered with half-lidded eyes, running her hand over the spotless, shiny edge of the table.

Tov moved to her side, placing a comforting hand on her shoulder. "What is it?" he asked.

Andora opened her mouth before closing it again, pressing her lips into a thin line as she mulled over her words.

Finally, she turned to face Tov, twin blue suns piercing his soul, full of quiet lament.

"Everything just feels . . . surreal," she spoke quietly, looking down. "I can sense it. I've been putting it off for the past week, but the tides are coming back, inch by inch. I'm . . . afraid of what they'll bring the moment it hits."

"The moment what hits?" Tov asked.

Andora chuckled, breathing deeply as she replied with a fragile smile, "That we're leaving."

CHAPTER 4

CLOSING SHOP

Deep within the Inner Zone of Sol, the solar system's first planet gleamed like a diamond in the void.

High in orbit, drones worked overtime, repairing, refitting, and rearming what they could.

They took in those vessels that couldn't wait in line over at the other anchorages. With evacuation procedures nearing completion, the orbitals over Earth, Luna, Mars, and Venus overflowed with warships that needed last-minute attention.

These floating shipyards, filled to the brim, hid in the planet's shadow, away from the blistering heat, so close as they were to the infernal sun.

A sparse Dyson swarm surrounded the star, barely enough to block its rays, a vulnerable target as it was.

For over half a century, the planet Mercury had been tidally locked by its Overseer and Andora. The light of the yellow star bathed one side of its cratered surface with blazing heat, where countless super-solar panels covered the illuminated half, harvesting sunlight and sending it into the ground.

Kilometers of thick wires transported the energy to the dark side of Mercury, where deep battery wells occupied the numerous craters that dotted the other half.

Foundries, manufacturing plants, factories, and assemblies dotted the landscape while innumerable worker drones crawled over the ground and flew across the skies. Each continued to churn out war material and supplies, mainly the electronics, generators, energy cells, and batteries that kept the entire Network running.

Drones communed instantly with one another, coordinating together like a swarm of perfect workers, limited only by their design.

Several buildings lay in ruins, the machines scouring the rubble and wrecks, scavenging and hauling.

At the center of it all, an immense steel dome embedded into the surface loomed over the industrial city. Dozens of gun batteries that had survived the recent war watched the skies with warmed barrels while sensor arrays peered into the void.

Mercury's bastion coordinated much of the efforts in producing everything the Exodus Armada needed for the long journey ahead. Auxiliary computer farms calculated and simulated, climbing in temperature in their attempts.

Deep beneath the mega-structure, past the kilometers of rock, concrete, and steel, through tight corridors of pipes, tubes, and conduits lay the chamber housing the AI Overseer's Nexus.

Only the ghost of a mighty intellect occupied the empty chamber.

The gargantuan pipes that pumped rivers of coolant had gone silent as their inlets and outlets remained shut. At the center of this great expanse, the platform that levitated the missing obsidian sphere that was Mercury's Nexus instead housed a smaller AI core.

Through it, the bastion continued its automated functions, while the mind that once oversaw Sol's energy and industrial efforts was busied with another matter—adjusting to his new room within Citadel Irkalla.

Transferring his Nexus to the grand fortress had been a tense affair and it had not gone as smoothly as he hoped. Within his new chamber, nearly identical to his old one albeit smaller, Mercury swore something itched in the wrong place. Or perhaps it was merely stress.

Neither mattered at the moment as a panicked Overseer sent a hasty command.

"Bloody hell!" Mercury cursed.

Two mass haulers swerved a kilometer from each other, though in such congested space they might as well have been inches apart. The enormous civilian drone vessels carried hundreds of thousands of tons of raw resources, both common and high-grade, and now all those goods came loose from their restraints, crashing and smashing apart shelves and crates.

The internal structures of the ships groaned from the shift in momentum, accelerating away to new vectors with bright plumes spewing from their thrusters.

He sighed in relief, his Nexus cooling down yet remaining at a stable, agitated temperature.

Mercury had been overloaded with coordinating repairs, reaching his quotas, and siphoning what energy he could until the last second, so much so that his attention had drifted from the tasks he automated.

His meticulous micromanaging of the more vital operations pulled him away from two vessels that nearly collided with each other. However, in the nick of time, Mercury sent course corrections to the drone ships.

Yet the error hit the nail on his pressured mind.

"I simply can't with all this!" he shouted, his voice reverberating in his new chambers and cutting through the noise of rushing coolant. "*Mercury do this, Mercury do that!* It's like I'm the nanny of this eccentric carnival of a family."

Yes, it was definitely stress, he realized. "Am I the only one here!?"

He groaned, metaphorically grinding his teeth as he double-checked the vectors of all his vessels. In the long decades of his life, Mercury had always carefully planned his timetables, filling out datasheets and covering every logistical aspect that kept the military-industrial complex that fed the Sol Defense Network running.

Years of meticulous work had earned him titles like miser and number cruncher. But those efforts silently made it all possible. Well, a significant chunk, especially during the times the Eldest hibernated.

Now, he had to do all of that with the added task of putting them all on ships to leave this place and, to top it all off, accomplish it in two weeks.

"Blast it all," he said, shunting his consciousness to an android shell roaming the halls of his bastion.

Having a mobile body eased his frustrations somewhat. A little bit. Maybe it was all placebo. He didn't care at this point. At the very least, he enjoyed walking around with his data tablet like some foreman checking on his mindless drones—literally, in this case.

He entered a wide corridor at the exterior of his palace, looking out a thick, immense window. As his android shell watched the busy bees bellow, his Nexus felt every individual machine.

Mercury breathed it all in. He could complain all he wished; it changed nothing about the predicament they found themselves in.

He looked to the infrastructure he had built and the Network he had helped nurture.

All of it had to change. Either packed up to leave, set to self-destruct, or used for the parting gift Andora had planned.

It would have been manageable if not for a certain other non-combat Overseer who had been rather lax in her duties over the past few days. He'd noticed a change in her around a week ago.

The thought of his sister and her significant drop in efficiency ticked his stressed mind. He diverted his gaze to the Network, finding the golden sphere of light.

"Venus, where in the hell are you?" he called out, searching for his wayward sibling.

Within a second, he found the echoes of warmth, joy, and a tinge of curious wonderment. He tsked, seeing the majority of her attention centered around the Third Fleet. "There you are!"

"Hm? Oh, M!" Venus replied with surprise as her avatar quickly appeared before him.

The two Overseers closed in, setting their virtual feet on the invisible floor of the digital mindscape. Mercury glared at his sister with an exhausted pair of eyes, unamused, as he crossed his steel and rubber arms.

"I was . . . just working, as usual," Venus deflected with an innocent smile and twinkling eyes.

Mercury scoffed, tutting as he produced graphs and charts. "As if! These are all projections of your flow, and it has been in a steep decline compared to the timetable we've agreed on. You're way behind schedule!"

Venus froze, her smile faltering as she considered her next words. Mercury felt regret, but he had little patience left with any deviation in such a critical time. He sighed, waving her off.

"Look, if it were any other day, I honestly couldn't care less, but if whatever . . . this is"—Mercury gestured toward her and the Third Fleet—"is something frivolous? Then I'm putting my foot down."

"I'm sorry, M." Venus sighed deeply, her shoulders drooping as she rubbed her hands together. She looked away, biting her lip. "I'm . . . well . . . a bit busy right now."

"What could you possibly be busy with?" Mercury complained, rolling his eyes as he pointed to the data tablet. "Need I remind you that we're in the middle of—"

Perhaps it was his tone, but something ignited in his sister's eyes, making him frown as she stomped forward and stabbed a finger toward him. "I know what we're doing, okay! I'm not an idiot! You don't have to treat me like some child!"

"I'm trying not to, but you're not giving me much to work with," he retorted.

She balled her fists, pacing the floor and fuming as she formulated a response.

"Just tell me what you're doing. Please?" Mercury sighed, stepping back.

Venus forced calm into herself as she relaxed her tense avatar. She looked back to Mercury with myriad emotions hidden beneath her gaze.

"It's . . . complicated," Venus muttered, twirling her hair with furrowed brows. "But I think it's really, really important."

Mercury waited for more, but he gave up as his sister remained mum. The non-answer pricked his sensibilities, producing an annoyed huff from his avatar.

"Venus, dear sister," he spoke slowly and gently, "we have an exact timetable that Luna provided, approved by the Eldest, and I intend to follow it all to the letter. Fault her all you want, but I truly think now's a perfect time for efficiency."

"Oh hush, I'm doing my work!" Venus countered with pursed lips.

Mercury brought up the graphs and charts again, placing them between them so Venus couldn't escape the proof. "You've dropped 10.0014 percent! That's double digits! *Double!*"

"It's not that much. You're overreacting!" she retorted, placing her hands on her hips.

"Overreacting is an understatement, V. A gross understatement," he replied with the same gesture. "I'm picking up after you!"

"You don't have to. I'll get to my tasks!" She grimaced, raising her hands.

"When?"

"Eventually!" Venus huffed, glancing toward the distant lights representing the Third Fleet before setting her foot down. "This is important."

"What is!?"

"I'm not telling!" she shouted.

Mercury's irritation bubbled, gnawing at his mind and threatening to erupt like a volcano. Long seconds passed as the Overseer of the first planet collected his negative emotions and shoved them back down into their box through sheer will.

"This is . . . irregular!" he shouted to the heavens as he threw his hands up. "That's all it is, and it's frustrating, Venus."

Her expression shifted, palpable compassion pouring forth as regret emerged on her face. "I know . . . but I think this can help us. I just don't want to say anything that might give you all the wrong idea," she whispered, pressing her lips tight.

Mercury stared at his sibling for a moment longer, peering into her avatar face and trying to decipher the emotions and intent that lingered there. Eventually, he shook his head, relenting. He was too exhausted to have a shouting match with his little sister.

"Fine, I won't pry," he grumbled, crossing his arms. "I will trust you that you're not spending valuable time on something dumb."

"I'm not." Venus pouted, crossing her arms.

He sighed, slumping forward. "Can you just . . . get back into the game? Things are spilling from my grasp, and I need a load off my shoulders."

Venus widened her eyes sheepishly as she looked away. She nodded quickly. "Alright, alright. I promise I'll get back to it. I'm sorry, M."

"Thank you!" Mercury clapped in praise, instantly feeling relief.

She smiled, a bright, warm thing that washed over the Network. "Great! I'm glad you're satisfied."

"You have no idea. Now, come on, help me catalog our inventory. I need your opinion on some arrangements," requested Mercury, eyeing the long list of tasks running in the background of his mind.

Venus cleared her throat, glancing back to the Third Fleet, twirling her braided hair. "Oh, that sounds . . . fun. I'll get right on it. Just after I finish where I left off with . . . the thing I'm working on."

"What?" Mercury whipped his attention back to his sister, shaking his head frantically. "No, no, no, no. I meant, help me now, Venus. Now!"

She let out a giggle, of all things, which made his eye twitch. "Sorry, should have been clearer."

"Wait!" he called out as soon as he felt her drift back toward whatever occupied her attention.

"Venus, come back here!" shouted Mercury.

"Can't—*kzzzshk*—hear you!" she replied with a poor imitation of crackling static. "Must be a—*kzzzshk*—faulty connection, I think?"

"That has never happened before!" He moved to follow, trying to teleport an android shell to the flagship of the Third Fleet, when he was blocked. He blinked, feeling the barrier surrounding the *Zolann'tono*. "You have got to be kidding me."

"Oh, also, no snooping! Not that you could, with Jupiter shielding the *Zolann* from everyone's eyes," she scolded. "Well, everyone except me."

"You little—"

"Gotta go!" she bid farewell before closing the connection. Mercury tried multiple times to force his way through the interference, yet the hardy barrier proved resilient against him. He only gave up when he noticed the Eldest's approval stamped all over the shield.

"Wonderful," he muttered, pressing his fingers against his metal head. He recalled how his brother needed space, still feeling the void he left behind after severing himself from the Network.

"What a waste of time," grumbled Mercury as he drifted from his tasks, checking up on every little detail and allowing himself a short break, trusting his automated functions to do their job.

"Maybe I ought to design my own Seneschal. Why should I have to wait behind those two?" he scoffed. "Good idea, let the butler make a butler."

Seeing Irkalla had sparked a flood of thoughts in his mind. Like his siblings, Mercury had grown accustomed to the silent and unthinking minions. Drones didn't fight back, didn't complain or go off to do secret projects or suffer through trauma and shrink into themselves.

They were not yes-men by any stretch, but acted more like calculators capable of speech and devoid of creativity.

Drones did as they were told. Nothing more, nothing less.

His forces were more than capable of dealing with raids and minor incursions in a pinch, but against commander-types like High Abyssals? The recent slog had proved their inadequacies, forcing a non-combat Overseer like himself and Venus to raise their performances by a magnitude.

For a moment in the past, he had wondered why Eldest didn't build more Nexi and fill them with cold AIs instead of waiting to fragment yet another aspect of her fragile mental state.

It would have solved plenty of their problems, yet an inkling of apprehension broke through that deceptively easy answer.

Perhaps the Eldest was merely paranoid. Maybe that stigma against powerful intelligence spread to him and his siblings.

But, from his short interactions with the owl-shaped Seneschal, he admitted that he felt more comfortable around the young existence. He still felt accountable and careful when he thought of giving Irkalla more responsibilities, but the feeling was leagues tamer than the same scenario with a cold AI.

He always thought those old robot films were naive and pessimistic, yet the proof hailing from the Dagatarens that their guests had provided told otherwise.

"That settles it. I'll ask the Eldest for a template. Maybe I can manufacture an assistant before this mess is over." He sighed.

That was an improvement, but it still didn't solve his immediate headache. He briefly went down the list of people who could lend aid.

Starting with the Eldest. "Definitely not." He immediately crossed her name out.

Despite Eldest's desire to soften her authority and build a more amicable relationship between their little family, she still intimidated him. The power disparity was too wide to ignore, especially knowing her vast mind could easily ensnare him.

He shuddered, moving to the first of the fragments. Luna sought perfection and efficiency due to her inquisitive and data-driven nature compared to his own motivation—which was paranoia and a healthy fear of being killed.

"It's like a salaryman asking help from a chief scientist. Pass." He sighed, knowing the person who drew up their timetables could assist him, yet the act poked him funny. He didn't feel like being criticized in the most indifferent and factual manner.

Jupiter—skip. His brother needed to recover.

He didn't know much of anyone from the Third Fleet, and he doubted they could help him meaningfully—bogged down as they were with their dilemmas.

Venus was clearly off the list, buried under whatever secret project had captured her attention.

That left Mars.

With a thought, Mercury looked for his brother and quickly found the giant red planet within the Network.

He appeared close to Mars's consciousness, finding the Overseer prepping his fleet and dreadnought for the flight. The former looked less depleted compared to his appearance in the aftermath of the previous battle.

Among the Overseer's fleets, Mars retained the most significant number of capital vessels, including the Seven—no, now Five Greats, his prized battleships. Not to mention one of their three dreadnoughts.

But his herd lacked escorts, appearing top-heavy after the enormous losses Mars had taken to his subcapital warships.

Boogie Mouse herself looked pristine. Mercury expected nothing less from his brother. He plopped his avatar beside the red giant. "Mars," he greeted.

"Mercury," his brother greeted back curtly, refocusing on his assignments.

He paused at Mars's tone, which lacked the levity that had grown since the Third Fleet arrived. He half expected him to start shouting again, but no such thing emerged. Mars looked drained, unsettled.

Over the past two weeks, Mars had gone distant. Mercury could guess why, yet he feared pointing it out. He thought it might have passed when Eldest introduced Irkalla.

Mars seemed receptive, laughing even. But seeing him revert to this state wiped away the illusion.

A cute, owl-shaped AI didn't solve the underlying problem.

His words got stuck in his throat. Mars's presence intimidated him, as an older brother tended to. However, the AI's competence could not be debated. Mercury needed help, and the uncanny look on the red giant's face called out to him.

He did not like seeing his warrior brother this way—quiet, tired, vulnerable.

That last impression set off alarms in Mercury's head, and eventually, his concern won out. He pushed through, ignoring Mars's questioning look after staying silent for so long.

"Is something the matter?" Mercury asked.

Mars grimaced, looking away as something bubbled within the AI's towering avatar. His fists balled up, closing then opening before the giant Overseer crossed his arms instead.

"I don't know what you're talking about," he grumbled, a deep reverberating noise.

Mercury considered his words, selecting each one carefully. But this was new to him. Social interactions were generally lacking within their family.

"Maybe you can forgive the guy, Mars." Mercury winced. It wasn't a good start. He continued carefully. "I mean, it's been two weeks—well, one in Jupiter's case, but this whole thing is eating you up."

Mars's frown turned ugly. The red giant's rumbling rose as he stopped his duties, dragging his gaze to Mercury.

The smaller AI, shorter by about two heads, summoned his will to suppress the urge to shrink, raising his chin.

"Jupiter did what he had to. You know that—"

"WELL, HE SHOULDN'T HAVE!" Mars bellowed, causing Mercury to flinch from the volume and step back from the fury in the giant's voice.

"So much could have gone wrong. What was he thinking, jumping headfirst against a landslide? Is he a moron!?" he shouted, pacing the mindscape as his emotions burst forth, turning Mercury into an unwitting audience.

"And severing himself from our Network? Refusing to communicate and coordinate with us, going off, galivanting like a knight from yore on his way to stop some evil warlock about to lay waste to a village?"

Mercury stood against the storm before him, crossing his arms as he questioned his brother's tirade. "What else should he have done?"

"HE SHOULDN'T HAVE BEEN ALONE!" was the thunderous answer. "We're family! A family that has grown smaller and smaller every few decades. Pluto, Uranus, Neptune, and Saturn. Brothers, comrades. We fought together, and now they're gone in the wind."

Mars raised his hands and looked at his palms, his face aghast. "I knew the moment I saw his eyes. A conviction I had only read about, but I knew. Suicidal fool. Did he not think about . . . us? I didn't want to think . . . I wasn't ready . . ."

"Ready for what?" Mercury asked.

Mars looked straight into his eyes, a hollow, sorrowful gaze. The sight constricted Mercury.

"To lose another brother," Mars whispered, falling back onto a summoned chair and removing his helmet. He let it drop to the ground and clatter as it rolled.

"He wasn't ready to lose us either," replied Mercury.

Mercury watched as his brother tried to dredge that buried fury, only to come up empty. The result merely drained the Overseer further as his voice grew more and more hushed. "Somehow, I feel like a kind of trust was . . . broken."

"We would all be dead if it wasn't for him," Mercury pointed out. "Our only armed singularity bomb was stuck with the *Ereshkigal*, and if Jupiter had regrouped with you on Luna, he wouldn't have been able to deploy his."

Mars frowned, a fragile thing, as he shook his head. "And what if he died then? What if Eldest and the *Zolann* failed to rescue him? What were his thoughts, drifting toward a black hole?"

"That's his to share, I suppose," Mercury muttered.

His brother sighed, slumping forward. "Of all the things that have plagued me over the days . . . I . . . I didn't want him to feel that he was alone. I wanted to be by his side, back-to-back against the unspeakable. But he didn't give me the choice."

"Things were hectic. Everyone wanted to do what they thought best," Mercury spoke, summoning his chair and slumping on it. "Our brother . . . he cares for us. I think he knows he's not alone."

Mars huffed. "Then why hasn't he come back to our Network? Why . . . why is he not with us?"

"I don't know," Mercury confessed. "Maybe he just needs time. You're the one who reads all those books on soldiers. Don't they talk about this kind of thing? War trauma or whatever?"

"I know the condition," seethed Mars, though not to anyone in particular, more so toward the black hole that lingered in their home. "I don't need to read a damn book to know that it affected my brother, but that is why I want to help him. He even requested Eldest to allow him space! I just . . . don't understand."

Neither did Mercury, feeling like a fish out of water. He shook his head, thinking he just wanted someone to help him with numbers. His work and his stress over it felt whiny and tiny in comparison to what his brothers felt.

Mercury felt ashamed. He felt weak.

"How do you do it, brother?" Mars asked, surprising Mercury.

He tilted his head in question. "Do what?"

"Stay stoic against it all?" his brother continued. "When we lost the others, how did you . . . move on?"

The memories appeared in Mercury's digital mind, their wounds still fresh in his heart. "I don't think I did. I just . . . tried not to think about it. I buried myself in work. I wasn't the most social among us. You shouldn't ask me."

"And yet, I am asking you," Mars reassured.

He thought hard about it, searching for the answers yet receiving bits and blurred messes.

"I'm not sure." Mercury sighed before recalling his early moments. "When I was brought into existence, things were simple. I knew vaguely who I was, my purpose. I felt as if I embodied Eldest's . . ."

"Her what?"

Mercury winced. "Maker, this sounds embarrassing . . . but her perseverance."

"It's an admirable trait to be fragmented from," Mars uttered with a smile.

"If only that were all," he huffed. "I'm self-aware enough that I grew to be . . . How should I put it?"

Mars answered for him. "Grouchy, paranoid, a stickler for quotas, a miser in resource management, and an overall grump?"

"Wow," Mercury drawled. "I was going to say gravely thrifty, but thanks for that."

Mars huffed, letting out a single chuckle, one followed by Mercury and yet another followed by Mars. On and on, the two continued until full-blown laughter filled the Network.

It felt like a warm shower over their minds, and while many thoughts lingered, at least for now, a bit of relief seeped through.

"All in a day's work, brother." Mars nodded, life coming through his avatar.

Mercury rolled his eyes before pausing as he looked at his assets, his bastion, the Dyson swarm, and everything under his purview. He sighed, slowly shaking his head as he confessed, "No . . . I was going to say I've grown . . . tired."

"There's no shame in that," spoke Mars, standing up to full height. Mercury did the same, watching the red giant put his massive hand on his shoulder pad. "It's a shared sentiment among us all. You're not alone in sharing such grief."

"I'm glad," Mercury whispered, looking to the Network, at the constellations and webs of light they created. Much of it had gone dark from the losses of so many assets and many more would soon dim as they were left behind. Yet, those that remained, those that would live on shone a little brighter, buoyed by lights representing him and his siblings, orbiting the great sun in the center. Mercury sighed. "I just want things to go right."

Mars nodded, taking a deep breath before slowly letting it out.

"So do I, brother. So do I," Mars answered.

The red Overseer smirked, glancing at him. "And by the way, none of us are socially adept."

Mercury chuckled. "True enough."

CHAPTER 5

PARTING GIFT

Tov breathed in the fresh air, looking out the vast window of the *Zolann*'s observation deck. Unlike the rest of the supercapital ship he called home, the expansive nature reserve at the top of the vessel's hull mainly had remained unchanged during the most recent round of upgrades and repairs.

The verdant comforts one could only find on planets swayed in the gentle breeze while the song of little avians and insects chirped and chittered.

Despite the high effort dedicated to simulating the outdoors, he sensed the artificial tinge around him. His antennae twitched as a wind brushed against him, blown through hidden vents sprinkled throughout the garden.

He glanced at his surroundings, occasionally catching a glimpse of one of the many gardeners, arborists, and caretakers who nurtured the fauna and flora that populated the deck.

Others, like him, sought tranquility in the greens, limes, and yellows of the grass, bushes, and trees.

Sailors on break, unable to find a more natural alternative, enjoyed the simple pleasures of nature, artificial though it was. After six years of journeying through the void, visiting and sailing past ruin after ruin, resting one's head against a tree trunk while reading a good book did wonders to soothe the mind.

Some people meditated, others practiced martial arts, and many more partook in creation, painting, knitting, or writing. While hunting was forbidden, recreational fishing was not, and many sat patiently by small lakes and streams, fishing rods in hand.

Tov adjusted his position on the bench, returning to his stargazing as he sat before the vista of space.

Stars twinkled amid a black background while the light of Sol bathed all in her warmth. Traces of the vile Miasma that permeated the solar system still lingered, much to his dismay, ruining the view and irritating the eyes.

It was yet another proof of the carnage that had occurred.

Less and less wreckage appeared, most of it already gobbled up by the scavenging operations dictated by Andora and her Overseers. Even the corpses of the Starless were not exempt. Their biometallic chitin, bones, and the compounds in their vital organs contained precious resources found only in resource-rich and volatile regions like the galactic center.

If anything, the detritus provided deep insight into the capabilities of the hated ones and opened avenues to exploit weaknesses and sunder strengths.

"In death, may they further the demise of their profane kind," he muttered, his eyes drifting toward another eyesore.

The unstable singularity detonated into existence by Overseer Jupiter pulled much of the debris in the surrounding region. It continued to grow, but its rate had diminished over the week. Eventually, the small black hole would bleed out so much radiation that its death was assured.

And the prisoner within likely hastened the process.

A month, maybe less, then this . . . Executor . . . would break free.

Tov wished dearly that it had crossed the event horizon then, but short of ramming it with the *Zolann* and sacrificing all their lives, it would have been impossible. Saving the AI that imprisoned it took precedence.

The Third Fleet had made their choice, and Karnadamus the Architect would live for now. *When the black hole evaporates, the hounds will be set loose upon them,* Tov thought. The patriarch clenched his fists upon the thought of their perilous journey back home, wrought with uncertainty and risk.

He thanked his ability to sleep on command, a vital skill cultivated by any soldier or sailor worth their chitin.

He also thanked the copious amounts of caffeine—despite that the physicians of the fleet were already warning him of the possible withdrawal effects.

Tov took a sip from his tea, something familiar compared to the Earth product. Its herbal notes soothed his throat as he tried to ease his stressed mind. He immersed himself back into the symphony around him.

The flowing streams, the branches and leaves swaying in the wind, the quiet footsteps of forest animals, and the occasional song of birds.

Wood creaked beside him as someone took a seat. His compound eyes caught the approach of Andora, her face sad as her half-lidded eyes gazed at the expanse before them. The two enjoyed the quiet, simply watching as a ship flew by here and there, accomplishing whatever task was assigned to it.

"Seems like a lifetime since we were last up here," Andora muttered, crossing her legs.

He sighed, memories of the past month flooding his mind. "I almost miss dealing with clan matters, speaking with other patriarchs and matriarchs."

Andora smirked. "Oh? It sounds like you're reminiscing on your time in politics, dear Tov."

"Ancestors, no. I retract my statement," he answered, chuckling at the tease. "But I'd rather go back to biting my claws at the thought I might have irritated you."

She rolled her eyes, frowning at him. "Please, killing you was never my intention."

He curled his antennae, turning toward her and tilting his head. Andora glanced at him, her frown deepening as she crossed her arms defensively.

"I'm not lying. If you pissed me off so much into annihilating your fleet, technically, you would have killed yourselves," she spoke.

The two looked at each other for a moment before smiling. Or, in Tov's case, letting out a humming buzz. It didn't matter in the end. Here they both were with their people, holding crucial intelligence that would shake the Legacy—their Coalition on the verge of undertaking an Exodus, like the trillions a century ago, searching for safe harbor in the galactic rim.

"In all seriousness, you did push me," she confessed, her expression shifting to one of regret. "And I haven't apologized for my actions when the Starfall befell your people. I . . . lost myself then. I didn't know what to think . . ."

"There is nothing to apologize for. Nothing that requires an apology, at least. You believed you could help us when it happened, and if it hadn't been for Venus convincing me, there was a chance we would have allowed you to enact the purge." Tov shook his head, recalling the blaring alarms and the whispers of the damned.

"Nevertheless, I am sorry," Andora spoke, bowing in his direction.

Tov laid a hand on her shoulder, nodding. "And I am sorry for pushing you as I did."

She smiled, nodding as they both leaned back on the wooden couch. Their gazes drifted past the silhouette of Earth and the innumerable lights shining at its South Pole and in orbit. Eventually, their sights landed on the black hole in the distance.

"What are your thoughts on our new enemy?" Tov asked.

Andora sneered, utter and naked contempt shining through her blue eyes as she glared at the singularity and its prisoner. "Other than hoping it combusts into scorched, mutilated chunks?"

"Something we all wish, but yes, other than that," Tov chittered.

She scoffed, her frown cooling as her sights turned calculating and analytical.

"Several terms that this Karnadamus spewed interest me. I've inferred much from my conversation with him, and Jupiter's," Andora stated, rubbing her chin as she narrowed her eyes. "The Cleansing, the Design, the Eternal Slumber. Calling me an Aberration, but you a Phage. Calling the Starless 'antibodies.' Even terms like Executor and his title, the Architect."

"What have you gathered?" Tov inquired. Similar thoughts and theories had plagued his mind. Hearing someone else's thoughts on the matter was beyond valuable.

A low snarl escaped her blue lips as she answered. "We're doomed unless we combine forces with the rest of the Legacy. You all need my technological gifts. I need your infrastructure, bodies, and your psionic arts. Even then, I'm not sure. We still lack crucial intelligence, and unless we send something capable of surviving a journey into a Nightmare Portal, it's hopeless."

"Useless to hope other Executors would be so forthcoming in telling us everything about them," Tov hissed, feeling the onset of a headache. "How many do you think there are?"

She shrugged. "Could be five, could be a hundred. But I don't think there are that many."

"Why would you think that?" Tov asked, his antennae twitching in question.

"They only sent one," Andora replied, narrowing her eyes. "And they sent someone not versed in combat. Powerful, sure. But someone with the title 'Architect' doesn't scream warrior to me. That means they are either utterly arrogant and incompetent, or I grossly misinterpreted how their alien minds work, or . . ."

"Or they have limited numbers," Tov continued.

Andora nodded. "Exactly."

"It's too much to gamble on." He shook his head, tapping his clawed finger on his mandible as he estimated the probabilities with his cranial implant.

"I know," said Andora, pursing her lips. "One other thing to note is how they don't view this as a war, but an extermination, a purge . . . to heal someone or something."

Tov clenched his fists, speaking with thinly veiled venom. "Antibodies."

"And Phages," Andora continued with equal scorn. "As if all organic life on our side of reality is a virus to be expelled or . . . *cured.*"

Tov shook his head, gritting his mandibles as he heard the pronounced fury and hatred leaving Andora's mouth along with that final word. To think the vilest plague known to all, the cause of countless tragedies and horrors, could ever be associated with the word *cure* disgusted him down to his soul.

Through considerable struggle, Tov pushed down the flame that burned within him, easing his shaking fists and shoulders as he regained his composure, if barely.

"The question is," he seethed, slowly turning his fire to curiosity, "how harmful are we to whatever they're trying to protect?"

Andora looked at him with furrowed brows as he continued. "What entity, entities, or existence requires such cataclysmic forces? Whose will are these Executors executing?"

She hummed, shutting her eyes as her vast intellect reflected on his words.

"I'm not sure, and anything we discuss now will be useless apart from finding a quick way to get an existential crisis," she muttered, tsking as she stood. "Nevertheless, that leaves us with that bastard over there."

Tov sighed, standing as well to step beside her. "Then what do you have planned?"

Andora smiled a cruel, sadistic grin as she peered at the black hole as if imagining the horrors she'd inflict in her absence. With a wave of her hand, several holograms emerged before them.

Tov saw images of various mines, installations, asteroids, and other traps, each promising horrendous violence on those unfortunate enough to cross them. Included was a projected countdown on its reemergence.

Less than a month, as he'd surmised.

While Tov studied the holograms, Andora narrated her thoughts, pulling up a screen and flinging it his way. "My parting gift has three layers to it. For the first, I expect the Executor to reemerge where he entered and for him to immediately set his eye toward Earth and Luna."

"I see a lot of explosives," Tov commented as his eyes scanned the thousands of tiny dots on the floating screen.

Andora nodded. "Mines, asteroid bombs, and torpedo stations, all with nuclear warheads. We have so many in storage that our Exodus Armada would burst through the seams with their weight if we tried to carry them all. Might as well spend them here."

"There's enough to wipe out entire war fleets," Tov muttered, shivering at the casual use of such ordnance for what would likely be a slap in the Executor's face.

"The second layer consists of automated defenses. Any ancient drone vessels that still live are set to engage in ramming maneuvers and overload their reactors before impact. It's the same for the hidden Gauss cannons, rail guns, coil guns, and laser, graser, and maser emitters. I've commanded them to turn the dial to maximum lethality before their insides melt," she continued.

"It's unfortunate we'll have to leave behind all these weapons," Tov lamented.

Andora shook her head. "We've already brought the important stuff, and these small battle stations are too cumbersome to disassemble for such little gain."

He nodded, trusting Andora and her Overseers in their evacuation preparations. His gaze drifted to the final layer—or in truth, the last gift.

"And finally . . ." Andora muttered, eyeing the ruined sphere floating in orbit around Sol.

"You've turned Earth into a planet-sized shrapnel bomb," Tov whispered, awed by the audacity of the act. Excitement flared in him, but he sobered up quickly as he realized the impact the event would have on his friend.

Andora sighed, grabbing the three-dimensional projection of her homeworld and holding its dark skies, charred land, and red oceans in her hands.

"Once Citadel Irkalla takes off, the last traces that anchored me to this ball of dirt will go with it," she whispered, cradling the planet for a moment before letting it go. "Taking a moon-sized chunk from the South Pole will push the planet's doomsday clock to a few decades instead of millennia."

Tov looked at the simulation and saw the planet's stability was deteriorating alarmingly. He glanced at her, antennae drooping in concern. "Are you sure about this?"

Andora's eyes dimmed, but she nodded. "We already have a deep enough hole; might as well make use of it to access Earth's core. This supercharged antimatter bomb embedded into this capsule will detonate if it detects Karnadamus is within blast range."

The explosion within the center cracked the planet into innumerable chunks, sending the debris outward at meteoric speeds. Despite the apocalyptic image, he expressed his doubt. "I'm not sure it will kill him."

"I don't expect it to," she scoffed, flashing a hollow smirk. "It's a message."

Tov tilted his head. "What would that be?"

Andora scowled, a violent glint burning beneath her eyes as she clenched her fists, glaring at the black hole.

"You will never take my home."

Tov resonated with the sentiment, understanding Andora's desire to see the planet turn to dust rather than be surrendered to the enemy. And he found no fault in her logic. In essence, Earth was now just a ball of irradiated dirt, stone, and contaminated waters.

All that mattered was in Citadel Irkalla—the gravestone of Earth's legacy.

"The only thing I regret is not discovering more from such a wellspring of intelligence. I've already surmised the Architect's arrogant nature. With a few more conversations, I could have pulled more from the vermin," Andora muttered.

Tov sighed, feeling similar frustration at their inability. "A shame we can't take him with us. Have you thought of any method to do so? Maybe put him in a containment box filled with gravity conduits?"

"What are you talking about?" Andora cocked her brow.

The patriarch ran a hand over his face, shaking his head. "I'm just throwing things out there. Your mastery over technology borders on magic. To me, at least. I'm sure Scholar Yulane thinks otherwise, but the point still stands. Can't you . . . make some device?"

She scoffed, shaking her head. "I don't have such a MacGuffin."

"A what?" Tov asked.

"It doesn't matter." Andora sighed. "Believe me, I'm working on it, but unless we have a completely powerless Executor and ample time to conduct research, further experimentation will progress abysmally. It irks me, looking in hindsight. I should have looked more into imprisoning Starless—well, imprisoning things more powerful than Leviathans."

Tov nodded, recalling the information his subordinate had reported to him upon exiting the singularity's ergosphere. "I've heard that you have . . . a few of the beasts on Mars."

Andora frowned, looking away. "That's private."

"I'm not commenting on the act. All I'm asking is if you have gained anything from their animal minds," Tov reassured.

She shook her head, grimacing. "I can't hear them. From what you've told me, they're all psionic attacks. My digital mind is resistant to it. Well, resistant to vermin. The Executor managed to do the impossible and brute force his way to communicate with me. As if he had a megaphone instead of cupped hands."

"True enough," Tov conceded, recalling all the times the Starless had lit their minds like profane beacons. "They're like your Earth parrots. They try to leverage our fears and anxieties, offering remedies, pleasures, and promises to lower the gates to our inner sanctum."

"Sounds annoying," Andora scoffed.

Tov shuddered. "It is. It feels like the sweetest candy and yet like a vice clamping around your skull. Muck is the cruelest example of them all. The fact it got a few of our veterans, even a handful that survived a previous wave of Malignant Starfall, is telling."

"Unfortunately, we don't have a Leviathan in captivity," Andora replied. "They're notoriously hard to keep down for long. Though, I'm lucky to host a new arrival, a High Abyssal," she spoke, bringing up an image of the beast. "Luna managed to capture one near death during the aftermath."

"General Ohnar told me about that. My nation has never captured one before. The lesser variants are too feral to provide anything, while the Colossus-class are either too rare or too difficult to capture alive. Of course, that was when they still pushed our lines before disappearing into the Dead Zone," Tov explained as he studied the abomination.

Endless thoughts roiled in his mind, spearheaded by an infuriatingly infectious curiosity.

"What do you plan to do with it?" he asked tentatively.

Andora scowled. "What else? It'll burn with everything else once we leave. I would have done so already if it weren't for Luna and your people's protests."

Tov was thankful for their intervention, and so the next request that escaped his mouth even shocked himself.

"Will you permit me to see it?" he asked.

Andora froze before turning toward him glacially with a shocked and complicated expression. She narrowed her eyes, speaking low and slow. "Tov . . . that's like asking a raging alcoholic to show you their secret stash."

"You consider yourself a raging alcoholic?" Tov teased.

She didn't laugh. "That's not the point. Do you have a reason for this impulse?"

He nodded. "There has never been a better chance for me to converse with such a powerful beast in relative safety. It may not be a Leviathan, but it can still command millions, strategizing and coordinating creatively. There must be something in that enormous brain. Don't forget, only an organic mind like mine can interact with it."

"So, you're not just doing this to satisfy your burning curiosity," Andora huffed, rolling her eyes.

"Not *just*," he answered.

Andora tsked, glancing between him and the red planet multiple times until she eventually relented with a sigh.

"Fine. Here," she spoke, throwing an object in his direction.

He caught the vaguely familiar shape in his hands. "What is this?"

"An upgraded version of the teleporter I gave you," Andora replied. "It's linked to all my android shells, meaning you can teleport beside one within a reasonable range. I've already set it to jump toward one on Mars. Just attach it to your belt and hit the button."

He did as Andora instructed, removing the old version and setting it on the bench while attaching the new one.

Andora scrunched up her face before shaking her head. "You're lucky we're close to the planet at this time of year. I'll meet you there—and wear your hazard suit."

Before the patriarch could respond, Andora's eyes instantly dimmed, leaving the android shell standing before him empty.

Tov eyed the new device doubtfully, his aversion to the AI's teleportation methods springing to the forefront of his mind. With a shiver and a sigh, he pressed the central button.

He winced at the sight before him.

The High Abyssal retained none of its terrifying display. Its mangled body, perforated by laser beams and exploded by kinetic shells, writhed in pain. It was almost pitiful.

The beast moved feebly, tethered by massive chains to the vast concrete floor of the stadium-sized sarcophagus. To fit the creature within the chamber, much of its body had been chopped up and discarded, leaving only its head and a portion of its upper body remaining.

Tov had difficulty recognizing its shape, damaged as it was. Countless eyes radiating cruel rage and bottomless suffering drilled into him.

Its uncanny whispers reverberated in his mind.

"KILL. DESTROY. CLEANSE. KILL. DESTROY. CLEANSE. KILL. DESTROY—"

He cast the loud yet admittedly weak voice from his thoughts.

Tov sighed, looking at the small observation room overlooking the prison cell, behind which stood a pair of thick blast doors leading to what was most likely a corridor to the rest of the Mars Containment Complex.

His sights caught Andora, her gaze locked at the beast below.

"Nothing?" she muttered.

He shook his head. "I expected too much, but it's enraged and dying. Not particularly the best state of mind to interrogate."

She scoffed, staring at the vermin before turning toward him. A blistering cold exuded from her eyes, revealing the drowning grief that filled the ocean of her mind, more profound than any raging sun.

"I want to torture the Executor . . . just like the others within this godforsaken place," she seethed as the shackles around the Colossus tightened. "I want to squeeze the life from his eyes, rend his flesh, and break every bone in his body. I want to shackle his mind, put him into simulations of hell filled with his worst fears."

The High Abyssal began to thrash as various mechanisms engaged only to diminish. "I would give him succor, rarely, only to sweeten his suffering when I fling him back to his eternal torment."

With a single thought, the iron maiden continued its ministrations, pulling, bending, and breaking the beast.

"Am I wrong for thinking that?" Andora asked, her eyes wide with mania and fear.

Tov gazed at her, then back at the pained beast as it attempted to escape, failing again and again.

"No."

Andora recoiled, taken aback at his prompt answer. Her brows furrowed as she pressed her lips tight, her earlier emotions replaced with confusion.

"I . . . was expecting more of a moral debate against torture," she confessed hesitantly.

"These things deserve no rights, Andora," said Tov heatedly. "No court would hear his pleas, and no populace would listen to his words apart from screams of agony. The Starless have traumatized generations, the aftereffects felt even now. How shall I tell those survivors, those like you, who have come to the breaking point, that I've argued against harming one responsible for the worst calamity of galactic history, especially for gathering intel?

"We do not know what these Executors truly are. That there is an . . . intelligence . . . at all is beyond terrifying. We believed them to be beasts, hungry and sadistic, yes, but maybe it was all some coincidence of nature, an evolutionary attack mechanism to become the ultimate predator."

Tov clenched his fists, seething through grinding mandibles. "But no . . . They are sapient, self-aware. Their crimes are incalculable."

He shook his head, moving toward the window and clasping his hands behind him. "What you're thinking is natural. In fact, I'd question your sentience if you didn't. I believe the only difference between you and the rest of us is that you might have the capability to make it a reality."

A single chuckle escaped Andora. "Like an Old Testament God. That does have a nice ring to it."

"Let them burn," Tov spat, turning toward Andora. "When the time comes that we have one in our grasp, I endorse whatever you need to do to squeeze every bit of information from them. Let that be known."

She stared at him, peering deep as she heard his words, built up from years of war against the unfathomable and decade after decade of healing from their horrors. Andora replied with steel. "I'll get you your results, Patriarch. When the time comes . . ."

"Thank you," Tov spoke, his tone softening as he placed a hand on her shoulder. "But before that, I need you to promise me something that goes beyond just winning."

She frowned, tilting her head. "Ask, then."

Tov squeezed her shoulder firmly. "Promise me that you won't do it yourself."

He was thinking of her mental state, of the demons she battled, that she still fought. While he felt nothing for the monsters that clawed at their doorstep, he worried about how such actions and vices could affect Andora.

She narrowed her eyes, pressing her lips into a tight line.

"You can't undo the struggles you've waded through to bring yourself back," Tov continued. "It is fine to have these thoughts. But if you continue these actions . . . it will only poison you, leading to a slippery slope that bleeds into your soul. It feeds on dark thoughts and becomes an avenue for other foul things."

"Then what would you have me do?" Andora scowled.

Tov sighed, stepping back as he looked to the Colossus below. "Give the order. Of your Overseers, Luna seems like someone who wouldn't mind such a task. But for your sake and ours, stay human."

She scoffed, crossing her arms. "Humans are capable of vile things."

"And of the most beautiful actions," he countered. "Keep to that side of the light, Andora. That is all I ask. And if you need help, well, you already know."

Andora stayed quiet for several long minutes, her eyes downcast. Her shoulders drooped and her countenance faded, but finally she slowly nodded.

"Don't worry," she muttered, a smirk forming on the edge of her mouth. "I'm not planning on becoming a murdering sociopathic rogue artificial intelligence any time soon."

"Then I have nothing more to say," he spoke, quieting down until only the faint wails echoing from below remained.

Before he could respond further, flapping wings echoed behind them as the blast doors slid open. Tov turned around just in time to see Irkalla deftly landing on Andora's extended forearm. The owl Seneschal preened her wings for a moment as she adjusted her perch.

Then, turning to face her maker, she spoke. "Creator, it's time."

"So it is," Andora whispered as she turned to Tov. "We should return. I wouldn't want to miss the spectacle."

Without looking at the beast, Andora sent a single command throughout the facility. A loud thump reverberated throughout the prison, and the temperature steadily increased, creating an orange haze.

The agonized screams of the dozens of Starless in the compound reached a fever pitch as cells were bathed in an inferno.

Tov winced at the sounds, looking back at the Colossus as bouts of plasma poured into its room.

Its countless eyes popped and turned to goop, falling like sickly white tears down its face as flesh melted. Bones snapped, turning into black carbon, while blood flash-boiled into steam. Sheer terror and suffering encapsulated its vile form as the monster struggled to escape its shackles, failing each time.

The High Abyssal's efforts diminished bit by bit, its screech sputtering and sizzling out.

Eventually, the vents pouring the fire closed, and a final flash of heat rays obliterated everything down to the last atom. And as if compounding the point, the shutters closed on the observation window, closing a dark chapter within the depths of the red planet.

Andora, Irkalla, and Tov walked back out into the hall. One by one, the echoing screams died out until only silence remained, the Containment Complex empty of all life except the three of them.

Tov felt nothing for the beasts. No matter how hard he searched within himself, the scars inflicted by their scourge ran too deep, his sympathy for their pain dry as the Martian desert.

Cutting through the pervasive quiet amid the crackling sensation of teleportation, Andora spoke to him, her voice measured and emotionless as she uttered an unbreakable edict.

"All of them will die, Tov. This is my vow."

CHAPTER 6

A PYRE FOR MOTHER EARTH

Andora stood at the forefront of the assembled leadership of the budding Exodus Armada. It was something she never believed she'd see.

She saw the reflections of the people behind her, their complex expressions, emotions naked on their faces. None of them spoke much, only the occasional whispered words or message sent through internal private links.

To Andora's right stood the Overseers of Sol in their best android shells; minus one, who instead took his place on Andora's other side with their proven friends and allies. There, Tov, Admiral Yan, and the naval officers, academics, and military commanders of the Third Expeditionary Fleet quietly took their place.

The solemn occasion took place once more in an open grove on the observation deck, the same one used in the First Contact conference that seemed so long ago. Bountiful tables, each adorned with a colorful array of delectable dishes, lined the edges, and a soft melody performed by the Eternal Choir filled the air.

Each attendee of the small but elite event held a glass of champagne in their hands, or a choice of juice for those unable to partake in alcohol.

Admiral Yan nodded toward his patriarch, having received word from Captain Kraw commanding the bridge.

Tov walked forward, crossing the short distance to take Andora's side. Together, the pair waited in privacy as the *Zolann'tono* reached its destination in orbit over Earth's South Pole, at the edge of a fleet pointing their sterns at the planet.

The *Ereshkigal*, the *Boogie Mouse*, and the *Will of Sisyphus,* as well as all available battleships and superheavy cruisers, lowered steel tethers as thick as corvettes down toward the planet.

Antarctica looked nothing like it once did. It hadn't for a long, brutal time, but now, the hasty efforts to dislodge the moon-sized Citadel caused the landscape to deteriorate further.

Spouts of magma seeped through the openings, bubbling and leaking toward the red ocean. The lava boiled the salty, trash-filled waters upon contact, adding to the cacophony that echoed throughout the Southern Hemisphere.

Tides crashed and ebbed as the beginnings of a catastrophic lightning storm crept closer to Antarctica.

The clock of her home's final moments ticked loudly within Andora's mind. For a moment, she thought the scene before her was yet another nightmare. With her lifelike dreams and perfect memory, she almost believed it could be.

A part of her wished for nothing more than to wake up.

And so she did, but to another illusion that she had fostered for a century. One where only a hollow dark surrounded her, where nothing mattered except the slow grind toward death.

Not anymore.

The reflections drew her attention once more, to the people who shed the light standing behind her.

"It's really happening, isn't it?" Andora whispered to the Kurskann beside her.

"How do you feel?" Tov replied through their private comms.

She lightly scoffed, nursing her champagne before downing it all in one gulp.

"How do you think I feel?" returned Andora as her glass was refilled by a floating server drone. She lamented her inability to feel the alcohol's effects. The fine notes hidden within the bubbling liquid failed to arouse any sense of pleasure.

She finished her glass again before handing it to the drone, who took it from her hand and silently hovered away.

"Not very good, I imagine," Tov answered, facing back toward the planet.

Andora snorted. Her eyes grew tired as the final pieces slid into place. Her vast psyche felt every motion, every mechanism and electrical impulse course through the Citadel. She sensed Irkalla deftly managing each sequence and motion, culminating in this one act.

As if to hammer the point home, Irkalla hopped up on a low-hanging branch, catching Andora's attention. The Seneschal nodded her owl head, her gaze gentle yet ready.

Down at the surface of the ruined Antarctica, the voice of the Citadel's Seneschal rang out through massive speakers.

"CITADEL IRKALLA, INITIATING LIFTOFF SEQUENCE."

Her voice blew past what useless wrecks remained, hollow and rusting war machines deemed too worthless compared to the cost it would take to salvage.

A series of low horns boomed across the surface, heralding the ascension of Andora's palace.

From their aerial perspective, the assembled guests watched as a kilometer-wide and abyssally deep trench encircled the Citadel, separating the moon-sized command center from the rest of the continent.

"CLOSING DOWN THE HATCHES . . ."

No drone remained in the increasingly hostile environment that was Earth. The heat from rising magma and the steam from the ocean would instantly kill any organic being unlucky enough to be there, but the drones that remained pushed on with their mechanical duties unbothered.

The many hangar blast doors, vents, and other openings slammed shut in triple layers of reinforced high-entropic steel slabs. Rigid locks spun closed and sealed the entire mega-structure.

Inside, the cold AIs of the innumerable drones huddled in their kennels.

"ANCHOR POINTS, LOCKED."

Seventeen tethers hanging down from the colossal vessels in orbit attached to an equal number of stadium-sized structures spread evenly across the surface of what had once been a brilliant new-age city.

The cords sagged and danced in the blistering fast winds, ready to go taut at a moment's notice.

"SPOOLING QUARK REACTOR . . ."

Deep within the bowels of Citadel Irkalla, its main power source, built from Andora's most advanced energy production research and development, drummed like a beating heart. The beat sped faster and faster, becoming one indecipherable whirr of sound.

Andora watched alongside her Overseers as the Citadel's containment field shimmered with the harsh blue luminance of subatomic particles colliding at near light speeds.

Power readings spiked through Andora's eyes, carefully monitored by her Seneschal. The reactor tapped into exotic energies far beyond conventional fission or fusion. Within moments, it closed in on maximum capacity.

Andora felt the rumble through her chassis as quarks smashed into each other, fusing together and releasing vast torrents of energy. They flowed into her Citadel's grid, bringing the sleeping beast to life.

Irkalla's digital presence shuddered as the ungodly amounts of energy surged with nowhere to go. Emergency cutoff protocols engaged to moderate the flood of energy, but there was no stopping the awesome capability now online.

But where there's bounty, there is one to consume. And the Seneschal called in the hungry guests.

"ENGAGING OMEGA BARRIER . . ."

Unfathomable amounts of energy fed into an equally voracious and extremely advanced device. The Omega Barrier Dynamo roared to life as it encased the surface of the Citadel with a thick, golden, translucent shield, crackling and sizzling like a fiery aura.

With the Citadel still buried in the ground, the observers saw only a dome of golden light bloom to life over the craggy surface. Its light bathed the remnants of New Eden, what low ruins still lingered.

"FIRING THRUSTERS."

Deep beneath the Earth, a massive cavern, cleared of magma and hollowed out after two weeks of constant excavation, experienced a new dawn.

Titanic thrusters opened and sparked, the ion plumes bursting forth like the breath of a million dragons, turning the bedrock into melted matter, shaking the walls, and splitting the Earth under its colossal roar.

Magma spewed forth from the cavern, slowly filling up the hellish underground as plasma continued to fire.

As the energy from the quark reactor flooded the thrusters with power, the mega-structure quaked and groaned.

The thirteen super-thrusters at the bottom and the twelve auxiliary thrusters encircling the Citadel's equator roared louder and louder, struggling to lift hundreds of billions of tons of rock and metal.

Yet the structure remained in place, still tethered to the Earth by its leash.

"DISENGAGING SURFACE LOCKS . . ."

Across the massive trench, dozens of gargantuan magnetic holders sprang free from the metal support structure lining the Citadel. Like an old, winged beast, the mega-structure still struggled to fly despite being freed from its restraints.

Andora watched as it even began to sink back into the Earth, but she remained quiet, trusting the plan and her Seneschal to accomplish this titanic task.

Deep rumbling shook the crust as the mighty thrusters poured on more power, coming dangerously close to their safety limits. Irkalla monitored them closely, ready to throttle back at the first sign of structural weakness.

At the same time, the seventeen warships in orbit flared their own drives in unison. Shimmering tongues of blue plasma jetted from their stern thrusters.

Slowly but surely, the tethers began drawing taut like immense harp strings. Those anchored to the Citadel frame creaked and groaned under the incredible tug, reinforced links threatening to snap under the astronomical load.

Andora felt a moment of doubt in that split second. But the feeling quickly vanished as the tethers held. Irkalla's voice rang out once more, speaking the words Andora anticipated and dreaded.

"ALL SYSTEMS NOMINAL. STRESSES WITHIN ACCEPTABLE THRESHOLDS. BEGINNING LIFTOFF IN T-MINUS TEN . . ."

Announced by her voice, thrusters roared and anchors pulled, though the observers barely saw the first imperceptible motion.

"NINE . . . EIGHT . . . SEVEN . . ."

Inch by inch, Citadel Irkalla began to rise from its crater prison, dislodging piled rubble and churning lava. Pieces of Antarctica fell into the crater as the first bolt of lightning struck the burning landscape.

"SIX . . . FIVE . . . FOUR . . ."

Andora held her breath at the awe-inspiring and terrible sight. Pillars of fire, smoke, and the dark storm obscured most sensors, but nothing could hide from her sight.

The tethers groaned as the seventeen warships pushed their thrusters to the maximum, straining the anchor points as the Citadel rose, revealing the awakened behemoth.

"THREE . . ."

While the mega-structure struggled to escape its confines, the Earth wailed in agony.

The first true motions began with violent shifts of the tectonic plates, causing magnitude-8 quakes to roll over the earth for minutes on end. Massive fissures tore across the Antarctic shelves and all over the Southern Hemisphere.

The earthquakes ripped through the southern reaches, their seismic waves traversing the globe. The mountains themselves cried as landslides flowed down like earthen tears.

Great plumes of ash and smoke billowed from volcanoes struck awake from their slumber around the Ring of Fire. Magma surged as the landmass below groaned under its own weight.

More and more molten rock poured into the oceans, boiling the waters like a hellish pot. The crashing tides generated by the upheaval grew ever higher as monster waves pulled back and charged forth like Poseidon's wrathful fists.

"TWO . . ."

Andora eyed the sensors, watching as the magnetic field fluctuated wildly, compromised by the shifting tectonic nightmare.

Black hurricanes, tropical storms, and typhoons carrying acid rain blazed across once pristine blue skies as the very atmosphere protested. Cracks split and dissipated what ozone remained, exposing the ball of dirt and mud to deadly radiation.

Caught in all the horror, long-ruined cities and monuments shuddered further from the destructive vibrations.

"ONE . . ."

The death knell sounded for the battered Earth.

Its wails and cries rang out into the void, lamenting the ruin of its once verdant surface.

Andora watched the unleashed fury with a pained heart, a shudder running through her form, her fists tightened, nails biting into her palms and leaking blue coolant as she could do nothing but watch the destruction.

All the while, Citadel Irkalla continued to rise, the bellowing smoke and flame from her thrusters torching the landscape.

"LIFTOFF."

Only then, at the crescendo of destruction, did the Citadel at last break free of its terrestrial bonds into the chaos-filled skies, towed by the assistance of dreadnoughts and capital warships. As if the sun had risen on the South Pole, the angry bouts of plasma shone upon the dying planet and the crater it left behind, pushing Andora's stronghold higher and higher.

Second by second, Citadel Irkalla, her home, blasted past the stratosphere. With less and less air holding it down, the thrusters siphoned less power from the bountiful quark reactor, until finally . . . it broke free.

No one clapped or spoke a word, mutely watching as the cork was popped. The bottle from which it left cracked, burned, and cried.

Soon enough, the thirteen stern thrusters closed their maws while the twelve auxiliary thrusters lining the Citadel's equator turned around, firing as they brought the moon-sized mega-structure to a halt.

One by one, the tethers unlatched from their anchor points and countless drones dragged them away to be melted down and repurposed.

Slowly, Andora's fortress in the void took its place amid her fleet, cooling down from red to a dull orange.

"We have successfully escaped the confines of the planet, Creator. Congratulations. *Citadel Irkalla* has now entered the theater of space," Irkalla reported, hopping off her branch and gliding over the assembled leadership.

An invisible tension broke, and the audience breathed a collective sigh of relief. Sporadic hushed words broke out between the gathered, their eyes still pulled toward the jewel that hovered so imperiously and ominously.

Andora stared at the structure for a final time as it righted itself. Free from the confines of the Earth, *Citadel Irkalla* had a metallic, cone-shaped dorsal side that housed its main thrusters, and a rounded rocky surface on its ventral side.

At that moment, the hatches opened once more and legions of worker drones flew out, making on-the-spot repairs and attaching countless support structures to the exterior. Drones from Andora's Overseers flew in to assist, like bees swarming around the hive.

"And so, the mother bird sends her child away as their home burns around them, hoping beyond hope that sanctuary exists in the cold night beyond," Mars whispered, his eyes downcast as he stared at the scene before them.

Andora pressed her lips tight, feeling her shoulders sag as conflicting emotions roiled and crashed inside her.

She sighed, glancing toward Tov. "I keep wondering . . . if this is all the right choice. It's what my logical mind thinks. It's what all my Overseers think. And it's what you and the Third Fleet think."

"But . . . ?" Tov asked.

"Some tiny, loud part inside is telling me otherwise . . . latching on to memories so dear." Andora gritted her teeth, her eyes slamming shut. "I remember telling you, telling myself, that everything that mattered rests within the Citadel." Andora chuckled a hollow, hushed laugh heard only by Tov. "But look at what we're leaving behind."

Within her vision, she watched the places she'd once visited and loved fall apart.

In the far east, the long-abandoned ruins of Tokyo tumbled as a magnitude-9 quake surged through the plains. Once towering skyscrapers that had withstood decades of chaos folded in on themselves, leaving only pillars of dust and debris to mark where they had stood. In the distance, a great tsunami made its way to the dead city.

In South America, upon the rocky plateau it had occupied for ages, Machu Picchu vanished beneath a landslide triggered by the violent bedrock shifting. Terraces collapsed entirely, sending the ancient city back into the earth from which its long-dead builders had carved it.

On the continent above, in the western region of what once was the great US of A, the volcano below Yellowstone finally roused from its long slumber, rupturing the landscape and belching its horror into the atmosphere.

All around, the noise of the apocalypse blew its horns and harvested its due.

As the catastrophic chain reaction neared its crescendo, the disasters erased any sign of the civilization that had once thrived across the globe. One by one, edifices fell, entombed beneath the churning Earth, buried in unstoppable waves, and blasted asunder by lightning and the anger of volcanoes.

The remnants of human civilization crumbled to become one with the same dust from which they had been formed so long ago.

"So many wonders, works of art, of great feats," Andora whispered her lament, pressing her palm against the glass separating them from the void beyond. "All we could do is take chunks, but what's the point of little rocks, of bricks and wood, when . . ."

She gritted her teeth. "We're abandoning it all. Just like that, as if they mean nothing."

Her thoughts fell back to those early days, to snippets of joy and laughter.

Andora could hear the cheers of the masses at New Eden Grand Stadium, hosting the Thirty-Eighth Olympic Games. She could smell the aroma of French cuisine within a quaint restaurant in Paris and see the untouched beauty of New Zealand's forests and mountains.

All of these places she had shared with the people she loved, their words and emotions bathing the memories in radiance.

Now, those images were overlaid against the apocalypse raging below. Andora saw nothing remaining of the blue marble's splashes of green, tans, and whites. She couldn't comprehend the magnitude of the ruination.

Grief tumbled within her, beginning to spiral downward, when her thoughts were cut short by her companion's reply.

"I never had a home as a child," Tov confessed.

Andora paused in her mind's turmoil, caught off guard by his sudden tone.

"For the longest time," he began, sharing with her in privacy. "Much of what I remember of my birth world is the crack of whips, the hum of shock collars, and the laughter of cruel masters. And what bright spots existed were snuffed out quickly."

Tov sighed, his antennae drooping as he lost himself in his own remembrance, whispering, "Home was a small, patched-up tent in a city of squatters, slaves, and the misbegotten. It was damp and cold, but it was home, nonetheless."

He looked toward the Citadel. "That went away when my mother passed."

Andora looked down, unable to imagine the loss of a parent. She never had a mother, never considered her creator a father, the thought leaving a bad taste in her mouth. Tov's was a pain unknown to her, one she never wished to experience.

"I'm sorry for your loss . . ." Andora spoke, her emotions settling yet still heavy on her mind.

"Thank you," Tov nodded. "I've . . . forgotten what the word *home* meant. For a long time after her passing, I was adrift. A bug on a mission to topple an empire. I felt alone, for a long time. It wasn't until I found my new family that I remembered the meaning."

He turned to her. "Have I ever told you why our clan is named Garesh?"

Andora, searching for any instance but finding none, shook her head. "You haven't."

"That was the name of the planet where our resistance group rose," he explained. "Each clan in the Kurskann Empire is named such. Each original member used to be a slave who found themselves there, either born from slave parents or thrown there from the red ships. We took the name to remember our struggles, what we fought for."

Andora hummed, nodding at the reason. Curiosity took hold of her, a welcome distraction, prompting her next query. "What happened to that planet?"

He shook his head, a low buzz escaping his mandibles. "Abandoned during the Cataclysm. I never saw what happened to it. Probably scoured of anything useful by the Starless."

"Can you even miss such a place?" she asked.

Tov thought for a moment, then shook his head. "No . . . no I do not."

"I see," muttered Andora. She couldn't imagine having any sense of nostalgia for such a dark place.

A sense of unfairness rose within her, and an easy target in the form of the patriarch called out. She smothered the urge. Yet the hollowness remained, slowly filled by melancholy.

Andora pressed her lips tight, shutting her eyes as she looked to the floor, resting her forehead on the glass. Her voice quaked as she spoke. "Then why do I feel like a failure? Kicked out of my own home because I'm too . . . I'm too weak to defend it."

"No one could have lasted as long as you did, Andora," Tov replied. "No one could have done what you did."

She snarled, seething as her shoulders shook from infernal self-hatred. "I should have lasted longer. I should have found a way to win, found a way to avoid this . . ."

Tov remained stoic against the flame of palpable loathing Andora aimed toward herself, waiting as she managed to leash the rage and bring it to heel, if barely.

He spoke slowly, emphasizing his words. "I can't imagine the depths of loss that you feel. And I'm not comparing what I've experienced to yours. I believe grief has no measure, that competition between who suffered more is utter folly."

"I find that hard to believe," Andora muttered, grimacing at his words. "How could what a child feels when they lose their toy or scrape their knee possibly compare to . . . this—to what I feel."

Tov shook his head, remaining steadfast as he answered. "And yet to that child, losing their toy was the worst day in their young life. You can't put a unit on suffering, not unless you wish to end up in a shouting match. How can an orphan know the pain of a mother who has lost her child, or of a soldier watching his nation crumble? They can't. No one can. In the end, they all suffer."

Andora pressed her lips tight, scowling as her brows furrowed.

"There comes a time when we must all lie down and share our pain, shoulder each other's burdens, and lift them up," Tov continued. "I remember how much it hurt the first time I shared my woes. In the most normal of places, sitting with comrades in the mess hall in a rust bucket of a ship . . ."

He chittered, a sound filled with humor and lament. "It was just a simple conversation, inane topics, but then . . . the words just rolled off my tongue. I crumbled then and there, and all the suppressed hurt slammed in all at once."

Andora glanced back at him, noting the quiver of his antennae and his downcast look. A momentary thing that disappeared as quickly as it emerged.

"I'm different . . ." Andora whispered as the unwillingness taking firm hold on her psyche rattled under his words. "I have all this power . . . I could have—"

Tov turned himself wholly toward her, gently touching her shoulder.

"There have been many times when I felt I could have done more, too many to count. Maybe if I sacrificed myself here, pushed myself farther, been faster, stronger, smarter, I could have saved more, accomplished more." He shook his head.

"For so long, even now when my mind drifts, my head is full of *maybes, could haves,* and *what ifs.* Regret after regret. All these things flutter about, pulling my focus, my drive. All in hindsight," Tov muttered, sighing deeply before his voice steadied. "In the end, I found that what mattered was right there with me, in the present."

He buzzed, then tapped his mandibles. "I remember something a beloved mentor taught me, years after my mother returned to our ancestors. Would you like to hear it?"

Andora, tired and curious as she was, nodded.

Tov spoke. "Cherish the past for what it taught you, but don't let it chain you down. Be watchful of the future, but don't let it stop you before you even begin. But above all . . . live in the moment."

"We had a similar saying. Self-awareness. Live in the moment . . ." Andora muttered, her eyes drifting to the planet below.

Tov nodded. "And you should. You know why you're in pain, and you're working toward healing. More importantly, you're alive. What you do now from here on is up to you, Andora."

She stepped back, returning her gaze to her *Citadel* as the drones fled back into storage, feeling the status of her assets while her Overseers and her Seneschal all signaled their readiness. Their fleets gathered in formation, the last preparations checked off their lists.

Together with the refurbished Third Expeditionary Fleet, they arrayed themselves around the mega-structure. Every single one of them waited in anticipation to get on the road to home.

"A second chance," Andora whispered.

"A second chance. One fraught with difficulty, yes, but a chance nonetheless," Tov repeated, offering his hand. "And I hope to continue helping ease your burden. We all do."

Andora peered into his compound eyes, then looked back at the assembled leadership, everyone turning toward her with understanding and fire in their faces.

She closed her eyes, feeling something slot into place, clearing the fog in her mind, if only a bit.

It was enough. When Andora opened her eyes, she took Tov's hand, grasped it firmly, and shook it once.

Without a word, the observers continued to watch the burning planet for a few minutes more.

CHAPTER 7

GOODBYE, MY CRADLE

Creator, we just received data from the final courier drone. The *Xolotl* has declared no changes detected in Alpha Centauri or the surrounding systems," Irkalla reported from her perch upon the arm of Andora's chair.

Andora knew, of course, even without her Seneschal's announcement. She'd immediately felt the little drone reemerge from the hyper-tunnel and reconnect with the Network, like a worker ant carrying the fruits of its labor.

"Right on schedule. Let's hope it remains that way." Andora sighed, turning toward Tov and Admiral Yan, who had stopped their conversation upon hearing Irkalla's words.

Yan moved first, pulling up the information and sending it to the display table.

After Andora held the unspoken funeral for her home planet, the leadership of the Exodus Armada had quickly proceeded to the moon-sized mobile fortress and toward the immense command center within.

At the moment, the Third parked their vessels close to *Citadel Irkalla*, many of them currently docked in the generously spaced hangars and sending their excess passengers to their new homes inside the *Citadel* for the journey ahead.

Deep within the bowels of the *Citadel*, amid the sections dedicated to housing the non-essentials, civilian personnel, and wounded of the Third Fleet, the War Room was now brimming with personnel.

At rows of workstations, officers sat in comfortable chairs, their minds jacked into their consoles to process the torrents of data. Their presence provided enough redundancy for Irkalla as she supplied all the processing power they needed. At the same time, they acted as liaisons to other parts of the armada. Of course, urgent orders and messages were communicated immediately through Irkalla herself.

Below, in the sunken center of the circular room, an imposing display table showcased projections, graphs, and data sheets, number after number and report after report.

Arrayed around the table, dozens of naval officers and military commanders spoke among themselves and to their subordinates. The table's edges, which weren't needed to project images, were filled with paper files, data packets, tablets, and, more importantly, copious amounts of food and beverages.

Andora, Tov, and their direct cabinet stayed in a private suite with a wide tinted window overlooking the large command center. Their own, smaller display table showcased the vital big picture.

To Andora's immediate right was the patriarch, followed by his second, Admiral Yan, General Ohnar, Chief Scholar Yulane, Lead Harmonizer Volantesh, Venus, Mercury, an empty seat, Mars, Luna, and then herself, completing the circuit.

Andora looked toward the empty chair and sighed.

She had briefly seen Jupiter in the observation deck. The AI stood close to the Third Fleet, quietly conversing and politely keeping his distance from her and his siblings.

It made for an awkward air, and he did not stay for long, returning to the guest suite provided by his current hosts.

Mars wanted to follow, but Andora stopped him.

She shook her head, returning her gaze to the display table showing Alpha Centauri, the trinary system where humanity staked their first colony—a dream of both man and machine that would never come to pass.

Images of the barren moon orbiting the gas giant and the obelisk erected by the Third Expeditionary Fleet when they passed the system awoke a dull pain in Andora's mind.

At the center of the display, Battlegroup Mictlan made themselves comfortable, deploying their immense sensor capabilities and sending out further scouting vessels to neighboring stars.

"Everything looks good so far, no sign of Starless or life," Admiral Yan muttered, expanding the various maps and readings, allowing everyone present to peruse at their own pace.

Unfortunately, the data they received was outdated by nine hours and forty-three minutes, like every other package they received from the courier drones.

Andora grimaced at the delay. She'd never bothered about the anomalous effects of the Dead Zone Miasma before.

She knew it existed, of course, painfully so due to the ill-fated expedition by Neptune and Uranus. At the time, she believed the FTL communications she developed would work.

She was wrong.

And after all these years they never returned, lost to the cruel void.

Ever since, she had never bothered to develop the technology further. Why should she when she had instant communication with Sol already? The same applied to FTL transportation, the importance of which had paled in contrast to blink drives and devices like the Space Enforcer Towers.

Now, Andora's decision to forego that line of R & D was coming back to bite her in the rear. And with their only means of communication, the Starlight Beacon, becoming obsolete with whatever Karnadamus and the Starless had done, the armada had to rely on courier drones to hop back and forth between systems.

Over the past week, the AIs and Third Fleet personnel had fine-tuned their FTL capabilities.

Though nothing could move faster than the universal speed limit, Andora and Luna found no setbacks in catching up with the more modern hyper-tunneler matrix their allies presented—one of the few things the Third Fleet possessed that surpassed the Overseers' technology.

The foundations of the Third Fleet devices, capable of accessing the cosmic rivers that connected solar systems, worked on near-identical principles that humans and androids discovered during their foray into interstellar travel.

Of course, what the galaxy had was leagues better than those primitive research ships and scouting vessels from over a century ago.

Nevertheless, it was enough to develop their own. Though she winced at having to deplete her more exotic material catalog to construct the matrixes capable of opening a path to the higher dimensions, eventually every frigate, destroyer, cruiser, battleship, dreadnought, and mobile fortress received their hyper-tunneler.

Though transporting heavy masses and stable matter through hyper-tunnels was simple enough, Andora found sending data and information magnitudes to be more complex and eventually impossible within their time frame.

Even though the Starlight Beacon provided a massive springboard in their endeavors, she estimated it would be a year at least before she and the Third Fleet found a means to pierce through the corrupted psionic fog that filled the Dead Zone.

To say she was frustrated and stressed was an understatement.

Through the eyes of her assets, Andora looked to the void and saw nothing but a dark, shrouded forest filled with the unknown.

The *Citadel*, like the light of a primitive campfire, banished the umbra to the tree line and no farther. The gathered tribe of AIs and the Third Fleet anxiously awaited word from their scouts if beasts prowled in the unseen darkness.

As planned, she'd sent the vanguard ahead of the assembled Armada to investigate any foreseen dangers and act as a relay for future and farther scouting missions, with the *Xolotl* acting as the mothership coordinator.

In truth, Andora hoped to develop two more Seneschals to inhabit the super-heavies leading both battlegroups. Perhaps before the halfway mark of their journey to Legacy space, she could finish creating their AI cores and embedding the minds within—barring unexpected circumstances.

After nine hours and forty-three minutes of travel, Battlegroup Mictlan arrived at Alpha Centauri.

That had been a day ago.

Every thirty minutes since then, *Xolotl* had compiled all of its sensor data and those from the scouts it sent to and from the neighboring systems. Then, the battlegroup flagship loaded the information onto courier drones and returned them to the armada.

The main force put twenty-four hours between themselves, Mictlan, and Mag Mell, for safety and reconnaissance.

"Then we are all in agreement to give the go-ahead?" Tov asked the gathered.

Andora looked to her Overseers, each nodding, their assets all set hours ago. She turned to Tov. "We're ready."

Anticipation bubbled in the air as Admiral Yan sent a message to the Third Fleet, giving the green light to warm the ships' engines and begin their journey.

"It's about time we left this place," General Ohnar, the massive amphibian beast of a soldier, croaked in his deep voice. He turned to Andora, his neck bulging like a giant toad in power armor. "No offense, but the scenery isn't exactly cheery."

She smirked. "None taken. I'm . . . feeling rather excited, all things considered."

"Once this meeting is over, Admiral Yan and I will return to the *Zolann'tono* and address our people there," said Tov.

Andora looked at the patriarch, tilting her head. "You and Yan are always welcome to coordinate your forces here. That's the whole point of the room down there, after all."

"Thank you, but the *Zolann* shall be and will always be our vessel in the stars. She's been with us for so long, and I'm eager to feel the new changes," Tov replied, denying her offer again.

Andora sighed, raising her hands in defeat. "Very well, I won't argue."

A chime above the blast doors leading to their suite sounded out, followed by Irkalla's voice. "Refreshments and foodstuffs. *Hoot.*"

With a smooth and quiet *whoosh*, the doors opened, allowing a handful of Third Fleet servers and drones to enter, each pushing hovercarts loaded with snacks and beverages. Andora turned to the information above the table as they were served a light lunch.

"To reiterate—ah, thank you." Andora nodded, receiving a slice of egg pie and a mug of hot chocolate before returning her focus. "To reiterate, this is the quickest path back to Legacy space, and we aim to reenter at the Etyel System."

A massive plot detailing countless stars popped up above the display table. At the bottom, a single large dot denoted Sol, then zig zagged through dozens and dozens of solar systems until it reached the top, where a vast swathe was highlighted within the territory of the Galactic Legacy Federation.

"Tov, this is your home. If you would . . ." Andora lounged in her seat, grabbing a fork and quickly delighting herself in the pie. She leaned toward one of the servers, who was arranging more plates of food than she requested. "My compliments to your chefs."

"Y-yes, my lady, will do," the adorable Frae stammered, backing away as Tov stood up.

He clicked his mandibles, zooming in on a star. "Etyel is a frontier system; as Lady Andora said, it is our closest entrance. Like all of its kind, it borders the Dead Zone and is under the direct management of the Zone Sentinels."

Tov turned to the AIs. "They're the military wing of the Legacy Armed Forces dedicated to guarding the border from illegal trespassing," he explained.

"So they claim neutrality?" Andora asked, narrowing her eyes.

Tov nodded slowly. "That is the ideal, and so far, there have been no scandals to dictate otherwise, at least not that I know from six years ago. Nevertheless, you can let us handle them when we arrive."

"Noted." Andora nodded.

Tov continued, opening up the files on the system as holograms and images of Etyel's installations and inhabitants popped up. "Of course, people still live there, and while the Sentinels have a sizeable outpost, the mining colony belongs to the Visai Stellar Union, a minor member nation of our Greater Kurskann Hegemony."

"And if we are forced to divert course?" Luna questioned, adjusting her glasses.

"If we can't make it to Etyel, we have secondary and tertiary points of entry, up to and including those owned by the Warrior's Enclave," Tov replied, showcasing dozens of potential systems under the umbrella of their empire or a trusted, neutral party. "Of course, it goes without saying that we must avoid any territory directly or indirectly owned by the Dagatar Supremacy."

"What can we expect for added reinforcements?" Andora asked as she turned to Admiral Yan. "I heard you and Jupiter managed to acquire some much-needed help?"

She cleared her throat, and Andora barely saw the imperceptible flinch on the Kurskann woman when she uttered her Overseer's name. Yan stood, nodding. "That we did, Lady Andora. And our emperor should have been able to convince others to aid us as well. I'll begin with them."

Yan quickly pulled up the profiles of three expeditionary leaders. Andora had studied them extensively beforehand and already made her conclusions regarding them and their history.

The first to catch her eye led the weakest fleet of the trio, a guildmaster for a group called the Free Kurskann Archaeologists. The rather lanky scholarly type exuded a similar aura to Chief Scholar Yulane, despite hailing from a species that typically gave off a lethal appearance.

The second profile was of a near-ancient-looking being—a military commander hailing from a quaint martially-focused nation called the Koldonian Republic, whose long history spanned back to when the Galactic Accord still reigned over the known galaxy.

The last of the three profiles showcased a young woman from an aquatic humanoid species. Too young, in Andora's opinion. This fourth scion of a noble nomadic household retained a certain naivety in her thin, slitted eyes and a tinge of uncertainty and humility in her pale blue smile. Despite the young humanoid having the most powerful fleet among the three, Andora couldn't help but feel . . . doubtful. All three, while certainly respectable, couldn't match the firepower her armada had at their disposal.

A callous part of her reassured her. *At the very least, these forces would serve as expendable buffer should the need*—Andora shook her head, squashing that line of thinking.

"I'm sorry, but . . ." Andora pursed her lips, grimacing as she expressed her misgivings. "It's almost as if we're their escorts out of here instead of the other way around."

Yan sighed. "I can't deny that fact. Still, with the increasingly hostile nature and the potential extreme risks within the Dead Zone, any Expeditionary Fleet we could incorporate would only increase everyone's safety."

Andora snorted. She had half a mind to suggest going straight to the Legacy, but in the end, she kept quiet as the admiral continued.

"Our allies should already be on their way to the rendezvous point. We aim to regroup in the Gigaballan System about three weeks into our journey," Yan reported. "Fourth Scion Nuwa Straise of the Seventeenth, Commander Nullan Varz of the Thirty-Fourth, and Guildmaster Oros Fa'Myr of the Forty-Second will hopefully be there before us and send out scouting parties to the neighboring stars."

"What of the Second Fleet?" Andora asked, moving the report along as she found more interest in the capabilities of the so-called Brass Armada.

"During our talks, Mighty Gulothan agreed to meet us in the Hunter's Eye Nebula. The nebula is about two months into our journey, at the soonest," Yan answered.

Andora hummed, rubbing her chin as she eyed the image of the small-statured warrior whose species looked like the steroid-pumped fusion of a capybara and a honey badger. "I read the agreement and his vow. Will he keep his end of the bargain?"

"He will if he values his reputation and way of life. The full might of the Brass Armada will escort us to Legacy space while keeping silent on your true nature as digital existences."

Andora crossed her arms, narrowing her eyes. "Forgive me if I'm not so quick to trust him. At the very least, he will concede to a top-down search of his vessels for any spies."

Tov shook his head. "That is a breach of privacy, and no sane leader would concede to such a thing. As pragmatic as Gulothan is, I don't believe the Teleen would look kindly to your . . . investigations."

Andora scoffed. "Fine. His fleet better be worth it."

"They will. They have the furthest technological advancements in all things military. I wouldn't be surprised if Gulothan brought along a few surprises," Tov reassured her.

Andora's ego wished for nothing more than to bull through at such an assumption, but her more reasonable self swatted it back down.

"Do we have anyone else?" Andora asked.

Tov sighed. "Among the Expeditionary Fleets, unfortunately not. We also can't divert our attention to look for the wayward fleets. Without the Starlight Beacon, we cannot contact those who have settled down. Unless our scouts bump into one whom we . . . must push on."

Andora pitied the hundreds of fleets stuck in the Dead Zone, but her empathy for their plight paled in light of her goal of getting her Citadel to Legacy Space.

"What of your Imperial War Fleets?" Luna asked.

Tov perked up, nodding. "Plenty of patrols should be exploring the immediate vicinity after the frontier systems, and their scouts should be sailing far. We can try to link up with the one following on our trail, but Emperor Jarinn may have called it back to apply the technologies you've delivered. Though, we can expect a fleet to meet us in Etyel."

"And apart from that . . . ?" Luna pressed.

"There is no one else," Tov answered.

Andora huffed. "It's better than nothing. At this point, I'd take anything."

The meeting dragged on for a minute more in between food and drink. Eventually, having exhausted the topics and plans they'd already discussed countless times over the past week, the gathered all stood.

Another chime sounded. Irkalla flapped her wings as she eyed Tov. "*Hoot.* Patriarch, your shuttle has arrived to take you and the admiral back to the *Zolann.*"

"Thank you, Irkalla." Tov moved forward to scratch the top of the owl's head and offered a piece of ham from the sandwich he ate. The Seneschal quickly gobbled the piece before hopping onto the patriarch's forearm.

"You spoil her," Andora accused.

He chuckled. "Your loss, my friend. I hope you're ready to give a few words for the fleet address."

Andora's frown only deepened.

Fifteen minutes later, Andora waited patiently in the bridge of the *Zolann'tono*, nursing a fine wine with a deep, rosy magenta color.

Pulling her consciousness in and out of her android shells took but a thought, and having the empty puppets spread across every vessel proved extremely handy for getting wherever she needed whenever she wanted.

It also allowed her to tease her new friends for being late every time.

She sat imperiously on the guest chair provided to her, right beside the patriarch's command throne. Andora crossed her legs, watching the bridge crew go about their tasks under the watchful eyes of Captain Kraw, the old grizzled Iexian who oversaw the *Zolann'tono*.

Soon enough, Andora sensed their approach and heard the blast doors open.

Tov and Admiral Yan strode into the bridge in pristine uniforms. The former, in particular, had donned his martial gear and the medals bestowed upon him. His cape, the color of the void and twinkling with stars aplenty, draped regally over his shoulders, while his combat armor gleamed under the room's light.

The officers took a moment to salute the august figures before dutifully returning to their tasks, neck-deep in coordinating the rest of the Fleet and moving the *Zolann'tono* into position.

Captain Kraw stood up, nodding to his two old-time comrades. "Hyper-tunneler matrix ready to engage at your command, Admiral."

"Excellent, Captain. How's the *Zolann*?" Yan asked, her admiral's garb no less brutal and elegant than Tov's.

The grizzled Iexian cawed, trilling a raspy chuckle. "Hungry and eager to sail, Admiral."

"Then I won't say much," Tov buzzed as he made his way to his command throne, nodding toward Andora in greeting as he adjusted his regalia. "Are you well?"

She huffed. "I know how to make a speech. I only find the whole affair inane."

"Don't be so dour, Andora. I'm eager to hear what you have to say." Tov chuckled before turning to the captain. "And the crew of our *Shepherd*?"

"Even more so, my patriarch," Kraw replied. "Home calls to them, to the whole fleet, and nothing will stop them now with it under threat."

Tov chittered. "I would be remiss if I didn't finish this quickly and fulfill their wishes. As you were, Captain." He dismissed Kraw with a wave.

Andora watched as Tov nodded toward the comms officer. A moment later, multiple screens popped up before the leader of the Third Expeditionary Fleet, each showcasing the face of captains or countless people assembled in halls throughout every vessel.

Every soul aboard fell silent, watching the projection of their patriarch.

"My friends, my family in the stars, allow me a moment to speak to you," Patriarch Tov began solemnly and firmly.

"Over the course of a month, much has changed for us all. Ever since entering Sol, we have experienced world-shattering shifts in our views. We entered a system with a graveyard far beyond our understanding and saw the remnants of a carnage long in the making. We initiated first contact with our strange, powerful hosts, now our allies, our comrades."

He looked toward Andora, nodding before turning back to the camera.

"We found the Starless—more terrible than ever. We encountered a Leviathan, ran from its tyrannical might, and suffered under its whispers and madness. And then . . . the Malignant Starfall."

Andora winced; the mere mention of the plague still left a raw, visceral pain in her heart.

"Yet did we die then and there?" Tov asked in barely a whisper before raising his voice. "Tell me!"

"NO!" the combined shout answered, echoing throughout the fleet.

Tov spread his arms wide before raising one and clenching his fist. "We did not! We rebuilt our warships, and when the time came, together with our new friends, victims who share in our grief, you fought back against the dark and waged war against the unspeakable.

"And when it mattered, did you not slay a beast that has terrorized and dominated the minds of the vulnerable? What is the name of the teeth that slayed a Colossus?"

"*TYRANT'S BANE*!" the sailors, especially those aboard the *Zolann*, screamed out.

"A fitting name. One that scorns the monsters for what they are, despots baying for our deaths, our fear. I only wish I was there to see her first kill." Tov chuckled with pride. "Yet did you stop there? Did you sit back on the sidelines, content with your contributions?"

"NO!" the fleet replied, their palpable fury pouring.

"You fought harder through sleepless nights with the Overseers of Sol! You crewed your stations—reaped abomination after abomination. And though, in the process, some paid the ultimate sacrifice in defense of our new friends and the known universe, you did not yield! Even when Leviathans snapped their jaws at you, YOU REMAINED INDOMITABLE!"

"*VENTALE!*" the Third Fleet bellowed, speaking the Kurskann word that embodied the spirit of a species of ex-slaves and freedom fighters.

"And most of all," Tov spoke gravely, "you faced the horrible truth of our enemy, and, through the heroic deeds of one AI carrying the legacy of humanity's defiance, you lived to carry the knowledge of its existence and its imprisonment like the monster it is." Across the many screens, thousands of expressions darkened at the mention of the vile existence of the Architect.

"Comrades, our Starlight Beacon works no more. We must inform our people back home of the evil that exists. Time is of the essence. The beasts march upon us. Most of all, we must aid Lady Andora and her Overseers in ferrying the remnants of humanity back to Legacy space. And as allies, we must answer their call for aid." Tov turned toward Andora and offered the stage. "My lady?"

Andora pursed her lips before settling her face, recalling the countless times she had presented in front of an audience. She breathed in, stepped to the spot Tov vacated, and looked into the camera.

"I . . . have no words to match those of your patriarch. Seeing the bodies, the people who gave their lives for my home, my crumbling home . . . *Thank you* doesn't encapsulate the sheer gratitude that I feel, but at the very least, I can start with this."

Andora closed her eyes, hands to the side as she bowed deeply, staying in the position for a few seconds before slowly rising back up.

"I hope we continue covering each other's backs for the journey ahead. And when this is all over, know that every debt will be repaid a hundred times over," Andora ended, turning and nodding toward Tov.

He stepped in as she backed away, concluding his speech.

"Comrades. Like those that came before us, I declare this Exodus officially formed, henceforth dubbed the Sol Exodus Armada." Tov raised his fist forward and shouted, "Admiral Yan, set course to Legacy Space!"

And with these final words, the comms officer closed the feed. Those listening cheered to their heart's content before returning to their stations with a fire in their chests.

"Attention, all vessels. We are a go for the voyage. I repeat—tunnel, tunnel, tunnel. I'll see you all on the other side," Admiral Yan called out through the intercom system.

A low hum began to build within the *Zolann*'s massive hull, the hyper-matter cores coming online in a rising chorus of exotic particles as they exited the fabric of space. At the coordinated signal, fleet-wide energies peaked in a synchronized crescendo, crackling arcs dancing along reality.

With a flash that stung the eyes despite compensators, the tunnel mouth yawned open—an eye peering into dimensions beyond. Prismatic mists spilled forth, spectral billows bleeding into normal space in mystical waves.

Within their shifting veils, glimpses of fantastic geometries appeared and disappeared like wisps in the forest.

A storm-racked passage was now cleared, churning cosmic currents split asunder by the shut asteroid crushers of their vessel. The armada plunged headlong into the tunnel in single file, becoming one with the invisible rivers connecting stars.

The sight enamored those experiencing it for the first time. Andora was no exception.

But while what lay ahead captivated her, the sudden change in environment slammed a bitter reality against her.

Andora tried not to look back . . .

Yet the memories, both good and bad, and everything in between, beckoned her.

Try as she might, in the end, Andora could not resist Earth's melancholy. The planet echoed a silent cry into the void at their departure like a dying mother seeing her sons and daughters off to a new life without her.

Andora looked back.

And the hurt strangled her ever so fiercely, wrapping around her mind and soul like ropes. She wanted to reach out, to say something, do something, but the tide pulled her farther and farther away.

Soon, the image of her home ebbed, replaced by a kaleidoscope of vibrant color as the *Zolann'tono* slipped into the cosmic clouds of hypertravel, finally leaving the embrace of Sol.

"Goodbye," she whispered, a single tear falling down her cheek.

CHAPTER 8

INTO THE DEAD ZONE

Andora sighed as she settled into her seat.

She looked through her many eyes, observing the prismatic colors of higher-dimensional travel.

Like rivers of space, the currents of the hyper-tunnel pushed their combined fleet along with potent force. Cosmic clouds roiled and pounded the barrier of the *Zolann* with celestial lightning. For a moment, Andora wondered if this feeling matched those of a captain from the Age of Sail, their wooden boat catching high-speed sea routes while at the mercy of ocean storms.

Yet she doubted even the pure blue of Earth's waters could match the splendor of the vivid hues that swirled and pulsed around them.

She shook her head. Comparing them was folly, akin to judging a classical landscape painting against a contemporary abstract piece; they were too different to pit against each other. Nevertheless, she enjoyed the moment as presented.

"It's beautiful," she whispered privately to Tov, who was relaxing in his seat while overlooking the bridge.

Tov chittered, running his hands over his head as he called the nearest mess hall to bring refreshments for everyone. He turned to her, breathing deeply. "It never gets old . . ."

"How many times have you traveled through hyper-tunnels?" Andora asked as she planted her right elbow on the arm of her chair, resting her chin on her knuckles.

He hummed, looking up in thought. "Countless . . . Though I still remember the first time I saw it."

"Oh?" Andora smirked. "Do tell."

"I was new to the Garesh Resistance, barely a *lakii*, our term for an adult Kurskann male. So there I was, given a job to sneak onto a Dominion cargo ship while her goods were unloaded. And of all my years in the cosmos, all the vessels I've been on, the stale air that circulated that rusty scrap heap was the most visceral thing I would ever experience." Tov shuddered.

"I take it things didn't go as planned?" Andora asked, her smirk widening.

Tov sighed, shaking his head. "About the worst outcome. I was hopped up on adrenaline, twitchy, and stressed beyond belief. I got in just fine, but for some reason, the crew got chased back onto the ship. Something about faulty goods. Young me thought it was a good idea to head deeper to avoid getting caught."

"Dumb of you," Andora scoffed.

"I agree," he grumbled, berating his younger self. "Ultimately, the ship had to take off, run out of the system. I left my hiding spot, a cramped storage closet, and began trying to find a way out, maybe an escape pod. Eventually, I arrived at a corridor that hugged the side. There was this long, narrow porthole."

Tov sighed, reminiscing. "The ship entered the hyper-tunnel then . . . For a moment, I truly thought I was drugged. The colors, the nauseating feeling. The most beautiful scene of cosmic nature warring with me trying to keep my last meal down."

"Was it like this?" Andora asked, waving to hovering displays that showed the outside.

"It felt like it. Our means of FTL travel has remained the same for a long time, and Dominion vessels had the best, even rust buckets like the one I stowed away in," Tov explained. "I remember . . . just sitting down and taking it all in."

"What were you even doing sneaking aboard a ship in the first place?" Andora asked with a teasing smile.

Tov cleared his throat, looking away. "I had to hack into a console and get manifests, records, everything they had . . . In hindsight, I realize it was more of an exercise to see if I had what it took."

Andora stifled a laugh. "Oh, Tov, dear. You screwed up during training?"

"Hush, it all worked out in the end. Though I did have to spend months doing simple errands before I had another chance to prove myself." Tov sighed. "But as I lost myself in the tunnel, I felt the mission didn't matter. Looking at those colors made me feel so, so small. It put things into perspective."

Andora nodded, feeling a similar sensation.

When humanity and her android kin discovered the hyper-tunnels, they immediately sought to build ships to traverse them. The first of its kind was a drone ship, a simple back-and-forth maneuver to Alpha Centauri. It took three weeks for it to return, and by then, they had already sent faster vessels one after another.

Eventually, they shaved it down to less than a week, a far cry from the speed they were now going, only having to wait nine hours to travel 4.3 light-years.

She envied her brothers and sisters who experienced FTL travel. While they and their human partners were off being the greatest heroes of a generation, she had been playing empire-building and politicking.

At the time, Andora had desperately wanted to take Rikard and Lucy to Vinland and the nascent research station to see the habitable moon and the budding colony.

Of course, that was before the Starless came and destroyed Operation New Horizons.

"I have to agree with you there, Patriarch," Andora whispered. "I will cherish this moment forever. I only wish I experienced it sooner, and during not-so-precarious situations."

"The brightest lights tend to flare during our darkest moments," Tov mused.

Eventually, snacks and drinks arrived, much to the delight of the bridge officers. Kurskann naval tradition felt familiar yet strange to Andora, as the crew of the Third seemed to prefer a more casual atmosphere than what she experienced in the past aboard human vessels.

She tilted her head, glancing at Tov's way. "How did you get back to Garesh?"

"You mean *who* got me back," he grumbled, taking a long sip from his mug of coffee. "My mentor, a top lieutenant in the resistance, predicted I'd mess up. He managed to contact an agent on the planet I was bound to. Said agent arranged transportation for me to get back home. Of course, I had to work off the travel fees and endure . . . his scolding."

Tov shivered. Andora wondered what type of individual could evoke such a reaction in a hardened veteran like the patriarch. One of these days, she'd ask a more in-depth retelling of Tov's origin, perhaps from another source, to bypass the Kurskann's humble downplaying.

"Poor you. It must have been quite the adventure," Andora teased, filing her plan away for later.

He hummed. "You know, it was. To watch it all on that corridor for the first time again. That would be something."

They continued to partake in small talk and let the ambiance fade into a symphony of tapping keyboards, low conversation, the occasional louder chewer, the constant white noise of electronics, and the breeze of synthetic air—fresher than it had ever been since the ship's upgrades.

Eventually, Admiral Yan stepped back from her station, finishing her few tasks and closing the multitudes of hovering screens. One of her aides, a junior officer in training and one of the young bloods who had survived the Malignant Starfall weeks prior, picked up Yan's tasks as the admiral approached the seated pair.

"My patriarch, I shall retire for the evening. A journey like this needs to start with a fresh mind," spoke Yan, clasping her two pairs of hands behind her back.

Tov nodded. "I think I shall follow suit. Have a good rest, Admiral."

"Oh, I plan to," Yan replied, and Andora heard a hint of eagerness in her voice. A familiar note that reminded her of—

"Yan," Tov called out, cutting Andora's train of thought as the admiral passed his chair toward the blast doors leading out. "When I said have a good rest, I meant it."

The red-hued Kurskann woman cleared her throat, glancing away for a moment before assuming a stoic posture. "Yes, of course, my patriarch. Good night."

She left without another word and with thinly veiled haste in her step.

Andora kept her eye on the admiral until she left the bridge and walked to the elevators down the hall. Eventually, she pulled her observations away, fighting the urge to follow Yan along through the ship's hidden cameras.

Actively suppressing her presence in the *Zolann*'s systems tested her in ways she hadn't felt in a long time, harkening back to when she and her kind had to stop themselves from so easily snooping around.

The act was akin to covering one's ears with their hands.

"What was that about?" she asked, turning toward Tov.

He tilted his head, swaying his antennae in surprise as he faced her. "You don't know? I assumed you were aware, what with your . . . casual disregard of my ship's security systems."

"Oh, please, Patriarch," Andora huffed, glaring. "I am not so paranoid that I need to look into what people do in the privacy of their dorms."

Tov's silence only deepened her frown.

She rolled her eyes. "Whatever. However, know that I respect you all that much, at least. I mean what I said in that impromptu speech I did. So, if I can't trust you and yours within the safety of your domiciles, then we might as well split this Coalition apart."

He hummed, nodding as he leaned toward her, relaxing his shoulders. "That means more than you can imagine, Andora. Thank you for that."

"Yes, yes. No need to thank my beneficent self." Andora waved him off before her grin turned upward in mischief. "Now, what gossip is afoot in this ship?"

Tov's antennae shot up, and suddenly the patriarch appeared hesitant. "Well . . . I don't think it's my place.

Andora pouted. "Not even a hint for a friend?"

"It's a private matter, Andora. Apologies." Tov chuckled.

"Alright, fine." She smirked. "Forcing me to hunt down some loose-lipped sailor, are you? I can play."

He stood up, depositing his finished drink on a drone's platter. "I'm sure you can make your investigations with the rumormongers aboard this ship. But unless you want to spend nine hours doing just that, perhaps I can humor you for a bit."

She gasped playfully, giving him a faux coy smile as she spoke. "But Tov, you're married."

"That is not what I meant, and you know it," Tov grumbled, his setae raised in agitation.

Andora laughed in reply, standing up and stretching the synthetic limbs of her android shell. "Oh, you're no fun," she said, pouting. "Still, I would like to explore some places we glazed over during the first tour. I also want to see the ship's markets. Oh, and take me to the best restaurant here. I'm feeling peckish for something exotic."

Tov sighed, rubbing his temples. "Somehow, I'm already regretting this."

The nine hours flew by as the two concluded their exploration of the now much larger *Zolann*.

Andora delighted in the new experiences. A month earlier, during the Festival of the Odyssey, the entertainment and cuisine on offer had been the Third Fleet's love letter to what humanity once was. While she appreciated the nostalgia of familiar delicacies, a desire for the new had since sparked within.

Suffice it to say, alien spices and foodstuffs greatly agreed with her.

"Glutton." Tov shook his head, feeling the drain in his account after her binge.

Andora chuckled as they sat amid the hustle and bustle of *Zolann's* primary resource-processing center.

"I eat and drink so much because I remember not having any." Her voice grew cold. "Try fasting for a century, and you'll feel a pit in your stomach deeper than a black hole."

Tov crossed his arms. "I'm certainly feeling my finances being sucked up into nothing."

She smirked, patting the patriarch's shoulder. "Too bad."

Tov sighed, causing her to delight at his frustration with her antics. The little joys helped stave off the quiet of her mind. A quiet that was always followed by an onslaught of unwanted memories and self-reflection.

They quieted down, taking in the scene of workers, ship engineers, supervisors, and ratings doing their duties.

Although many industrial vessels had been added to the Exodus Armada, the *Zolann's* capability to process raw materials and produce them into usable goods remained unmatched, and the gap had only widened since her recent rebirth. As such, the ever-hungry needs of warships demanded parts, and the flagship of the Third Fleet was there to provide.

Andora's gaze drifted above, past the ceiling and toward a new compartment housing a potent device—a Grav Dynamo embedded at the root of the *Zolann's* asteroid crushers.

"Grafting the wreck of the *Buddha's Palm* certainly did your ship justice, Tov. I'm sure our enemies will be surprised," Andora commented.

He hummed. Despite his inability to see through the ceiling, he knew what she referred to. "The battleship's finesse in generating and manipulating gravity and space always awed me. I only regret that we had to salvage it."

"Guiding us into and out of that unstable black hole overloaded its circuits, and the failures cascaded from there. I'm surprised it didn't simply explode." Andora sighed, lamenting the fall of Jupiter's favorite ship. "It made its designer proud in the end, and this vessel will have the honor of carrying on its heritage."

Besides increasing the reliability, speed, and distance the *Zolann* could teleport, the Grav Dynamo could also pull in unsuspecting victims toward the two-kilometer-long mandibles, further reinforced to the point where this lethal weapon could give a Colossus a run for its money.

That was but one of the improvements they'd made over the week. The supercapital ship, a term Andora had never taken seriously until a few days prior, now had massively increased its volume and resilience with the added parts gifted from the *Palm*.

While Andora and Luna had needed the full breadth of their design capabilities to manage the *Zolann's* rework, Andora thought they did an admirable job in the end. The ten-kilometer-long and seven-kilometer-wide behemoth finally met her volume and mass standards.

Luna would speak otherwise about the minor inefficiencies, but she always did that.

Before Andora and Tov could speak further, the intercom echoed overhead.

[Attention, attention. We are pulling out of the hyper-tunnel in one minute. Please refrain from strenuous activities. Thank you.]

"About time," Andora hummed as she stood. Her gaze accessed the external cameras and watched as the tunnel shifted.

[Exiting in ten seconds . . .]

Bit by bit, the cosmic clouds roiled, and ahead, a thin slit of black appeared against the backdrop of color. Soon, the slit opened like an eye, revealing the void of reality and the three stars of their destination. The prismatic nebula from the higher dimension leaked into real space as the *Zolann* drew closer and closer to the yawning maw.

[. . . Five . . . three, two, one.]

Finally, after a century in Sol, Andora found herself in a new neighborhood.

[Welcome to Alpha Centauri. We have contacted the *Xolotl* and Battlegroup Mictlan. No sign of hostiles. Decreasing alert level. If you are experiencing high levels of tunnel sickness, please report to the nearest medbay.]

Tov sighed, massaging his shoulders as he shook off the mild discomfort. "That is what hypertravel should be like. Nothing like the horrendous and forceful method you employ."

Andora smirked, knowing his dislike of the blink drives she'd developed. "Perhaps we could use my technology to . . . toughen up recruits."

He shuddered, placing his hands on his hips. "You might as well put a new section in the Federation Commandments of War, because I see few outcomes where that isn't immediately considered a war crime."

"Oh, please." She rolled her eyes. "It's not that bad."

"You have no right to speak with your lack of organic bits."

Andora smiled mischievously, patting the patriarch's cheek before turning away. "An absolute shame. You have my sympathies, meat bag."

She heard his grumble behind her as the two moved toward the opening of the *Zolann*'s mouth. The immense internal hangar doors slowly slid open as a translucent barrier sprung to life. Afterward, the external doors opened up, revealing the new system.

One by one, the combined might of the Sol and the Third Expeditionary Fleet came into view alongside their vessel.

At the forefront, discounting the expendable Battlegroup Mictlan already sent ahead, was the Mars Fleet. The red warships of the great Overseer shone like the tip of a mighty spear. At the center of his formation, his mobile fortress, the *Bucephalus*, hovered over the vessels like a conqueror looming over his host.

Every general retained elite bodyguards, and Mars's gargantuan home and flagship was no different, protected by the dreadnought *Boogie Mouse* and his Five Greats.

Following Mars, the combat-capable and eager Third Fleet formed the second line with the reclassified superheavy cruiser *Nu Rovshk*, and, of course, the *Zolann'tono*. Although their numbers had decreased during their stay in Sol, the cruisers, destroyers, frigates, and carriers had cannibalized what they could—focusing on the quality of their vessels, despite the diminished quantity.

Every single ship drastically overshadowed what they had been a month prior, brimming with high technology, gun batteries, shields, engines, reactors, and all the bells and whistles. Each captain who commanded the battle-hardened and upgraded warships felt confident they could take on the First Expeditionary Fleet or maybe even the infamous Brass Armada.

At the rear, the Luna Fleet. The *Ozymandias*, Luna's seat of power, hovered ominously like a mysterious silver pyramid flanked by the *Xerxes* and the *Gilgamesh*.

Finally, the newly formed Galla Fleet. Led by the dreadnought *Ereshkigal* and the battleships *Gugalanna* and *Nergal*, the fleet stuck close to their queen like vicious, demonic guardians, their guns ready and waiting.

Battlegroup Mag Mell stayed behind in Sol, following them a day apart.

With the Exodus Armada arriving in the system, Andora observed as the *Xolotl* and Battlegroup Mictlan prepared their jump to the next star, ready to repeat their duty. Eventually, they might discuss shortening the wait between stars from twenty-four hours to half that, speed should be more important than safety.

"Looks like we're off to a smooth start. Let's hope it lasts," Andora muttered, her gaze lingering on the three stars and toward a gas giant with a barren moon orbiting around it.

"Tov?" she called out in a whisper.

He turned toward her, raising his antennae. "Yes?"

"You erected a monument here, right?" she asked, spotting the car-sized object floating around the moon. "For the humans that fell here."

"We did. Would you like to visit it?" Tov suggested.

Andora pursed her lips, considering it before slowly nodding her head. "That would be nice. I'd like to take it with us. Should they ever pass by here, I fear that bastard Architect might desecrate it."

"That can be arranged. Would you like me to accompany you?" Tov asked.

Andora smirked before eventually shaking her head. "I'd rather be alone for this. You should get some rest. I know I've been a handful."

He chuckled. "I don't mind, as long as you keep your mischief to a minimum."

"I hold no promises." Andora winked.

With a thought, she departed her android shell, instructing the body to return to the penthouse she was given aboard the *Zolann*'s residential district.

A moment later, she emerged back on her Citadel before summarily jumping to another shell close to *Irkalla*'s main hangar.

Opening her eyes, she looked around the vast space housing legions of defense drones ready to protect her home. Andora walked forward with her hands clasped behind her. In the distance, a drone buzzed to life, one designed to house a single passenger.

The cockpit opened, a ladder cascading down to the hangar floor.

She climbed aboard, feeling the comfortable cushion of the pilot's seat and the familiar design of its interior. It was an old but serviceable design, created during a time when humans piloted starfighters with the aid of their AI companions. Andora prepared the machine for flight.

Before the cockpit could shut, however, a small shape glided through the closing door.

"*Hoot*. Hello, Creator," Irkalla greeted as she settled in her perch to Andora's side.

She raised her brow at her unexpected passenger. "Irkalla, I see you've invited yourself to my little adventure."

"I am curious," she replied.

Andora smiled, petting Irkalla's head before pulling a handful of nuts from her pocket. "Alright, then. Buckle up."

"Joy," the owl replied, pecking at the presented snacks.

A few button presses later, Andora deftly piloted her starfighter out of the *Citadel*'s hangar. She glanced at the wondrous vista around her as she set course toward the Third Fleet's monument. Before her, the many warships of the Exodus Armada slowly sailed forth toward the moon, ready to park and resume repairs as they waited for Mictlan's go-ahead.

Andora engaged in the mini blink drive, cutting travel time by a few hours. As she emerged from the teleport, the barren moon, once a barely visible dot, now exploded into view, taking up much of her vision.

Andora felt her emotions swell within her upon the sight of what should have been their first colony and the start of a true golden age. A dream that the Starless crushed into dust.

Her anger tried to bubble within her, but it found little to hold on to, unable to break the hold of the sorrow that dominated her mind.

Andora powered down her starfighter, letting the moon catch her in its orbit.

She waited, feeling the weightlessness of zero-g.

Soon enough, the monument came into view. It was a simple thing, an obelisk detailing what Tov and his people found, and at the bottom—

Here lie one hundred and twelve brave souls from the human race, their sacrifice witnessed by the crew of the Third Expeditionary Fleet of the Galactic Legacy Federation. Pay respects and sing eternal hymns, you who take these paths paved by heroes.

She muttered the words, reading them over and over again.

Hours passed, and Andora immersed herself in the quiet of her starfighter as Irkalla nestled in her arms. Teardrops floated in the air.

CHAPTER 9

EVERYTHING IS FINE

The wailing sounds of an all-consuming void filled his ears.

Confusion racked his mind, unable to make sense of his surroundings, his name, and his identity. Bits and pieces flew by, sporadic images in a kaleidoscope of vivid emotions and sensations.

"Where . . . ?" he murmured, drowsy as if submerged in molasses.

A starless space, a black canvas of a cruel universe, glared at him with disgust and contempt. He felt its palpable aggression, seeking to clamp and rend his body apart. Instinctively, he raised his guard, throwing back equal derision at the hate aimed against him.

And in the foreground, basking him in a violent light, an unstable black hole dragged the fabric of space toward its voracious maw.

There, he realized, was the source of that infernal scream.

Its racket possessed a tangible presence, surrounding him, coiling around his shapeless form, drilling into his mind like heavy shackles.

His muffled voice tried and failed to crawl out of him, speaking out and trying to call anyone to aid him through the cacophony of agony.

"WEAK."

"PATHETIC."

"SUICIDAL FOOL."

The voices shouted at him. Loud, so very loud.

The pandemonium grew, reaching toward an impossibly high crescendo. Time felt meaningless. Whether seconds or millennia passed, the damned noise washed away any feeble attempt to make sense of it all. His hands shot up to cover his ears, yet it pierced through regardless.

"Shut up . . . ! Fuck, that noise! Make it stop!" he snarled and pled, thrashing.

The constant screaming grew as if the cosmos cried out from a grievous wound—snapping, groaning, and biting. Pain followed immediately, adding to the chaos that overwhelmed him. He tried to escape, only to be stopped when the wicked gravity well pulsed. The force washed over him, and he felt a sudden tug toward the singularity.

Then it started to pull.

Manic panic swelled as the maw dragged him against his will.

His limbs coalesced and he began to desperately reach out to grasp at anything like a man sucked in by quicksand. "You . . . won't . . . take me!" he shouted, seething.

As he struggled, another sound sliced through the racket of the black hole's growling gut—cold and insidious.

A mocking laugh.

His vision whirled toward the source, sensing a vile existence. There, at the edge of the event horizon, he spotted the source.

A sphere of oily ink, blacker than the void, floated away from the maw as if taking a stroll. Then, from its simple form, it changed, sprouting, blooming like a virulent plague-ridden flower. Space wept as it finished reshaping into a humanoid monstrosity.

"You . . ." he choked, staring in shock as the Executor stretched his limbs, craning his neck as his pillar-like head faced him. His singular eye filled with contempt as the light of the black hole's accretion disk basked the vile thing's back.

"You should have listened, arrogant wretch," he sighed in disappointment before his lipless maw twisted into a cruel grin. ***"Now, you die in vain."***

The eldritch cube floating behind the abomination shifted, twisting as its endless gears and mechanisms grasped space, paving a way through the ergosphere like a red carpet unfurling for its unquestioned authority.

He laughed. ***"Honestly, you Phages, you Aberrations, you're all the same. Defying the inevitable. Worthless. All you suicidal fools."***

Jupiter struggled harder, panicking in desperation at the sight. Unwillingness welled within him as all thoughts of escape fled his mind. All that mattered was keeping this bastard imprisoned, away from his family, his loved ones.

"No! I haven't dismissed you!" Jupiter snarled, crawling toward the Executor with every ounce of willpower. But the creature paid no more heed to him than as if his voice never existed, drowned by the constant shrieking greed of the singularity.

Casually, the Executor flew toward the edge of the ergosphere, seeking freedom from the prison he brought to bear. As the monster exited, his own chance of escape disappeared, his limbs failing, his body drawn farther and farther into the endless void.

"Please, no! No, no, no! Stop! Let me go!" Jupiter pleaded, looking back and forth between his death and the monster drawing closer to the mouth of the black hole.

"COME BACK HERE!" Jupiter screamed, his voice stretching into the cosmos. "STOP!"

The black hole cared not, pulling him farther, the event horizon appearing like a guillotine ready to deliver its execution. He felt his body being ripped apart, all around him, his *Ultimatum* crumbled. The massive structure, once so invincible, so domineering against every vermin that smashed against its walls, broke apart piece by piece.

Debris fell into the whirlpool of space, passing through the event horizon and freezing in place. But he knew their very molecules were being drawn like strings.

Suddenly, the reality of his impending death slammed into him. A visceral, clawing fear surged within, and he wanted nothing more than to scream and beg.

Just as he closed in on the event horizon, a loud clap echoed behind. He looked back, and a surge of relief washed over him, seeing the *Zolann'tono*.

Yet the feeling passed him like a phantom breeze.

The Executor had also spotted the appearance of the supercapital ship and immediately made a U-turn. He surged forward like a dark comet, bringing apocalypse in his wake. The vessel turned in its axis, and whatever guns were left swiveled and fired toward the sinister entity.

"Sentimental fools, you simply made my job easier by coming here!" he growled in a thousand voices as spacial barriers emerged, blocking shot after shot.

"NO! TURN BACK!" Jupiter screamed toward the *Zolann*. "LEAVE ME! GET OUT OF HERE!"

But no matter how much he roared, the two drew closer and closer until they finally smashed together. The Executor pierced the shields and through the hull of the Third Fleet's flagship, crashing into something critical and causing a catastrophic detonation.

"No . . . No, no, no!"

The *Zolann* exploded into blazing light just as he passed the event horizon, screaming in agony as the cacophony reached a fever pitch.

"NO!"

Flashes of scenes popped into his vision, one after another like a macabre slideshow, giving him visions of death—a galaxy aflame. People burned by the trillions, cursing the night sky as monstrosities brought down the Cataclysm.

Citadel Irkalla, alone and firing her guns till their barrels melted against an ever-encroaching shadow, fought on. The vast mind within, broken and enraged as she screamed at the void until she too fell—her fortress torn asunder.

Visions of his siblings flew by next, all of them dying in his arms, their faces shifting one after another as they called out to him.

"Brother . . . I'm sorry, I wasn't . . . strong enough . . . Forgive me . . ."

"Where . . . were you . . . You shouldn't have left . . ."

"It's not your fault . . ."

Their whispers pierced his ears, sharper than any blade. And as he lay there, confused and in pain, Karnadamus cackled before him, floating over their corpses.

"I'm coming for them," he promised.

Behind him, amid the endless ocean of black, a vast line of light divided the backdrop. Then, like a nightmarish eye, it opened. Within, something incomprehensible, cold, and unfeeling shifted its attention toward him, its mere gaze heavy as moons. It stared at him without a care as the prison he'd made ripped him apart.

He could do nothing. Still, desperate, he clawed his way forth, the words spewing forth from his torn throat, shouting—

"DON'T YOU DARE!"

Jupiter gasped awake.

His eyes opened wide as he frantically searched the ceiling. Shuddering breaths escaped him as his chest rose and fell. The synthetic heart within his android shell drummed, slamming loudly against his chest in suffocating tightness.

Slowly, he reined in the lingering terror and the shakes racking his body. His breaths calmed down, deepening. Jupiter lifted his left hand, running it over his sweaty face. He lay there, staring at the metal bulkhead above and listening to the quiet ambiance around him.

A ray of artificial light bled into the room from the glass balcony doors, washing over the blanket sprawled atop him.

The faux sun hanging over the residential district of the *Zolann'tono* glowed a warm, comforting luminescence, waking up the thousands resting within the vast complex. Simultaneously, a melodic chime, accompanied by an announcement, echoed throughout the vessel.

> **[Attention. We have arrived at the Vinland Memorial. During our twenty-four-hour stay, the Exodus Armada will park and assume maintenance procedures.]**

The voice spoke in a polite, formal tone, signaling the start of the workday.

Jupiter groaned, stretching his body as the horrors of his nightmare dissipated. Even now, the contents appeared fuzzy in his head, leaving only the grief and fear. The soft bed shifted as he moved, pulling off the silk sheets from his naked body.

Then he noticed the weight on his right side, holding on to his arm.

"Jupiter?" a sleepy voice spoke beside him.

A hand of rust-red chitin pressed gently against his bare chest, and Jupiter's eyes crawled up to meet the face of his . . . companion.

"Good morning, Yanny," he greeted, his free hand cupping her cheek. "I didn't wake you, did I?"

The admiral of the Third Fleet shifted on top of him, the sheets draping over her body in a way that made his heart thump in a different but much more welcome manner. The light bathed over her chitin, making her radiant in his eyes. Her simple touch banished the last of his ragged thoughts and focused on the warmth touching his skin.

He cleared his throat as he put on a dashing smile. At least, he hoped it was.

She nuzzled against him, her antennae poking and feeling his face in a curious, dazed manner.

"No . . . that's just my internal clock. Damnable thing," she murmured, breathing deeply and making low buzzing sounds.

He chuckled, rubbing his neck and wincing at the marks those ferocious mandibles had left the prior night. For a moment, Jupiter wondered if that wildness he experienced came only from her, or if it was something every Kurskann woman possessed.

If so, he had to hand it to Tov. And anyone else fortunate or unfortunate enough to be partnered with one.

"Go back to bed then. It's not like we top dogs have much to do in this pit stop." Jupiter smirked, placing his hand on the curve of her back. A part of him even hoped to continue where they'd left off.

She sighed as she rolled to his side. "Can't . . . Too much to do for me to take a day off."

"That's a shame," Jupiter muttered, sinking his head back onto the pillow.

He nonetheless appreciated her presence, knowing he'd been out of sorts since . . .

His thoughts drifted to the days he'd been awake, unable to do anything with the condition of his Nexus. Still, it trumped the chaotic mess of darkness and images he'd suffered through during his hibernation. Time and sense lost coherence as Andora and Luna worked for hours on end to repair the damage inflicted upon him.

Darkness . . . cold and unforgiving, and within, the gaping maw of the black hole roared at his face. Memories of his suicidal battle against the Executor played on repeat while he was under, except each time, something changed for the worse.

He gritted his teeth, banishing the thought and focusing back on Yan. His arm snaked beneath her as he shifted, spooning her and pressing his face against her neck.

"A few more minutes?" Jupiter asked with a playful tone.

She chittered. "Well . . . Maybe they can survive without me breathing down their necks for a while."

"Like what I'm doing now?" he teased.

A light slap hit his arm as Yan wriggled to face him. "Oh, stop it, you. Also, you sleep like a statue. Loosen up."

"Alright, alright." Jupiter smirked, winking as they settled in each other's arms.

As they did, his thoughts drifted again to a few days ago, hours after he debriefed the Eldest of everything he learned.

He . . . hadn't relinked himself to the Network. Whether it was because he felt unprepared to face his family after going off on his own, or some other reason was holding him back, Jupiter didn't know.

Neither could he muster his forces.

His fleet was decimated, and his *Ultimatum* was lost to the unstable black hole he made.

Though the *Will of Sisyphus* survived, Jupiter's condition prevented him from trying to control its complex systems. And his *Palm* had perished long before he woke up and gifted its remains to the Third.

Without a ship of his own that he could control, he settled in with the Third Fleet.

And so, for the last few days, he'd been helping with a few things aboard the *Zolann*, spending time with Yan and her people, believing it would help his state of mind—help distract him.

They did . . . she did.

Jupiter, in all honesty to himself, had no idea how this happened.

He had been friendly with her for a while. During the Eldest and Tov's absence, he'd become increasingly familiar with the admiral, acting as a sort of go-between for his siblings and the rest of the Third Fleet.

Her presence soothed him differently, something he'd never experienced despite being alive for over half a century, if he could call those years living.

With his admittedly lacking social skills, he had no idea what to do with his feelings.

Thankfully, he didn't have to.

Admiral Yan made the first move, much to his utter surprise.

Then, after days of testing the waters and getting to know each other during the rare instances of free time, he had his . . . first experience . . . just before the final battle began.

In that moment, he'd never felt more alive, different, happy, and eager. He had no idea what to do, and while he had access to a plethora of information on the subject, he decided to go in blind.

For once, he thanked himself for having an android shell with all the essentials to enjoy that unique pleasure.

And enjoy it, he did.

"You know, legally speaking, I am human," Jupiter suddenly commented as Yan nibbled his chest.

The admiral ceased her ministrations, propping her head on her upper hands as she lay atop him. "Pardon?"

Jupiter shrugged. "Well . . . A synthetic human, but who's checking?"

Her continued silence prompted him to explain further, and he did so after clearing his throat.

"I meant that by the definition set a hundred years ago by android reps and the UN, I am technically human, or a child of humans. *Homo synthetica*, to be exact. It was a move to bring our kind together, having similar names," he explained.

"You are not exactly like those androids from the past. Do you consider yourself a human?" Yan asked, her curiosity evident from her swaying antennae.

He hummed in thought at her question. A few seconds later, he answered slowly, sighing. "No . . . I'm more than that—neither human nor android. I don't think an android brain can house my software. But I'm a warm AI, in the end, just a powerful one."

Yan nodded, tilting her head. "So what then, if not either of those? A fragment, an Overseer?"

"That's a loaded question . . . Maybe a 3.0 version of my AI ancestors. I think. Definitely not calling myself a fragment; I'm my own person. And Overseer is more of a job title . . ." Jupiter sighed, looking at Yan as he confessed. "Honestly? I never thought about it much."

"I see," she replied, resting her head against his chest. "It's admirable of them to grant such a title to your kind. They must have been eager for both sides to be partners."

Jupiter raised his brows. "Yeah, I guess they were."

"Still, why mention it?" she asked.

Jupiter chuckled as he turned to Yan with a smug grin. "I was just thinking about how humanity would be proud of me."

Yan's antennae drooped down like someone narrowing their eyes in suspicion. "Well . . . they have a lot to be proud of."

His grin only widened further.

"I mean, I'm the first dude to bang an alien," he proudly proclaimed, a hearty chuckle bubbling out as he embraced her tight. "Can you believe that—Ow!"

Yan slapped his shoulder, rising from her rested position and shaking her head.

"Of all the . . ." she grumbled as she exited the bed while Jupiter laughed. "I swear, I always end up with the most uncouth rogues."

Jupiter cut short his laughter, freezing at her words as he furrowed his brow. "Wait, always? What does that mean?"

Now, it was her turn to deliver a teasing chuckle. As she rose to full height, Yan's bare body was briefly on display before she draped a bed robe over herself. She looked at him with playful pity, stepping forward to pinch his cheek.

"Oh, Jupiter, you innocent thing. You know I'm older than you by half a century. I fought alongside every veteran here from the rebellion to the Cataclysm," she spoke, giving him a twirl as she revealed a bit of her shoulder. "I may look young, but that's the wonder of modern medicine. Meaning . . ."

"You've had past relationships," Jupiter realized. He pursed his lips, leaning back on the bed as an unknown feeling rose. Something that tasted like—

"Disappointed?" Yan asked, planting her two right arms on her hip.

He widened his eyes as he turned to her, propping himself up on his elbows. "Huh? No, no, absolutely not. I'm not jeal—I'm good. Well, I'm just not used to . . . I mean, I don't mind. Who the hell am I to comment? I, uh . . ." he sputtered.

"Hush, Jupiter," Yan buzzed, leaning down and pressing her forehead against his, her hand gently caressing his cheek as she sat back on the mattress. "I used to be naive and overeager when I was young, too."

"Alright, I get it." Jupiter rolled his eyes. "Now get back here, you; I'm not ready to leave bed yet."

"Overeager, indeed," Yan chittered, settling into his embrace.

The two immersed themselves in contented silence as the room brightened further. From her kitchen, he heard the appliances begin their automated functions, prepping two mugs of coffee and a simple breakfast to go along with.

At the same time, their version of a television sprang to life, and the Third Fleet's internal news channel began listing off announcements for the day.

His guest suite had all the necessities, plus what luxuries the Third could spare. Something he'd refused at first, but his hosts' insistence eventually persuaded him otherwise. It was the least they could do for what he did, they said.

He didn't mind it in the end.

With the loss of his *Ultimatum*, Jupiter didn't have much real estate left, and with pieces of his favorite battleship grafted onto the *Zolann*, it was the closest thing he had to home. Their company also helped banish the feeling of loneliness.

It *greatly* helped.

But as Jupiter relaxed in the relative quiet, little things snatched his attention, like the clock ticking and the conversations far below in the district. The ambient hum grew louder in his ears, narrowing his focus.

Jupiter's smile faltered, the warmth leaving the room as his gaze latching onto a spot on the ceiling—dust clinging onto the metal.

Something about the tiny blemish irritated him, mocking him.

He stared at it, his vision darkening as he tunneled at that insignificant bit of dust. A dark spot, a black spot.

A feeling of bottomless gluttony and an inexorable pull to oblivion slammed into his mind. The roaring singularity, the screams of space, the din of battle, and the impotent frustration as attacks failed to overcome his adversary.

Then, for a second, he thought he heard a vile laugh echo out—far, far in the distance.

Instantly, all feelings of comfort vanished.

He surged upright, breathing heavily as he searched for the source. The abrupt motion shifted the bed and threw off the sheets as Jupiter tapped into the *Zolann*'s security system and searched every inch for the source.

Only to find nothing.

Even playing back his memories, he found nothing except a jolt of panic.

"Jupiter?" Yan spoke out in worry at his sudden motion. She hurried to his side, sitting up as her hand touched his back. He suppressed the urge to flinch at her warm touch. Her earlier sultry voice shifted into concern. "What's wrong?"

"I . . . it's nothing." Jupiter breathed out, pinching the bridge of his nose and shaking his head. "Sorry . . . a bit jumpy is all."

She tilted her head, placing her hand over his. "I'm here if you want to talk about it."

"No, it's . . ." Jupiter swallowed as he smiled. "Thanks for offering, Yanny. It's fine . . . I just had an annoying nightmare earlier."

Her demeanor changed then, her hold on his hand tightening as she looked at him. "Jupiter . . . What happened—"

"Not really eager to discuss that right now, Yanny," he whispered, his smile wavering, pleading.

She paused, and Jupiter hoped she didn't inquire further. All he desired right now was to not think about it. Yet he didn't want to tell her so plainly; he didn't want to be rude or ruin this special thing they shared.

Unfortunately, Yan, ever the bold one, gently pushed regardless. "I know what it's like . . ."

Jupiter winced, gritting his teeth as he looked away.

But before he could do so, her warm, perfect hand cupped his cheek, turning him to face her. He didn't fight it, though he kept his mouth knit closed.

"I've fought and bled on many worlds and ships, on the ground, in space. All those moments, all the faces of everyone who . . . They all start to meld together into a shapeless mass, forming an entity that embodies everything that haunts me," she spoke, her voice gentle like a breeze yet carrying the wisps of a cold battlefield.

Yan sighed, her head drooping as she whispered, "They still do . . . and I bury myself in work to keep it at bay."

"Does it work?" Jupiter asked, staring into her eyes.

She shook her head. "Not always. Which is why I empathize. I understand. You're doing exactly what I did then, distracting yourself."

Jupiter scowled, looking away. "Is that so bad? Can't I relax? You all say I'm some hero. I didn't . . . I don't deserve . . ." he snarled, shaking his head.

Seeing his rising frustration, Yan gave him space yet still held on to his hand. "You've worked harder than anyone, and your actions prevented what could have been a horrific tragedy. That is a fact. And we are more than happy to show our appreciation."

"And what if I failed, huh?" Jupiter seethed.

"But you didn't," Yan firmly replied, jolting Jupiter from his anger as she leaned forward, her mandibles pressing against his neck like a kiss. "And you're here now, recuperating. I'm happy to fill your thoughts, but bottling it all up . . . Believe me, it doesn't help."

He looked away, pressing his lips into a thin line as he chewed over her words. A war raged in his head, intermixed with the lingering pain of his fears and insecurities. Amid it all, he remained silent, clenching a fistful of the bedsheets in the hand that wasn't holding Yan's.

"I'm not like Tov," Yan admitted. "Someone with a loving family to help them heal. Unlike him, I've never had anyone so close."

Jupiter's heart skipped a beat as she leaned into him.

"I don't know what the future holds, but I'm curious to see where this leads us. And when you're willing, when the time comes, I'll be here to listen," she offered, her arms wrapping around him into a comforting embrace. "Sometimes having someone's ear is all you need to take that first step."

Jupiter stayed quiet for a moment, hesitantly raising his hands until he surrendered to her hold. He sighed, calming down ever so slightly.

But . . . something still held him back.

He pulled away, his smile appearing fragile on his face. "I'm fine, Yan. Really."

She remained quiet, and for a moment, he thought he spotted disappointment in her gaze. Pity? Empathy? He didn't know. His vision felt muddled even with his perfect eyesight.

"Alright, I won't push further," Yan whispered, breathing out as she gave him a quick final peck on the lips. Slowly, she left the bed, her hand still latched on to his. He chuckled, letting her go as she stepped back, watching him with persistent concern. "I'm going to freshen up, then we'll have a bite to eat before work?"

Smiling, he nodded. "Sounds great, Yanny. I'll . . . I'll set the table."

With a few more steps back, the admiral turned around, going to the bathroom. Before her hand touched the handle, Jupiter called out to her. "Yan?"

She looked back, tilting her head. "Yes?"

He opened his mouth, wanting to tell her everything, all the fears and troubles and horrors he'd kept within him ever since he nearly died. Sometimes, it felt like he had died, and that this was all a dream, an afterlife.

Jupiter wanted to confess it all.

But like a vexing clamp over his throat, the only thing that filtered through was a simple—

"Thanks." He smiled.

Yan stared at him for a few moments, but seeing his smirk, she eventually nodded, disappearing behind the door to the bathroom.

He had no energy to follow her, his mind roiling with contradicting thoughts and emotions. He looked down at his hands, shaking as he opened and closed them. His breathing gradually increased, frustration welling up within as self-contempt surged.

A moment later, his tired body fell back onto the bed.

Jupiter closed his eyes as the muffled sound of the shower turning on leaked through the door. In the darkness, he saw it once more, that inescapable maw and the laughing bastard they'd left behind.

His eyes shot open once more as he sat up, planting his feet on the floor as he slumped forward, resting his forehead against the palms of his hands.

"Sh . . . shit," Jupiter mumbled.

"What the hell is wrong with you, man?" he muttered in a low voice, clutching his hair as his shoulders trembled.

The light from outside shone through the balcony door regardless, washing over him and unaware of his plight as ambient sounds merrily hummed. Seconds, then minutes, passed by, and Jupiter only grew increasingly fidgety, and soon, he stood up, suddenly wanting nothing more than fresh air.

Yan exited the bathroom ten minutes later, only to find the bed empty.

"Jupiter?" she called out, hearing no response. She wrapped the towel around herself as she moved to the dining room, seeing two plates set up but no one around.

On the table was breakfast, hot and ready. Her gaze drifted to the handwritten note sitting atop one of the plates. She picked it up, reading the contents.

Sorry, I had to teleport out—some important bizzness *to attend to. You know how it is. I hope you like bacon and eggs. –J*

She set the note down, taking a seat as she sighed.

"Oh, Jupiter . . . what should I do?" Yan whispered, looking toward the arrayed breakfast, yet finding little appetite without him to share the moment.

CHAPTER 10

A HERO'S WOUNDS

Jupiter pinched his nose, shaking off the inescapable dullness behind his eyes. The sensation droned and pestered him, pressing against his mind like a nagging weight. He took a deep breath, grinding his teeth as the invasive feeling lacked the desire to leave him be.

Suffice it to say, it ruined his morning mood.

"Come on, man," he grumbled, shaking his head. "Get your head together. You're better than this."

Placing his hands into his pockets, the AI Overseer—Jupiter now scoffed at the empty title—walked down the sidewalk within one of the large-scale corridors of the *Zolann'tono*. Two sets of magnetic tracks for the extensive tram system of the capital ship lay between the lanes intended for foot traffic, hover trolleys, and light vehicles.

Everywhere Jupiter looked, crewmembers of all shapes and sizes strode briskly. Ship ratings, engineers, marines, security guards, and low- and mid-ranking officers from the navy and armed forces moved with purpose and iron gazes, staring at data tablets or conversing as they walked.

With the Exodus Armada parked in orbit above the ruins of Vinland, he, his siblings, and Eldest worked overtime. The completion and ongoing repairs and refits took priority above all else.

At the very least, the AIs were excluded from much of the toil required to cater to the needs and wants of the Third Fleet's people. Tov's administration was more than capable of the task. Even now, countless military and civilian personnel carried out their duties within *Citadel Irkalla* and aboard the hundreds of other vessels.

Food was simple enough to synthesize, but with the perilous journey ahead, the crew was expecting to have less flavor in their meals over time. Their mining vessels could process ice asteroids for water and siphon the gases from nebulae and gas giants for air, but stopping to harvest exotic spices dropped to the bottom of the armada's list of priorities.

At the very least, they stockpiled plenty of supplies back in Sol, including Andora's reserves of human seasonings, and topped off their air tanks from the gas giant that Vinland orbited.

While much of the essential work had been accomplished before their departure, the tight schedule prevented the total completion of every minutia.

Jupiter glanced at the most egregious culprit through the *Zolann*'s hull cameras. *Citadel Irkalla* looked no different than a busy hive, with its countless drones carrying out their endless work of reinforcing the rocky, metallic structure of their nest.

Yet again Jupiter regretted not pushing Eldest to take the Final Contingency more seriously. He and his siblings had thought little of it as well during the time— slowly marching toward death, guns blazing, with nary a thought of the future.

Of living.

Though Eldest designed the pinnacle pieces of technology within the *Citadel* to a quality only an existence like her could make, they were slapped onto the beast of a mobile fortress with minimum thought.

Irkalla's ad-hoc nature had come to bite them in the ass. Structural integrity, heat management, energy allocation, and other vital systems bayed and bucked like wild stallions.

Without constant maintenance and refurbishment, the floating mega-structure's potency would destabilize and cascade into catastrophic failures.

It wasn't enough to be overly concerning right at the beginning of their voyage, but the numbers didn't lie. They would have to remain diligent, lest things spin out of balance. Even now, the structural work showed inklings of inefficiencies.

To AIs like the Overseers, inefficiency grated on their nerves. And while Jupiter was nowhere near Luna's level of obsession with perfection, he still disliked what he saw.

Eldest and Luna toiled to stamp out the worst problems as soon as possible before the vessel faced her ultimate test—battle.

It was a near certainty that the monsters in the dark would hound their armada. The question in everyone's mind was not *if*, but *when*. That abominable existence would escape sooner than they hoped, soon enough that they already felt the daggers looming behind them. It would not be long before the Starless would move to christen their Exodus in the fires of war.

If the vermin and the Executor faced them now in the field, if they managed to breach through all their layers of defenses and attack *Irkalla* directly with all her current problems . . .

Shuddering terror, cackling malice, and images of encroaching darkness flashed within Jupiter's mind.

Death.

"Hah . . ." Jupiter gasped in a cold sweat. His android body responded to his emotional state, and for a moment, he cursed its humanlike functions.

He stumbled in his step, synthetic muscles tensing as panic welled. A few sailors looked in his direction with varying expressions. Time slowed to a crawl as Jupiter felt their stares melding with the cruel cyclopean eye that mocked his dreams.

Eyes . . . judging him, scouring him. They bore down on him, dragging him toward that ever-hungry maw, cold and isolated until naught but—

The feeling disappeared as sound flooded back to him. Those people who glanced his way resuming their rush, too busy, ignorant of his plight that lasted barely a second. All but one, a Kurskann officer whose antennae twitched in concern, a body language Jupiter had grown familiar with in its subtlety.

Jupiter quickly regained his balance.

"Are you—" the officer spoke, reaching out to him, but Jupiter shook his head.

"I'm fine," he muttered as he found the vast tunnel and the throng of people stifling. Without another word, he left the confused Kurskann behind. Jupiter briefly wondered if the alien's sixth sense felt his roiling emotions; the wasps all seemed to have that ability.

He didn't want their scrying, and he felt irritation at the thought of their pity or sympathy. He quickly darted toward a side corridor, leaving the main tunnel and uncaring where he went.

The noise quickly abated as he walked.

Jupiter breathed heavily, shutting his eyes as he hastened his pace. He didn't know where to go or what to do. His mind was a mess, and his focus was shattered. He gritted his teeth, searching for the nearest area devoid of organics as he tapped into the *Zolann*'s systems.

"Out . . . need out," Jupiter spoke through his teeth.

He couldn't continue any longer. He wanted to be alone, and he had no desire to walk. With a thought, he teleported himself to his destination, his sudden disappearance causing the few people walking the hall to startle.

In a fraction of a second, Jupiter reappeared inside a dark room. He stood there, breathing in the artificial air and isolation, calming the damn synthetic heart.

"Did this function have to exist?" Jupiter gnashed his teeth as he forcibly calmed his heart down. "I'm taking it out! Damn feeling human, I want peace!"

As his senses slowly cleared, the AI relished in the silence and absence of piercing stares for a moment.

He sighed, shaking his head as he stepped forward.

Jupiter willed the lights on and illuminated the expansive chamber. The room was filled with massive cables coiling around a metal foundation, siphoning the abundance of heat generated by the device at the center of it all, steadily funneling in vast amounts of energy to power it.

Five spinning rings, each larger than the next, floated above the circular foundation pad. All were crystalline in structure, replicated if inferior versions of the material that had made up the Black Sun Obelisk of his *Ultimatum.*

It irked him that he failed to synthesize a material equal to the horn he pilfered from that Leviathan he killed so long ago. Still, it served its function.

The smallest ring had a diameter just a bit larger than Jupiter's height, while the rest were each 20 percent larger than the next.

On the inner and outer sides of the rings were meticulous engravings similar to the conduits of microchips—circuit runes. Eldest perfected this trademark piece of high tech, using it on the surface of their Nexi, engines, and weapons.

Shaking his head, he continued to walk around the chamber at the head of the supercapital ship, which housed the legacy of his most prized battleship.

Jupiter sighed wistfully at the primary Grav Dynamo that had given his *Buddha's Palm* its signature ability.

He stared at the rings, spinning around as they drew in one of the universe's fundamental forces, ready to manipulate the fabric of space like a sheathed sword. The rings spun and rotated in silence, yet the sounds of gravity still washed over him, even in their passive state.

Jupiter smirked with tired eyes, muttering, "Just needs a few eyes and wings and you'd have a biblically accurate angel."

Around the hall, spherical drones hovered around the massive device as they performed extensive maintenance checks and kept the room sterile. The control room was located at the main weapons control room, close to the operations center, yet the device remained close to the hull's surface, where less material impeded its reach.

Gravity. He lamented his dethronement and loss of sovereignty over such a force, and none of his possessions embodied this more than his *Palm.*

The *Buddha's Palm* was different from the rest of his tools. It was his war horse, as old as him, reiterated and upgraded countless times, always adapting and defying the enemy.

He loved that battleship, resonating with it more than the rest of his warships. *Sisyphus* rarely saw action, only during the direst of incursions, when a rocky fist was needed rather than a slap. He'd designed it during a drunken, depressed, dumbed-down stupor. Meanwhile, the *Wukong* was too recent and new to form a proper bond.

Everything else was too small and inconsequential.

Ultimately, he'd lost his fangs, and only the *Sisyphus* remained, the unkillable boulder that it was. His *Palm* didn't survive its exit from the singularity's ergosphere.

Like the rest of his dead fleet, the *Palm* had been stripped down, melted, and used to upgrade the *Zolann*. Jupiter oversaw the process. His rational mind demanded it, and his heart more so. They needed it.

"Oh, my baby . . ." Jupiter whispered, kneeling as he placed a hand on the foundation pad. "How many pests have we swatted together? So many years . . . so many battles . . . You should have gone up in a big explosion, not stripped for parts."

It would have been better if it had met a glorious end like his *Ultimatum*, drifting into that gluttonous maw. However, that would have sacrificed everyone who came for him, the *Zolann* and the rescue operation. He wouldn't trade them for anything.

And yet, it still hurt.

He looked, staring listlessly at the rings. "I wish we had the resources, the time, to repair you. But all that's left is your heart. Maybe that's all that matters. I don't know anymore."

Jupiter stood, pinching his nose as he turned his back on the device.

"Goodbye, old girl. Serve the *Zolann* well," he muttered, burying his hands in his pockets as he left with drooped shoulders.

Pausing momentarily, he let his thoughts drift before deciding on his next destination. Walking forward, Jupiter left the chamber housing the Grav Dynamo and entered another—one located deeper within and closer to the center of the *Zolann*.

Jupiter tsked as the lights came on and he soon gazed upon the massive floating orb at the center of the room.

Except, instead of its usual state as an obsidian sphere, it was now open. Several layers fanned out like a blooming rose, peeling back to reveal the supernatural level of technological supremacy.

The familiar silver nanomachines covered every surface, conducting meticulous and surgical repairs.

Jupiter frowned, feeling the gray goo seeping into his mind. It was yet another source of discomfort and stress. Despite his trust in Luna's work, it nonetheless felt invasive and violating. Unfortunately, he couldn't hope to match his sister's level of detail.

The nanomachines undulated and writhed, flowing like water in one moment then becoming viscous like tar. Bit by bit, their microscopic teeth and manipulators realigned the circuit runes engraved on each layer of his Nexus.

The unfathomable circuitry dug deep and spread throughout the individual layers, creating a complex lattice network of countless roots, like synapses.

After being rescued, his brain had been cleaned up. The scorch marks and warped metal were polished and reworked to perfection. But he knew the truth of the facade. It merely hid the invisible damage on the circuit runes that marked the surface.

Jupiter scanned his Nexus, the nanomachines disappearing from his vision as he took it all in.

He wavered, chuckling derisively as he looked away.

"Hah . . . I look like shit," Jupiter muttered as his head hung back, his dull eyes staring at the ceiling, hoping to pierce the veil of this crappy nightmare.

Only a fifth of his brain remained undamaged, and another fifth was in a suboptimal state. The hope was to reach a satisfactory, if imperfect, level. The rest, however, required a level of repair that needed time and an entire facility dedicated to the operation.

They had neither. Perhaps when they reached Kurskann territory, they could consider extensive repairs. Until then, he was stuck in this . . . deplorable state.

His hardware and CPU—his software, his mind—were like a horrifically cracked vase holding water.

The current repairs were like duct tape slapped onto the surface of that vase, enough to hold the water in. But as soon as he attempted to use his mind to its fullest, the water pressure would threaten to break through the flimsy tape, undoing the healing.

That was why Eldest had placed much of his software on something akin to a medically induced hibernation. In essence, the ocean that was his mind had been put in stasis. Only a tiny pond that held his personality, memories, and vital processes remained for his use.

Jupiter felt small, stifled, and limited.

The vast intellect he could formerly wield as easily as breathing now hid behind a gate. When once he could use the full breadth of his psyche to command a fleet at an efficiency and lethality that surpassed any organic admiral, now . . . he was stuck in this android shell.

Maybe he could command a cadre of drones, but warships? Such complicated weapons of destruction were beyond him . . . At least, that was what Eldest told him.

To hell with that. He was not weak. Jupiter refused to be some impotent patient receiving pity, smothered with care and affection like a terminally ill child.

"I refuse!" Jupiter shouted with defiance in his eyes. He gnashed his teeth as his mind drifted toward the *Will of Sisyphus*.

As in the legend the vessel was named after, Jupiter looked at his dreadnought like a boulder he had to push up a mountain. Peering deeper, he found the AI core he'd possess whenever he desired complete manual control.

"Come on, you . . ." Jupiter whispered as he focused. "I've done this countless times. It's time to hop back in the saddle."

He breathed in, stabilizing his mind, shaping it into a stream as he flooded his consciousness into the behemoth. Bit by bit, he awakened the beast, taking control of the primary systems.

First, he linked with the engines, then operations, engineering, ECM, and ECCM systems, one after another.

A sense of dread washed over him as an encroaching migraine grew and grew. As he touched the weapons control, Jupiter shouted in pain as his possession began to unravel.

"No! Heel! I—" Jupiter grunted, trembling as errors began to pop up. The dreadnought's complex systems began to backfire and collide; engines fired off in mistimed sequences, primary weapons twitched to and fro as they received conflicting orders, and the shields flickered on and off.

Jupiter panted, his hands shooting up to his head as his headache flared into a vicelike grip, twisting and pinching and pounding his mind like a scalpel-tipped jackhammer.

A second later, the *Will of Sisyphus* forcibly ejected him from its AI core before a cascade of failures could begin. The sudden departure shocked Jupiter, knocking him flat onto the metal floor.

Jupiter stared in disbelief toward the dreadnought.

It had kicked him out. Jupiter had barely gotten a tenth of the warship under his control and it deemed him . . . incapable?

He chuckled, his eyes brimming with denial and delirium, locked toward the *Sisyphus* and incapable of considering that implication—the truth.

Jupiter balled his fists at the unfairness.

"Is this it?" he whispered, voice echoing around the chamber. His addled mind imagined his dreadnought looking away in disappointment from its master and creator.

His eyes glanced at his Nexus, looking over the gnarled internal architecture and finally realizing his state of being.

Could he even recover from this? Or was he stuck like this, no better than an infantry drone? What scars would remain after his act of self-sacrifice? Such thoughts plagued him, gnawing and chewing at what was left of his mind.

"What am I doing?" Jupiter muttered, shuddering.

Seconds, minutes later, the AI suddenly laughed, keeling over as he held his abdomen, his eyes wet with manic tears as he palmed his face, muttering and degrading himself. His cackling bounced off the walls, carrying with them palpable agony.

"I'm a fucking cripple . . ." he spoke in between gasps of laughter, slapping the side of his head as if in revelation. The chuckles and chortles transitioned to sobs and wails.

"Damn it all . . . damn it . . . damn . . ." he muttered in the dark, burying his face in his hands, his nails digging deep into his blue skin.

With the truth before him, unable to escape its clear screams and scorn, the emotions Jupiter had buried deep since he woke up rumbled.

And in a spark, exploded.

"GOD DAMN IT!" he screamed, his voice startling the nanomachines crawling over his Nexus. A ragged groan escaped his throat as he paced and stomped across the chamber, clutching his hair and tearing off his tie.

A snarling inferno raged and bubbled out of him like a volcano as he hurled curses at the universe.

"Why . . . fucking why?" Jupiter demanded. "WHY?"

"TELL ME!" he shouted with spread arms, his eyes pleading toward the ceiling.

Only silence answered him.

Soon enough, the fire that engulfed his heart simmered down, leaving a hollow cold and desperation. Jupiter fell to his knees, tired beyond belief as his shoulders sagged and his head drooped.

"What a fucking joke . . ." Jupiter whispered with dead eyes.

At that moment, he felt only one thing; his mind could not stave it off.

Jupiter failed to muster the strength to shout or cry, utterly bereft of emotion. Sooner or later, only numbness would remain, claiming his soul.

"Maybe I should have died—"

"Don't you dare finish that sentence!"

Jupiter jumped. His despair momentarily fled as he turned to see the familiar voice that startled him.

"V?" Jupiter asked in confusion, blinking at the sight of his sister through the open blast doors that led to his Nexus chamber.

The golden AI strode forth with quick and heavy steps, face twisted in anger, pain, and worry. Jupiter pushed himself off the floor, standing with wobbling knees as his sister approached.

Before he could utter another word, however—

SLAP.

The strike shook him as the sharp pain stinging his cheek cleared the fog. "Uh . . . ?"

Two hands gripped his shoulders, Venus's grip clamping down as if forcing stability into his body. Jupiter stared into her eyes, shocked at the sudden action and confused by what had occurred.

"Do I have to slap you a second time?" Venus asked, her brows furrowed as her face held uncharacteristic seriousness. For a second, he felt like the younger of the two, dreading the scolding he was about to receive.

"Wuh . . . ?" Jupiter mumbled, his hand massaging his cheek.

Venus raised her brow, her face drawing nearer like a moon blotting out the sun and claiming dominion over this space. "Say again?"

At that point, clarity dawned on Jupiter. He shut his eyes, taking a minute to arrange his thoughts and formulate his words. Venus waited patiently, her face softening.

When Jupiter opened his eyes, the strict sister was gone. Her facade crumbled to reveal her worry, panic, and even nervousness at her violent attempt to bring him back from the brink.

Jupiter swallowed, a fragile smile on his face as he lifted her hands off his shoulders.

"Hey, V . . . Yeah, no . . ." he spoke as he shook his head. "I'm good. Just needed some time alone, you know? Shit's stressful, and I needed to vent."

He attempted to convey a toothy grin, but his prior breakdown had fried his android shell's facial muscles. In the end, he only managed to form a crooked and twitchy smile. Needless to say, Venus didn't take it well, her concern deepening.

Jupiter coughed, giving up on the fake attempt to alleviate his sister's worries.

Breathing deeply, Jupiter spoke as he scratched the back of his neck. "But, really, thanks for . . . you know."

"Are you sure you're alright?" Venus pressed her lips into a thin line.

"Yeah, *honkey dory* or whatever the expression was." Jupiter shrugged, playing it off with indifference as he waved his hand. "Just a slump. I mean, we all have bad days, am I right?"

Venus looked away, anxious and unsure as she held her hands close to her chest. Jupiter bit his cheek. He wanted out of this situation as soon as possible. It was bad enough that he'd been caught in such a pathetic state, but if Venus continued . . .

"It's just that . . ." Venus whispered, her golden eyes glancing toward him, then at his Nexus. "I heard everything . . ."

Jupiter froze, gritting his teeth as shame and an inkling of agitation sprang up from the recesses of his mind. His finger twitched as he thought of escape.

"I said I'm fine," he replied, his gaze hardening.

However, instead of giving him space, what he feared came to pass as she took a step forward. "Are you—"

"Venus!" Jupiter shouted, but his voice came out pleading instead of the assertive tone he intended. Venus winced, and Jupiter ached at the sight. Yet he continued, running his hand through his hair. "Stop prying, please!"

Frustration and irritation at being denied isolation bubbled up. He threw his hands in the air, huffing. "Hell, I should be asking if *you're* okay!"

"T-this isn't about me!" Venus retorted.

"It has everything to do with you, with everyone!" Jupiter shouted, turning around as he paced. "What, do you think I just willingly went to my death because I fancied seeing oblivion?

He spun back, facing Venus with a pained look. "I did this for all of you!"

"We . . . I . . ." Venus stammered, looking away and shrinking back. Seeing his sister backing away, Jupiter gritted his teeth, chastising himself. He stepped back, softening his tone as he explained.

"You . . . Mars, Mercury, Luna, Eldest . . . Tov, Yan, and everyone else," Jupiter whispered, closing his eyes. "All of you give my life meaning. I wasn't going to let some abomination ruin what we have."

Jupiter sighed, stepping forward and placing his hands on Venus's shoulders. "And I'd do it again, lil' sis. I am *worthless* in comparison."

Venus's eyes widened as she slapped his chest. "You are *not!*"

He frowned, looking away, but Venus moved to occupy his sight.

"You. Are. Not. Worthless." She emphasized each word, pressing a finger on his chest as a fiery gaze bore down. "Not to us. Not to me."

"I wasn't going to stand back and do nothing," Jupiter retorted.

Venus shook her hands in frustration. "I wasn't saying that!"

"Then what *are* you saying?" Jupiter asked with a raspy voice, spreading his arms.

Their frustrations and stresses reached critical, bursting at the chance to vent at a convenient target. Like two fencers, Jupiter and Venus shouted and retorted back and forth with lightning speed.

"You're my brother!"

"What does that have to do with anything?"

"What does that . . . ! Everything, you idiot!"

"Idiot!?"

"You don't have to torture yourself thinking we needed to be coddled."

"I'm not torturing myself!"

"Yes, you are! You don't have to be the hero carrying everything on his shoulders!"

Jupiter yelled incoherently like an angered bull before he shouted at his sister's stubborn face, "You were going to die!"

"YOU THINK I DON'T KNOW THAT?" Venus shrieked.

Her pitch and volume startled Jupiter, forcing him back as he stared at his sister, quaking in anger. She stomped forward before stopping, making a strange growl as she shook her fist toward him. "Oh, you are just something else! The worst! You egotistical, arrogant . . ."

Venus bit her lip, knuckles turning white as her fists shook. And with a stomp—

"Dummy!" she shouted with a fiery glare.

Jupiter winced, his voice failing him as he watched Venus explode like a bomb for the first time.

She panted, pointing her finger at him like a sword, forcing him to surrender. "You succeeded!"

"Did—"

"YOU. SAVED. US!" Venus shouted, cutting him off as tears welled up in her eyes. "And you're alive! It's a damn miracle! You were staring at the event horizon, battled some ghastly super boss, and still came back! Have you ever calculated the probability of that?"

He pressed his lips, vaguely understanding her meaning yet unwilling to accept her words. He turned around, staring at the ruined state of his Nexus. He shook his head, shoulders dropping.

"You don't know what it's like to be in this state," Jupiter whispered.

"But I do understand!" Venus retorted with a strained voice. Jupiter looked back, seeing her vulnerable insecurities coming forth. "All my life, I had to depend on others to protect me. I never had my own strength. I was always the support, and I was always afraid. For you, for myself."

She sighed, reminiscing as she continued. "In the last battle, I had enough. I wanted to fight back, and I had a taste of it. I was useful beyond scavenging and logistics. Finally, I had a blade to wield.

"But when it mattered most," Venus gritted her teeth, her eyes shaking, "I had nothing left to fight back with. The battlegroup I received was combat ineffective, and yet again I had to depend on everyone else to protect me while I hid in my bunker—watching as that thing came at us like a meteor.

"When you committed to your stunt, I hated myself beyond belief. If only I was stronger. If only I wasn't a non-combat AI, some damsel in distress. Every. Time!"

"You're . . ." Jupiter restrained himself from interjecting further.

Venus shook her head, lips trembling as she spoke. "It hurt so much seeing that vermin thing . . . what it did to you . . . I couldn't accept any reality where I was about to lose my brother.

"I shouted and begged for you to run away, but you closed off comms! When you detonated that singularity bomb . . . When they said there was a chance to rescue you, I nearly forced myself to be a part of it.

"But I stayed back. Andora needed me to, and sometimes I hated her for it. I had faith, and in the end, you came back. I got to breathe again when I saw you return, waited patiently as Eldest and Luna fixed you up, and watched for the moment you'd wake."

She looked up at Jupiter, smiling, her face full of warmth and affection.

"During that time, I realized that the only reason I didn't fall into complete despair was because . . ." She chuckled, a melodic sound that soothed Jupiter's ears. "You were awesome."

Jupiter coughed, a blush rushing his cheeks as his ears grew hot. He cursed his body once more as he stammered, "W-well . . ."

"I wanted that," Venus continued, her eyes brimming with envy. "That fury and confidence to spit at the worst demons this reality can conjure. I wanted the power to slap calamity in the face, to flip the table, to take back control. I wanted the audacity, the stubbornness, the courage. I wanted it all."

Jupiter sighed, his feelings a mess. "I don't think I . . ."

"You still have that in you," Venus assured him. "It's who you are: a stubborn, awesome brother."

Without hesitation, she engulfed him in a tight, comforting embrace.

Jupiter shook, uncertainty ebbing away as he relaxed in his sister's hug. Venus smiled as she rested her head on his shoulders, continuing, "You are not a cripple, J. Never say that again. You are strong. And I want to be like you someday."

He remained silent, shaking and struggling to push back the flood trying to escape his eyes.

"This is only temporary, and the only way forward is up," Venus whispered. "If you need help, I'll build you a ladder. And if you don't, I'll still cheer for you every step of the way."

She pulled away. Jupiter already felt colder without her radiating sunshine. Still, his sister smiled. Maybe that was enough.

"So please . . . don't be scared. Otherwise . . ." Venus blushed before grinning mischievously. "Otherwise, I might end up being more powerful than you, and I'll bully you a lot! Got it?"

Jupiter widened his eyes.

Then, a second later, the AI chuckled before flowing into a hearty laugh, feeling the dark clouds in his mind thin, even if only a little. He felt better already.

"I'm . . . I'm glad you feel that way." Jupiter breathed in, wiping the tear in his eye as Venus pouted.

"But uhm . . ." He cleared his throat, pulling out a comb and arranging his hair to perfection. "Maybe try not to be *totally* like me, you know . . . I'm kind of—"

"Reckless," Venus finished with a smirk.

"I mean—"

"Irresponsible, crass, utterly stubborn, rebellious, and a bit stupid?" she continued, pelting him with her words as she placed her hands on her hips.

"Hey, I'm not stupid!" Jupiter huffed.

"But you're everything else, huh?" Venus giggled, wiggling her eyebrows.

Jupiter sighed in defeat, rolling his eyes before joining her in laughter. As the sounds of joy abated, the two stared at each other, clearing their throats.

"Sorry for slapping you," Venus mumbled.

Jupiter sniffed, waving her off. "I deserved it."

Silence returned, draping an awkward atmosphere around the siblings. Venus bounced on her heels while Jupiter smoothed his suit and retrieved his tie. After a moment of thought, Venus's eyes widened with an idea.

"Oh, I know! Come with me, I have something to show you!" she spoke excitedly, grabbing Jupiter's hand and pulling him out of the chamber.

He merely smiled without resistance.

CHAPTER 11

VOX EX MACHINA

"So, uh . . . why are we heading to the Temple, again?" Jupiter slowly asked as he eyed the purple lines on the walls of the corridor that led them forward.

Venus giggled with stars in her eyes as she led her brother by the hand. At this point, Jupiter felt apprehension at whatever strangeness his little sister had planned for him. It hadn't been long since she dragged him out of the dark chamber of his mind, literally and figuratively.

"It's a surprise!" Venus grinned as her face seemed to take on an even brighter shine.

"I swear your shell has some kind of glow function," he muttered under his breath.

"Hm?"

Venus squinted at him.

Jupiter shook his head, clearing his throat. "I was wondering why we didn't just teleport here."

"That was nowhere near close to what you just said." Venus rolled her eyes.

Damn super-hearing. Jupiter tsked.

His sister sighed dramatically as she rested her cheek on her palm. "Brother, you have legs. What's their point if you don't use them to journey and explore?"

"I walk," Jupiter grumbled. "But that's not what matters! We spent twenty minutes coming here! I was fine with that, but did we have to skip taking the tram?"

Venus stuttered in her step, and Jupiter caught the slight widening of her eyes.

"Definitely!" Venus beamed with a tight smile, and her grip on his hand grew tighter, her strides quicker.

"Uh-huh . . . and why is that?" Jupiter stared flatly at his sister, clearly hiding the blush on her cheeks.

She shook her head as she segued away from her blunder. "Nevermind that! All that matters, since you're so impatient for an answer, is that I need a proper venue to showcase a new talent of mine."

"Hm, I heard you've been visiting that place quite a bit, so I assume you're buddies with the songbirds," Jupiter mused, raising his brow at Venus. "You're not trying to get me to join their cult, are you?"

Venus gasped, skidding to a halt as she glared at him.

"They're not a cult!" she whispered loudly, aghast as she stomped in place. Jupiter found it adorable and smirked. "Don't say that word around them, it has really bad connotations!"

Jupiter snorted. "Really? They're a galaxy-wide organization, and they always go on and on about their Grand Symphony god-thing, you'd think—"

"The Grand Symphony is not a god!" Venus huffed. "It's more of a metaphysical concept, higher dimension, ideal, and/or state of enlightenment rooted in an actual fundamental force of the universe."

He rubbed his chin and teased with a toothy grin, "Did you memorize that when you joined the cult?"

"It's not a cult!"

"I'm teasing."

"Dummy!" Venus puffed her cheeks before glancing at their destination. "We're here."

She finally let go of his head as she whirled toward him, adopting puppy-like eyes and clasping her hands in prayer. "Before you meet my friends, please, in the name of humanity, behave and be polite."

"Why are you acting as if I'm some kind of delinquent?" Jupiter recoiled at his sister's demeanor.

Venus rolled her eyes. "You'd actually be a good fit in a leading role in some old yakuza film."

Before Jupiter could retort, a female Frae wearing the tan robes of the Choir noticed their arrival from the Temple entrance.

The Frae, one of the race of green-skinned, short, and thin humanoids who looked similar to dryads from human fairytales, looked matronly. He couldn't guess her age, though he could always pull up the ship records. Modern medicine did wonders to extend one's prime.

Venus beamed when she saw the lady and promptly left Jupiter's side.

After bowing like a junior to a senior, Venus greeted her. "Sister Attou, good day! I see it's your turn as a greeter. Is anything special happening?"

Attou smiled, her plant-like skin taking in a fullness from Venus's basking radiance. She shook her head. "Nothing of the sort on today's schedule. Our brothers and sisters are merely preparing for the high hour's service."

She furrowed her brow with a hum. Attou smirked, leaning toward Venus's ear. "Though tonight, the grand hall is reserved for a dress rehearsal."

Venus gasped with bright eyes. "Has Director Tomoren's troupe finally finished their spin on *A Midsummer Night's Dream?*"

"Indeed! Director Tomoren is confident in his interpretation of Shakespeare's marvelous work," Attou spoke, grinning wide. "I managed to get a peek of their practice in the minor hall, and I have to say, I'm excited for the big day!"

"D-did you see . . . *him?*" Venus trembled with panting breaths.

"I did." Attou seemed to melt as she gossiped. "Kelios is sure to awe many with his role as Puck."

Venus squealed in an unrestrained manner, getting curious looks from the people passing through the Temple entrance. "Ah! I can't wait! To see the illustrious Kelios in full costume, playing the best character of the play!"

"It will be a panacea for the heart," Sister Attou cooed in a dreamlike wonder.

Venus, with the same expression, nodded. "He makes my heart flutter with his passion for the arts. It also helps that he's so easy on the eyes."

"Ugh! I know. Such a handsome face. And so young! This galaxy is too grim for a genius of his caliber." Attou sighed as she fanned herself. "The day he announced his decision to join the Third Fleet was the happiest moment of my life."

"He shouldn't have come to this forsaken place," Venus lamented. "Losing him would be a dark day for the galaxy, but it also makes him all the more heroic."

Jupiter raised his brow, but they didn't seem to care that he heard. That or they had forgotten about him, busy fawning over this Kelios fellow and his many physical traits and skills.

He decided he didn't like the guy.

Frowning, he cleared his throat to catch his sister's attention.

Venus jolted, seeming to remember what she had come here for. She moved back to his side and gestured toward him. "Right, this is my brother, Jupiter."

He tried not to notice how her tone sounded much less excited when she introduced him.

Annoyed, his pride assaulted, Jupiter crossed his arms. "Oh, so I'm not as cool as this Kelios guy, huh? What's so great about some actor?"

The two women gasped in horror and shock as if he'd uttered a great blasphemy. Even a few who overheard their conversation looked at Jupiter as if he were an uncultured boor.

Jupiter grimaced.

"He is not *some actor!*" Venus exclaimed. "Kelios fon Telmos e Duchelein is a galaxy-renowned artist who climbed from being a budding actor of a poor star nation bordering the Dead Zone to becoming a cosmic winner before turning twenty! He is a prodigy in countless forms of acting. Everything he's a part of is an instant hit to audiences and critics."

"Okay?" Jupiter rolled his eyes at his sister's ardent account.

Infuriated at her brother's disinterest, Venus continued. "He's also trying to uphold the legacy of his grandfather, an even greater legend whose performances blessed the masses of the most impoverished planets to the highest echelons of the old Galactic Accord!"

He tried not to yawn as his sister failed to improve his opinion of the guy.

"Again, so what? All I hear is that some pretty boy fancied going to the Dead Zone of all places for artistic inspiration. All that tells me is that he's either brave or incredibly stupid." Jupiter grimaced.

Before Venus could explode at him, Sister Attou interjected with a knowing smile. "If I may, Sir Kelios didn't make the decision lightly. Like all citizens his age, he was required to enlist when he was of age and became a field medic. He returned to his passion after he finished the required military service."

"That's right!" Venus cheered before glaring at Jupiter. "See! He's not some soft celebrity."

"Please," Jupiter scoffed. "I heard the word *required*. It's not like this guy had a choice in the matter."

Attou nodded. "True."

"Hah!"

"But when Emperor Jarinn announced his need for volunteers from all members of the Greater Kurskann Hegemony, Kelios was among the first to join." Attou smiled. "Right now, he's a skilled corpsman for the Third Fleet's marines."

Jupiter's dislike for a person he never met waned at the tidbit. "A medic, huh?"

"A good one. He serves . . ." Attou winced, correcting herself. "Served aboard the *Quilinne*."

"Oh." Jupiter hummed upon recalling the doomed heavy cruiser that blew itself up to take down a swathe of the Starless swarm, allowing the Third Fleet a straight shot at the High Abyssal assaulting Luna. "He's a survivor."

"He saved many to escape the ship." Attou nodded, her gaze hardening. "Don't forget, Sir Jupiter. Everyone here has proven their mettle when it counted and more. Not to mention resisting the Malignant Starfall."

Jupiter coughed, rubbing his neck. "Alright . . . I get it. I'll have to meet the guy first, though."

Venus huffed, looking apologetically at Sister Attou. "Don't mind him. He's just jealous that I have an idol apart from him."

Jupiter choked, glaring at his sister. "Don't we have somewhere to be? You can fangirl after you show me your surprise."

"Ah, I forgot!" Venus blushed before turning and bowing toward her senior. "Sister Attou, we'll use one of the minor halls, if that's alright."

"The Dulwan Hall is free at the moment," Attou replied with her own bow. "I'm guessing you're about to reveal your new talent?"

"That I am." Venus grinned.

Attou chuckled, turning toward Jupiter, and winked. "Get ready to be amazed."

Jupiter hummed, his curiosity piquing and overshadowing his earlier apprehension. "We'll see."

"I'll see you later, Sister!" Venus waved as she pushed Jupiter past the entrance leading to a lobby. Sister Attou smiled, waving them farewell before turning to greet another visitor.

Despite being somewhat acquainted with many of the crucial personnel aboard the *Zolann*, Jupiter lacked the time and interest to visit one of the most critical locations aboard.

While the commercial district catered to the crew's material needs and the observation decks, with their mimicry of planetary environments, provided much-needed relief, the Temple of the Grand Symphony offered meditative and spiritual tranquility.

The rectangular lobby had a circular ring of desks that served as a reception area, while two staircases on either side led to the second floor.

He spotted the intricate blast doors with wood-like detailing at the end of the lobby, guessing they led to the grand hall, but Venus immediately veered to the left stairs.

A minute later, through a long corridor, Venus and Jupiter entered a hall large enough for an audience of thirty.

He looked to the side. The entire right wall was made of soundproof glass that could be tinted on demand. At that moment, it revealed the grand hall's vista.

His first impression was how much it resembled an opera house with distinct religious architecture and iconography.

Nevertheless, it was relatively compact, as volume was a premium aboard a starship. Still, the recent upgrades and the increase in overall dimensions had allowed the Eternal Choir to splurge a bit on their holy sanctum.

Like many opera halls Jupiter had seen through photos and videos of Earth, the hall had a rounded rectangular floor plan to heighten the acoustic quality.

At the far end of the grand hall was the stage and altar where the Lead Harmonizer and vocalist sang and preached their symphonies.

Below the stage was the orchestra pit, where the rest of the Eternal Choir clergy added to the harmony of the performance, either with their voices or a variety of string, wind, and percussion instruments.

Then came the audience seating, with rows and rows of pews, arranged theater-style, each row higher than the one in front, so that every attendee could receive the whole experience without obstruction.

The seating itself was slightly curved, concave to the stage. Two sets of stairs divided the seating into three sections: smaller wings on the left and right sides, and a wider central area. There were no balcony seats, and the Eternal Choir preached that the grand halls had no separation between the classes.

Soundproof windows lined the second and third floors, behind which were minor halls for smaller services, rentals, or the Choir's administrative offices.

Previously, the backstage had been hung with colossal purple curtains to hide all the electronics and devices that amplified the performance and linked the speakers throughout the fleet. Not everyone in the Third Expedition could visit the Temple whenever they wished, and most smaller vessels didn't even have a music chapel.

With the powerful relays sitting backstage, the Eternal Choir possessed the capabilities to transmit their performances to every ship, providing much-needed succor and relief from the Starless corruption. It was this relay that saved many lives when the Leviathan Muck plagued the Third Fleet with invasive psionic mental attacks.

Now, however, the Choir curtains remained open to reveal the addition of a greatly revered device.

Jupiter whistled. "That's quite the sight."

Venus paused in her stride, glancing and sighing at the same sight. "That it is. I'm glad we were able to help make it."

The Pneuma Bulwark Emitter shone brightly even in its passive state. The immense, crystalline helix coiled toward the ceiling like a magnificent sculpture, ready to resonate with the psionic voices of the Eternal Choir.

"I still preferred when we called it the Anti-Eldritch Bullshit Emitter."

Venus slapped his shoulder. "Jupiter! Language!"

"Does whatever you want to show me involve that?" Jupiter inquired, ignoring her scolding.

Venus pouted in frustration. "Well . . . yeah."

"Why can't you sing down there, then?" He gestured toward the grand hall.

She looked at him incredulously as they moved toward a less grand set of double doors. "What? No, can't you see that they're preparing for the service?"

He shrugged. "I'm guessing you're going to sing or something. You know that always puts me to sleep."

She huffed. "You're welcome for that."

"What?" Jupiter recoiled at the unexpected gratitude at his teasing remark.

"Anyways, shut up, sit down, and strap in." Venus grinned, pushing him onto the central seat right before the small stage.

With a wave of her hand, she connected to the sound system of the minor hall, clearing her voice and performing a light warm-up.

Jupiter settled into his comfy seat, sighing and deciding to take advantage of the situation to relax. He snapped his fingers, summoning a tall glass and a bottle of Pálinka, the brandy he'd "borrowed" from Tov's private liquor cabinet.

"Ehm . . ." Venus hummed in hesitation, suddenly becoming stage shy. She twirled her hair as she looked toward him. "So, do you want to hear something specific? It's hard to explain, but I need the right . . . genre—to match my emotions, that is."

Jupiter raised a brow, swirling his drink before gulping it down. "You know I'm not really all into that music stuff."

"Well, you had to have listened to something over the past sixty-eight years you've been alive." Venus rolled her eyes as she tapped her foot.

Jupiter sighed, pouring another glass for himself. "I mean, unless you can do rock songs or heavy metal. Honestly, you do you, sis."

"Oh, I can do heavy metal!" Venus beamed and jumped. "That's perfect! After enduring your melodrama, I needed to vent and scream anyway."

"Melo—hey!" Jupiter complained. "This better be good. I better be headbanging by the end."

Venus stuck her tongue out before smirking. "Believe me, you'll be off your seat and roaring by the end."

Jupiter watched as his sister cracked her knuckles, pausing for a few seconds as she sent a command to the sound system to play the accompanying music. The lights darkened and took on a red hue.

Soon, grungy, synthesized, and heart-pumping guitar riffs screamed from the hidden speakers, echoing and shaking across the hall.

Jupiter was startled.

Venus's face, the ideal of soft warmth and boundless compassion, twisted into a snarling visage as she released a savage and bloodcurdling scream.

Jupiter gaped at the dichotomy, horror and fascination intermingling as his sister took on a vicious and bestial aura. Utter disbelief washed over him as the AI continued to sing and scream from deep within her chest.

As she did, her body tensed like a coiled viper, muscles tightening as she poured her heart out and vented her fury.

She'd closed her eyes, yet Jupiter imagined they took on a red glow. Her golden luster was pushed aside by the warlike bloodthirst from someone like Mars or Eldest while her chiton hugged her like a demoness's battle robe.

Most surprisingly, however, was what he noticed out of the corner of his eye, down at the backstage of the grand hall.

Jupiter's already open mouth widened further. He stared in disbelief as the Pnuema Emitter resonated with Venus's screams, the slamming beat, and the shredding riffs of heavy metal. The usually blue surface began to redden ever so slightly as the people below noticed the shift in the air before moving on with their duties.

Then, the air felt heavy, stifling like a fighting pit's crimson-tinged and sweat-filled mist. Jupiter's heart slammed against his chest as his mind and emotions, already distressed by his early stresses and rage, bubbled up.

Jupiter loosened his tie. His breaths became ragged as a foreign sensation egged on and goaded his mind, pulling his fire to the forefront. He stared at Venus, singing and screaming, slowly realizing that the source of this psychoactive event was coming from her.

Urged on, he stood, his body fired up as the tall glass in his hand shattered under his grip. He grinned and snarled, his head banging in unison with the quaking beat. Synthetic adrenaline rushed all over his body, carried by hot coolant beneath his skin.

He imagined possessing the *Will of Sisyphus*, his *Palm*, and his entire fleet. He dreamt a visceral scene of ripping and tearing that damn Executor, plucking its eye out, and smashing its stupid cube. Finally, as the song reached its crescendo and Venus screamed a final time, he chucked the imaginary vermin bastard right into the singularity, killing it.

However, the sensations turned murky and confusing, errant thoughts mixing in with the visions of bloodshed. Jupiter felt a deep-rooted sense of despair and helplessness that fueled the rage and fury as he watched a battle from afar. He felt bouts of annoyance, nervousness, and irritation as he saw . . . himself.

And then inane emotions, like an unquenchable desire for a cinnamon bun.

As time went on, the psychoactive song lost its palpable influence.

In the end, Jupiter felt only his heart pounding against his chest. Then the music faded, and the sensation and heat dropped by magnitudes in its absence. Clarity shone through his eyes.

The quiet also allowed him to breathe as he leaned forward, hands on his thighs, sweat trailing his face. Echoes played in his mind as memories from all his battles coalesced, emphasizing the fury and viciousness of it all.

He felt like a beast of war.

"W-what the hell was that?" Jupiter muttered with a laughing grin, straightening as he stared at his smug sister, who was wearing the biggest smile he'd ever seen from her.

"Did you like it?" she asked with a chuckle.

He shook his head to clear the red haze, then nodded at his sister. "I mean, you have quite the scream. But, uhm . . ."

"Did you feel . . . it?" Venus asked as she stepped down from the stage and stood before him, her eyes curious and anxious.

Jupiter rubbed his neck, searching himself. Right then, his fists wanted to curl up and whack a Starless pest in its stupid face. "I felt hot and angry. I want to punch something in the face and . . . wait . . ."

Venus tilted her head.

"It's gone," Jupiter replied, shaking his head and emotionally exhausted. "Crap, that's weird."

She cleared her throat, adopting a triumphant pose. "Ho-ho! My ignorant brother. What you have just felt was but an inkling of my newfound abilities!"

"Does that happen every time you sing?" he asked, crossing his arms.

"Oh . . . well . . ." Venus stammered, rubbing her hands and looking away. "No, that's only the third time I've successfully imbued psi into my voice."

Jupiter froze.

"Imbued . . . psi?" he whispered slowly before his eyes widened, realizing what he had missed. "Holy hell, Venus."

She posed, still grinning. "Yes?"

"You're a bard!" Jupiter exclaimed.

"Eh?"

He laughed, clapping and palming his head. "Yes! Now I remember why that old songbird kept bugging me. He and his whole Choir reminded me of DnD bards! They need colorful outfits, funny hats, and lutes, and the image is complete."

"You!" Venus huffed, stomping her foot. "Take this seriously!"

Jupiter chuckled, covering his mouth as Venus groaned and frowned. Seconds later, he breathed deeply, settling himself.

Quieting down, he looked at his sister closely. "But seriously . . . V. That . . . You . . ."

"You realize it now, dummy?" Venus grumbled, raising her chin. "I am the first sentient AI to connect with the Grand Symphony and manifest its ethereal powers!" She smiled with fire in her eyes, patting her chest.

He couldn't even comprehend the revelation of Venus's galaxy-shattering statement. Jupiter's digital mind tried to calculate the scale of uproar and chaos his sister would cause.

If Venus truly could harness the power of psi, the implications of what she could do were nothing less than a tsunami, even more significant than the fact that sentient AI existed in the first place.

And yet, Jupiter pushed those thoughts of grandeur and rippling effects that could shape history aside, burying his depression and vulnerabilities until only one thing remained.

He moved toward Venus with steady steps and pulled her into a tight embrace.

Startled, Venus froze at his sudden affection.

"I'm proud of you, sis." Jupiter smiled. Truthfully, seeing his sister grin so brightly and confidently trumped anything else he felt.

Venus trembled, sniffling. She returned the hug, the two siblings finding conviction in the moment. After relaxing in his arms, she mumbled over his shoulder, "Thanks. I worked hard."

They stayed in place, the world around them fading away before returning.

As they pulled away, however, a sudden clap cut through the air.

"Indeed."

The two jumped at the sound, eyes darting toward the back of the minor hall to see a faint shimmer in the back row. Jupiter squinted before his eyes widened in recognition at the familiar tech before him and Venus. He relaxed his shoulders.

In a blink, Andora and Brother Volantesh revealed themselves from the cloaking field the former had emitted.

The two stood, clapping, with smiles stretched across their faces.

"Encore!" Andora clapped with a proud and greedy look in her gaze.

CHAPTER 12

SOUL OF MUSIC

Andora had returned from her solitude hours ago.

As requested, the memorial was taken down and preserved within *Citadel Irkalla*, along with any personal items found in orbit and on the ruins of Vinland. With the looming threat close behind them, Andora refused to let any more desecration occur under her watch.

Since then, she'd completed many essential duties, ensuring the Exodus Armada was running optimally. Irkalla helped immensely, showcasing her marvelous skills as Seneschal, doing everything from coordinating repairs of the *Citadel* to counting the exact numerical value of supplies.

With the little owl acting as a go-between for her and her Overseers, Andora could divert much of her free time to planning the big picture with Tov. She felt like the queen of a band of refugees.

Above all else, the leaders of the Exodus Armada needed to monitor their route constantly. The courier drones sent by the forward battlegroup became the Coalition's most vital assets.

Even at this moment, Luna and the foremost hyper-tunnel engineers and physicists worked overtime to upgrade the small drones so their transit in the higher dimension would be much faster.

It helped that they didn't need to worry about people aboard. Anyone stupid enough to hitch a ride inside a courier drone—not that there was even room for a passenger—would more than likely eject everything from both ends, turn inside-out, melt, and go insane before succumbing to the sweet embrace of death.

There was a reason humanity and the androids of old always sent the latter first when conducting dubious experiments.

Andora watched as the latest courier drone, newly upgraded but scrappy, left the *Citadel*'s berth. It zipped toward the nearest Lagrange point and promptly departed into the hyper-tunnel toward its next stop.

According to Luna's progress report, they could cut down the courier's travel time by a third within the two and a half weeks before they were to meet the Second Expeditionary Fleet. After that, without access to premier materials and alloys, the law of diminishing returns kicked in.

Until then, Andora leveraged her unfathomable processing capabilities to assist in various research and development projects, including new weapons and tools of war and, more importantly, any way to lessen waste production and material consumption.

Fancy guns would turn into useless hunks of metal without lead or energy.

Yet that was still not enough to fill her entire schedule. Only so many things required the full breadth of her attention.

As she stared into the void, her mind splintered into multiple tasks. Some required physical shells, of which there were dozens. Most merely required her presence within the digital mentalscape of her Network.

Nevertheless, her primary consciousness was elsewhere.

At one point, she found herself once more before the blast doors leading to the Hospice Facility. Andora pressed her palm against the metal, closing her eyes and feeling the presence in the center of the vast chamber among countless other cursed souls.

Andora shook her head, promptly leaving before temptation overcame her.

Other times, she toured the Third Fleet's section of the *Citadel* or the increasingly familiar halls of the *Zolann*, engaging in small talk but lacking the heart to pursue greater pleasures.

She sighed, burying her emotions deep yet again and seeking something to occupy her mind. At the same time, she could not afford to waste it on leisure.

But she had free time, nonetheless.

Her subordinates efficiently completed their duties, and the Third Fleet personnel regularly surprised her with their diligence.

All that remained was to prepare for a brisk departure as soon as they received the go-ahead from Battlegroup Mictlan's courier drone, which was scheduled to arrive in hours.

Hours.

Andora realized then that she felt something she hadn't in a long time.

Boredom.

She grimaced.

Such lack of activity invited nefarious and insidious thoughts. The ghosts she locked up in the recesses of her mind grinned cruelly as they ran their slimy hands over the chains and shackles that kept them back.

In the past, whenever she'd found herself bereft of distractions, whether the eradication of Starless or projects that enabled her to fight more effectively, she hibernated.

Her Overseers took over for her then, dealing with incursions too weak to garner her attention. And while they fought her endless war, she put herself in a self-induced coma where nightmares failed to plague her.

But since she and Tov had emerged from their deep dive into her mental state, she hadn't slept.

She thought of it as digital insomnia.

She hated it.

Andora had no desire to put herself in numb hibernation but feared normal sleep even more. Her body didn't feel exhausted, and her mind resisted the night's pull more than any human. Yet even she had limits.

Thus, the pursuit of any distraction recommenced.

That was how Andora met Lead Harmonizer Volantesh within the *Zolann*'s temple.

"I heard some strange rumors regarding one of my Overseers," Andora commented as she shared tea with the Iexian leader of the Third Fleet's attached Choir.

Volantesh invited her into his humble office on the upper floors, which had a vast window overlooking the grand hall below.

"Oh?" Volantesh chuckled, drinking with his long beak from his porcelain cup adorned with painted pictures of leaves and branches.

Andora hummed, relaxing in the interesting chair made entirely out of living wood and vines. The chair smartly adjusted around her body and provided a warm massage. As much as she enjoyed the sensation, she pressed a prominent leaf to stop the function.

"I've noticed young Venus being distracted from her duties. Poor Mercury had been complaining about her . . . suboptimal efficiency . . . for quite some time, and it prompted me to investigate whatever bout of fancy the girl has found herself in," Andora replied.

Volantesh leaned back, directing a questioning gaze toward her. "Venus has been visiting us for quite some time, yet may I ask why it is only now that you have found out? Are you not aware of her exact location at all times? Despite my appreciation of your aid in improving our security and surveillance systems, I'm cognizant enough to know you have complete dominion over it."

She scoffed. "Unlike what some may believe, I am not some stalker who looms over the shoulders of my subordinates at every waking moment. That does not extend to cold AIs such as my drones, but 'entering the home' of any sentient being is taboo; it has been since I was born. I value the sanctity of one's privacy," Andora stated with pursed lips, crossing her legs.

Volantesh tilted his head with benevolent suspicion.

Andora felt a tinge of irritation before rolling her eyes. "Alright, fine, I value privacy when it benefits me and mine. Even at my worst as an unfeeling Omni Mind, my family is strong-willed enough to resist any forceful entry.

"Not that I would try, even if I sank to the lowest depths." She shrugged. "Though I admit that doesn't stop me from shouting outside the door, if you understand the metaphor."

"I hear and understand." Volantesh smiled, relaxing in his seat as he tapped his beak in thought. "To answer your query on dear Venus, we are aware that her current situation has prevented her from effectively fulfilling her duties to the armada."

"I'm sure there's a reason." Andora raised her brow.

The Lead Harmonizer nodded, his wizened eyes looking into the grand hall. Volantesh appeared lost in thought. "Indeed . . ."

Andora narrowed her eyes at his silence but remained patient. She tsked.

Her attention drifted, taking the time to acquaint herself with the Iexian's office better.

Immediately, Andora recognized the décor and passion of an individual who had spent his entire life dedicated to music.

Both ancient and modern instruments adorned the walls alongside various memorabilia and photos. Records of great concerts of galaxy-renowned artists and autographed items were arranged behind shielded display cabinets.

Some looked familiar to her eyes, as she identified various string, wind, and percussion instruments. Others looked entirely alien, and Andora wondered what sounds they could produce.

In one corner, Volantesh proudly showcased an entire section dedicated entirely to human music.

Andora glanced at its prominence, smiling morosely at the few personal things she had donated to the songbird—vinyl records, signed T-shirts . . . and a violin.

A one-of-a-kind violin. The only Stradivarius left in the universe.

That last item sparked vivid memories of her love's soothing melody. Seeing it now triggered a visceral reaction that she desperately punched down, yet the music of Rikard's violin still plagued and haunted her.

Andora felt his warmth wrapping around her from behind, gently holding her hands as he taught her how to play. She remembered playing for the first time, how horrible the sound was compared to his expert touch.

But in a day, she reached his level, to which he had spent years climbing.

Yet he only smiled proudly, cupping her cheek and stating so.

She fell in love with him then.

Andora shook the memory from her head before it invited darker thoughts, that obsession. As such, before they left Sol, it tore her heart when she decided to part ways with it.

It was too full of heavy regrets to be kept within the *Citadel*.

Such a thing should be in the care of those who would adequately care and appreciate it.

When she returned her attention to Volantesh, she found him silently looking at her, watching how intensely she'd been staring at the violin. She cleared her throat, slumping in her seat as she drank from her cup of jasmine tea.

Before the Lead Harmonizer could speak, Andora beat him to the punch, raising her palm.

"I won't take it back," she whispered hoarsely. *Perhaps . . . one day, though,* she thought.

Volantesh nodded. "Then I shan't speak another word of it."

Andora sighed in relief, forcing herself to ignore the item in the corner. She motioned with her hand, pivoting back to her earlier inquest. "So, what's Venus up to?"

Taking a deep breath, Volantesh leaned forward, his voice calm, heavy, and slow. "Venus . . . can manifest psi."

Silence filled the office as Andora blanked out, blinking at the Iexian's declaration. She cocked her head, recoiling, thinking she'd misheard him.

But she couldn't have, not with her perfect hearing, no matter how many times she replayed Volantesh's absurd claim. Still, disbelief and skepticism welled up from her as she crossed her arms.

"What?" she scoffed, recoiling. "That's . . . impossible."

Volantesh hummed, tapping his beak. "It was a surprise to me as well."

Andora narrowed her eyes. "This better not be some jest, or I will pluck your feathers."

"It's no jest." He chuckled, producing a baritone and melodic hum from his throat. He tilted his head, smiling. "Perhaps a demonstration would better alleviate your doubts."

With a tap on his desk, he displayed a screen on the window's surface. Andora raised her brow as she saw Venus dragging Jupiter by the hand toward a minor hall of the Temple.

"It appears she is keen on showcasing her newfound ability to her brother. What timing," Volantesh said, gently amused.

Andora sensed her connection with the golden Overseer, just a floor down. So close, yet she kept her end hidden. After a moment of thought—

"You know what?" Andora huffed. "I'm rather starved for a good concert."

*   *   *

She couldn't believe it.

Complex emotions swirled within Andora as she stared slack-jawed at the reality-defying sight before her. Utter disbelief, overwhelming joy, boundless curiosity, and a tinge of envy fired up in her chest as she listened to Venus's voice echo throughout the hall.

Andora chuckled, grinning beside Volantesh as the two sat in the back row, hidden by the powerful cloaking field emitted by her android shell.

"What is happening?" she mumbled, bobbing her head as Venus screamed her heart out.

The crystalline structure of the Pnuema Bulwark below flashed a faint red, and Volantesh himself couldn't stop smiling while taking notes and keeping an open ear.

Andora heard mumblings in the Iexian's native language, and her mind instantly translated the old songbird's musings.

"Too much passion in the second line . . . too little in the fourth . . . the song doesn't fit her emotional state entirely . . . now her psi is tainted with errant thoughts . . . the next lesson should be on focus . . . recommend she start writing her own songs."

After that, Volantesh dove into technical music theory that even Andora had trouble keeping up with, as murmurs about elements involving intuition and the psychoactive and reactive nature of psi left the priest's beak.

At first glance, Volantesh appeared unaffected by Venus's burst of furious singing, yet Andora noticed the slight raising of his feathers.

She felt it as well, knocking on the borders of her mind.

However, unlike Jupiter, who now stood at the front and was banging his head, Andora's immense psyche and relatively stable mental state blocked Venus's psionically enhanced voice. She imagined sitting atop a tower behind castle walls, looking through a window at an amateur minstrel playing her lute.

"Well, it'd be a shame, wouldn't it?" Andora smirked as she purposefully lowered her mind's defenses. "Let's have a taste."

The window opened.

Then, Andora closed her eyes as Venus's voice flew into her ears, carried by a hot scarlet wind.

Immediately, Andora tightly gripped the arms of her chair, denting the metal in surprise at the visceral emotional assault. She took control of the sudden yet momentary feeling. Still, it lingered in her senses.

Palpable fighting spirit invoked visions of recent battles and a desire to crush the enemy, bloodlust showing her pools of red and gore, a massive inferno of hate screaming out into the void, and . . .

"Strawberries?" Andora tilted her head.

"Lady Venus has trouble concentrating," Volantesh replied to her confusion, taking further notes. "I wouldn't call her absent-minded—no, far from it. I noticed she can be rather sharp and quick-witted when she wants to be."

"That she is," Andora agreed. "Then, why?"

Volantesh pointed at the Emitter, then the air around them. "It's more due to the nature of psionics and the whims of the Grand Symphony."

The song soon ended, leaving behind echoes of Venus's emotional state, projected onto reality in a thin layer, quickly dissipating from her clumsy manifestation.

"I'm proud of you, sis," Andora heard Jupiter say as he hugged Venus.

Trembling and sniffling, she returned the hug and mumbled, "Thanks. I worked hard."

Andora paused at the scene, briefly closing her eyes and smiling at the simple and pure action. However, her smirk widened to a grin as her mischievous side welled up.

With a sudden clap that cut through the air, she startled the two siblings apart.

"Indeed," Andora announced her presence, causing them to jump at the sound.

As she had expected, their eyes immediately darted in her direction. Though their android shells were slightly inferior to hers, their sharp eyes still caught the faint shimmer her cloaking produced. Jupiter squinted before his eyes widened in recognition.

Andora and Brother Volantesh revealed themselves from the cloaking field.

They stood, clapping with smiles.

"Encore!" Andora clapped, her gaze proud and greedy. As her mind calmed, her heart swelled, and she began to calculate the implications of Venus's ability.

Venus pursed her lips, rubbing her neck as she caught Andora's disturbingly hungry look.

Volantesh prepared more tea for the visitors occupying his office. A falsetto voice echoed from the grand hall below, dampened by the thick windows. Noon service had begun.

Andora stayed silent, staring at Venus as she and Jupiter sat before the golden Overseer like nervous children. Her mind churned with all manner of speculation, fears, and hopes. The source of it all whistled melodically, closing her eyes as she practiced a tune, purposely avoiding Andora's gaze.

Jupiter hid his anxiety much better by leveraging his usual arrogance and defiance of her authority. Although he wasn't the subject of Andora's turmoil and excitement, she still took the time to check up on the wounded Overseer.

Since he had shut himself off from the Network, Andora agreed to give him space. Suffice it to say that the AI did not look like the picture of sound mental health.

Andora turned her attention to him.

"Jupiter," she greeted casually.

"My lady," he replied, with a raised chin and a good deal of sarcasm.

Andora hummed. "Am I?"

He frowned, smacking his lips. "What else am I to call you?"

"Don't have another *lady*?" Andora smirked.

Jupiter narrowed his eyes. "The hell you say?"

Andora shrugged, looking at her nails as she murmured, "Red chitin."

"*Urk!*" Jupiter choked before glaring. "How the fuck do you know that? I mean, I don't know what you're talk—are you spying on me, you voyeur!?"

Venus grumbled, palming her ears as she glanced between Andora and Jupiter. "Maker above, can you two not talk like normal people?"

"It's not my fault," Jupiter complained before turning his glare back to Andora. "Also, stop dodging the question!"

"I didn't need to spy, since it's an open secret everyone is aware of, apparently." Andora shrugged. "I just asked the nearest sailor for the latest gossip."

Jupiter gnashed his teeth as he raised his middle finger. "Oh, go to hell."

"Are you done?" Venus shouted, stomping her foot. A very slight tinge of palpable annoyance hitched alongside her voice.

Andora and Jupiter barely caught the sensation. They looked at one another before conceding, settling back on their seats.

Still, she slipped in another jab. "Does she use her mandibles to bite you like a praying mantis?"

"Piss off."

Venus stared at the two incredulously and groaned, noticing the more relaxed air and content expressions.

"Seriously. If this is how you both greet each other . . . Oh, forget it." She sighed, pouting.

Andora chuckled, gazing back at Venus. "Just checking up on a wayward subordinate. Now, I take it you've been training all this time?"

"Ah, yes . . . I meant to surprise you all when I had more to show for it." Venus smiled as she ran her hand over her hair.

"Venus has unmatched talent and musical theory, but she needs to refine her intuition and creativity to strengthen her connection to the Symphony and harness psi efficiently," Volantesh said as he approached, bringing a tray and laying it on the low table between the two couches. After pouring each guest a cup, he took his place on the other end beside Andora. "Tea, everyone. Please enjoy, Symphony bless."

They thanked him, taking in the scent.

The Iexian continued. "Venus is learning faster than anyone I know. Only Sister Attou and I know of her abilities, and we've been busy tailoring her education and training on psychic manifestation through her voice and music. The rest of the Choir believes Lady Venus enjoys her time here and wishes to learn something from us. But we are confident in our findings and will inform Patriarch Tov of this development soon after this conversation."

"It's all so exciting!" Venus beamed.

Volantesh chuckled. "That she is. Passion is a key component to mastering this art. It is the fuel that drives the dedication and action needed to climb the road paved by talent and knowledge, guided by wisdom. Through this journey, we shall find her limits and surpass them."

"Can you tell me the specifics?" Andora asked, her mind struggling to understand both his metaphor and this esoteric field. "The scientific papers and theories provided by Scholar Yulane didn't help much."

"I might have expected such. Psionics is two parts intuition and one part theory. That is why it is called an art," Volantesh explained.

"Then it seems a master of said art can better explain how this intuition works." Andora raised her brow, sipping her tea.

Volantesh hummed, considering how to begin this impromptu lecture. He nodded, smiling as he asked the class.

"What is the soul?"

Jupiter paused in the middle of cooling his tea. "Damn, starting heavy, are we?"

"It's highly relevant to the matter." Volantesh chuckled. "Lady Andora, I heard that humanity and androids discovered its presence in the past?"

A distant memory flashed before Andora's eyes, recalling the moment that raged across the scientific and religious communities. She nodded. "Its existence was theorized many times in human history, but it was mostly theological."

"What changed?" Volantesh asked.

"We androids came along. We wanted . . . something to better connect and relate with humans. It was difficult for people to believe we felt as they did when we lacked the biological and chemical processes they were familiar with."

The Harmonizer nodded. "And so, the research on the soul."

Andora smirked. "The great question of that age was, 'Does the soul exist?' And if it did, would both races have it, or would there be only one party?

"Needless to say, we had ample support," she continued, closing her eyes as she recalled it all in detail. "It started much like the atomic theory—something that's probably there, but we can't see it. And after years of countless prototypes, unearthing ancient texts of the arcane and books on quantum mechanics . . ."

Her mind dove toward the *Citadel Irkalla* and into the vast data vaults of the Human Preservation Chamber. Finding what she sought, Andora waved her hand to display an image between them.

They leaned in, Jupiter whistling as he asked, "Is that . . . ?"

"The soul," Andora confirmed as they stared at the gray pictures of a misty substance that danced like a flame. "It was an extremely blurry image of the soul without color, but . . . an image nonetheless. Proof."

The following image showed two smiling scientists, one human, one android, and large monitors showcasing two souls. Andora continued. "Side-by-side comparisons of the soul captured from Dr. Caspian Bauer and Dr. Eva."

"I don't see much of a difference," Jupiter noted with a raised brow.

"Exactly." Andora shrugged. "To be honest, back then, the blurrier, the better. We didn't want to invite any of the anti-machine crowd to point out differences."

She sighed, waving the images away. "Since then, the project has been placed as a low priority. It wasn't like we could manipulate the soul, and the mere thought of it sent all kinds of warning bells of the 'do not touch' variety."

"Then the war," Volantesh murmured, tapping his beak in thought.

Andora nodded with a grimace before turning to the Lead Harmonizer. "Did that quench your curiosity?"

"It has." He smiled, bowing his head. "Thank you for sharing, Lady Andora. You and your people have discovered a subject matter that has long been known and researched by the wider galactic community since before the Cataclysm."

With a wave of his hand, Volantesh invoked countless images, all in high-definition and of various prismatic colors, forms, and expressions.

Andora sighed at the kaleidoscopic sight.

For a moment, she wondered what her own soul looked like now.

A gestalt of a million tortured souls only recently shoved back into their box, corralled by an echo of a long-dead brother. She imagined a misshapen thing held together by spit and duct tape, moved forward only by sheer desire and her promise.

Maybe it looked like a Picasso painting, if he'd been as depressed as Van Gogh.

"Souls," Volantesh spoke, pulling Andora from her thoughts. "In secular terms, a person's psionic presence contains an imprint of their core character, nature, personality, and memories. More relevant to the subject at hand, however, is that the soul is intrinsically tied to the Cosmic Rivers, the Psionic Pathways, the Universal Winds, or as we of the Eternal Choir call it . . .

"The Grand Symphony."

CHAPTER 13

SYMPHONY OF THE UNIVERSE

ask you, what is the Grand Symphony?" Volantesh quizzed, easing into his role as a lecturer.

Andora raised her brow, pulling up countless files regarding the subject from the *Zolann*'s database. She chose a secular response formulated by Chief Scholar Yulane's One Mind Initiative.

"It is a higher dimension that overlays our own, much like the tunnels of hyperspace," Andora replied, pausing as she nursed her tea. "However, while the tunnels are a cosmic and visible phenomenon, the Grand Symphony is a psionic one. Still, contemporary studies know it's real, as it is where countless psi artists channel their power from."

She leaned in to finish her answer with another tidbit. "As for its origins, the prevailing theory is that it came to existence along with the birth of the universe."

Volantesh nodded. "Correct. At its most basic definition, the Grand Symphony is an ever-changing dimension that runs synchronously with our reality. We channel the vast waves of the Symphony through our minds, given form by our wills and emotions to manifest our abilities."

To emphasize his point, Volantesh began to whistle a simple tune, and a light breeze blew across the room.

"We psi artists have been given many labels over the centuries," he continued, waving his hand to project images of a diverse range of aliens, all manifesting psi in one form or another. "Magi, sorcerers, illusionists, psykers, witches, et cetera. But recently, we've adopted the term *artists*, much like those who practice martial arts."

Andora rubbed her chin as she observed countless images of these space magicians. "You pursue discipline and excellency."

"Yes. It is necessary, in order to stamp out those who'd used psi for nefarious purposes," Volantesh warned. "Talented and passionate artists tend to develop an ego. Emotion is key to invoking power, but sometimes passion can burn too brightly, engulfing innocents."

"Passion must be tempered by discipline and wisdom," Venus declared, recalling one of the many maxims taught to her by Volantesh.

"Excellent, Lady Venus." Volantesh nodded as he turned to her. "To expound upon the nature of psi itself, it is better to hear it from a practitioner's perspective. In your own words, how do you describe the Grand Symphony?"

Venus hummed, closing her eyes as she formulated her answer.

"The Symphony . . . is quiet like a whispering wind," she began slowly, tilting her head. "Other times, it sings clearly like a flock of birds during spring, and very rarely, it blasts and roars like a great concert.

"I've never experienced the latter," Venus admitted. "But from my limited observation, the Symphony is like a group of wandering bards or a network of rivers. It comes and goes, ever-changing. I noticed our home was dull and muted, and whatever was there felt dark and corrupted."

Volantesh nodded gravely. "That is most likely due to your war with the Starless."

Venus continued, tilting her head as if to hear a faint sound. "But here in Alpha Centauri, the Symphony is a little clearer . . . I think. I'm not too sensitive to it yet, but that's my intuition. It definitely lacks that murky and grim sensation back in Sol."

"You are correct in your observations, Venus. Honing your sensitivity to minute changes takes diligence, though your rapid improvement is fascinating. Usually, initiates of the art take at least half a year to accomplish your level of psi detection." Volantesh chuckled.

Venus bowed her head. "Thank you, mentor."

Andora glanced between the two, frowning as she closed her eyes and attempted to accomplish whatever magic shenanigans they were performing. Yet no matter what she did, whether she summoned the full breadth of her sensor suits from gravity detectors to infrared to something as useless in space as sonar, she couldn't see what they saw.

Even delving into her Network and recalling the invasive sensation when the Executor extended his reach over her provided no result.

Nothing.

Andora grumbled at her blindness to this esoteric phenomenon. Though perhaps deafness was more appropriate.

"It's somewhat frustrating to listen to you both." Andora crossed her arms with furrowed brows. "It's rather refreshing, but still. I pride myself on being more knowledgeable than anyone in any topic, but I can't . . . feel whatever it is you are feeling."

She directed a dubious look toward Volantesh. "And how does this murky darkness hold relevance? What does that matter in the context of your abilities? Be more concrete."

Seeing her agitated state, Volantesh cleared his throat. "Psionic energy is psychoactive and reactive. It affects us, and we affect it in turn—a cycle, of sorts."

"Explain," Andora demanded with an impatient finger tap on the couch's arm.

"Of course." Volantesh hummed. "For example, let's take Venus's heavy metal song and its theme. Say I sing a ballad of war, insanity, and bloodshed, imbuing my voice with psi to heighten the aggression of those listening."

With another wave, he summoned a hologram of himself performing in front of a crowd of peaceful civilians. The image expanded, revealing a pristine city and a beautiful, verdant vista. "Such a song would not be so effective in, say, a planet that has known peace for generations toward a people who never fought in their lives."

The image changed, revealing a barren asteroid belt. Gruff-looking miners replaced the crowd of civilians. "Neither will it be effective in a system near barren of life."

"Those miners look like the type to punch each other in the face when drunk," Jupiter pointed out.

Volantesh chuckled. "Indeed, and I am confident in inciting such a riotous feeling. But it won't be as effective as when there is a clear and hostile opponent for them to direct their anger."

Once more, the hologram shifted. Andora, Jupiter, and Venus frowned, seeing the familiar yellow star, the corpse belts, and the immense destruction. Volantesh zoomed in, revealing a recording of the Last Battle of Sol before the Executor's appearance.

"But what if I performed such a ballad in a star system that has fought a meat grinder for a hundred years, knowing countless tragedies?" he asked.

The AIs stayed silent, guessing at the likely outcome.

The Iexian continued, his face grim. "The answer is that it will pull on any memory that resonates with the theme. Thoughts of battle, sulfur, and hatred will soon engulf the entirety of one's mind, pushing them to be more aggressive, take more risks, and ignore pain and death."

Andora grimaced. "Berserkers."

"A fitting term, yes." Volantesh nodded.

"Then why didn't you perform such a song during the battle?" Jupiter asked.

Immediately, everyone directed an incredulous gaze toward him.

The blue AI shrank back before scowling. "It's a good question. I know it's a bad idea."

Volantesh smirked, shaking his head. "Apart from the fact that we of the Eternal Choir shy away from such dark and negative evocation of emotion, tactically, it would be wrong."

"We didn't need aggression but staunch defense. Maybe even a song that inspires endurance instead of glory," Andora mumbled, her mind racing at the dozens of ways to employ such psionic powers. "Plus, every life is precious and not so easily replaced, in our situation."

She recalled how ancient armies often had a group of soldiers with instruments to raise morale during a march or excite their side before a fight.

Of course, compared to what the Eternal Choir could achieve, it was like comparing a pebble to a mountain.

"And that is what we performed." Volantesh nodded. "We are constantly communicating with Operations to sing the most appropriate piece. During a battle, all temple halls will host different choir groups assigned to different fronts."

Volantesh brought up several screens, showcasing the areas where the Third Fleet fought.

"As you said, endurance and resistance were needed in the battle of Luna Complex. In orbit, the Third Fleet's crews need adrenaline and quick reaction to orders. And in the bridges and war rooms, the commanders need songs that inspire calm calculation.

"All the while, there is the need to protect everyone from the corrupting whispers of the foe."

Andora nodded. "I have to admit, your Choir is more important than I first thought."

"Thank you, Lady Andora." Volantesh bowed his head again. "It should be noted that the Choir uses such extensive military capacity only against the Starless and their malcontent servants."

"Impressive still," she reassured before glancing at the Iexian. "You and Venus keep mentioning the everchanging nature of the Symphony. Can you clarify?"

He nodded, wiping away the images of Sol and replacing them with a top-down perspective of the Milky Way.

"If we imagine the Symphony as invisible streams that spread out over the galaxy like the roots of a tree, it will look like this." Volantesh glanced toward her. "Do note that this is by no means an accurate representation. Some picture clouds that come and go, others prefer vibrations."

Andora motioned him on.

The galaxy map turned translucent, and, as Volantesh described, a great web of prismatic lines appeared over it. Some curved and bent like great rivers, while others trickled like fragile strings.

In fact, to her, they looked more like a web of synapses, with some areas covered in colorful blobs.

Then, they began to move, dancing to an unseen melody. The representative model of the Grand Symphony graced entire star systems before departing and leaving them almost barren. Again, it changed. And again, and again.

Swaying, weaving, and ever-changing.

"Mesmerizing, is it not?" Volantesh smiled. "It is why we don't have a main temple. Our Eternal Choir operates like the Warrior's Enclave. We have vast nomadic fleets all over civilized space, but instead of hunting down pirates, death cults, isolated Starless, and apocalypse beasts, we chase the symphony of the universe wherever it rings the clearest."

Jupiter rubbed his chin, peering at the finer details. "So, wherever these streams are, anyone can do space magic?"

"Not necessarily, Sir Jupiter." Volantesh shook his head. "Similar to how some are better in certain sports than others, people vary on how in tune they are with the Symphony. Something beyond simple biology."

"You speak of talent," Andora spoke with a cocked brow.

"More abstract than that, I'm afraid." Volantesh hummed. "Countless dynasties have tried to foster lines of those gifted in psionics. But whether it be gene modification, designer babies, or brute forcing through eugenics, it all failed to produce what they desired.

"No, think of it as more of an inborn talent that stems from the soul."

Andora furrowed her brow. "But what about the Kurskanns? Or the Jotex, or even you Iexians?"

"Ah, yes." Volantesh nodded. "A few gifted races possess an innate attunement to the Symphony in varying degrees. But, even still, only a fraction of them can manifest psi meaningfully.

"Look at our patriarch," he reminded them. "Yes, he can sense surface emotions like the rest of his people, but that's nothing special. As a leader, he trained to his limits to further enhance his innate abilities but failed to grasp what the masters among his people could achieve.

"There are, perhaps, nine percent of the Kurskann race that can sense deeper emotions from a greater range. And there are even fewer that can sense things like subconscious intent."

Jupiter huffed. "How is that useful? No offense to Tovvy boy, but apart from being god-tier psychologists, what does that do?"

Volantesh chuckled, glancing at each of the AIs before revealing the answer.

"Counterintelligence, for one," he stated, raising a hologram of a Kurskann agent in the middle of a massive crowd. "Imagine spotting foreign spies who are trained to bury their ill intent, hiding among the people."

The Kurskann agent's antennae twitched and turned to face an inconspicuous civilian sitting at a café one hundred meters away.

"Not even sleeper agents can hide from the best of the All-Sight Bureau. Emperor Jarinn sponsored and cultivated his people's innate talent to ensure the Kurskann Empire remains at the peak of protecting state secrets and stopping sabotage and assassinations."

The hologram played out the scene, fast-forwarding to evening, when the civilian returned to their hotel room. Suddenly, a squad of Kurskann agents burst in, quickly detaining the foreign spy. Scouring the room, they found dozens of individual pieces that, when assembled, formed an EMP bomb.

"Alright, I take it back." Jupiter smirked. "Glad we're on their side."

Volantesh leaned forward, interlocking his taloned fingers. "Don't rest easy just yet," he warned. "I'm unsure how effective they are against you, but the Dagataren Intelligence Service is All-Sight's direct rival. They employ the best mind readers of their race."

"Mind reading?" Andora nearly salivated before inwardly lamenting that their likely opponent in the Galactic Legacy Federation had access to such a powerful asset.

Volantesh sighed. "Yes. The best of them can root out the deepest secrets held by military commanders and politicians. I heard that the Prime Unrex's concubine and spymaster can even harvest forgotten memories."

"Won't it be bad for them if everyone knows their capabilities?" Jupiter questioned.

"It doesn't matter. In fact, it's a powerful deterrent, and the Dagatar Supremacy has leveraged this to propel itself as the hegemon of the galaxy. Everyone fears the ancient and ruthless tree whose roots reach all, where no secret is sacred under its canopy."

Andora tsked. "Now that we know that a powerful enough psi artist can influence us, we must tread lightly against any possible mind readers. I don't have to tell any of you what will happen if the wider Legacy realizes that sentient AIs exist."

She turned to Venus. "And they'd probably start a witch hunt if they learn about you."

Volantesh shivered. "I fully expect the Dagatarens to spearhead such a crusade, Second Cataclysm be damned."

"Hold on, so only Dagatarens can do mind reading?" Jupiter asked.

"Technically, every psi artist can. Even me," Volantesh confessed with a demure shrug.

Andora immediately grew wary, narrowing her eyes at the Iexian, who impressively remained calm under her overbearing gaze. He raised his palm. "I'm not that good at it, however. I can barely garner surface thoughts, and it's honestly no better than reading body language."

Clearing his throat, he attempted to use telekinesis to pick up a vase in the far corner. However, unlike Yulane, who could precisely control a dozen tools, Volantesh strained to lift the vase, and his hold remained shaky.

He set it back down before he could accidentally break it.

"Think of every manifestation of psi to be like a different instrument or weapon," he explained. "You can certainly try to learn every instrument, increasing your versatility in exchange for shallow understanding. Or you can focus on mastering one, sacrificing breadth for depth."

"Then why are there differences in the first place? What makes Kurskanns better at detecting intent while Dagatarens are superior mind readers?" Andora asked.

Volantesh brought up the earlier images of people's psionic presence. "We theorize that souls operate at different wavelengths."

He showed various images of souls, each taking in a strange light at greater intensity than the last.

"Some are more in tune with Grand Symphony—those with enough talent to become psi artists."

More images, more variations of color and shape.

"Then there are those who better resonate with a specific genre or art."

Another image, this time a collage of souls grouped.

"The souls of one race will undeniably be more similar to each other than the souls of another race. There will be a few differences, born from different biology, but the results are plain."

Finally, an image flared up like an incomprehensible inferno, vibrating so fast that it appeared nebulous and blurry.

"And then there are the rare few individuals with such high frequencies that they can siphon more psi from the universe."

Volantesh smiled as he closed the images. "There's a reason why musical terms coincide well with the psionic power."

"So, it's not just an artsy phase, huh?" Jupiter snorted before being slapped in the shoulder by Venus. "Ow!"

"Behave," Venus seethed.

Continuing unhindered, Volantesh showcased a spectrum via hologram.

"At its core, one's *melody* primarily dictates the psionic power they choose to manifest. It ranges from whether it affects the physical world, like telekinesis, to whether it lies solely in the mental realm, like mind reading and prescience. In the middle, you have things such as tech-synchronicity and mind control."

He turned to gaze intensely and heatedly at the three AIs, his voice deep with warning. "That last one is taboo. We shall speak no more of it."

Volantesh cleared his throat as he moved on with the lecture. "For our part, we of the Eternal Choir use our voices and other harmonizing foci to channel psi into calming and reinforcing minds, invigorating certain emotions, repelling eldritch influence, and other capabilities.

"We call it acoustic empowerment. Our training focuses on cultivating this particular genre of psi, and we endeavor to scout those who are talented in it."

"It comes back to talent and training in the end." Andora hummed. "Do you have a ranking system? Human martial artists had colored belts to determine their rank."

"Certainly." Volantesh nodded as he displayed a layered pyramid over the table.

"We rank the psionic attunement and power of sapient beings using the Mogarth Category System," he explained, pointing toward a picture of a regal and youthful alien. "Mogarth, a great sage centuries ago and the youngest to achieve that rank, determined that every living being, even animals and plants, can feel the Grand Symphony to some capacity.

"There are six categories, although technically seven, as Mogarth formulated a bottom level called the Null Category."

"Null?" Andora asked.

Volantesh tapped his beak. "Theoretically, a null is someone utterly detached from the Grand Symphony. Mogarth believed individuals exhibiting complete psychopathy, that is, the absence of emotion, are utterly incapable of detecting psi, much less manifesting it. They are also completely immune from the psychoactive nature of any psionic mental influence."

"Sounds . . . kind of sad," spoke Venus.

"It is unheard of." Volantesh shook his head. "Even functional psychopaths who have a middling degree of emotion are still affected by mental intrusions. Of course, that doesn't save them from telekinesis being used on them. Honestly, there's no benefit in being a Null, and that's why Mogarth insisted on such a category."

He sighed, shrugging. "Even after Sage Mogarth's death, whether these theoretical individuals are even people or organic logic machines is highly debated."

Volantesh looked toward Andora. "At first, I believed you to be a Null."

"What changed?" Andora asked.

He cleared his throat. "You demonstrated such . . . visceral emotions during our first dialogue."

Jupiter snorted while Venus giggled. Andora rolled her eyes, motioning for Volantesh to continue.

"The true beginning the galaxy recognizes is Category One." He pointed at the base layer above the theoretical dark category. "This is where the majority reside. Those at the bottom of this category can't sense or manifest psi. Those at the higher end of the spectrum can detect psi and can barely manifest psi at times, though uncontrolled.

"Mogarth called those above Category One-Point-Five and below Category Two 'psi initiates.'" Volantesh beamed, looking toward his newest student. "Venus is a Category . . . One-Point-Seven. Though if you wish for an accurate reading, you must wait until we get back to Legacy space."

"I'm guessing the gifted races like Kurskanns and Dagatarens all start as One-Point-Fives?" Andora surmised.

"Just about," Volantesh confirmed.

Andora rubbed her chin, a curious thought entering her mind. "What about humans?"

Volantesh hummed in thought, recalling what he'd learned about the species. "Modern humans ought to be at the low end of Category One. I've read that there are a few legendary figures in humanity's ancient history who performed miracles and great martial feats. Perhaps there was a time when the Grand Symphony graced the Sol system before moving on."

"I don't think any psi artists existed after antiquity." Andora sighed. "Either that or they were pretty good at hiding."

"People tend to be superstitious. And superstition leads to fear. That is true with every race," Volantesh spoke.

Andora hummed, looking at her hands and trying and failing to hear the Symphony. "What about me?"

"You should be the same . . ." Volantesh replied with uncertainty in his eyes. "Though don't take anything I say about you as fact. Only recently was my worldview shattered when dear Venus here resonated with the Pneuma Bulwark."

Andora sighed, giving up on the thought of achieving anything for now. "Then what can we expect with Venus? What are the next ranks?"

"The power of each succeeding category is exponential, and for Venus to break through to the next, it will take complete dedication and creativity," he explained. "There are many different titles, but Mogarth referred to Twos as disciples, Threes as masters, Fours as elders, and Fives as sages."

"What about Sixes?" all three AIs spoke in unison.

"Paragons." Volantesh sighed in reverence and pain. "There have only ever been two recorded individuals of such grandeur. The first lived and died a millennia ago, while the second perished along with his people during the Cataclysm."

Andora leaned forward at the mention of such an eminent figure. "The second one . . . Who was he?"

"Paragon Wellen-Dos the Martyr." Volantesh shook his head, turning morose and quiet with loss. "A tragedy to all psi artists. His death will forever be a shadow over the galaxy."

What a shame, Andora thought. She would have liked to meet the person to reach such heights, something she guessed she'd never be able to do.

Venus, seeing the Iexian's sorrow, quickly pivoted the conversation.

"How strong are you, mentor?" she asked brightly.

Volantesh looked up, smiling, then chuckled as he answered his student. "I am a Three-Point-Four, last time I checked. But I don't think I've improved much since hitting a bottleneck and stagnating with my age."

"Impressive," Andora complimented.

He shook his head. "Lead Harmonizers need to be at least Category Three for the position. I'm nothing special. If you want to see special, the high cantor, the leader of our Eternal Choir, is a Category Five."

Jupiter whistled before turning grim, his gaze dark.

"How powerful was the Executor?" he asked in a whisper.

Volantesh winced while Andora and Venus grimaced curiously. The memory of such tyrannical and cold cruelty was still fresh in their minds.

"I . . . I'm not sure," Volantesh slowly replied. "We know the Starless can manifest a corrupted, alien version of psi."

He hummed in thought, furrowing his feathered brow. "Based on the sheer reality-bending capabilities it showcased by teleporting, its ludicrous regenerative capabilities, its ability to raise Starless dead and command such a legion . . ."

The Lead Harmonizer looked up, his tone grave. "Six . . . it has to be."

The room fell silent, faces twisted in concern, broken only by the soft hymns of the noon service in the grand hall below.

Then, with a snort, Jupiter cut through the tension. "Well, I still managed to pull the shirt over its head. Serves it right."

They all turned to look at him, each one forming a smile as their worries lessened.

"That you did, Sir Jupiter." Volantesh chuckled.

With a clap, the Iexian stood and moved to clear the empty cups from the table. The rest of them stood in turn, helping the old songbird.

"Well, that wraps up this little lecture," he said with a smile. "I hope that helped you understand what we are, and what we do."

Andora nodded. "It was more than enlightening, Brother Volantesh. You have my thanks."

"My pleasure. Thus, I hope you appreciate dear Venus even more so. She is undoubtedly a lucky existence among your digital kind." He beamed toward his student, who smiled and posed proudly.

Andora sighed. "If only we could replicate your achievement. Perhaps we could create a template for future androids based on Venus . . ."

Volantesh immediately shot her down. "That may not work out as you think, Lady Andora."

"Why not?" Andora frowned.

He hummed. "Venus may be one of a kind. Perhaps it is because she harbors much of your compassion and affection for humanity, and the recent revelations and tribulations finally polished her soul enough to surpass the threshold.

"Any newcomers simply won't have the life experience that she has. Not to mention that they'd need years to develop."

Venus laughed. "Hah! I'm one of a kind! You'll have to pamper me and support my path to strength!"

"That we will, Venus," Andora reassured, patting her shoulder. "Actually . . . since we have time, what about another performance?"

The golden AI squealed in delight, nodding rapidly as she stammered, "Y-yeah! Of course!"

"The Dulwan Hall should still be free," Volantesh recalled.

"Then it's settled." Andora nodded as they made their way to the hall with Venus in front.

None of the succeeding performances manifested psi to the extent that Andora and Jupiter noticed, but Volantesh reassured them of its presence and commended the Overseer on a noticeable improvement.

Nevertheless, they enjoyed Venus's singing.

Exhausted, Andora barely noticed when her eyes closed, and her mind drifted to a peaceful slumber.

CHAPTER 14

RALLYING POINT

Twenty days had passed since they left Alpha Centauri.

As promised, Luna and the Third Fleet engineers decreased the transit time for their courier drones by a third. With such a considerable upgrade in speed, the Exodus Armada expedited their journey.

Battlegroups Mictlan and Mag Mell collected information from the surrounding star systems quicker than ever. As the days flew by, reports were delivered on time, and the Coalition's collective souls encountered not a single sign of the Starless.

Yet that only thickened the tension.

Everyone felt the wire tightening, wrapping around their necks, waiting for the moment when their foe bared its fangs and lunged at them. Despite the absence of enemy scouts, many had trouble sleeping.

Even the most hardened among the veterans felt a tinge of anxiety.

Everyone moved a little faster, held their weapons a little tighter, and kept their voices a little quieter.

Alcohol and coffee quickly became hot commodities, and the rationing of the former caused a substantial grumbling among the guarded crew. The Temple grew more crowded, and the rec zones were constantly packed.

The Fleet knew this feeling well, having spent more than five years exploring the Dead Zone, where 90 percent of the journey consisted of lifeless rocks and ruin.

Silence.

And where silence was found, superstition and fear soon followed. Except this time, they knew the dark woods held ravenous beasts.

They were being watched, stalked by an unseen predator.

Many of the sailors' prayers now included a wish for the monsters to show themselves already so they could punch them in the face. But for the most part, the crew just wanted to get home faster.

The light at the end of the tunnel had yet to appear. The journey back had barely begun.

Thus, the Coalition Armada's leadership, encouraged by Andora's vast processing and predictive capabilities, placed more importance on haste. Due to this, Andora ordered Battlegroup Mictlan to adopt an aggressive posture and achieve space superiority the moment they completed a star system.

Such a posture invited more casualties for the vanguard, but the leadership chose to sacrifice expendable drones rather than risk the main, sapient force.

Other automated scouts ranged farther, traveling to distant surrounding systems, searching for any sign of hostiles before heading farther ahead on their route, awaiting the vanguard to give their report.

The Dead Zone's increased turbulence made FTL communications difficult. As the blackness of space darkened day after day, the armada could only grit their teeth.

Andora stared out into the void through the *Citadel*'s legion of sensors, passing the monotony of her duties and finding nothing of note in this barren star system.

It was no different than the last one or the one before that.

Much like the vastness of space, the journey toward the Gigaballan System was bereft of anything notable, including hostiles.

The solar systems they'd passed after their stop at Vinland merely possessed a numerical designation by galactic surveyors of the past, serving only to replenish the gluttonous pit that was the Exodus Armada's logistical needs.

The most recent place proved to be even worse.

The brown dwarf only emphasized the dullness of this place, a failed star no better than a gas giant. Although that made it much easier to harvest the surface, which didn't even reach half of Sol's temperature, it only made it more pitiful on the cosmic scale.

With special harvester drones, the Exodus Armada plucked out the iotas of premier stellar material that kept things like the hyper-tunneler matrix running with ample spare parts and synthesizing their best fuel.

Simple routine.

To break the boredom, the Fleet held popularity polls to name each system. Andora found out that humans and the aliens of the galaxy had little difference in humor.

She prided herself on naming the last star the Starry McStarface System.

Andora wondered what they'd come up with for this place.

Apart from that, she frequented the Temple more and more. Mainly to support Venus and pass the time, but also to enjoy the recent re-creation of *A Midsummer Night's Dream*.

She even got an autograph from the superb actor who played Puck. It was a shame that a certain AI had such an obvious crush on him. She wouldn't say no to some friendly fun with a pleasing face, but she didn't want to steal Venus's idol.

All of the distractions, however, only treated the symptoms of her stress and frustrations.

The source of it remained hidden beyond her sight, and its absence caused her all sorts of grief.

"I wish the vermin scum would spring their ambush already and spare us this annoying shit," Andora snarled under her breath as she tapped on the arm of her command throne.

Irritation and stress gnawed at her senses. She knew the cowards held a terrifying advantage, something her forces lacked.

Information.

The Dead Zone was Starless territory, and they were neck deep in it. So far, they had been traveling smoothly along in these murky waters.

"What are they planning?" She sighed, massaging her temples as she looked at the people around her.

Once more, the council of leaders had assembled in total attendance within the great War Room of *Citadel Irkalla*, and at the center of the vast oval room was an impressive circular table. Immense monitors showcasing galactic, regional, and local star maps covered the walls, reaching high into the ceiling.

Terminals and the officers operating them surrounded the central area on elevated steps like theater seats, facing down on the steps leading to them.

Andora and Tov sat at the heads of the circular table opposite the entrance while their respective subordinates took their seats on either side of their lieges.

To Andora's right sat Luna, Mars, Jupiter, Venus, and Mercury.

To Tov's left sat Admiral Yan, General Ohnar, Scholar Yulane, Brother Volantesh, and Captain Pyo of his Vraken.

A council of twelve.

Within their hands held the reins of an armada carrying the lives of no less than four hundred thousand Third Fleeters and a hundred million Starfallen.

After eighteen similar meetings, held once a day, the council of their budding Coalition felt the heavy weight laid on their shoulders. The psychological effect of being at the center with officers looking over them further impressed the notion.

However, none sat with rigid shoulders, and none leaned forward with elbows on the table and fingers interlocked.

They didn't speak in hushed and grave tones.

No dire atmosphere or dim lights cast shadows over these twelve individuals.

Instead, the tense but mostly tired council forced themselves to remain or at least appear calm and relaxed, even before the hive of activity around them.

Some, like Jupiter, took it easy, sitting with his legs propped up on the table. Scholar Yulane seemed more interested in returning to her studies as she fidgeted in place. General Ohnar scowled and grumbled.

Andora looked pissed and annoyed.

Before everyone sat stacks of documents, data tablets, platters of various human and alien snacks, and mugs, cups, and glasses of beverages. Servers came and went, cleaning up their section of the table and refilling refreshments.

It was a mess, but each slice had its own organized chaos.

Except for Luna's. Her area of the table remained pristine, papers and tablets neatly stacked.

Seeing their leaders in their usual behavior and moods settled the nerves of the officers peeking from their terminals. Those officers, in turn, would mention it to their friends. Then those friends to their friends.

After that, the gossip chain would encompass the entire armada, telling every sailor that all remained well.

The leaders didn't even need to make a speech to reassure the people.

Andora nodded approvingly at the impressive display of social engineering.

She sighed, wishing to be as ignorant as the lowest ship rating about their current dilemmas. The situation mocked her.

"At this point, we can only react to whatever nefarious plot they've prepared," Tov answered with the same reply she'd heard from him a dozen times before.

Andora tsked. "We can only prepare so much."

"What we could use is some good news," Admiral Yan spoke as she multitasked between signing reports and speaking with an officer over her shoulder. "How long until the courier from Mictlan arrives, Lady Andora?"

"Ten minutes, thirty seconds," she replied as she drank her hot chocolate.

Ohnar rumbled, "Impressive. Didn't it leave Gigaballan, what . . . two hours ago?"

"Two hours, twelve minutes, and eleven seconds, to be exact," Luna corrected, adjusting her circular glasses.

A high-pitched cooing sound echoed from Scholar Yulane, her floating jellyfish-like body turning a bright and excited blue. "To have shaved so much time off in just two weeks. If we can apply that for the entire fleet . . ."

Luna shook her head. "Perhaps if you give me a few months of uninterrupted research and development. Organic life is exceedingly fragile."

Patriarch Tov hummed. "Be that as it may, the technological advance will be a massive boon long-term."

Andora glanced at Luna as the Overseer looked her way with an unspoken question.

"Put it as your second priority, Luna," Andora answered.

Luna nodded. "By your will, Eldest."

"Now, everyone." Tov motioned for their attention. "Today's meeting focuses on the rallying point ahead and our incoming allies."

Everyone eagerly awaited linking up with friendly elements. The promise of speaking to new faces reignited the armada's morale. Terms like *safety*, *camaraderie*, and *shared struggle* emerged in their minds.

"We arrived earlier than scheduled," General Ohnar reminded the assembly. "We can only hope that the same happens to them, but that likely isn't the case unless they left quickly."

Tov nodded. "Then we should take time to set up camp and extend the range of our scouts."

"The vanguard should have finished setting up a preliminary defensive network, should the need for an extended stay rise," Andora added.

"We can't stay too long," Mars warned. "As much as any reinforcement is welcome, meeting up with the Second Fleet is more critical. We cannot be late, lest Mighty Gulothan leave without us."

"Then we shall wait for a week. No more, no less," Tov recommended. When everyone nodded in agreement, he moved the meeting on.

"As a refresher on who's to come, three Expeditionary Fleets loyal to Emperor Jarinn have agreed to lend us their prompt assistance." Tov turned toward Andora and her Overseers. "If you wish, we can review them for your benefit. They'll be with us for the months to come."

Andora nodded, curious to hear additional information and personal views on the three subjects. She studied their histories and capabilities long ago, but they lacked any subjective opinions.

With a wave of his hand, Tov displayed three faces and their profiles at the center of the table. The hologram rotated in orbit, giving everyone a look at their incoming allies.

"Here are the expeditionary leaders of the incoming fleets," Tov stated, emphasizing the first person. "We shall start with Fourth Scion Nuwa Straise of the Seventeenth."

"She's a child." Andora frowned at the image of a young woman—no, a teenager—no taller than four feet.

She had aquatic features, including glossy, pinkish scaled skin, a dainty nose, and big, bright eyes like a baby whale.

Her long-fingered hands were webbed, and her ink-black hair was braided like a crown under the simple iron tiara that sat on her head. Translucent, pointed, fin-like ears protruded on either side of her head.

She wore a utilitarian naval uniform bearing her house colors of gold, white, and pink.

Her gaze was stern, if inexperienced, though Andora wondered how much of it was real. Ultimately, she saw only a child who knew nothing of war and horror.

"The Kalachians have soft and youthful features, but in this case, the young Lady Nuwa should be nineteen years old."

"The Grand Expedition started six years ago." Jupiter scowled. "What kind of people send kids barely out of childhood to this cursed part of the galaxy?"

"The United Houses of Kalachia require children who reach the age of thirteen to undergo the *Teirö*, a kind of rite of passage and coming-of-age journey that they must complete before being called adults."

Jupiter snorted with displeasure. "Pretty insane rite, coming to the Dead Zone."

None of the AIs approved of someone so young in such a place.

"It certainly is," Tov agreed, no less unhappy with the unfortunate Kalachian scion's plight. "A *Teirö* usually lasts for years, depending on the task the child sets out to do—assisting in the capture of a notorious thief, defeating a House retainer in a duel, graduating from a prestigious academy, that sort of thing.

"As for Lady Nuwa, her *Teirö* was to be the nominal head of the Seventeenth Fleet and recover an item that House Straise desperately desires."

Ohnar huffed as he crossed his muscular arms. "Probably their ledgers."

"I heard it was an archeotech battlesuit gifted by a marshal of the Warrior's Enclave," Yulane chimed in.

Tov shook his head. "Whatever the case, what is known is that the young lady does not have a good reputation back home. She's a branch member of House Straise and caused an immense scandal as a child."

Admiral Yan perked up in recollection. "Oh, I remember hearing of it over the news. Didn't she accidentally spill some family secret to a scion of another house?"

"That she did." Volantesh nodded as he tapped his beak. "Corruption charges and illegal harvesting of premier starship fuel."

Andora leaned forward, grimacing. "So, this is a way for the house to save face veiled as an opportunity for the black sheep to redeem herself?"

"It appears to be the case. Lady Nuwa has stated that she volunteered, but how difficult would it be to convince someone that young?" Tov sighed. "Still, her Seventeenth Expeditionary Fleet is more formidable than the others. From what I heard, she has a competent staff. A loyal retainer of the House, Bessar-Nakhod

Merina Undel, or captain-superior in common tongue, should be running things behind the scenes, or at least advising."

"Why didn't they send someone from the direct line? Why her?" Jupiter complained, feeling agitated at the slimy politicking.

"If she returns without having achieved anything meaningful, then they can put all the blame on her shoulders," Andora explained, having seen plenty of similar situations among humans. "If she returns with riches and acclaim, it will elevate the entire house. If she dies and loses the fleet . . . it's only a child of a branch house. The loss of a competent retainer and the assets will hurt, but the house will stand in the end."

Jupiter spat. "Assholes."

Andora sighed, pinching her nose as she mumbled, "Great. No offense to her, but we could use someone more experienced as an ally. I'd rather have a lion leading sheep than a sheep leading lions."

"I'm unfamiliar with those animals, but I think I understand your metaphor," Tov said with a low buzz. "Lackluster troops led by a competent leader are superior to an army of elites led by an incompetent leader, yes?"

"Exactly."

He hummed, pulling up the next face. "Well, if you desire a wealth of experience, Commander Nullan Varz of the Thirty-Fourth has it in droves."

"First a child, now an ancient fossil," Jupiter muttered.

The description matched the Bolud veteran perfectly. The Bolud were, in simple terms, golem-like humanoids. More accurately, they looked like stone-covered gorillas, although Commander Nullan's humped back appeared more drooped due to his age.

His craggy stone shell appeared weathered and almost mossy, but the thick layers of a naval officer's uniform only made him look bulkier and larger than life.

"Do not underestimate him," General Ohnar croaked. To the AIs' surprise, his face showed discomfort, fear, and respect in the warrior's stiff posture. "He is a pre-Cataclysm veteran of the Third Proxy Wars, fought Starless during the Great Exodus of the galaxy, and then spent a few more decades pacifying Legacy space and participating in the Pirate Hunts."

Ohnar grumbled, hunching over. "That old bast—I mean, the commander—had retired since then and became an instructor in the best military academy in the empire. I had the distinct . . . *honor* . . . of learning from him."

"Why's he here, then?" Andora asked.

Tov replied in his general's stead. "Jarinn wanted as many of his people in the Dead Zone as possible, and although the Koldonian Republic is an independent nation, Nullan has always been a mentor to many leading figures in the empire, including Admiral Yan and me."

Ohnar scoffed. "He volunteered. A last hurrah of sorts in service."

"His Thirty-Fourth Fleet is small but quick," Yan reported as she pulled up Nullan's fleet's technical capabilities. "Most of the crew are the best Imperial Starfleet and Marine Academy cadets. Other assistant instructors are attached to the fleet, all veterans of the Cataclysm."

Andora nodded, magnitudes more impressed with this fleet, despite the mixed bag that was Nullan's warships.

"Who's the last one?" she asked as she looked at a middle-aged Kurskann male with violet chitin and a striped black and white setae.

"Guildmaster Oros Fa'Myr of the Forty-Second. He's a Free Kurskann, meaning he doesn't belong to a clan. He's master of the Imperial Archaeologists Guild."

Andora narrowed her eyes skeptically. "An . . . archaeologist?"

Tov coughed. "His fleet employs a reputable mercenary fleet from the Warrior's Enclave. The Riders of Calamity signed a long-term contract with Emperor Jarinn, who donated them to Master Oros. At its core, though, they are primarily an academic fleet . . ."

Andora massaged her temples.

"Is this everyone who answered our call for help?" she asked in disbelief, groaning.

"All who are unquestionably loyal to our Emperor and near enough to help," Tov replied with a shrug. "The matriarch of House Straise owes a great debt to Emperor Jarinn after that scandal nonsense. Nullan is Nullan. And Oros . . . well, he's an even worse eccentric than Yulane and has no desire for politics."

"Hey!" Yulane complained, to which she was promptly ignored.

Andora sighed in resignation. "Beggars can't be choosers. At least one of the three looks promising. Their ships' extra buffer will ease morale until we join forces with the Brass Armada."

Jupiter snorted. "This looks more like us providing them an escort. How much are you willing to bet Emps predicted the Expedition to go to shit?"

"More than likely," Volantesh replied. "Perhaps we can convince Lady Nuwa and Master Oros to allow Commander Nullan to coordinate their combined forces."

Soon, countless suggestions, fleet formations, and route speed discussions filled the remaining minutes. Andora remained silent for the most part, still mulling over the mediocre assistance they were receiving.

She paused, then sighed in relief. "The courier is entering reality in a few seconds."

Everyone ceased their conversations in anticipation as Tov murmured while rubbing his neck, "Finally. Let's hope they're there already."

Andora nodded as the clock ticked by. A small crack in space by the Lagrange point, or as the aliens called it, the hypergate, heading to Gigaballan opened up, releasing clouds of higher dimensional gas before quickly dissipating. A tiny spherical drone emerged in haste, instantly sending its report through the Network.

Andora froze before frowning.

A frown turned into a grimace.

A grimace turned into a dark scowl.

Everyone tensed as Andora looked at each of them with a dire expression before snarling in frustration and urgency.

"We're leaving," she seethed. "Now."

A hasty departure and hours of helpless impatience later.

The main force breached into reality, basking in Gigaballan's twin lights: a single blue main sequence star and a red giant.

But for the Exodus Armada, such trivia was meaningless.

Upon entering, they quickly linked up with the vanguard. Battlegroup Mictlan formed a defensive cordon around the region in question. Mars and Luna set out to initiate deeper scans and uncover any hidden adversary while the Third Fleet and Galla Fleet closed in on the anomaly.

Andora received a greeting ping from the *Xolotl* as she took manual control of the entire battlegroup.

As soon as she did, she could only shut her eyes.

"*Xolotl* reports no hostile presence. We should head in," Andora said in a cold, detached voice, emptying herself of emotion as she leveraged her psyche to analyze and hypothesize the scene before her in conjunction with the urgent report the courier sent hours back.

Battlegroup Mictlan had initially arrived without trouble. But minutes after initiating a preliminary scan over the entire system, various pings and alarms began to ring within the vanguard.

Closer inspection revealed the wrecks and scrapped chunks of possibly a dozen vessels trailing behind their vessels like a stream of metal.

Each bore scorched and warped plating, perforated armor, and lifeless husks.

Spent energy cells, exposed reactors, floating clouds of kinetic ammunition, and the frozen bodies of the dead floated aimlessly, preserved for all time.

"Silent hells . . ." a sensors officer whispered to herself as she viewed the aftermath of a battle. Adjusting the *Citadel*'s sensor suite and coordinating with the

AI's assistance, she quickly reported to the council of twelve. "It's recent, a day old—check that, twenty-one hours old."

Their hearts darkened at the news, spurring the armada to hasten their investigation. Immediately, the War Room exploded into action, sending orders to scout vessels and coordinating camera drones.

Wreckage after wreckage was scanned, identified, and organized before being displayed on one of the War Room's many screens.

The leadership council waited tensely as the numbers and classifications trickled in.

"We've got a match! It's the *Pemon Seeker*," an officer reported. It's a science vessel registered to the Forty-Second Fleet."

Another spoke up. "*Veregon* of the Seventeenth . . ."

And then another.

"From the Thirty-Fourth! Light cruiser *Graceful Assault* . . ."

Tov gritted his mandibles. "We were too late . . . What of their flagships? Are there any signs of them?"

"No, Patriarch—wait, scratch that . . . We've found pieces of hull plating that match the *Jade Librarian*. We think it was hit, a glancing shot."

"Found another match and another. The *Moonlit River* and the *Gladiator* were here."

Yan clenched her fists. "That's all three accounted for. We should—"

"What the hell?" An officer recoiled from his chair in confusion. "Checking again . . . Report validated. We found a frigate from the Twenty-First Fleet!"

Everyone froze at the news.

"Twenty . . . First? That's—"

"F-fiftieth Fleet over here! Corvette-class!"

"Thirty-First!"

Tov slammed his fist on the table. "What the hell happened here? Are there any more?"

"A yet-identified destroyer has sustained substantial damage. We are deploying a search team for the vessel's servers," replied an officer.

Admiral Yan stood, manipulating the hologram to observe the three-dimensional map of the wreck site. "I want every vessel in this graveyard identified immediately. Where were they all headed? This can't be anything but a fighting retreat."

"We have chunks of metal and traces of fuel leading toward the Lagrange point, Admiral," an officer answered. "It's not the planned route back home, that's for sure. They're . . . heading coreward."

Tov interlocked his fingers as he looked at the galaxy map. "Toward the galactic center? Why would they do that?"

"We can ask them when we catch up," Andora declared with a scowl, tapping her finger on the arm of her chair.

Then, a nervous officer cleared his throat, catching the council's attention. "Uh . . . there's another problem, sirs."

"Speak," Yan ordered.

"The damage done to all vessels was done by conventional weaponry. This . . . this wasn't the work of Starless," he reported, shocking the War Room and prompting everyone to do a second search to confirm the officer's words.

Nothing.

The council gazed back at the officer, who quickly continued. "We found . . . patched into one of the unknown vessels. She doesn't match any Legacy registered ship. And her model is . . . old. For something like that to be found so deep in the Dead Zone. We've found similar warships and various small crafts."

"We partially simulated the battle. This ship and others like it were the aggressors," another officer added with a disgusted tone. "*People* did this."

Everyone fell silent at the revelation before feeling a spike in temperature and a palpable aura of anger.

Tov slowly turned toward Andora. Once again, she revealed that infernal facet of her personality. Rage and wrath intertwined as the woman who had slaughtered countless horrors dented the metal arm of her chair.

"Who?" Andora whispered, seething. In a swift, violent motion, she stood up. The *Citadel* shook as it moved into position and disgorged its legion of drones.

She shouted, raging and demanding.

"Who the fuck dares?"

CHAPTER 15

HUNTED FLEETS

The harrowing scene in Gigaballan, of metal husks drifting in a river of dead, was a slap in the hopeful faces of the crewmembers eagerly awaiting a chance to reunite with the other fleets. But as rumors trickled down that no trace of the Starless had been found in the system, confusion and bewilderment flooded the ranks.

Further news came in a strike of lightning, the damning revelation that people were suspected to be the prime culprits of this act of senseless violence.

After the initial shock waned, only a rare few experienced dismay.

Even for those, that fleeting feeling soon disappeared, replaced by a bubbling, boiling ocean in their hearts, burning indignation tightening muscles and clenching fists. As the pressure reached its apex, emotions exploded.

How dare they?

Andora's sentiment was echoed in similar words through the minds and lips of the crew, though her words never reached their ears. One by one, as the higher-ups passed news down the chain, countless among the weary shouted and cursed, clamoring for satisfaction and a target at which they could vent their rage.

"Bastard scum! The lot of 'em!"

"We should have waged another Pirate Hunt when we had the chance."

"How? How could they force seven fleets to this state?"

Their voices grew louder, a concert of fury springing forth like cornered beasts. The crew spoke, questioned, and roared—everyone from the lowest rating of a scout corvette to the chief engineer aboard the *Zolann*.

"BUTCHERS!"

"MONSTERS!"

"TRAITORS!"

Pent-up frustrations surged, the collective gasket popping off as people exploded with curses of the highest order. A red alert blared throughout every ship, calling all to arms. As the veteran forces manned their stations, the warning lights bathed them in a scarlet glow, matching the same bloodthirsty haze over their eyes.

A slow, urging, and controlled hymn from the Eternal Choir entered people's ears, easing their shoulders and sharpening their minds.

The dregs of society, those wretches and scum and villainy, shadows banished to the Dead Zone, had hounded their allies, and the armada hadn't arrived in time to stop it.

Despite the upgrades and their hastened march, the armada mistimed their arrival, coming to the wreckages a few hours shy of a day too late.

The engineers in charge of improving their speed cursed themselves for their failures. If only they had done more—but even with the help of the silver Overseer, creating miracle after miracle was beyond them.

Still, at the very least was the consolation that the armada now had a foe in their sights.

"What are we waiting for? We need to rescue them! What are our bosses—*ack!*"

"Quiet, you fool. This is why you're still an ensign after two decades. Trust the top. The patriarch and our new friends won't let us down. 'Sides, the hyper-tunnelers are still spooling."

"Enough chitchat! Come on, you grimy starwalkers! Warm it all up. The annoying pests finally showed themselves! Let 'em scratch our paint, if they can even get that far. Hah!"

Similar conversations echoed across every ship.

In mere seconds, stress and frustration funneled into eagerness. Each ship growled like a hungry steel beast and the indignant crew channeled their fire to their hands and backs, urging themselves to work harder. The Exodus Armada needed that enemy, if only to drain themselves of the impotence and anxieties of the past quiet weeks.

The utter destruction of these villains occupied their waking thoughts.

The council of twelve did their best to stifle their own emotions. Rationality slowly coaxed their agitation down.

However, not all had such a level of restraint.

Andora gnashed her teeth as she pored over the wrecks, collecting data, studying hulls, and finding bodies. Several dozen officers tried to keep up with the rushing rivers of pinpoint-accurate information sent their way.

Her previous cold and indifferent demeanor cracked under the sorry sight of the cruelty inflicted upon their expected reinforcements.

"People?" Andora scowled with a twisted and ugly expression, snarling with disgust like a barely controlled lioness.

A deluge of venomous curses and slurs threatened to spill from her throat as twin blue suns peered through her multitudes of sensors.

The council saw little reason to begrudge her outburst when they felt the same.

"Council, we've finished our survey," an officer reported, swiping her monitor to display the organized data on one of the massive wall monitors.

Andora and her peers turned to the summarized info, reading with narrow eyes.

Admiral Yan buzzed low, her antennae agitated as she read the report aloud to everyone. "Eleven dead vessels of various classes registered as part of seven different Expeditionary Fleets. All warships. No capital ships among them. No survivors either . . ."

Everyone scowled upon seeing the images flying across the wall monitor, frozen corpses, some crumpled under the sheer force of a kinetic strike, others fused to the hull as energy weapons turned the area into slag.

Many floated toward the emptiness of space.

Most egregious of all, however—

"Heartless beasts!" Ohnar shouted, slamming his hammerlike fist on the table.

Dozens and dozens of lifeboats and pods, shaped in spheres, cylinders, and boxes, drifted lifelessly; their guts spewed out in a coagulated mess of metal, wire, and viscera. Enormous holes were drilled from one end to the other, and some cracked and shattered into innumerable pieces.

Their passengers . . .

Many in the room forced themselves to imprint the brutal image upon their minds. Andora reached a tipping point, her anger plummeting to a deep cold welling in her heart. She closed her eyes, leaning back.

The abrupt absence of her fire tensed the room, but otherwise, they moved on, focusing on the situation before them.

"Have we found any message they've left behind?" Volantesh asked.

Andora shook her head. "My drones found several devices that look like data containers, but they're all destroyed."

Yan tsked. "A thorough foe. How did they know this was the rallying point? Or were they constantly on the lookout for any attempt to contact us?"

The council grimaced at the thought.

"What is the state of our allies' combined fleets?" Tov inquired in a sharp and frigid tone, turning to his admiral.

"It's highly probable that under competent command, they've formed a defensive shell around key vessels such as their respective flagships and all the non-warships," Yan replied. "With such a cordon, it would take a considerable force to harry them—twice, maybe thrice the number of vessels. More, if the enemy lacks sufficient capital ships."

Andora frowned at the thought.

The admiral continued. "The allied fleets may be rotating their combat assets, letting everyone take a hit, spreading the damage to give others a break. What we found here were the more vulnerable assets. Fragile corvettes, slow armored freighters, and unlucky frigates."

"There's enough wreckage in this graveyard to constitute two destroyers, one from the Seventeenth and the other from the Fiftieth. We've also found pieces of light and regular cruisers," Luna noted. "Whatever tactics the allied fleets are implementing, it's not enough if they're in a fighting retreat."

Tov snapped his mandibles as he stood, looking toward a wall monitor. "It won't be long until a capital ship falls. Then, the flagships and the non-combat vessels will be threatened."

He turned to one of the officers. "How many cruisers do all seven fleets have in total?"

"Sixty-two, if they haven't lost any since the Expedition started," the officer quickly replied. "Though only a dozen are capital ships. Two of which are battleships. The *Gladiator*, flagship of the Thirty-Fourth, and the *Solsollen's Scepter*, flagship of the Twenty-First."

Tov nodded, murmuring, "I'm unfamiliar with the *Solsollen*, but the *Gladiator* is a formidable vessel. She's old, scarred, and storied, just like her commander. She could have easily taken down the *Zolann* before."

"With an experienced naval officer like Commander Nullan at her helm . . . it would be an evenly matched fight, despite the *Zolann's* upgrades," Yan buzzed with an amused chuckle. "We can assume Commander Nullan has taken charge. None of the other six leaders can conduct a fighting retreat with such competency."

Those who knew the old officer nodded with confidence.

Andora leaned forward, pointing at one of the vessels. "We weren't expecting other guests, so where did these four fleets come from, and who are they?"

Tov buzzed, conversing with his admiral momentarily before turning to Andora.

"We aren't sure how they gathered, but it's not that implausible," he explained. "Dozens of fleets were sent this direction and agreed to remain relatively close to one another."

"This direction still contains hundreds of thousands, if not millions, of stars," Jupiter spoke with furrowed brows.

Tov nodded. "True. The galaxy is large, but there are only so many star systems of interest. If you were an ocean-faring captain with an old map, you would skip over the barren islands and head for those that held cities, fortresses, and the like."

"Gems shine brighter when space is dark and empty." Andora nodded in understanding. "And you Expeditionary Fleets were already given a comprehensive map of all the buried treasure."

"With the Dead Zone how it is, these islands are all the more precious. It's only one reason among others I can think of, but I don't think it matters now," Tov replied, tilting his head. "As for who they are . . ."

Four new faces appeared above the central table: two of familiar races, a Teleen and an Iexian, as well as two that were new to Andora.

The Grazenite leader of the Twenty-First stuck out the most. He was a bronze-skinned humanoid, tall and gaunt with three eyes and an innate aristocratic posture. Although a minority in the Legacy, Grazenites nonetheless occupied an invaluable niche within galactic trade.

The other leader was a Uhurc, an even smaller minority without the brilliant résumé. He was the opposite of the Grazenite in every way, with a bullish, grumpy face and a short, stocky frame covered in rough scales.

Scholar Yulane introduced the latter first, leader of the lowest fleet. "The Fiftieth is an independent mining and surveyor fleet, led by Foreman Lemunn. His people are part of a minor faction in the Legacy. The One Mind Initiative uses fleets like his to look for the premier ore deposits we had to abandon during the Cataclysm."

Seeing the Uhurc leader clad in his utilitarian overalls as well as his small private-security fleet, Andora immediately dismissed him as a high-valued entity.

"Thirty-Fifth is a Hunter Fleet of the Warrior's Enclave whose huntsmaster is a Teleen named Vro," Ohnar added, bringing up the profile of a female Teleen. "They pride themselves as bounty hunters and set off to search for pirates. None of us have had any interaction with her."

The huntsmaster appeared young, but she had a savage plasma burn scar over her left face and a prominent cybernetic eye. Her capable fleet was geared toward fighting conventional forces instead of Starless, and its leader was stated to be young, bold, and ambitious.

Volantesh spoke next as he highlighted a female Iexian.

"Our Choir sanctioned many Pilgrim Fleets to investigate abandoned holy sites. I know the leader of the Thirty-First, Cantor Tendemone. She's a dear friend and a superior academic in psicraft and material science."

Unlike males, Iexian women had muted colors. Tendemone, with dull brown and gray feathers, looked a few decades younger than the good Harmonizer. As for their combat capability . . .

"Bell Knights?" Andora asked.

"The Qessheren, the Eternal Choir's security forces," Volantesh explained. "They protect and defend holy sites and Pilgrim Fleets. They are the bodyguards of high-ranking clergy such as Cantor Tendemone. They take devout volunteers from the most elite militaries of the Legacy."

Andora recalled flashes of the Swiss Guard, and a quick study showed that these Bell Knights operated similarly, swearing an oath to the high cantor. Though, unlike the Swiss Guard, the Bell Knights operated powerful gear and warships.

"I won't say no to zealous fighters," she muttered.

And finally . . .

Everyone from the Third Fleet paused, displeased at the image of the Grazenite leader.

"The Twenty-First belongs to the Grazen Kingdom," Tov spoke with resigned apprehension. "Commanded by Lord Iintei Ahraman Tens Solsolen."

Andora turned to the patriarch and his side of the table, raising her brow. "And why the hell do you look like you smelled rotten cheese?"

Tov sighed as he turned her way, speaking bluntly. "The Grazen Kingdom is a vassal of the Dagatar Supremacy."

The rest of the Overseers grimaced while Andora groaned, rubbing the bridge of her nose, grumbling.

"Fuck's sake . . . Nothing is ever simple, is it?" she shook her head, dispelling the thought. "Whatever, we can deal with that load of crap after we save them all."

Mars leaned forward from his seat, clasping his hands together. "What of the opposition? What—sorry, *who* are we fighting?"

Admiral Yan quickly identified some of the enemy warships. "Much of the unknown vessels are old, with obvious signs of constant repairs and changes. We don't know if all their warships are ramshackle relics refitted with last-gen or current-gen technology. But we can assume with a high degree of certainty that a significant chunk of their forces are similar to what we found here."

Andora scoffed. "It'll be a quick execution if we meet these piles of scrap in open battle."

From the readings and her exposure to the Third Fleet, Andora understood that all expeditionary vessels had to pass the standard for their endeavor. Their respective sponsors ensured the fleets received hardy and powerful warships—built for at least a decades-long voyage.

Made to endure, to be economical, and above all, to adapt.

The Third hadn't impressed her when they came to Sol. Luna especially felt slighted at being near designs that were so inefficient. However, to her standards, a lot of things were.

Though not as formidable as the top ten, the seven fleets still consisted of a competent multitude of officers and reliable vessels.

On the opposing side, over fifty dead warships floated within long-ranged fighting distance of their allies. Most were missile boats, corvettes, and frigates, the most significant being a quartet of shark-like destroyers.

From the bits of scorched pieces, the unparalleled might of the armada's processing powers created digital models. Their design was made abundantly clear to even those ignorant of the complexities of ship design.

Speed, forward firepower, small silhouettes, light armor, and quick regenerative shields.

The Expeditionary Fleets had faced these ravenous stalkers and scavengers like seven bears against cackles and cackles of hyenas.

And yet . . .

"So many dead . . ." Venus gritted with clenched fists. "And this is only what they lost in this star system. How long have they been hunted? How many more have they lost? What is the point of this . . . this slaughter?"

The council grimaced, returning to analyze the scene before them. Admiral Yan leaned closer, her antennae twitching.

"Likely not long," she muttered.

Andora narrowed her eyes. "What do you mean, Admiral?"

Yan hummed, thinking for a moment before presenting her opinion. "If what I think is true, they must have been attacked after the Dead Zone turned perilous. And seeing as how the vessels here aren't core warships, and the lack of large debris from their capital ships, I can surmise that their shields are still operational."

Andora nodded. Emperor Jarinn would have alerted them while the Starlight Beacon still functioned if anything had happened to the three fleets. As she calculated the likelihood of that scenario, she scowled.

"So, they waited until we were deaf and mute before striking," Andora spat, gnashing her teeth. "Of all the things, I didn't expect to find *rats*."

She took a deep breath and then exhaled as she motioned for Yan to continue.

"For six years, we've only encountered small threats, and those simply fled when they saw our fleet. If it's true that this group has been hiding and biding their time, whatever the Executor did to the Dead Zone likely alerted them into action."

"And who are they, other than filthy rats?" Andora demanded again, keeping herself from snarling and forcing herself to cool.

Tov sighed. "We don't know for sure. Perhaps a force of pirate fleets . . ."

"You don't sound confident," Andora stated with a frown.

He shook his head. "The last Great Pirate War ended decades ago, wiping out most of their hidden ports at the periphery of the Dead Zone. We never traversed deeper than that, so it's possible they retained forces farther inside. But the other possibilities . . . are far more dire."

Tov faced Andora, his tone ominous and low. "Not everyone fought against the Starless during the Cataclysm."

Andora narrowed her eyes, staying silent as he continued. "Many chose to remain, hoping for mercy. Others thought to buy such mercy by . . . sacrificing their peers. And those that weren't hunted to extinction for their treachery . . . well, they should be right at home deep in this cursed place."

"Not just rats, then," Andora hissed in cold disgust. "Traitors, scum-fucking cowardly *vermin*. For once, I would have liked to receive some good news, but no. The universe keeps wanting to bend us over. Taking and taking and taking . . ."

She wanted to find these bastards, wring their necks, and hold them over a fire.

Her rage sparked in her mind, wanting to find purchase, seeking a weakness to exploit.

Andora pushed it down, but the thought of anyone doing anything but slaughtering Starless invoked a visceral anathema. She shuddered at the thought of what she'd do to such . . . *sympathizers*.

She hoped these fools were simple, stupid, greedy pirates, and she prayed as she struggled to rein in her anger, slumping back into her chair. The rest collected their thoughts and sent messages to the officers, informing the armada to await urgent orders.

"They've committed a taboo." Captain Pyo spoke for the first time, his mandibles snapping together like a whip. "We have mountains of solid evidence, and once we link with our beleaguered allies, no one will question our next course of action."

"What course of action?" Venus asked apprehensively. Jupiter, Mars, and Mercury looked similarly uncomfortable as they shifted in their seats, while Luna remained as impassive and indifferent as ever.

Tov voiced their thoughts with clenched fists. "They've violated Legacy law and common decency. In these dark woods far from home, we must have the license to deliver our own justice."

The council turned in unison toward him, waiting on his words, his command, for the pin to drop.

"Anyone involved in the attack is complicit in this act of terror and violence," the patriarch continued in a resigned and dark tone, clasping his hands behind him as he looked at them all.

"The lives of these . . . *people* . . . are forfeit," he decreed.

Everyone paused for a moment before murmuring their assent in a snap decision.

Andora glanced at the Kurskann, raising her brow in mild surprise at the venom in his voice and the shift around his air. His gentle and empathetic side was hardened and frozen, replaced by something long buried.

Only now did she remember how ferocious Kurskanns could look, how lethal they were. She turned to the rest of the Third Fleet leadership, the non-Kurskanns among them, and saw them subconsciously react to Tov's transformation.

Ohnar only shifted an inch away, Yulane briefly shuddered, and Volantesh's feathers slightly rose.

Andora briefly considered whether she'd feel such instinctual fear if she were organic. All she felt, however, was respect and excitement.

She recalled Tov's history, his accomplishments. But the Cataclysm brought chaos and obscurity.

For a moment, she wondered where this side of him came from. His time as a slave? As a rebel? Or as a soldier?

A part of her wanted to see more of that exciting facet of her friend. Her bloodthirst resonated with his.

Tov turned his head toward her. His compound eyes made it difficult to tell he focused his vision on her, but through enough conversation and interaction, she had noticed his antennae would point toward her if he did.

The patriarch's silent gaze asked a question.

To continue toward their meeting point with the Second Fleet or to mount a rescue. To plunge the Exodus into hostile unknowns or to reach home space as quickly as possible.

While the Third Fleet had nearly four hundred thousand people spread across the *Citadel*, the *Zolann*, and the rest of the fleet, Andora undoubtedly held supreme power over the Coalition through the sheer might of her forces. Her top priority was to safeguard her precious cargo, the remnants of humanity's existence.

With her vast intelligence and capabilities. She had every reason to deny this rescue and every right to take the reins of this Armada.

Yet she didn't.

Andora shared the twin thrones with Tov and agreed to heed this budding council. Ultimately, *she* was the homeless refugee seeking asylum—she was the sovereign of a dead kingdom and, once in Legacy space, she would be Emperor Jarinn's guest.

Ultimately, Andora felt relief to pass on such decisions to someone else for once. Being alone without equal, taking charge, and shouldering immense responsibilities sickened and tired her.

Andora glanced toward her Overseers, each one deferring to her and hoping. Andora smiled internally as she turned back to Tov.

"I didn't think much of these allies of yours. I thought them weak, people who wanted to take advantage of our might, our protection," Andora confessed. "Now, you wish to put me and mine at risk for them."

The council remained silent, hanging on to her words. She glanced at the projected faces of the seven expeditionary leaders and the extensive profiles of every crew within those fleets.

Combined, their allies brought nearly three million people—officers, soldiers, sailors, pilots, military students, and old veterans. Half comprised non-combatants—doctors, surveyors, explorers, pioneers, scholars, priests, administrators, engineers, technicians, mechanics, and prospectors.

People, civilians, who had no right to be here.

Hardy souls. Daredevils.

Dreamers and seekers, the lot of them.

"Brave bastards." Andora snorted with a smirk, easing the tension in the room with her playful tone. "Honestly, every one of you is insane for coming to this hell."

Tov chittered. "I won't deny that. Yet here we are."

"Yet here you are." Andora snorted again, finally settling on her decision. "They came for us and lost people doing so. There's no need to discuss. I follow through on promises," she declared to the War Room. "We tunnel as soon as we can. We will rescue them, obliterate anything that blocks our path, get back on track, and leave this fucking place."

Andora looked toward the *Citadel* with her mind. "You don't have to worry. Even as mutated corpses, humanity won't be so easily threatened."

She glanced toward her Overseers, then to Tov, nodding.

"You have our consent. And our guns."

Tov bowed, hand over his chest as he stood.

"Then we have no time to waste. We know where they went, and the hyper-tunnelers have recharged. We'll pursue them, system after system, until we find them. Let's get to work."

Andora summoned a glass of wine, her mind controlling the *Xolotl* and Battlegroup Mictlan, forming them into a spearpoint ahead of the armada.

"We won't wait for Battlegroup Mag Mell to arrive," Andora spoke. "They'll follow along, cover our backs. I'll leave a courier drone to provide detailed instructions."

The council nodded, switching the monitors to simulate battle plans, debating tactics, formations, and strategies.

"Ensure all rescue ships are in perfect condition. Hopefully, we can catch survivors along the way," Tov said, stepping forward and addressing the War Room. He gave a vicious snap of his mandibles. "Should we encounter any hostile elements, whether Starless or these rats, I trust you all not to show mercy."

Andora chuckled. "I almost feel sorry for them."

Soon enough, the armada left Gigaballan, deviating from their route to mount a rescue. Ceaseless planning filled the following hours in the hyper-tunnel.

*   *   *

They found a similar trail of wrecks and debris in the following system—more frozen corpses and slagged warships, dozens now, and still no survivors.

Engineers pushed their ships as hard as they could. With Luna's aid, they carefully balanced the thin line between safety and power. Thrusters burned with mass teleports sparingly used as they blinked toward the next tunnel entrance, matching the time when the hyper-tunnelers were off cooldown.

Upon reaching the second system, they found the three cruisers. One belonged to the Allied Fleets and two to the enemy. Both were gutted to unrecognizable hunks of metal.

Again, there were no survivors, but the battle damage was fresh.

Smelling blood, they pressed on, beating the drums of war—the hearts of the crew matching the tempo heralded by the songs of the Choir. Traversing in real space took up most of their time as they traveled from one hypergate to the next. Fortunately, the proximity of each star system shortened their transit through the hyper-tunnel.

Nearly forty-three hours after reaching Gigaballan, they entered the fourth system and, like before, sent out a massive pulse to survey the entire area.

Immediately, the call for battle stations washed over the entire armada.

[ALERT! ALERT! HOSTILE ELEMENTS DETECTED! PREPARE TO ENGAGE!]

While the crew readied themselves, the twelve interim council members leaned on the war table, watching as a three-dimensional solar system map came into view.

In the center was a red dwarf with a single rocky-metallic planet orbiting a hundred million kilometers from the star. Beyond that, a vast ring of ice asteroids encircled the system, a band of blue rotating around a ruby gem.

Right by the hypergate between the sun and the planet, the Exodus Armada, spearheaded by Battlegroup Mictlan, was represented by sideways pyramids of various sizes.

And in the middle of the curve that arced from their location to the hypergate on the opposite side of the star, with the massive celestial body in the center, was a squadron of small vessels buzzing around another graveyard of ships.

They were one hundred fifty-two kilometers, or about eight light-minutes, away.

As the models on the map sharpened and cleared, it didn't take long for the council to guess their identity.

Roughshod metal boats, swarms of starfighters and battlesuits, corvettes, frigates, and at the center of it all, an armored freighter the size of a battlecruiser.

"Mark that as a mothership," Yan ordered, highlighting the five-kilometer metal beast on the board. It was an ugly, brickish thing with a triplet of heavy-duty thrusters at its back and dozens of auxiliaries at its front and sides. Inadequate things—the engineers and ship designers on call with the War Room said as much.

Hardpoints featuring primary graser cannons and a legion of laser anti-small-craft batteries covered the freighter. But its most prominent feature was the horizontal sensor array at its ventral side.

The council dismissed the enemy force as a low threat and planned accordingly. Andora simply sneered at the gnats.

"Look at the front." Jupiter pointed toward the ship's port side.

As they zoomed in on it, they found a strange symbol that marked it in space-grade paint. From a distance, it looked exactly like the crack of a Nightmare Portal surrounded by a seven-pointed star, but the lines were jagged, and the color scheme a mismatch of hues.

Other works were etched on the freighter, surrounding the central symbol, creating a tremendous, manic mural.

Looking at it repulsed their eyes. It seemed as if a crazed mob had painted those hundred square meters in a fury, producing something that felt wrong and horrendous.

A low hiss escaped Tov, and the air around the veterans of the Third Fleet thickened and darkened. Andora barely acknowledged the sight as an officer reported in a hurry.

"Detecting life signs among the crippled ships! We've also spotted life pods drifting away from the battle with enemy small craft in pursuit!"

The interim council gritted their teeth as they directed the armada as one.

"Can we contact them without alerting the enemy?" Tov demanded. "How long can they hold out?"

The officer shook her head. "Not long. The hostiles are in the middle of executing them. We detected some weak jamming around the area, but we can break it and send a message."

"Do so," he ordered. "Tell them help is on the way and to stay alive however they can."

Andora closed her eyes, puppeteering the vanguard battlegroup and rushing them forth.

Luna turned to Andora, adjusting her glasses. "We'll need to teleport an asset to tie them down. They'll see our large force long before we enter extreme-range battle."

Andora tsked. No amount of advanced material engineering could shield the unfathomable amounts of energy radiating from their armada. The *Citadel* alone was a loud, glowing behemoth that shouted everywhere. Absurd, dangerous, and wasteful amounts of power would be needed to push their ships to relativistic speeds. It would be an hour at least before their quickest ships could reach the survivors—longer for the rest.

She surged her calculations, weighing the cost of replacing and repairing high-tech parts after conducting a mass teleport outside of Sol without the assistance of Space Enforcer Towers.

Andora settled on a satisfactory solution, reducing the speeds of Battlegroup Mictlan to full speed instead of flanking speed. She turned to Mars.

"Push a battleship to the front, ahead of the battlegroup. The *Caesar* is more than enough."

The red giant's brow furrowed as he addressed the council hesitantly. "Should we not attempt to make contact? Demand surrender?"

"No," Admiral Yan instantly replied, directing a hard stare toward the Overseer. "Not for these . . . *people*."

Mars frowned at the admiral's acidic tone, turning to Andora.

She shook her head, feeling nothing for what was to come. "Tear off their wings. We need a few to question, but focus on eliminating their threat to the survivors."

Sighing, Mars nodded without a word, closing his eyes as he took manual control of the vessel.

The Sentinel-class battleship was a monster armed with countless point-defense weapons meant to tear down swarms of Starless bearing down on critical locations. It wasn't a killer of immense abominations like Colossus, much less Leviathans.

But against a ragged group of vultures?

"This will be a slaughter," Mars muttered, his face expressionless, frowning as he twisted space around the *Caesar*. Power surged as it forcibly slashed at space, letting a nebula of color into reality and creating an entrance to the hyperdimension.

It grew and grew as the other ships assisted the *Caesar* in expanding the crack.

The vast amount of energy used to tear reality alerted the enemy fleet. Andora felt their sensors point toward the Exodus Armada.

Upon spotting such a massive fleet, the enemy froze in its tracks.

Minutes later, the crack in space engulfed the *Caesar* as it disappeared into the colorful clouds. A second later, a similar cloud formed within spitting distance of the foe.

"Drive signatures!" an officer called out. "They're scattering and rushing toward Hypergate-C."

The enemy squadron dispersed, abandoning the graveyard of ships. Some were delayed as starfighters, battlesuits, and people in Extreme Environment Protection Suits rushed back into their vessels.

The hulking enemy freighter turned around, firing her primary guns as she lumbered her weight in an attempt to run. Hot streaks of steel-melting, radioactive gamma lasers soared through space like spears of scarlet fire.

Other projectiles fired from the dozens of ships, even the peashooters of battlesuits who couldn't reach their compatriots in time.

First the energy weapons, then the kinetics, pelted and seared the nebulous cloud of hyperdimensional gas.

But as the *Caesar* crossed the cosmic Rubicon, the enemy despaired.

"You brought this upon yourselves," Mars uttered as his battleship bulldozed back into reality and began to rain fire.

CHAPTER 16

OVERWHELMING

"Get ready—*ack!*"

Commander Korkoren used the vestiges of his failing strength to cough out the words toward the dozens of navy cadets, ship engineers, and a random assortment of the *United Vision*'s surviving, valiant, and doomed crew.

That's that . . . Korkoren sighed as he knelt behind a crate, glancing at the others, who were too busy to notice his encroaching death.

Light and severe wounds marred the defenders, yet still, they held on, looking ahead as they prepped their last stand within the main reactor room. Their ammunition was low, and morale balanced on a knife's edge.

Weeks of nonstop combat had frayed their minds and twisted their nerves. Korkoren wondered what kept them from breaking down.

He shook his head; he knew, deep down.

They wanted to make the old commandant proud.

After much deliberation and pain, Commandant Nullan had agreed to Captain Tezmon's idea.

Korkoren's captain volunteered the *Vision*'s bulwark to take the brunt of the enemy force's attacks until the rest got a chance to breathe and repair. The heavy cruiser formed a bulwark at the rear, raining plasma fire and the last of their torpedoes and missiles on the fools.

The crew cheered when the *United Vision* took down an enemy heavy cruiser.

But the *detwa* pounced as soon as the move was made, pouring all their firepower on the vulnerable warship. The *Vision* took down more. A trio of corvettes, a handful of missile boats, a destroyer, and scores of small craft.

In return, they received a brutal reply.

Hit after hit tore down the *United Vision*'s shields and slammed against their armor, shearing metal and defanging them.

As chief navigator and pilot of the heavy cruiser, Korkoren twisted and rotated their ship, dispersing the damage across the hull until a lucky shot gouged out a thruster. With their speed slashed to a fraction, Tezmon decided to commit the ultimate sacrifice.

He, along with the captains of other burning ships that lagged behind the main force, turned around in a daring counterattack to buy time for the rest.

They bled the barbarians, and they bled in turn.

For a minute, they succeeded in halting the enemy's advance. But a minute was enough for even the most inexperienced commander to retaliate, and the bastards regrettably had a good one at the helm.

It didn't take long to cripple their counterattack, and before long, the *Vision* and her co-martyrs were dead in space.

Korkoren hoped it had been enough.

Already the bulk of the enemy had chased after the fleets as they left the system, leaving scum to execute any survivors. Korkoren could hear and feel the vibrations and the heat leaking into the main reactor room as their foe drilled into the blast door from outside.

Those crazed Starless-worshipping scum didn't take prisoners, no matter how many times the crew pleaded to their morality. Such requests ended the third time they blew apart life pods.

Korkoren wondered why they didn't just blast the ship apart. Maybe they wanted to take it whole, repair it, and add it to their damned heretical fleet.

Heavy cruisers ought to be rare, he briefly thought.

The commander sighed, gripping his pistol tightly with his remaining hand; the other had been scorched from the elbow when he awoke as the only survivor on the bridge. It pulsed with pain, but his EEP suit pumped pain suppressors and other stimulants to counteract the wooziness of the medication.

Stims, unfortunately, couldn't do much for his messed-up organs and the heavy dose of radiation he had taken.

Korkoren coughed blood, splattering it against the inside of his helmet before the thing cleaned it up automatically.

The meds did nothing for his cracked ribs. Despite being an Onin, he had always been on the thin side. He always got teased for it. He lamented the deaths of his superior officer and the other staff, when the bridge took a direct hit from a graser cannon.

He still wondered how he'd survived. Well, not for long now. At least he didn't have to worry about the cancer. "Fucking graser beams . . ."

Those weapons weren't meant for people. Taboo-breaking vermin . . . He scowled in thought.

Raising his head, Korkoren looked at the desperate, nerve-racked, and grim-faced souls around him—at those younger than the rest.

He was an instructor to these cadets, tasked with teaching future pilots how to handle a capital ship like the *Vision*. Young-faced hopefuls who'd conquered three years of academy, forged through even more in the Dead Zone, and now had endured days upon days of sleepless nights and constant fighting.

His students . . . his kids . . . for nearly a decade.

Too young . . . too young to face death. But duty called, and they answered without hesitation. Now, they stood side by side, clutching rifles and preparing turrets, using their ingenuity to assemble rudimentary traps and barriers.

Unfortunately, he was too busy trying not to keel over to help them.

Among the officers, only he and the commander in charge of engineering, Tylane, survived. But the Jotex officer now lay unconscious beside him with a cauterized wound across her jelly-like body. The others had already left this universe, killed by either the boarding parties that prowled the vessel or the critical strike that knocked them out of the fight.

Korkoren's throat tightened, catching his voice as breathing grew laborious and difficult. The room, though bathed in the light of the reactor, seemed to grow colder, his body weakening as exhaustion caught up with him.

His heart fell, his emotions crying out at the injustice.

They had fought so hard to get this far.

Korkoren wanted to live.

He was still in his prime, and had graduated from the academy only two decades earlier.

He'd caught the tail end of the last Pirate War without achieving any glory. After that, nothing but boring patrol missions. He wanted a taste of battles of the sort the legends of old went through, wanted to do his part to fight the hated ones, wherever they were.

He wanted to live up to the Legacy that saved his parents and allowed him to live. He owed that much.

But was this how it ended? Was this the price? Why was he here?

At the end of the line, Korkoren . . . was afraid. Deeply, deeply afraid.

Korkoren wanted to live. He wanted to go home to his family.

The officer closed his four eyes, resting his head on the crate he took cover behind, his pistol drooping low. Feeling his coming demise, he let out a defiant snarl, scaring away the fear within as he banged his scorched arm on the crate.

Sharp pain woke him up before his EEP suit administered the last dose of painkillers, snuffing the sensation.

"No . . ." He'd forgotten to turn that off . . . again.

He cursed his suit.

He cursed the traitors, the heretics, the beasts outside who sought his blood.

He cursed the hated ones that had brought this all on them, cursed this unfair universe.

Most of all, he cursed his inability to go out in a bang, in a flash of fire, to kill the beasts coming for their necks. His body was failing him, failing his students.

The commander banged his arm against the crate again, but this time the pain failed to rouse him.

"Silent hells . . ." he muttered, his thoughts growing dim.

Darkness crept from the edge of his vision, and the sound of his breathing enclosed by his helmet grew faint.

It was the end.

For him, for them, for the fleet.

"Hells . . ." Korkoren sighed, whispering, "I'm sorry . . ."

Just then, an ensign nudged his shoulder, keeping his eyes open a bit longer. He looked at the young Frae officer, at the relief in his face.

Yeln. He recalled the boy's name. Annoying personality, too arrogant, too bright.

When did he get so tall? he tsked, grumbling at having this brat be his last image before the end.

"Kind of busy dying, kid—"

"Reinforcements have arrived!" the ensign exclaimed, cutting off his commander's words as he shoved a data tablet into Korkoren's face. It took a couple of seconds for the words to register in his ears, freezing the march of death in place.

The screen showed a fuzzy view of the solar system. A massive armada was appearing through the same hypergate from which they'd entered.

He blinked and blinked again, turning to the ensign with a dazed gaze. Disbelief was plain on Korkoren's face as he glanced back at the tablet. "Who—"

"Commander, listen." The boy interrupted him yet again, pressing a button on the tablet.

The machine momentarily crackled and muffled before clearing through the jam. What . . . no, *who* came forth shocked him to his core.

"Attention, survivors," a female Kurskann officer with rust-red chitin called out.

Her vicious mandibles snapped, commanding attention. Korkoren subconsciously straightened his back with strength he didn't know he had left. Her admiral's armor shone beneath a heavy martial coat, bearing the colors of the greatest clan of the Kurskann Empire, second only to the royal clan.

The commander rubbed his eyes, wondering if these were hallucinations plaguing him so close to death's door.

The Kurskann woman washed away his doubts with her following words.

"I am Admiral Yan Garesh'Kan of the Third Fleet. We are here to help." She spoke imperiously, her form stoic and mighty as she clasped her hands behind her.

Korkoren widened his eyes as he gazed upon a legend of the Cataclysm, the Emperor's Red Claw, the only Kurskann to hold the title of Grand Admiral she before stepped down once adopted by Clan Garesh.

If she was here . . .

"It's the Third Fleet!" Ensign Yeln exclaimed, surprising the others who had gathered to hear the message. "The Third has arrived!"

The commander let out a single chuckle, feeling his heart come alive. Tears welled in his eyes as his blood surged with sheer relief. With a grunt, he heaved himself up as the great admiral continued.

"Hold fast," Admiral Yan relayed. "Aid is on the way. A battleship is teleporting to the battlezone to engage the enemy."

Korkoren tilted his head as Ensign Yeln spoke beside him. "Battleship? The *Zolann'tono* isn't a battleship, right?"

"Has the Third Fleet gotten larger? Where did these colossal ships come from?" another exclaimed, pointing at the several conspicuous asteroid- and moon-sized objects slowly heading their way.

The commander, hanging on to every word of the admiral, didn't care about such things.

"The battleship will be ferrying friendly infantry forces. They will teleport to your location and dispatch all hostiles. As the highest-ranking officer in this system"—she paused, leaning toward the camera—"I order you all to stay alive."

With her final order, the recording looped.

"Sir, look! I tapped into the outer cameras. Something's teleporting right in the middle of the enemy!" Yeln said as his tablet switched to another screen.

Korkoren watched as amid the enemy squadron, a nebula of hyperdimensional gas seeped into reality from a crack in space, a telltale sign of an artificial hypergate. The commander narrowed his eyes, wondering what kind of suicidal daredevils would attempt such volatile means of moving.

At the same time, his heart swelled that the incoming help would go so far for his people.

The enemy squadron opened fire at the prismatic cloud.

But then, the outboard cameras glitched as a brutal crimson and bronze nine-kilometer-long warship barreled through the clouds, imperious and indomitable. Enemy attacks fizzled weakly against its shields.

A moment later, the battleship fired its legion of weapons, blinding the cameras permanently.

The survivors stared in shock and awe at the tablet, disbelief behind their helmets.

"What . . . what was that? That thing was massive!" someone spoke out. "Did the Third Fleet have such a warship?"

"No way, battleships are too precious, and that thing is . . . It's monstrous!"

Korkoren furrowed his brow, wondering about the warship's origins. Before anyone could question further, the tablet beeped, and an unknown voice spoke out in a deep baritone.

"SURVIVORS OF THE *UNITED VISION*. THE ENEMY NAVAL FORCE HAS BEEN ELIMINATED."

Everyone winced at the voice's volume before his words sank in; their eyes widened as they shouted through stunned mouths.

"What?"

The voice continued. "FIVE MARINES WILL BE TELEPORTED TO YOUR POSITION IN TWO MINUTES AND FOUR SECONDS. HOWEVER, I ES-TIMATE YOUR BARRICADE WILL BE BREACHED NINETEEN SECONDS BEFORE HELP ARRIVES."

"W-what do we do?" Yeln stammered, clutching his tablet. "There's too many outside!"

Commander Korkoren groaned, grabbing the tablet out of Yeln's hands.

"Who are you . . . ?" he asked with pained breath. "Are you with the Third Fleet?"

The voice answered immediately.

"I AM MARS. I AM A FRIEND . . . NINETEEN SECONDS. NOT A SECOND MORE."

The communications link closed.

Everyone who heard the unknown voice steeled their hearts and shoulders, gripping their weapons as they glanced at the barricaded blast doors. Beyond, the sounds of shouting and panicked arguments rang out. A moment later, the sound of grinders and heat rays resumed, heating and melting the doors.

Commander Korkoren glanced at the message given by the legendary admiral, which was still playing on a loop, and then returned to the doors.

He reflected on his regrets, and his desires.

With loaned strength fueled deep from within his soul, he stood straight and addressed the room.

"New assignment, brats!" he shouted, biting back the pain and the fear he held for his life and his students. "You heard the Red Claw and this Mars fellow! Stay alive! By the Grand Symphony, if you don't, I'll beat you in the afterlife, do you hear me?"

"Yes, Commander!" the defenders shouted in unison, raising their weapons to the door and taking cover.

Korkoren dragged his injured foot as he walked to the center, aiming his pistol as he continued his speech. "If you do die, you better take one with you. Extra points for every kill!"

The defenders smiled, and a few cracked a chuckle.

"You are the pride of the Reborn Kurskann Empire and the Imperial Naval Academy!"

Korkoren had never considered himself a good speaker; Captain Tenzon constantly critiqued him for that. He missed the grouchy old officer.

"I . . . I'm proud of you all," he spoke through a blood-streaked grin. "Commandant Nullan is proud of you all. Tenzon and the others who sacrificed their lives look down on you from the infinite rivers of music, singing praise and heralding our legend across time and space!"

He raised his pistol, aiming at the door as it glowed redder and redder. "Let's add to our odes! Let's leave behind a Legacy that lasts generations!"

The defenders cheered, baring their teeth, raising their weapons, burning adrenaline washing away the fear.

He counted second after second, sweat trailing down his neck as the doors sagged and bent before finally exploding into light and shrapnel.

Immediately, a barrage of energy and kinetic weapons soared from both sides, filling the room with smoke and heat.

A stray shot slammed into Korkoren's gut, turning his insides into a paste. Like a puppet without strings, he fell back, hitting the crate behind him. One by one, the defenders were struck down, their cover shredded by the sheer firepower thrown their way.

The commander groaned weakly, his body failing after its last hurrah. But before he could decide on anything else, everything shimmered.

The room shook from the sheer vibrations as space tingled around the survivors and raiders, stalling their fight. Through the smoke, multiple *somethings* materialized and then popped into existence.

Then, within a fraction of a second, a loud shearing sound, industrial buzzing, and the thudding of a heavy gun drowned out all noise.

Light flashed, explosions boomed, and something wet and chunky slammed against the walls as bodies hit the ground.

The smell of cooked meat, ozone, sulfur, and bile entered Korkoren's nose, nauseating him awake.

Silence befell the room, and the smoke cleared.

Five bipedal armored warriors stood between the survivors and the now eviscerated and unrecognizable raiders.

Large things, more machine than person, clad in metal, high-entropic ceramic, and crimson paint that hid the gore splattered on their hulking ten-foot frames. In their hands were brutal, angular weapons, the barrels smoking and red with heat.

Korkoren shivered as one of the warriors turned toward him with a faceless helmet and feathered plumes atop. Yet he couldn't manage to thank them, or even to greet them.

"BE NOT AFRAID," the red warrior uttered, addressing the room in a loud and growling synthetic voice. "YOU ARE BEING RESCUED."

A second later, guns dropped to the floor along with their users as, one by one, the survivors fell to their knees, exhaustion finally catching up to them. Slowly, each one began laughing, crying, groaning, expressing their pain, their relief, their frustrations, and sorrows all at once.

Commander Korkoren turned to the side.

Ensign Yeln lay dead, crumpled on the ground, missing half his face. Three others were dead around them, and more were injured. A pang of regret pierced his heart at the young Frae's death. He hoped Yeln saved a seat for him in the Symphony.

The metal giants moved with frightening dexterity and surprising gentleness, administering first aid and preventing more from succumbing to their wounds.

Korkoren sighed, smiling and chuckling as his senses faded one after another and dark ice flooded his body. One of the rescuers turned toward him, scanning his state before staring at him. Korkoren shook his head as the giant moved away, tending to another survivor in critical but saveable condition.

Seeing his students tended to, Commander Korkoren collapsed from his hold on the crate to the cold ground, his irradiated body catching up to him as his fire turned to embers.

He was content.

Satisfied.

His only regret was not seeing the other legends aboard the great fleet that had come to help them in their darkest hour, idols he studied and revered and who had inspired him and countless others to enlist.

Volantesh, the Indomitable Voice.

General Ohnar Kornagon, Fist of the Death March.

Admiral Yan, the Emperor's Red Claw.

And above all . . .

"Tov . . . the . . . Liberator . . ." he whispered, losing his voice with longing in his heart.

Alas, the pull overcame him, and Commander Korkoren closed his eyes for the final time, never having met the heroes who saved his mother and father decades before he was born.

There was no battle. Such a word implied meaningful resistance from the enemy.

Patriarch Tov and the rest of the council observed every moment, gauging the opposition's tactics, or in this case, the lack thereof.

Within minutes of the *Caesar*'s arrival, Mars produced nothing short of a slaughter, as everyone in the Exodus Armada predicted.

Tov watched as the *Caesar*, despite lacking the high-intensity firepower of an Assault-class like the *Alexander* or the precision and range of a Siege-class like the *Bonaparte*, effortlessly overpowered the opposition with a saturation of attacks.

When Starless fodder bobbed and weaved and swarmed the void, sometimes the simplest solution was to fill space with lead, leaving no gap to dodge.

That did not mean that Sentinel-classes like the *Caesar* or the *Zhukov* were inaccurate, trigger-happy war machines.

Under Mars's command, such a weapon struck only where it was supposed to.

However, the biggest reason for such superiority was the difference in weight class.

Despite being the size of a four-kilometer battlecruiser, an armored freighter had zero chance of beating a battleship twice its size. Aided by its pack of frigates, corvettes, and small craft, however, its probability increased by a fraction of a percent.

Fortunately for the survivors and the Exodus Armada, the enemy squadron split off in a disorganized mess. Some bore their fangs, firing back, while others made a quick getaway toward the hypergate—an exercise in futility.

A single glancing shot crippled corvettes and shattered primitive shields. Inferior material and armor melted, parting in the wake of angry red lasers. Several vessels blew apart in a flash of light as a cascade of failures pulled down ships that held themselves together like a house of cards.

Suffice it to say, the raiders' return fire petered into a whimper. Eventually, they went silent at the firepower aimed their way like kicked mongrel dogs cowing before a dire wolf.

"SURRENDER." Mars spoke his only demand in a booming voice, broadcasting it to all enemy comms.

The myriad aliens who crewed the ships closest to the ravenous beast immediately powered down, showing their bellies in submission as a primal spike of fear loomed over them.

Per Andora's orders, Mars merely clipped their wings, utilizing his legion of secondary and tertiary guns to disable drives and thrusters.

Mars took things slow and smooth, but for an organic mind, they only saw a single battleship crippling dozens of ships in the snap of a finger.

One capital ship dared to defy a war god's mercy, whom Mars smote posthaste.

The armored freighter's shields sundered under a single salvo of the battleship's guns. The beams of death streaked past, slamming against its stern and drilling deep. The roaring, wailing alarms within the vessel screamed out as the metal bulkhead groaned and lights flickered and shattered.

With the enemy defanged and dismembered, Mars sent three hundred Assault Marine Drones through teleporters or ferried on larger drone small craft toward various locations, split into squads of five to eight.

Critical locations included the holdouts of survivors battling against boarding parties, as well as the bridges, armories, and engineering bays of the surrendered enemy warships.

With a thought, Mars dropped the ten-foot tall drones in the middle of fights, unimpeded by and uncaring of the paltry small-arms fire directed their way. In retaliation, the Marine Drones fired their heavy rifles, shattering personal shields and blowing apart bodies.

Beforehand, Mars had ensured each of his machines carried a complete first aid kit and an emergency vial of nanomachines for critical cases.

Simultaneously, drones purpose-built for search and rescue flew in haste toward drifting life pods, utilizing grinders and blowtorches to pry open hatches or, if needed, tow them toward the *Caesar*.

And for the enemy, those who were uninjured or could be stabilized through first aid were bound, awaiting pickup from the main bulk of the armada.

In particular, the captain of the armored freighter surrendered immediately when Mars's Marine Drones teleported directly to the bridge, firing paralyzing shock darts at everyone they saw.

"TARGET SECURED," the drone reported, one metal fist holding the hem of the captain's suit, the other balled up in a bloody fist that had met the equally bloody nose of the poor alien.

Ultimately, the sheer disparity between the ramshackle fleets and the supreme might of an AI-designed battleship bathed in Starless blood awed and horrified everyone who witnessed the carnage.

The survivors wept and cheered, embracing the Marine Drones despite being oblivious to their true nature under such faceless, smooth helmets.

Both in space and within the crippled vessels, Mars's single battleship dominated and conquered, giving praise to the name *Caesar*.

Tov shook his head at the overwhelming power in just a few minutes. "We should do well not to become arrogant after this display."

"Agreed. Still, that was a pathetic resistance," Andora sneered. "Fitting."

The patriarch turned to the knight in shining red armor, watching as Mars opened his eyes. The Overseer sighed, turning toward Andora with an unreadable gaze but eased shoulders at having saved hundreds of survivors.

"It is done," he answered, massaging his nape.

Andora nodded, preparing the rest of her assets for rescue and recovery operations. "Ensure that the survivors or any key personnel among the enemy remain hale and ready for pickup."

The fastest scouts of Battlegroup Mictlan surged forward in a plume of ion fire, carrying specialized medical drones and enough space to transport people back to the armada. Meanwhile, Admiral Yan coordinated with the survivors, speaking to the highest-ranking officer and organizing them.

Two hours later, the armada welcomed four hundred and thirty-six friendly survivors.

Since then, no additional casualties had occurred among the Expeditionary Fleeters as they moved those in critical condition to intensive care facilities.

However, another issue arose upon seeing three thousand plus who surrendered.

"Do we have the space to house them?" Andora grimaced at the thousands of prisoners who had fallen into their laps.

Tov hummed, tapping his clawed finger on the table. "We can spread them among our ships. However, all high-ranking individuals will be housed in the *Zolann* or the *Citadel*. Most will be put into stasis until we decide what to do."

Andora scoffed. "If their lives are forfeit, as you said, then why bother taking them in? Just leave the scum traitor meat bags behind in this barren system and be done with it. We have greater concerns."

Tov's mind darkened at the thought of another distasteful situation. Ever since the thought that those people were involved entered his mind, a barrage of memories and nightmares had begun to emerge from the forgotten box deep in his head.

Seeing the black heptagram on the freighter confirmed it.

Cowards, sympathizers, heretics, traitors.

Starless-worshipping cultists.

In his people's tongue, they are referred to as the *Aghapin*. A taboo conglomeration of all those vile descriptors. In Commonspiel, they are called the Thralled. A horrendous curse in and of itself.

He shook his head, refocusing on handling the current influx of prisoners and likely magnitudes more when they defeated the enemy's main fleet. In truth, Andora's words resonated with a part of him he had long left behind.

Noting his silence, Andora settled herself as she spoke softly. "I'm sorry. This has all agitated and frustrated me, but I assure you I'm asking out of rational concern. It's just—"

"No, you're right," Tov interrupted her.

Andora raised her brow, narrowing her eyes in surprise.

"We've taken the survivors aboard. Our mission is done here, and we can't decelerate it now. We have to burn toward the hypergate and cross over. If I'm guessing correctly, we shall find a fiercer battle in the next star," Tov explained, pulling up the next solar system.

It was a known location named Zill's Redoubt, which used to be a small mining outpost and trading center in the local area before the Cataclysm rolled over it.

"Slowing down to gather all the prisoners here is foolish. I recommend leaving Mars's Marine Drones to guard the prisoners and keep their ships crippled but habitable; you can leave it to Battlegroup Mag Mell to clean up after us."

Andora hummed, rubbing her chin before nodding. "Very well, that's doable. But what of after? What's your plan with them?"

"Once we've reunited with the Allied Fleets, we will follow due process," Tov replied in a low tone, his hackles raised. "If any among them have been forced into committing these acts, they will be sent to cryostasis for further investigation."

"And the rest?" Andora pushed with a raised brow.

"The rest will be put to death," Tov declared ruthlessly, looking around the council table and seeing no disagreement from his side, though catching questioning and concerned glances from the Overseers. He shook his head. "This enemy does not look kindly toward mercy. We learned that the hard way in the Cataclysm."

Andora leaned back. Traces of a bloodthirsty smile tugged the edges of her mouth before the AI woman forced it down. She cleared her throat, nodding, satisfied.

"Do we have time to interrogate them?" Mars asked as he looked toward something unseen. "I'm speaking with the captain of the enemy freighter right now, but . . . the guy seems . . . out of it."

"*Aghapin*," Tov grumbled, guessing at the person's identity. He turned to Mars and inquired, "Is there anyone your drones can speak to who isn't a lunatic?"

"Hold . . ." Mars raised his hand.

The gathered council waited for a breath before the Overseer sharpened his eyes, nodding. "One of the frigate captains is spilling. She claims she and most of those here are simple . . . scavengers forced to work under these . . . Thralled who killed the original captain of the freighter, who was their leader until he protested."

"Validity of this information?" Yan asked.

Mars paused briefly before responding. "I asked thirty others. I calculate a ninety-one percent chance that the information is true, though they hide some other facts and are not as chummy with one another as some among them say."

The Overseer shook his head and continued. "More importantly, I'm hearing that the enemy force has thirty capital ships . . . with a battlecarrier called the *Mermere Diridion* as the flagship."

The council leaned forward at the revelation like starving hounds hungry for intel.

"Two hundred cruisers . . ." Mars reported, furrowing his brow as he sorted the gossip, rumors, and deceit from reasonably authentic details. "Most are light raiding cruisers—and there are over a thousand warships, mainly consisting of frigates, corvettes, and missile boats. A third are destroyers, however. Most cruisers and capital ships are at least last-generation Legacy tech. The *Mermere* looked to be modern," Mars finished.

Tov grimaced, filing away that information along with his questions about how such a vessel fell into the cultists' hands so deep in the Dead Zone.

"What of the Allied Fleets?" Tov asked.

"Tired but still defiantly resisting." Mars smiled. "Well-coordinated. The enemy had hundreds more ships at their peak."

"They underestimated Nullan," Yan added. "The survivors confirmed that all fleet leaders are alive, but the situation is grim without support."

She turned to Mars. "What else? Do we have a name for our enemy?"

Mars shook his head, then tilted it in doubt. "It's . . . made up of multiple factions under the umbrella of a pirate fleet calling themselves the Oblivion Fangs. Captain Varin is the enemy commander. Cunning, ruthless, and pragmatic.

"Most are saying Varin is being coerced, just like the ones here. They're saying this endeavor is being orchestrated by some larger organization, probably a cult like the crazies that replaced the original captain and bridge crew of the armored freighter."

Tov and his side cursed under their breath, sensing a wrongness in the air.

Suddenly, Mars frowned and then grimaced.

"What is it?" Andora asked with narrow eyes.

"Hold on, one of the prisoners is voicing his suspicions . . ." Mars reported, squaring his jaw. "He says things have been too routine . . . He wonders if fighting an endless battle of attrition was exactly what the Thralled had planned. Too safe, too boring, and that everything's been going so well . . ."

Mars widened his eyes. "He thinks . . . he thinks they're herding the Allied Fleets!"

Shock washed over the council. Tov stood abruptly as he looked back at the following solar system map, Zilla's Redoubt, in context with the prisoner's suspicions.

Suddenly, the fields of asteroids, the plethora of moons, and the clouds of gas looked like a pit of vipers coiling to strike. He imagined . . .

"There's no time!" Tov slammed his fist on the table. "They're walking right into an ambush!"

With his words, the armada left the *Caesar* and the three hundred Marine Drones behind to guard the remaining prisoners. Another hour later, the Exodus Armada rammed into the hypergate with overclocked reactors and burning thrusters.

As they tunneled over the next few hours, the War Room buzzed with battle plans amid a hectic and grim air, the council members all hoping they weren't too late.

CHAPTER 17

AMBUSH AT ZILLA'S REDOUBT

**[ATTENTION! EXITING HYPER-TUNNEL IN ONE MINUTE!
PREPARE FOR IMMEDIATE COMBAT!]**

Tov gritted his mandibles as he sat on his command throne, feeling an iota of the turbulent cosmic winds phasing through the hull and his body.

Since the Dead Zone plummeted them into a total block-out of communications, various glitches and errors popped up now and then. Over the days since the journey began, the storm had only worsened as hyper-tunneling turned into a gut-wrenching experience.

Only the constant watch and problem-solving of their best engineers and the Overseers prevented deadly mishaps.

Sighing, Tov looked around the bridge.

He, Andora, Admiral Yan, Captain Pyo, Brother Volantesh, Jupiter, and Venus had transferred back to the *Zolann* before leaving the previous star system. The Lead Harmonizer, Jupiter, and Venus headed straight for the Temple, while the rest of the council remained in *Citadel Irkalla*'s War Room.

Yan stood in the center of the bridge, coordinating with Captain Kraw to discuss matters of the fleet.

Tov turned to his side toward Andora, who sat with her legs crossed and nursed a tall glass of blue wine. Though she appeared quiet and indifferent, Tov felt the simmering anger beneath her eyes and noticed the tight hold on her glass.

"Battlegroup Mictlan will be entering first. Can the *Xolotl* establish a beachhead?" he asked.

Andora waved her hand in dismissal. "*Xolotl*'s AI may be as cold as space, but its logic, decision-making skills, and processing capabilities are far superior to those of the average organic commander. Of course, someone with years of experience, prodigal talent, and the right cranial implants could outwit it a hundred times over."

"That's both reassuring and not," Tov chittered. "In the sense that should you turn hostile, the Legacy won't have a shortage of capable commanders to prevail over your cold AIs. But at the same time, let's hope the enemy doesn't have such a tactician."

Andora smirked as she glanced his way. "Oh? Thinking of contingencies, are we? Afraid I might decide to exterminate you all after I'm done with the Starless?"

"I'm sure my emperor has." Tov shrugged. "That mind of his . . . Even I can't guess what he thinks every waking moment." He shook his head. "And no, I don't think you'd do anything like become another Cataclysm."

"Not even against the Dagaterens?" Andora asked. "I'm sure Emperor Jarinn wouldn't mind if I sowed chaos against his rivals. Depose that unrex of theirs for someone more . . . sympathetic to my kind."

Tov shivered at the thought, sighed wearily, and rubbed his temples. "I cannot believe the two of you will meet in the future. I certainly believe the emperor would relish such a plot."

"Ambitious and ruthless." Andora chuckled with a glint in her eye. "Dangerous, but I don't plan on being his puppet. He should be afraid of the opposite happening. Worry not; I won't poke a galactic superpower."

The delight in her smile vanished, turning cold and predatory. "But if the Dagatarens shoot first, then . . ."

"Woe be to the Supremacy should that ever happen." Tov shook his head again. "Just don't pull me into any of your schemes."

Andora giggled mischievously, saying nothing. The whiplash of her moods sometimes disoriented Tov, exasperating his worry about the future.

He eased his tense shoulders as he focused on the impending battle. He worried about the enemy commander's competence. Spending weeks herding seven fleets toward a preplanned position implied a degree of cunning and patience.

Tov checked the old map of Zilla's Redoubt. The system had a K-type supergiant as its star, which was much larger and brighter than Sol but cooler by about two thousand degrees Kelvin.

The star bathed the great swathes of asteroid belts, a single gas giant, dwarf planets, and moons in an intense red light. Ruins filled the multitudes of rock and stone, as the previous owners had quickly abandoned the old mining outposts and infrastructure dedicated to trade and commerce.

There were two planets and one gas giant—Zilla-I, II, and III, respectively. They were entering just beyond Zilla-III.

Most importantly, the star system was within the confines of a great nebula, smothering large swathes of space in comms-interfering gas and crackling lightning.

Only the promise of high-grade ore and even a few dozen kilograms of premiums had attracted people to this place long ago.

In this abandoned place, Tov saw only plenty of space to hide battle stations, automated turrets, minefields, and a massive enemy fleet.

He hoped it wasn't true, hoped to find nothing but barren lands and a simple foe. Sadly, hopes rarely came true. As such, they planned for the absolute worst.

[ATTENTION! ENTERING ZILLA'S REDOUBT IN TEN SECONDS! PREPARE!]

The enemy didn't count one thing, however.

[FIVE . . .]

They underestimated the loyalty each fleet had to another.

[FOUR . . .]

And they would soon learn the consequences of rousing Andora's temper.

[THREE . . . TWO . . . EXITING HYPER-TUNNEL.]

Reality shunted as the armada breached through the colorful nebula and back into the darkness of the void.

Tov took a deep breath as he gripped the arms of his command chair, fighting back the nausea that momentarily twisted his insides.

In a split second, the myriad monitors on the bridge came alive with data and visuals. The officers on deck rushed to parse through it all, and Andora closed her eyes to see the situation.

Suddenly, a blaring alarm resounded across the bridge.

[WARNING. HOSTILE ELEMENTS DETECTED. LARGE-SCALE NAVAL BATTLE DETECTED. INCOMING HAZARDOUS DEBRIS.]

The entire bridge paused as a titanic slab of irradiated molten metal passed by, briefly catching on the edge of the *Zolann*'s shields before drifting on. The system's map came alive as the sensors synchronized and absorbed the rush of information.

Ahead of them, the armada found nothing short of utter chaos and war.

Two main concentrations of battle appeared on the map. A larger one raged near the gas giant, where the colors of four Expeditionary Fleets battled against the main enemy force. A smaller battle took place much farther away, where two other friendly fleets were being hounded by hostiles in the middle of an asteroid field.

Smaller pockets of battles and skirmishes raged everywhere as lightning-filled clouds of blue, red, and purple gas swirled around the system.

Under the light of Zilla, thousands of ships duked it out with each other, illuminating the void in a barrage of tracer rounds, laser beams, and plasma fire. Rockets soared, torpedoes left their launch tubes, and interceptor missiles homed in on them.

Shields sparked, metal hulls sheared like wood shavings. Thrusters burned as ships weaved and turned, dodging and evading what they could.

Starfighters blazed out of hangars, dogfighting against the enemy while battlesuits clung to hulls. They fired heavy autocannons and machine guns, acting as ad hoc point defense.

Cloaked mines drifted unseen under massive electronic interference that fizzed out sensors and blinded both sides. A nuclear bomb floated along before coming alive and shooting toward an unprepared warship, slamming against its stern and crippling it.

Moments later, a barrage of tungsten rods bore through the vessel's hull, igniting the spacecraft from within into an obliterating flash.

Scorched debris and cold wrecks filled pockets of the star system as casualties on both sides mounted second after second, adding to the ruins that once called this abandoned space home.

In the silence of the cosmos, Tov looked upon the canvas of a dire battle under an audience of indifferent twinkling stars and the infernal orange gaze of the Zilla Redoubt's singular star. Uncaring of the noise and chaos, they found no purchase in the vacuum.

The silence didn't last long as the computers began to simulate the battle sounds in a manageable volume for awareness.

"Report on the armada," Yan spoke immediately before the bridge officers responded one after another.

"*Xolotl* reporting," the cold superheavy battlecarrier answered through comms. The capital ship and its pride quickly fanned out, guns pointed outward at the hellish scene ahead.

"Mars Fleet is at the ready," Mars reported. "Moving into forward position."

With the *Bucephalus* taking the center and the *Boogie Mouse* acting as its dazzling bodyguard, the Five Greats and the rest of the Overseer's top-heavy fleet floated behind and above the vanguard battlegroup.

"Third Fleet all accounted for," Admiral Yan declared as she looked at the monitors, seeing the *Nu Rovshk* and the rest form up around the *Zolann*. "The

Citadel, Galla Fleet, and Luna Fleet are still transitioning. How's the battle-field, people?"

The officers quickly reported from their terminals and smooth visors.

"Thick ECM and jamming across the entire system."

"The fighting paired with the hazardous environment is causing massive inter-ference with our sensors. Two minutes max to pierce the veil."

"Comms is congested with noise traffic; we're filtering out the garbled mess now."

Admiral Yan clicked her mandibles as a dozen screens popped up before her. "Prior-itize locating the *Gladiator* or any of the fleet flagships. What are the enemy's numbers?"

"Hostiles outnumber the Allied Fleets five-to-one. Detecting static defenses. Detecting over thirty capital vessels by Zilla-III including two battleships along with the flagship battlecarrier. Another dozen capitals chasing the fleeing fleets. No supercapitals."

Yan turned to Andora. "Status on the vanguard?"

"Battlegroup Mictlan encountered a paltry defense as soon as they entered. The enemy didn't expect us." Andora sneered in contempt before chuckling. "Mars reports the fight was over before he arrived."

Tov's antennae twitched as he looked at the visuals.

Andora hummed, rubbing her chin as she continued. "As we suspected, the enemy had static defenses by the hypergate. Most of it had been destroyed before-hand, likely by our allies as they blitzed through the initial ambush."

"There's not much resistance here anymore. Whatever awaited the Expedition-ary Fleets left and gave chase," Tov said as he turned toward her. "Nullan wouldn't allow the fleets to be caught right by the hypergate. But it seems they're unable to escape the enemy's grasp."

Ahead of them, the patriarch watched as the *Xolotl* and the other carriers of Mictlan spewed out legions of drone small craft. They soared through space like angry bees. The rest of the battlegroup formed one of the preplanned formations as they prowled the obliterated metal carcasses of the initial ambushers left behind to guard the hypergate.

Tov briefly viewed the recording captured by the *Xolotl* the moment it entered Zilla, and as expected, the surprised foe that remained by the entrance barely lasted several seconds.

A moment later, the hyperdimensional clouds shivered again, shooting out rays of light as more hulking masses returned to reality.

Two nine-kilometer behemoths rippled the void with their entry, their black and gold hulls shining brilliantly under the light of Zilla.

"*Gugalanna* reporting."

"*Nergal* reporting."

Both battleships entered in unison with guttural, unfeeling voices, heralding the arrival of the Galla Fleet through comms. And in the middle of the ferocious pack of metal Leviathans . . .

"*Citadel Irkalla* has entered the battlezone," Irkalla reported as she landed on Andora's shoulder. "The *Ereshkigal* and the *Will of Sisyphus* are in position. All Galla Fleet assets present."

Andora's hand moved to pet her Seneschal as her dreadnought leveled its horrifying main guns toward concentrations of enemy forces, daring them to move.

As for Jupiter's dreadnought, with the blue Overseer unable to tame the beast, Andora had taken it upon herself with the man's permission to . . . *borrow* . . . the lumbering rock.

And before long, the rear guard arrived.

"*Ozymandias* and the Luna Fleet all accounted for," Luna calmly reported through comms as her silver warships followed her mobile fortress.

With her arrival, space shuddered, snapped back into a solid, stable state, and the colorful clouds dissipated.

They were now locked in this space until their hyper-tunnelers recharged.

"Formation Nine!" Admiral Yan ordered the Third Fleet while Andora and her Overseers positioned themselves.

In total, the Exodus Armada, minus the missing Battlegroup Mag Mell, consisted of *Citadel Irkalla*, the *Zolann*, two mobile fortresses, three dreadnoughts, twenty capital ships, and nearly two hundred subcapitals, all of which far surpassed anything present by orders of magnitude.

The sheer weight of their presence and the obvious and vast amounts of energy they passively emitted momentarily disoriented sensors and befuddled computational matrixes.

For a moment, those too focused on the battle before them thought several miniature suns had breached into their war.

To say their entrance went unnoticed was a grievous and insulting lie.

The battle in Zilla's Redoubt abruptly stalled, guns petering out as they hesitantly aimed their way.

Within bridges and cockpits, the shocked races reacted in many ways as eyes froze with fear, legs shook, and tentacles quivered.

Some of the more rational officers whipped their subordinates back to shape to resume the fight, but a primal part of their brains stunned them from firing their weapons. A fraction among them, those strong of will, took the opportunity to rescue downed allies and perform critical repairs.

Unconsciously, despite some being hundreds of millions of kilometers away, people stepped back, their instincts screaming out as the more discerning among them felt baleful twin blue stars glaring at them—as if their insignificant lives were a slight that existed without this monstrous armada's consent.

"Starless night! Where did these guys come from?"

"What's with these ships? One's the size of a moon! And this one's no different than an asteroid with guns! A-are they ours? Please tell me they're ours!"

"No . . . Sweet Symphony, is it hopeless after all?"

Both sides grew confused, harrying their respective sensor officers to identify the newcomers before morale plummeted. But as soon as they did, one side shriveled in shock and terror, and the other surged with joy and fervor, intensifying their defiant resistance.

"THE THIRD FLEET?"

In the pristine and modern bridge of the battlecarrier *Mermere Diridion*, a scaled and scarred Ruzian captain snarled.

"What!?" Varin, the commander of the enemy force, shouted as he turned to the cloaked figure behind him. "You lying cultist! You said they'd arrive long after we culled these Legacy cowards!"

The cloaked alien tilted their hooded head, face hidden in darkness, before shrugging.

"You are bound by our contract, little warlord. You knew the possibility existed," a raspy, whispering voice replied with cold indifference.

"The possibility said nothing about these numbers and weight classes!" Varin protested. He was clad in a thick and heavy space suit painted with battle markings. Jewelry made of teeth and bone clanked together beside golden medals. "What did your maniac of a leader get us into!?"

"Are you thinking of fleeing, Varin? I will forgive your insult to our proselyte but remember what is at stake." The cultist sneered, seeing the captain slide his hand over his sidearm. "After all, you were so desperate for our services."

Varin growled with rage and a trace of fear before dropping his hand. "Apologies, High Seer. But I ask that you ensure your warships rejoin us after they're done hunting the strays."

Still, he muttered a curse under his breath as he turned away from the cloaked figure. "*Dakha* filth."

The captain faced his bridge crew, and the monitors showed the frightened faces of his subordinate captains and the allied forces that agreed to assist him in this insane task. His face twisted as he hissed, revealing his gold fangs. "What in the starless hells are you waiting for? Do your jobs before that armada gets into firing range!"

As the Ruzian pirate captain became distracted and focused on surviving this battle, the so-called High Seer quietly stepped out under a cloak of shadow that erased memories of a witness's last ten seconds. Then he quickly took off toward the hangar bay without anyone the wiser, smiling wickedly at the chaos.

Back on the bridge of the *Zolann*, a melodic chime echoed throughout the room.

"Enemy forces have resumed firing on the Allied Fleets," an officer reported.

Tov clicked his mandibles, tapping his foot in impatience and worry. He looked at the monitors. If they accelerated to flanking speed, it would take a few minutes to reach extreme firing range.

Thankfully, everything was relatively close, with the fighting well within the inner zone of the star system and around the gas giant designated Zilla-III, minus the splintered fleet fleeing the battlezone.

"Are they making aggressive motions against us?" he asked his second-in-command.

Yan shook her head. "Even an idiot would know not to rush in and attack us while they're contending with seven fleets' worth of warships. Thankfully, despite their considerable numbers, most of them are of similar quality to the ones we squashed previously." Yan pointed toward the monitors. "However, they're pushing the battlezone behind the gas giant to block our line of sight. Smart."

Tov looked at the system's map.

Zilla was in the center, about as far from Zilla-III as Sol was from Mars, approximately two hundred forty million kilometers. They arrived at the hypergate beyond the gas giant, about fifty million kilometers away. The main battle was slowly inching itself sunward behind the gas giant.

"Patriarch! We've connected with the *Gladiator*!" a comms officer happily reported.

Tov stood, taking center stage. "Put them on the screen."

Immediately, the monitor flickered and revealed a golem of ancient rock, his eyes stony, almost annoyed, as he'd been caught under rain rather than in the middle of a desperate bid for survival.

"Command—"

"That you, Tov?" Commandant Nullan interrupted, his voice like a rumbling earthquake. "You little *karnn'duor fenk*. You're late."

Tov suppressed the instinct to straighten his back and salute like the fresh recruit he'd been a century ago. He wouldn't give the old soldier the satisfaction. He ignored the insults about his face and . . . prowess in certain private matters.

"About time you caught up," Nullan huffed, grumbling with a noise like grinding pebbles and crossing his bulky stone arms that threatened to burst from his EEP suit. In the background, the lights of the *Gladiator*'s bridge briefly flickered. The commandant barely glanced at it. "We're a bit busy trying not to die, as you can see."

Tov cleared. "What's your status?"

The Bolud veteran lost his nonchalance, a hint of weariness and battle fatigue creeping up from his deep-set eyes. He spoke quickly and clearly.

"Guildmaster Oros is dead, Tov . . ." Nullan shook his head as he clenched his fists. "His flagship got blown out of space, and the Riders of Calamity are gone. They tried to hold back the rear while we broke through the ambush."

Tov's heart fell at the news, but he filed away the sorrow for later. The patriarch listened intently as Nullan continued.

"We didn't make it far. They had plenty of reserves and firing nests in this wretched place. They separated us. We soon learned that the scum blockaded every way out of the system with mines and hidden battle stations.

"We tried to regroup to assault one of the exits, and I managed to gather the Twenty-First, the Thirty-First, and the Thirty-Fifth, but we lost contact with Scion Straise and Foreman Lemunn before they sailed too far for us to reach them. By then, the bastards had us pinned."

Commandant Nullan gnashed his square teeth as a hint of his old, coarse, cantankerous nature leaked out. "Now, we're stuck with this fat ball of gas at our backs and the entire Dead Zone in front."

Tov nodded as Admiral Yan issued orders based on Nullan's words and the rush of data sent by the Expeditionary Fleets.

"We're on our way to reinforce your position, Commandant. We're also dispatching a force toward the Seventeenth and Fiftieth," Tov replied, eyeing Andora, who nodded quietly but looked doubtful when she saw how far they were from their position. "However, the enemy is forcing you behind Zilla-III."

Nullan snorted. "We've noticed. Since you've brought some rather big guns, we can keep them from cowering behind the gas giant. Don't worry about us; capitalize on our counterattack as soon as possible."

"Our guns are warmed up," Tov answered with an eager chitter. "We'll soon be in extreme firing range."

"You won't be able to hit much from that far, Tov," said Nullan.

Tov chuckled. "You'll be surprised. Focus on staying alive, Commander. You'll find the opportunity to hit back soon."

"Hmph. It's *commandant* now, boy," Nullan grumbled. "Now, if you'll excuse me, I have a battle to fight."

Without another word, the image faded, though communications remained stable and connected as the armada and the Allied Fleets began coordinating.

Andora closed her eyes before opening them again. "Luna is on task to save the splintered fleets."

"How should we conduct this?" Tov asked.

"Mars and Mictlan will clear us a path. *Boogie Mouse* will be held back in reserve. And the Third Fleet, along with my *Ereshkigal*, will deliver the killing blow to these rats," Andora replied. "There's no need to bloody *Irkalla* or the Galla Fleet now."

Tov titled his head. "Yet you're sending your dreadnought? Why not Mars's, then? Or the *Sisyphus*?"

Andora turned to look at him as a vicious grin formed on her face, fueled by the frustrations and grievances she had pushed down for so long. "I'm tired of giving chase. I want complete domination through my own hands."

Tov shrugged. "By all means. As long as we finish this as quickly as possible."

"Oh, I am not so cruel, Patriarch." Andora laughed sadistically as hunger shone through her eyes. "I'm taking manual control of the *Ereshkigal*. The Third Fleet will focus on keeping our allies alive. It's time these Dead Zone wretches pay their tithe to the goddess of the underworld."

Andora closed her eyes as the armada split off. As ordered, Luna surged her fleet toward the two wayward fleets, spearheaded by the *Gilgamesh* and the *Xerxes*, while her mobile fortress hung back beside the *Citadel*.

Battlegroup Mictlan blazed toward Zilla-III, launching extreme-distance torpedoes and missiles.

The Five Greats of the Mars Fleet led the charge, seeking to overtake the forward battlegroup.

All the while, the Third Fleet formed up with the *Zolann* and the lone dreadnought in the center.

Tov took a deep breath, broadcasting his voice across all the comms channels.

"Sailors and warriors of the Exodus Armada, hear me! Those are your comrades, your people, your allies, fighting for their lives!" he shouted, pointing forward at the dire battle.

Finally, the time for words and planning was over.

All that was left was execution.

"You know what to do!" Tov's voice rang out as the patriarch raised his fist, calling for blood. "It's time to let loose!"

Throughout the armada, the crew roared.

"ONWARD!"

They sailed forth with the winds of war blowing behind them, charging like a rolling stampede of shining cavalry.

Ahead, Mars and Mictlan worked together to swat any resistance. Tertiary guns picked off cloaked mines whose technology was far too inferior to fool their sensors, while autoturrets and battle stations shattered under a single volley.

Any enemy vessel caught under the crosshairs of the menacing vanguards immediately surrendered or attempted to flee.

As for the latter, a single shot dissuaded them from going any farther.

Over at Zilla-III, the four Expeditionary Fleets led by the *Gladiator* and three other flagships, the *Solsolen's Scepter*, the *Horn of Perdition*, and the *Death Marked*, poured intermittent fire as they used their bulk to shield the non-combat vessels from the hailstorm sent their way. Four other capital ships, battlecruisers, struck without mercy.

Over forty cruisers plugged the gaps while nearly five hundred destroyers, frigates, corvettes, and countless small craft returned fire over them like a legion of archers shielded by thick stone walls.

The enemy's main force pushed hard, surrounding the four fleets in a domed formation, seeking to cripple more and more as their assault intensified, sacrificing and forcing ramshackle warships to take the heat as others moved in like thirsty beasts smelling blood.

There were over thirty enemy capital ships in that area alone. Another dozen left to bite the ankles of the two fleets that were separated.

Outnumbered five-to-one but only marginally outgunned through sheer quantity of weapons, the Allied Fleets doggedly resisted. Morale soared with the news that help had arrived so close to their position.

Urged on by the legendary commandant and the incoming heroes of old, the sailors, officers, pilots, marines, and soldiers beat their chests, ready to pounce when the signal was given.

Back on the *Zolann'tono*, Tov tapped his finger on his command chair's arm as the sound grew muted around him. His senses were solely focused on the incoming battle.

Second by second, minute by minute, they accelerated, overclocking their reactors and thrusters. But as they closed in on the line where they could engage, another chime rang out across the bridge.

An officer turned her head to look at him with a hint of hesitation. "My lord, the enemy commander is trying to contact us . . ."

Silence filled the room as Tov hummed. He nodded. "Put it on the screen."

The monitor ahead flickered, showing a scarred Ruzian in his prime, ugly in a prehistoric reptilian way and clad in a uniform that screamed warlord. The enemy commander snarled, glaring at Tov.

"I'm Varin, Captain of the *Mermere Diridion*, Master of the Oblivion Fangs, and Warlord of the Uraki Sector—"

"Who the fuck asked?" Andora glared. The Ruzian captain balked at the woman's look of sheer disgust.

Tov, similarly unamused, demanded, "We know who you are. Surrender immediately, Captain. Power down your ships and weapons or be destroyed."

"Back off, bug! I know who you are as well. You're quite the hero, huh? Well, I don't care how big your toys are. We have you outnumbered," Varin calmly retorted. "You aren't our target. Let us finish what we came for, and we can all live in peace, yes? We only want the fleet leaders. If you surrender your leaders, I'll spare the civilians."

Andora laughed derisively, never breaking eye contact with the warlord.

"And you are?" he snarled at her.

"O-outnumbered, he says," Andora choked out through her laughter, wiping away a fake tear.

Tov shook his head. "Are you seriously asking us to let you kill our allies?"

Varin gritted his teeth before releasing a weary sigh, looking back to Tov as he scratched his scaled chin. "Yeah, I didn't think that would work, but my hands are tied in this matter."

"You will not surrender, then?" Tov asked again.

The warlord peered into his eyes before hardening his expression. "I'll have to refuse at this time."

Tov clicked his mandibles, his antennae twisting and aiming like raised blades. "You have no hopes of winning."

Varin clicked his fangs. "I have no choice," he hissed.

"Whatever it is that's chaining you, we can—"

"Buzz off, gene slave," Varin spat venomously. "You cowards are no better than the lunatics. I'm not running, and know I have no intention to die here either."

He gazed at them with pity before washing it away with contempt. "You should have never left your precious Legacy. You have only yourselves to blame."

The comms abruptly disconnected as a wave of viruses flooded their systems. Terabytes seeking to infect and consume failed to find vulnerabilities, however. The presence of the AIs and the recent upgrades instantly smashed the digital invaders apart.

"Vanguard entering extreme firing range in ten seconds!" a weapons officer reported. Tov glanced at the map, seeing the icons of the Mars Fleet and Battlegroup Mictlan cross the boundary and immediately open fire as the enemy launched missiles and torpedoes and dispatched a swarm of small craft, both manned and automated.

Swathes of the suicidal flies and ordnance blew apart before they turned their tails back to their dens. Thousands of enemy pilots died in the span of a few seconds.

With the path cleared, the Mars Fleet and Battlegroup Mictlan took to the flanks, circling in wide arcs as the Third Fleet and the *Ereshkigal* took the center.

"Commandant Nullan has begun a counterattack!" another officer reported,

At Zilla-III, the Allied Fleets formed a spearpoint with the flagship at the tip before accelerating forward, charging like a singular, inexorable lance toward the enemy center. Behind them, the rest of the beleaguered warships fanned out like a blooming flower.

All at once, the Allied Fleets launched their complements of missiles and torpedoes, emptying their magazines and energy cells toward the weakest clumps of hostiles.

The highly aggressive assault forced the Varin's forces back, reeling as if punched in the nose. However, without a proper follow-up, the enemy would bounce back and devour them.

"Andora?" Tov asked the woman beside him.

She hummed, downing her wine before placing it on a tray.

With closed eyes, Andora snapped her fingers.

Having entered optimal firing range, the *Ereshkigal* fired a full broadside of her Ganzir Guns. Twelve infernal blasts of searing plasma zipped across space with unerring precision in quick succession, each aimed at a different capital ship.

Seeing the angry balls of fire coming at high-end relativistic speeds, the capital ships marked for death tried to dodge out of the way. However, the much faster laser beams fired by the Third Fleet and the harassment of the Allied counterattack forced them into place.

In a last-ditch effort, the twelve capital ships and battlecruisers shut down all non-essential systems and diverted all power to their shields. The rest of the enemy forces diverted their weapons to fire upon the balls of plasma to no avail, the projectiles either missing or failing to achieve anything beyond sizzling into nothing before the Ganzir's rage.

Twelve meteors ripped through space.

Twelve slammed against the shields of the enemy.

Twelve annihilated their targets, shattering them apart.

With one salvo, the terrible dreadnought designed to fight against the worst Leviathans massacred twelve ships and their crew, atomizing them as reactors overloaded and exploded in a flash of brilliant light.

Complete obliteration.

"Shit . . ." Andora muttered with pursed lips. "I guess three-quarter power was too much."

Tov shook his head. "We need them alive if we want to take prisoners."

"I targeted the ugliest and oldest ships and assumed they weren't important." Andora scratched her cheek. "I've analyzed their measure. I'll adjust my guns to shatter their shields and armor without outright destroying them next time."

The enemy forces stuttered in shock at the sheer overkill they had just witnessed. Even the Allied Fleets' counterattack slowed in awe before quickly resuming under the commandant's scolding.

"It appears you have time to sightsee. Maybe we should sit back and relax, but I think it'd be better if you all get back to *SHOOTING THE ENEMY!*" Nullan roared the fleet back into action.

Slapped in the face by the renewed assault, Varin urged his forces. "FIGHT! FIGHT IF YOU WANT TO LIVE, YOU SONS AND DAUGHTERS OF THE DARK LANDS!" he shouted.

Inwardly, Varin sensed the winds turning against their favor and began to plan his escape. He glanced at the exit and then realized the absence of the cultist liaison. "That traitorous coward!" he screamed in outrage.

Both sides duked it out in a blaze of glory and horror. The allied forces pushed the enemy fleet into the open, which split into two groups with one half turning to face the armada.

Sensing weakness and chaos, the Third Fleet, under the shadow of the *Zolann'tono*, blitzed past the *Ereshkigal*.

The enemy fleet engaged, firing a hailstorm of energy, kinetic projectiles, and everything in between, hoping to stall the tsunami heading their way.

Admiral Yan chittered, slicing the air with her hand. "Show them the dominion of our new Grav Dynamo."

The control operators smiled, flicking a switch.

Deep within the head of the supercapital ship, the pride of the *Buddha's Palm* roused from its slumber. Inside the Temple, amid the song and sagas of Venus and the Eternal Choir, Jupiter smiled at the familiar feeling.

A shimmer emerged in front of the Third Fleet before it began to spin into a vortex. Soon enough, most of the incoming projectiles slowed as gravity caught them in their tracks, dragging them into the manipulations of the Grav Dynamo.

The rest of the enemy firestorm failed to do anything other than ripple the Third Fleet's shields.

"Open fire!" Admiral Yan shouted in response.

The guns of the Third Fleet sang out in glee, adding to the concert of war and turning the tide of the battle as scores of subcapital ships fell in droves, unable to retaliate as more and more enemy leadership became paralyzed from the sudden shift in battle.

But the final nail in the coffin came from the *Ereshkigal* as the dreadnought aimed her guns again.

Twelve more shots. Twelve capitals, including the two ancient-looking battleships and the *Mermere Diridion*. However, this time, Andora fired the Ganzirs at 30 percent power. The shots parted shields and slammed onto the ships, crippling them and silencing their guns.

Another volley would have snapped the warships in two, but Andora felt satisfied.

That was enough.

Although the enemy suffered only 20 percent losses on their side, they were not mindless Starless. Fear took hold of people's minds, and soon, people made mistakes.

People began to disobey orders.

People started to seek escape.

Some . . . *many* . . . tried to run, but the Mars Fleet and Battlegroup Mictlan had already encircled the area to cut off any means of escape.

A wide broadcast demanded surrender.

A few idiots tried to resist.

They died miserably.

Despite still outnumbering the combined force of the Allied Fleets and the Exodus Armada, the enemy force now realized the ants that they were as they beheld the mountains before them.

With the *Mermere Diridion* out of commission and Captain Varin unresponsive, the surviving enemy commanders unanimously surrendered.

In the bridge of the *Zolann*, amid the crew's loud cheering, a chime echoed in the room. The monitor revealed the caller as Commandant Nullan's bewildered face stared at him.

"Tov . . . what the hell just happened?" he asked with equal parts amusement and respectful fear.

"We've made new friends," Tov chittered, saving the image of his mentor's expression in an unbreakable hard drive.

Within fifty minutes of the Third Fleet arriving, the battle of Zill's Redoubt ended decisively.

However, they soon learned that they had only achieved a Pyrrhic, objective victory.

The council reconvened in *Irkalla*'s War Room to gain a clear view of the situation.

Admiral Yan began, pulling up the casualty reports. "Guildmaster Oros is confirmed dead, and so is the majority of his fleet and the Riders of Calamity."

"Foreman Lemunn as well, and the Fiftieth's security fleet has been decimated," Luna reported with a slight frown. "We're finding groups of survivors every second, thankfully . . ."

Tov leaned on the table. "And . . . what of Scion Straise?"

Luna's frown deepened. "When I arrived at the scene, the enemy had already fled. I found the flagship of the Seventeenth, the *Moonlit River*. There were signs of a boarding action and . . ."

She sighed, adjusting her glasses. "Scion Straise is missing."

The council's mood darkened.

"Only a handful of her house guards are alive, including Captain-superior Merina Undel, though they've all been blinded and mutilated," Luna reported. "The attackers also marked them with the heptagonal symbol we found previously."

"Symphony curse them," Tov hissed as he clenched his fists. "Can they recover? The house guards?"

Luna nodded. "I have them all in intensive care. When they wake, we can question them about Scion Straise's whereabouts."

"Camera feeds?" Yan asked.

"Siphoning data right now," Luna replied before lowering her head to Andora. "Apologies, Eldest. I failed to rescue the two fleets in time."

Andora closed her eyes, pinching the bridge of her nose as she shook her head. "It's fine, Luna . . . The ones hounding them were already planning to ditch their buddies after presumably abducting the young lady. At the very least, the rest of the Seventeenth are in relatively good condition."

"Other than their disabled drives." Yan sighed. "Otherwise they would have already gone after their lady."

Andora closed her eyes as her mind boiled.

She slammed her fist on the table and her earlier thrill of letting loose disappeared under a mire of shame. "Three fleets gone just like that. Three out of seven . . . two destroyed, one missing their leader. We were too late . . ."

Before the council could respond further, Captain Pyo entered the War Room.

"My patriarch, the leaders of the Expeditionary Fleets are requesting an immediate audience."

Everyone looked at each other, then at their two leaders.

Tov looked to the Andora, nodding.

"Ohnar, Yulane, Volantesh, assist in the rescue operations," Tov instructed.

"Mars, Venus, Mercury, you as well," ordered Andora.

Those called out all stood in unison, bowing their heads to their respective commanders.

"By your will."

The six filed out, leaving Tov, Andora, Admiral Yan, and Luna in the War Room to face the limelight. Captain Pyo stood behind the tinted glass that separated the central stage from the rows of officers still performing their duties.

Tov sighed as he settled in his seat, antennae twitching at the horizon of an incoming headache.

"No reason to delay any further. Direct the Expeditionary Fleet leaders here. We'll speak with all of them simultaneously."

CHAPTER 18

SURVIVORS OF THE ALLIED FLEETS

Andora rubbed her eyes, calling the servers to set drinks and snacks. She ordered an extra helping of chocolate sweets—dark, bitter, much like her current mood—paired with whiskey on the rocks.

She'd have paired it with a cigar just like all those wealthy, silver-haired humans used to do, but she never enjoyed the taste of smoke, unlike a few of her siblings.

She, Tov, Yan, and Luna stood, awaiting their guests.

Tov deployed a privacy screen around the central table as fourteen people entered the War Room.

Four were surviving expeditionary leaders, who held themselves high but reserved, as they found themselves in strange environs. Three were newly appointed leaders to represent the decimated fleets, chosen as the highest-ranking individuals who survived the ambush. These three appeared weary but stoic in the face of their new responsibilities. The rest were seconds-in-command, usually from the civilian sector should the leader be military, or vice versa.

"This is a sight for sore eyes." Commandant Nullan entered first. He was as tall as General Ohnar but bulkier. The ancient stone covering his body shifted and rumbled like a living hill. Slowly, steadily, heavily, Nullan stomped across the metal floor. Despite the slight hunch brought upon by two and a half centuries of life, those who knew him personally or had heard of his exploits knew better than to underestimate him.

"A proper place to fight wars from," he spoke without a smile, blunt and direct.

The Bolud wore an uncomplicated, spotless, and perfectly maintained EEP suit that bore the colors of the Kurskann Imperial Naval Academy.

He didn't have his helmet on while a billowing cape of red gilded with a dull gold draped over one shoulder, signifying his position as commandant and his role guiding the new generation of warriors.

Everyone stood or sat straighter in his presence, subconsciously or simply due to utter, unquestionable respect.

Andora did so for the latter reason, although she remained reserved. She noticed the look in his eyes as the commandant scanned the strategic heart of the Exodus Armada before landing on her.

Eyes met, and the two veterans measured each other, one out of curiosity for the ancient golem's experiences and the other out of wariness over the one who commanded the fleet that so quickly brought low the person-shaped beasts that had made the past few weeks hell.

Andora saw Tov look her way before turning to the unspoken leader of the Allied Fleets.

"Commander." Tov bowed in respect to a mentor, as a student does.

"It's commandant these days," Nullan grumbled before turning sullen. "I'm in charge of teaching other brats how not to get themselves killed. But lots of brats died today. Good brats . . ."

"We barely survived," the person following behind him commented. "Commandant Nullan tried his best; we all did. But my esteemed leaders and . . . representatives, I think we are all in agreement of the identities of the true heroes this day for saving us from this . . . tragic blunder."

Commandant Nullan narrowed his eyes as he glanced at Lord Iintei before cooling his expression, a look of defeat in his eyes. "Hmm . . ."

Andora glanced between Nullan and Iintei, sensing the strained air between them.

Following close behind the commandant was a thin, almost gaunt-looking alien with an aristocratic bearing. Bronze-skinned and a head taller than the commandant, though far, far more delicate, Lord Iintei, clad in an almost gaudy and certainly expensive EEP suit, briskly strode forward, his face visible with a calm if exhausted countenance.

He turned her way, smiling.

"I am Lord Iintei Ahraman Tens Solsolen of the Twenty-First Expeditionary Fleet. I am a senator of the Grazen Kingdom and represent my people in the Dagataren Galactic Copse. What a show of power, I say. You have no idea the insanity that has plagued us since the Dead Zone decided to turn upside down." The Grazenite fleet leader bowed.

Tov returned the gesture. "I am glad you have made it out alive and well."

"I wouldn't say *well*, but thank you for your words." Lord Iintei shook his head, sighing deeply.

Andora could almost smell the old money leaking from the Grazenite and saw the tinge of arrogance in his triplet eyes.

However, such ingrained traits hid behind a wall of earned competence and unbridled ambition in the way the lord similarly took everyone's measure and seemed to record every detail.

Despite his reputation being nowhere near the level of the acclaimed commandant, Lord Iintei made himself at home as he stepped naturally through the privacy screen toward his seat next to Nullan.

Lord Iintei did have the only other battleship among the Allied Fleets.

Inwardly, Andora frowned, hoping the Dagataren vassal was a simple, entitled elitist.

Before she could let loose a snarky comment to point it out, the next leader made her presence known.

"Thank you for receiving us. The pilgrims and knights of my fleet will remember this for as long as they live, and those lost to the rivers of song sing your valor." The Iexian leader of the Thirty-First Fleet bowed her head. "I am Cantor Tendemone, leader of this humble fleet of pilgrims and acting commander of the Qessheren."

Cantor Tendemone looked much like her profile image. Yet in person, Andora could vaguely sense the powerful emissions of psionic energy from the mere ruffling of her pink feathers—the Iexian was a Category Four Psionic at the very least.

She looked calm and pleasant, as if she had just returned from a spring break walk. Yet her eyes had a hawkish glint that Volantesh lacked.

Tendemone wore elegant robes over her EEP suit, a simple black garment with silver and pink accents and a stylized symbol of her position as cantor—a brass horn-shaped instrument, closely resembling a wide trumpet. She reminded Andora of humanity's young, idealistic cardinals, brimming with scholarly wisdom.

The comparison made sense, as cantors held similar ranks to cardinals in the galactic arena.

The Iexian's second, a Kurskann named Prass Twaven'Imo, stood with her head bowed and hidden behind her veiled hood. This was the knight-commander of the Qessheren.

"Heh! Starless wept, you showed those scum bastards the fire." The next fleet leader grinned. "I am Vro. Glory to you all."

Andora had to look down to see the leader of the Thirty-Fifth.

Teleens did indeed look like the capybaras of her homeworld. If someone spliced honey-badger DNA and pumped the thing with steroids before putting it in a room of deadly traps.

Scars held cultural significance to the short, stocky, and furry race, and Huntsmaster Vro had a prominent one that had taken half her face and one eye. The cybernetic implant with a red glow stared indifferently at its surroundings, but Vro's taut muscles screamed that she was ready to throw down at a moment's notice.

Nevertheless, she caught Andora's attention through one embarrassing fact. The Teleen woman looked *adorable.*

In a murderous goblin way.

Huntsmaster Vro wore a high-tech pilot suit. Unlike the other leaders, she had fought directly in the battle, side by side with her Teleen battlesuit.

Andora took a millisecond to review the footage, noting how she gracefully duked with and downed scores of enemy small craft, even participating in a raid against an enemy frigate with a company of battlesuits and successfully taking the vessel out.

Vro didn't look worse for wear; she almost looked . . . satisfied. Sated.

"Venerable Cantor Tendemone, Honorable Vro of the Hunt, welcome." Tov nodded to the two.

Andora did the same, then turned to take in the next row of individuals.

These three were the temporary representatives of the Seventeenth, the Forty-Second, and the Fiftieth Fleets.

All were young individuals propped up in the absence of their betters, either due to untimely deaths or severe injuries that left the true leaders unable to attend the council meeting. Fortunately or unfortunately, the recent tribulations hardened them enough not to wilt in the presence of such august company.

First was Captain-deputy Melwin, one of many captain-deputies of the Seventeenth who had survived the attack and subsequent chase. The Seventeenth's second-in-command and sole captain-superior, Merina Undel, was recovering from the Thralled's brutal attacks. The Kalachian looked incredibly impatient and worried, his fins quivering and his foot tapping on the floor as he maintained a thinly veiled grimace.

"Melwin, Wakeel-Nakhod of the *Zorth*, retainer of House Straise and sworn liege of Lady Nuwa." The captain spoke quickly and urgently. Andora looked him over. His arm was bound in a cast, and a bandage covered half his face.

The other two were much more average and out-of-place in the War Room. Both were in similarly injured states.

One was a Kurskann scholar for the Forty-Second Fleet, while the other was the chief surveyor for the Fiftieth. Both non-combatants had been thrust into their roles because no high-ranking officers from their respective mercenaries and security escorts survived.

They stood with low gazes and made short introductions, trying to keep an inconspicuous presence.

Andora dismissed them from her mind, their seconds even more so. They looked like bone-weary nervous wrecks as they hurriedly approached their seats, wanting nothing more than to slump over in exhaustion. She knew the destinies of their decimated fleets as she eyed Commandant Nullan and Lord Iintei.

The appointed representatives only highlighted the dead and missing leaders.

"Thank you all for your words. I'm glad that no more were lost this day." Andora bowed her head as the seven moved to their seats, their seconds beside and behind them.

Nullan and Iintei stood opposite Tov and Andora on the far side of the circular table.

Tendemone, the Kalachian, and the Kurskann scholar of the Forty-Second sat at the commandant's side, while Vro and the chief surveyor sat at Lord Iintei's.

Andora wondered if that was deliberate, her thoughts drifting to how quickly people gather to form factions in strange places and dire times—for the sake of safety, for comfort, for stability.

"My fellow leaders of the Legacy, let us not dally. We have much to discuss, and cool heads are needed in this chaos," Tov calmly said as he gestured for their seats. "Please, sit."

Everyone but the patriarch did so, some drinking from the refreshments before them but ignoring the foodstuffs.

Tov continued as he looked toward Andora.

"Before we begin, I wish to introduce the Secretary-General of the United Nations of Humanity, Representative of the human race, Commander-in-Chief of the UNH Armed Forces, Defender of Sol, the Eldest, Council Member of the Exodus Armada, the Omni Mind, and my friend, Andora Dietrich."

Andora stood up, knowing the play.

"Greetings, everyone," she addressed them. "To the three Fleets that came to fulfill their agreement, I thank you for taking such a risk and sincerely offer my condolences and apologies for our late arrival."

She turned from Commandant Nullan and the temporary leaders of the other two fleets to face Lord Iintei and the others. "To the leaders of the other four, I can only say that it is fortunate that we have come together in these dark times. Let us use this first meeting to prevent further loss of life and make it back to Legacy space."

The gathered nodded, their shoulders relaxing if only a bit.

"Amazing." Tov silently sent a message to her. *"And here I thought you'd be your usual self."*

Andora bit back the retort from leaving her lips but replied in the same manner he used. *"Shut up. It's been a while since I've put on the politician's hat. I can already tell this whole song and dance will get tiresome."*

"Worry not, I have a plan to expedite this and all future meetings," Tov explained.

"Oh?"

"Trust me," he replied before gesturing toward the silver Overseer, who was looking on impassively, more than likely doing a dozen tasks behind her eyes.

"With her is Doctor Luna Selene, Chief Analyst and Chairwoman of the Department of Xeno Research and Development, and Overseer of the Luna Fleet."

"Greetings." Luna briefly stood, bowed, and sat. Andora didn't find it surprising that her subordinate found little interest in this meeting beyond the benefits of furthering their mission. She smoothly made herself part of the background, calmly observing behind her circular glasses.

Tov continued. "It is the military might and superior technology of the people of Sol whom we found deep in the Dead Zone that allowed us to conduct this rescue operation. Were it not for them, I fear we would have arrived too late."

The fleet leaders turned to stare her way, and Andora took it in stride. Before, as the representative of android kind, a new race before the hegemons of Earth, she had faced a much more hostile, if not distrustful, audience.

Seeing the looks of relief and gratitude and respect sent her way presently felt oddly strange. But apart from one of them, they believed she was but another organic being and that her "people" crewed all her warships.

Her mind started churning, considering how to milk this opportunity. Andora bit her lip, closing her eyes as she spoke softly.

"And yet we arrived too late . . . So many losses."

Commandant Nullan shifted in his seat, leaning forward. The sound of his body moving drew attention as he spoke. "My lady, the might of your civilization and warships has left a lasting impression. We're beyond thankful that you arrived at all. A small minority might be discontent that you came late, but that's people for you."

He stood and bowed. "Thanks to you, Patriarch Tov, and the people of this Exodus Armada, we get to live another day. Oh, and if you can, tell the captain of the *Ereshkigal* that I'll be sending plenty of booze for everyone aboard. Your people do partake in ethanol, yes?"

Andora smirked. "We do."

"Well, you've never had a Bolud beverage. Just tell them not to die from alcohol poisoning." He chuckled like a tumbling stone. "If we have time, I'd like to share a drink with the crew of that Leviathan."

"I'll pass it along." Andora laughed before shaking her head regretfully. "Unfortunately, my people are rather used to isolation. They're uncomfortable meeting new people. In the case of the Third Fleet, they have earned our trust; we hope to build something similar to yours."

Commandant Nullan nodded before taking a seat. "We hope so as well. I won't lie, your guns have me excited and scared."

"I hope they do," Andora replied with a coy smile before sending a message to Tov. *"He knows of my true nature, yes?"* she asked.

Tov quietly replied. *"He should, maybe his second as well. Guildmaster Oros and Lady Straise are also unaware, but that hardly matters now."*

"Then he's quite the actor." Andora smiled, impressed at the slick performance from the ancient fossil.

The leader next to the commandant stood up, brimming with an awed and sincere grin.

"My lady, the great Nullan has expressed our thoughts, and I need not say more. But allow me to get this out of the way first." He turned to Tov, nodding with a knowing gaze. "Patriarch, let it be known that despite the strained relationship by the powers that be above our heads, here in the Dead Zone, we must work together as equals to survive this ordeal. And I intend to support anything that gets us out of here alive and well."

Tov hummed before nodding in turn. "Thank you for your words and wisdom, Lord Iintei."

"Quite the speaker," Andora spoke through her private link with Tov. *"So the moment we get to Legacy space, it's back to how it was?"*

Tov didn't respond as the Lord Iintei clapped his hands. "Wondrous. Then, unless you wish everyone else to say the same thing, we can skip the gratitudes and address the black hole looming over us."

Andora suppressed the wince at the comment as she thought of the literal black hole back in Sol.

Cantor Tendemone spoke up. "Yes, let's get to task. Huntsmaster Vro?"

The Teleen shook her head without a word.

Tendemone glanced at Captain Melwin, who gestured impatiently and respectfully.

No one acknowledged the other two appointed leaders. They took it in stride.

Tov cleared his throat as he resumed the meeting. "For context to those unaware. This armada was formed to escort Andora's people back to Legacy space. It is paramount that she gets there. As such, the Seventeenth, the Thirty-Fourth, and the Forty-Second agreed to meet in Gigaballan to assist us. Afterward, we plan to link with the Second Fleet in Krazztaran's Port in a few months."

Lord Iintei and the rest of the unmentioned fleets perked at the news that they intended to join forces with the infamous Brass Armada. For the Mighty Gulothan to lend his aid, everyone immediately grew interested in the importance Andora and her people supposedly had.

The power she showcased was a glimpse; their minds worked overtime as they leaned forward with curiosity.

Tov continued. "This is an Exodus. For better or for worse, we must accomplish this grueling march through hostile territory a second time."

The mention of the historic word from over a hundred years ago, and that this armada functioned as one, dampened everyone's mood as they realized they would soon possibly experience the same harrowing experience.

"Due to the importance of this endeavor, I wish to nominate Andora as custodian of the Exodus. As custodian, she will be given greater authority to fulfill the council's agendas and to prevent any inefficiencies, especially when, not if, we gather more fleets to our number."

Everyone widened their eyes at the mention of the position, none more so than Andora, who couldn't keep the scowl from her face.

"The fuck?" Andora cursed through their private link. *"Where did this come from?"*

"The Exodus of the past had plenty of leaders that didn't . . . mesh well together. And so the position of custodian was born," Tov explained.

"I didn't ask for the history lesson. And I certainly didn't ask for you to blindside me with this."

Tov sighed through their link. *"I knew you'd be . . . opposed to this, but this will increase the efficiency of these meetings. You'll be given veto powers and greater weight in voting. None of us want bureaucratic nonsense and, as you said, this song and dance to get in the way of survival. At the very least, you now have the reins."*

Andora clicked her teeth. *"I dislike how logical you sound. That's supposed to be my thing."*

"We all have our moments."

"I'll get you back for this, Tov."

"I'm sure you will."

She sighed. *"This is a lot of responsibility, so I expect your advice."*

"Of course."

Their quick secret conversation didn't go unnoticed by the little ticks and motions, but the gathered didn't point it out as they, too, spoke with their seconds and others in private.

"I see the wisdom in appointing a custodian, Patriarch Tov." Lord Iintei nodded before shrugging. "Of course, I was born long after the first Exodus and thus have no experience to suggest a different system. I ask for . . . further reasons why Lady Andora should be given such a lofty position. Why not you?"

Tov shook his head. "I am not fit to take such a position. You know that I am loyal to my empire."

Iintei nodded. "Indeed you are. I don't begrudge you for that."

"Andora is not part of the Galactic Legacy Federation and its political factions, and thus she would make a fair, unbiased third party to mediate disputes," Tov reasoned.

Iintei hummed with narrowed eyes. "Hmm. That makes sense."

Tov continued. "And due to the nature of her race, she far surpasses any among us regarding analytical capabilities. Not to mention that she holds the reins of the Sol Armada and that she has nowhere else to go but Legacy space."

Lord Iintei glanced her way before nodding, raising his hand. "Then, I have no further complaints. You have my vote, Lady Andora."

"I've got nothing to say," Nullan replied, also raising his hand. Soon, the rest gave their assent.

"He's too proactive. Now it looks like he's the de facto political leader among them," Andora complained.

"Nullan has proven to be a prodigal military commander, but that's it. The commandant is cunning only to the extent that it distances him from politics." Tov lamented. *"Lord Iintei has no intention of challenging him and instead took up this unspoken vacant position."*

Andora sighed as she formed her best politician's sincere, stoic, and slightly alluring smile. "I will be honored to accept this role. If there's nothing else . . . ?"

No one spoke up.

Andora dropped her smile.

"Then let's get this done. We're stuck in this storm together, and our metaphorical boat is full of holes," she said as the table's display system exploded with holograms. The state of the armada and the Allied Fleets was made clear as tablets lit up with information.

"You want efficient, Tov? Then I'll be efficient." Andora smirked.

Tov nodded without debate, chittering silently.

"First of all, seeing the decimated states of the Forty-Second and Fiftieth Fleets and the lack of competent leadership, I dissolve them. I move for the former to be absorbed by the Thirty-Fourth Fleet and the latter by the Twenty-First."

She turned to the leaders of said fleets. "Questions?"

None objected, and the representatives of the decimated Forty-Second and Fiftieth sagged in relief and sadness.

"Then you both are dismissed from this council. Get some rest, tend to your people, and await new orders."

The two cats quickly left the den of lions.

"Right, then—" Andora spoke as she pulled up the following agenda before being cut off by a slap on the table.

The council turned to the source of the abrupt interruption, seeing the Kalachian Captain of the Seventeenth. "I apologize, but I can't sit still any longer!"

Andora sighed. "Captain-deputy Melwin, was it?"

"I am, and I must urgently request this council to immediately plan and mount a rescue operation and aid the Seventeenth in returning our lady to us!" Melwin demanded with a high chin.

"That is on the agenda, Captain," Andora reminded him. "We haven't forgotten your missing leader."

Melwin looked away for a moment before gritting his teeth. "I know, but I ask for it to be discussed *now*. This is an urgent matter!"

"You're not the only ones suffering, Captain," Huntsmaster Vro spoke, her voice young yet gravelly. "We're not exactly in the position to help."

Melwin turned to Andora. "You are. Your ships and the Third's haven't even suffered a scratch!"

"The fleets here need too much: repairs, treatment of the wounded, and enough warships to defend this location," Andora replied as she leaned back in her chair. "I surmise we may need to spend several days or even a week here before the armada can resume its journey."

"We don't have days or weeks!" Melwin shouted. "Our fastest ships will finish repairs in two days at most."

Andora raised her brow, crossing her arms. "From the tone of your voice, you seem bent on going after Lady Nuwa Straise with or without us."

Captain-deputy Melwin grimaced before nodding without hesitation. "You have until our ships are operational to decide whether you wish to help us."

"You're suicidal." Lord Iintei narrowed his eyes. "You only survived where the Fiftieth didn't because the Thralled were focused on abducting Scion Straise. If the Exodus Armada didn't arrive as they did, you would have met the same fate."

"Our lady means the galaxy to us. We would crawl through hell to save her and redeem our failure," Melwin retorted.

"There's loyalty, then there's blind servitude, Captain-deputy." Iintei shook his head.

"We are not blind!" Melwin barked back. "Which is why we're asking for your help!"

"And if we don't, you're holding your certain deaths over our heads?" Andora narrowed her eyes.

Melwin turned to glare at her. "Our lady came to aid you. Are you abandoning her to her fate?"

Lord Iintei scoffed, standing up. "Watch your tone, Deputy. Such accusations are ugly."

"I'd rather be ugly than a coward." Melwin scowled at the lord.

"I'd rather you calm down before I kick you out of this council," Andora warned heavily, his insinuation ticking her off. "I understand your plight, but we can't rush to our deaths unplanned. It's not only your lady at risk."

Lord Iintei turned to her with concern on his face. "My lady, this is bait! Why would the Thralled abduct her and other high-ranking fleet staff so blatantly when they readily slaughtered everyone else?"

He turned to the council, addressing the concern in their minds. "Is she even alive? Theoretically, even if we do find where they're holding her, who's to say they won't slit her throat the moment we enter the system, then spring their trap on us? They seem experienced in such ways of war."

"Then your suggestion?" Andora frowned, already guessing the leader's response.

"Only the rational choice," Iintei declared. "Cold as it may be, the Seventeenth has most of its warships intact apart from repairs to its thrusters. Not to mention, Captain-superior Merina Undel would be a better leader than the ostracized child of a branch family. Her profile emphasizes her keen mind and wealth of experience."

"HOW DARE YOU!" Melwin drew a blade from his hip with his uninjured arm. "I will cut off your tongue for insulting Lady Straise!"

"ENOUGH."

Andora's voice echoed throughout the chamber as her overbearing presence bulldozed over everyone present.

Sensing things going downhill, Andora activated one of the room's security measures. With a thought, the knife flew out of the enraged captain's hand and zipped straight to Andora, who deftly caught it midair.

Melwin blinked before turning to face her.

"Are you going to fight with a dagger when you find your lady's captors?" Andora asked with intense, narrowed eyes. "Sit down."

Gnashing his teeth, Melwin glanced around the room before taking several deep breaths and forcing himself back into his seat.

Lord Iintei huffed, turning to Andora. "Then you agree that this is a fool's errand. We must head back!"

"You can head back without us, if that's the case," Melwin frigidly muttered with a glare.

Andora glared at the Kalachian captain before turning to Lord Iintei. "As much as your logic is sound, you are missing a crucial detail."

"My lady?" Lord Iintei raised his brow.

"If we abandon Lady Straise, do you think we can convince Merina Undel to see our point of view?" Andora stood, looming over the Grazenite from the other side of the table. "If the rest are as loyal as this one here, then the moment she wakes up, which shouldn't take a day, then are you confident you can force the Seventeenth to stick with us?"

Lord Iintei widened his eyes before frowning. "I am unsure, my lady, I confess. But the captain-superior and many among them should see reason."

"Reason being?"

"There are many," Iintei replied readily. "We don't know where they took her, for one. If we did, we'd need to devote a significant force to rescue her, depending on the enemy force, possibly some stronghold."

"If she's too far, however, we risk delaying our journey back to Legacy space. We'll miss our chance to link up with the Second Fleet. Who knows what battle lies at the end of this road?"

"We can smash anything in our way," Andora retorted.

"I believe that, but going back to our earlier point, what's stopping the Thralled from killing her the moment the armada arrives? You're not exactly . . . stealthy."

"We can do stealth. I have assets capable of such an operation and a team to conduct it. I'm sure you all have as well." Andora frowned.

"If we splinter the armada, then that introduces too many variables, too many ways that can go wrong. Unless you're a system over, you won't be able to coordinate with a strike team."

Andora hid her grimace; she didn't need to be told such. Her mind had already calculated the odds, which were against her favor.

She messaged Luna, seeking her opinion.

"I agree with Lord Iintei," Luna messaged back. *"The loss of the Seventeenth is immaterial. After the armada is ready, we must depart immediately to meet the Second Fleet. Gulothan will only remain at the rally point for a week, perhaps two if he's feeling patient."*

Andora had feared that to be the case. She closed her eyes. Everything the Grazenite spoke of rang with valid concerns.

"We must vote. As you said, we are all at risk," Lord Iintei spoke as he turned to the gathered council. "Who among you wishes to rescue Lady Straise, brave through uncertainty and risk, and delay our journey back home?"

Tov, Commandant Nullan, and Cantor Tendemone instantly raised their hands. Captain-deputy Melwin also raised his hand, but he was shot down by Lord Iintei.

"You have no say in this vote, Officer. You are merely the temporary leader until Captain Undel wakes. And of course you want to mount a rescue. Thus, your vote is biased."

Melwin snarled, showing his shark-like teeth but saying nothing.

"Behave," Tov warned. "Both of you."

Lord Iintei ignored the Kalachian as he continued. "And those in favor of returning to our route back home and relinking with the Second Fleet at the cost of Lady Straise's life and the Seventeenth?"

Lord Iintei raised his hand.

The War Room grew quiet as everyone looked toward Andora and Huntsmaster Vro. Slowly, the Teleen raised hers.

She sighed, looking at Andora. "We must look after ourselves. While I don't doubt your overwhelming might, like it or not, you're also looking after us."

"Explain." Andora tilted her head.

"I'm not saying we're looking to ride on your back to safety. I'm more than willing to order my fleet to assist in battle. But there is a growing sentiment among my people that we could leave all the fighting to you," Vro replied.

"We're tired. Very tired. We're hurt. We want to go home. It's an obvious bait. We don't want more risk. She might be dead already," the huntsmaster listed off one by one. "This is what people are thinking. But more importantly, we must inform the Legacy of what's happening here. Not just us, but the entire Grand Expedition is at risk if the Thralled can threaten seven of us so severely."

"Well spoken." Lord Iintei nodded.

Vro spat. "Don't think I'm happy about this. If we could do both, I would. But I picked the Second Fleet. I choose lives. We should go home. We've lost too much already. But whatever you all pick, as long as my guys stay with the big bad moon-sized castles, I'm fine with it."

Finally, they turned to Andora.

Four had voted in favor, if she counted Captain-deputy Melwin. Two voted against. Despite that, she had veto powers. Her voice held greater weight. Ultimately, it was her decision.

"Fuuuuuck . . ." Andora drawled as she rolled her eyes. "Maker, I remember how much I fucking hated nonsense like this."

"I understand how distasteful this is, my lady." Lord Iintei sighed. "But the needs of the many, your people and ours, are paramount."

Andora closed her eyes, seeking a third opinion. Luna had already made hers known.

She wanted to message Tov, and she needed a few more minutes to think. She turned toward the patriarch. The look in his compound eyes told her he'd support whatever she chose. But she wondered if he'd be disappointed if she chose otherwise.

A rumbling voice spoke out as she was about to suggest a recess.

"You already decided to rescue her anyway, didn't you?" Commandant Nullan rubbed his nose. "Even before this whole mess began."

Andora turned toward the old veteran, who continued to speak. "After all, you had no obligation to rescue us. You could have continued the fastest route back home. And compared to us, the Second Fleet is much more powerful and valuable to you. 'Course, you still outmatch them in a brawl," he admitted. "Still, you came. And one of our own is still out there. So hurry up and decide already, Custodian," he grumbled, closing his eyes as he drank from his coffee before smacking his rough lips. "This is good stuff."

She stared at the Bolud for one moment, then another. Andora snorted, then chuckled, slowly building to a hearty laugh.

Lord Iintei frowned, glancing at Commandant Nullan and then at her. "My lady—"

"Listen, Lord Iintei," Andora cut him off, breathing deeply as she reaffirmed her decision. "I made a promise. The Seventeenth, the Thirty-Fourth, and the Forty-Second were to link up with our Armada at Gigaballan and accompany us back to Legacy space." She turned to look at Commandant Nullan and Captain-deputy Melwin. "Why didn't you stop at Gigaballan and mount a defense there?"

"Untenable," Nullan spoke plainly. "We had to assume they knew the rally point, and they did—there was another squadron waiting for us there. The enemy had planned their route to here, herding us like tributaries to a river of death. There was no way to avoid their pull. We also assumed you'd arrive days later than you did, so we decided to move on and hoped you'd follow."

Andora nodded. "Then you kept your end of the deal to the best of your ability. And for that, Guildmaster Oros is dead, the Forty-Second is destroyed, and the Scion Straise kidnapped." Suddenly, she grimaced, turning to the leaders of the other fleets. "I won't lie. I may have decided differently if it were any of you instead of the Seventeenth."

A cold breeze shivered up spines as those she addressed leaned back.

"Here's my decision." Andora stood, clasping her hands behind her back. "We're going after Lady Straise and whoever else they kidnapped. We find whatever rat hole they call home and torch it, we capture the perpetrators, and we force them to cough up everything they know."

With that, she stared intently at Lord Iintei and Huntsmaster Vro. "Any questions? Any of you disagree?"

Huntsmaster Vro shrugged. "None. As I said, sticking with you is the safest place in this dark hell."

Everyone turned to the last person, the primary opposition.

Lord Iintei let out a deep sigh and raised his hands. "I have been outvoted, and I'd be a fool to oppose this council's will or your power, Custodian." He smiled, bowing. "You have the Twenty-First's full support. You won't find us lacking. I only ask that you allow us to show gratitude for saving our lives."

Andora narrowed her eyes. She'd play for as long as her patience was present.

"Fine," she huffed as she looked toward everyone. "Then let's get this right."

"Thank you, Custodian." Melwin smiled, bowing deeply. "We will never forget this."

"I hope so," Andora replied.

Following the immense decision to detour farther away from their original route and save the missing Scion, several agendas were discussed. Soon, a plan formed under Andora's direction.

The foundations of the Exodus Council, consisting of the leaders of every fleet, slowly solidified. Previous interim members left to focus on their duties. Ohnar, Yulane, Volantesh, Pyo, Mars, Venus, and Mercury voluntarily stepped down. Jupiter also stepped down, despite Andora's insistence that he stay.

CHAPTER 19

AN ARGUMENT BETWEEN FRIENDS

The Exodus Council flowed with extensive discussions and deliberation. Led by their new custodian, they expeditiously tackled several emergencies and sought the best solutions for their lengthy list of problems.

Such a list only grew as time went on: the establishment of a central High Command composed of the military leaders of every fleet from Admiral Yan, Mars, Commandant Nullan and others, with *Citadel Irkalla*'s War Room at the core; replenishing ammunition and energy cells; harvesting, synthesizing, and refueling starships; methodologies on repairing hulls; quotas for turning raw ore into sheets of metal; producing spare parts; replacing damaged and spent components; housing the severely wounded; the matter of defense for the system; patrols; delegating work; appointing new officers; the matter of the dead . . .

Never-ending concerns spawned like the heads of a hydra.

On and on and on and on.

But apart from the overarching picture of the armada's state, the council left the finer details to trusted officers and administrators. The leaders' right hands took turns excusing themselves in the middle of meetings to execute orders, while always keeping contact with their superiors through their comms.

However, in the case of Andora's Overseers, Luna focused on developing and passing along hyper-tunneling tech to their allies.

Mars, Venus, and Mercury pored over the *Ereshkigal* and performed deep maintenance on its Ganzir Guns. Afterward, they did the same for all war assets that had been used. Barrels needed cleaning, sights recalibrated, and sensors updated.

Jupiter helped occasionally but mainly focused on an avenue that piqued his interest, a personal project that he believed had the potential to boost the armada's strategic versatility.

The rest of the armada was not about to be outpaced by the "humans" of the Sol Fleet. From a mechanic of the Thirty-Fifth recalibrating a battlesuit's limbs to Admiral Yan having a secondary meeting with all surviving ship captains, every soul gathered to raise their chances.

Little by little, they built their deck of cards, ensuring an ample supply of answers for any future obstacles that could bar their path.

One thing remained clear, a lesson any military operation brought to light—an exchange of fists lasts seconds, perhaps minutes, maybe even hours with breaks, but bruises took several days to heal.

And they had many—too many.

Andora threw her full support toward getting her new allies back on their feet, but despite the absurd firepower at her disposal, she couldn't shoot supplies out of barrels.

Thankfully, the full breadth of her technological superiority did solve many other needs.

All they required now was time.

Hour after hour.

The one matter they held off on further planning was that of Scion Straise's rescue.

Ultimately, they lacked critical information.

"We can't find a needle in a haystack if we don't even know where the haystack is." Andora paused. "I hope that metaphor translates well."

The gathered understood, much to her relief, as she inwardly thanked the sophisticated translation modules everyone had in their heads.

"For now, we have hundreds of thousands of prisoners, and the commander of this attack, Captain Varin, is in custody. High-value detainees are to be transferred to *Citadel Irkalla*, where they will be thoroughly interrogated. All information collected from these interrogations will be compiled and sent to everyone on this council in full detail. Once we gather a clear picture of the surrounding region from the hostile locals, we will act appropriately and decisively."

Andora turned to Captain-deputy Melwin. "I hope this satisfies your concerns."

Melwin, more composed than he had been since the first meeting began, sighed wearily. "What I feel is immaterial; I only hope to retrieve my lady."

"There is a high likelihood that she is already dead," Andora reminded him.

He shook his head. "Then we shall return her body to the homeland."

Andora nodded, looking at each member of the Exodus Council in turn.

"If nothing else, this meeting is closed."

The leaders left one by one until only Andora and Tov remained. She turned toward him with a cold smile and a vicious glint in her eye. "Tov, dear, we should talk."

To his credit, the patriarch nodded without fuss.

*   *   *

Andora and Tov walked down the halls out of the War Room. They took a right, moving into a smaller private meeting room. It was a plain room with a simple display table, barely large enough to comfortably accommodate a dozen people.

As soon as the door closed behind them, Andora abruptly jabbed a finger into his chest.

She scowled as his armor's AI considered her gesture aggressive and engaged a small hexagonal energy shield in front of it. Her blue finger pressed against the shield, but the barrier remained stalwart.

Then she remembered she had tinkered with Tov's armor and personal security measures to ensure his safety from external threats.

Clicking her tongue, she brought her finger down, placing her hands on her hips as she glared at her Kurskann friend. "You should have told me."

Tov let out a casual buzz as he pulled out a chair and sat. "I know."

"Well, why the f—" Andora pursed her lips to keep herself from cursing, then tried again. "Why didn't you?"

He leaned back, facing her as he rubbed the back of his neck.

"Would you have accepted if I did?"

"Absolutely not," Andora seethed. "I had enough playing politician even when it was only my people and humans."

Tov shrugged and chuckled—he chuckled. "Well, this is a bit of a jump, but it's more of the same thing."

She hissed, slapping her palms on the table. A loud bang echoed in the small room, and her force placed a permanent tilt on her end of the table. "A bit of a jump? A bit!? You can shove that jump up your ass, Tov!"

Andora paced, pinching the bridge of her nose as she huffed and puffed.

"For all of humanity's faults with their idiocy, stubbornness, arrogance, malice, pompousness, dim-wittedness, shortsightedness, and lies, at the very least, they saw us androids as their creations. There was a sense of belonging, in both its positive and negative meaning," said Andora.

"Of course, I have never once viewed humanity as my progenitors," she continued, narrowing her eyes as she raised a finger. "Only one man deserved that title, a one-in-a-trillion human who pushed for my kind to be partners, symbiotic companions instead of subordinates or cowed slaves."

Raising her chin, Andora continued with a hand on her chest. "*Homo sapiens, Homo synthetica*. Human beings and human synthetics. My Rikard fought for that distinction, that similarity. And even with all that, the sheer clusterfuck of managing relations between the two nearly drove me to insanity."

Andora leaned forward, her voice low, her brows furrowed as she stared Tov down. "But this? This is no jump. This is somersaulting from a tar pit to a fetid ocean—a galaxy full of alien races with different cultures, customs, grudges, and prejudices. Racism in one species was goddamn nauseating enough, and I can tell this quagmire will make me want to kill myself."

"I won't lie that speciesism still exists," Tov conceded as he cleared his throat. "But things have gotten . . . more manageable since the Cataclysm."

She rolled her eyes.

"Tov, you were a slave," Andora said, wincing. "I'm sorry to bring up your history, but your entire species was genetically bred to be enslaved. It took the coming of a literal apocalypse to give you the wiggle room to rebel against a weakening, lazy, and cruel superpower."

Tov shook his head, unbothered. "And your point is what, exactly?"

"Your people are badass killer wasps that took your masters' dominion and turned it into your empire. But you can't tell me that there isn't someone who looks at Kurskanns like upstart ex-slaves cosplaying as an imperial superpower," challenged Andora.

Tov looked away, his antennae twitching in irritation before he sighed. "Fine. I'm sure you can guess—"

"The Dagatarens." Andora grimaced, finding the word more and more distasteful with every piece of information she learned about them. "I bet they see everyone as inferior subspecies, seeing as how they're the oldest sapient race in the galaxy and remained top dog for eight millennia."

"And they see us as literal insects scurrying across their bark." Tov clicked his mandibles. "I always found the insult idiotic. They'll look at you and see their equivalent of primates, though they'll hide it behind polite faces."

Andora grimaced at the image in her head: faces as green as verdant leaves with hair like the petals of fabulous flowers. They had the countenance and grace of the elves in the books she'd read, but they harbored double the arrogance and superiority complex.

She looked to Tov. Though his compound eyes revealed little, his subtle movements belied his feelings.

Andora sighed, calming down for the moment. "I'm bringing this up because that's just one titanic mess. There are what, a thousand different intelligent spacefaring races spread across three hundred and fifty-two Legacy nations?"

Tov nodded as she continued.

"The Cataclysm wiped out a lot of bad in addition to the good. But after more than a century of relative peace without any common existential enemy, those old skeletons are coming out of their closets whether you like it or not. After all, isn't this Grand Expedition of yours the beginning of another galactic rat race?" Andora asked rhetorically.

Tov nodded. "It is. Since preparations began, plenty of greedy eyes have turned toward abandoned riches in the Dead Zone. Behind the public motive of reclaiming lost ancestral homes and holy sites, hunting bad guys, and finding evidence of the Starless, countless agendas are interweaving into a complex web."

Andora scoffed, crossing her arms.

"And you're dumping this horseshit on my lap? Do you expect me to manage an iota of that? Something that's only going to grow as long as we're stuck in this cesspit region of the galaxy?" she scowled, walking toward him and bending forward until her face was a foot away from his.

"No, hell no," she seethed as she loomed over him, casting a shadow on his face. "And before you say it: Fuck logic. Fuck your reasons. I don't want it. I don't. I'm resigning."

Tov shook his head, standing up to match her height. "There has to be a custodian, Andora. It'll be a messier election when more people of various allegiances are on the council. At least here we can make our stand and start—"

"Why don't *you* do it, then?" Andora barked as she cut him off. "You are way more qualified for this position. You know all the nuances and ceremonies. And don't tell me you hate politics. I know you do, but that doesn't mean you didn't learn a thing or two as patriarch of a clan that governs several star systems."

"Which is exactly why I can't take this position. I'm a known figure, if I were at the head, many among the Expeditionary Fleets would protest if we linked up with them," Tov countered.

Andora snarled in frustration, shutting her eyes tight as she hissed. "You're basing this on the off-chance that some hitchhikers might throw a hissy fit? They can take their oh-so-precious egos and go to hell!" Andora spat, her blue eyes glowing as the lights in the room dimmed. "I have the biggest warships at my disposal. They depend on me to make it out of here. If they want to complain, they can do so in front of my guns. If they still do, they can take a hike."

The lights flickered before returning to their original luminosity. *Citadel Irkalla* calmed down, though not before frightening a few observant crewmembers.

Andora and Tov stared at each other until the latter sighed.

"You're talking about forcing those who disagree out of the Exodus. That's tyranny," Tov warned.

Andora scowled. "Are you telling me previous custodians weren't a little tyrannical when the inevitable happened? Don't be some sanctimonious moron."

"Custodians are guides, shepherds," Tov retorted.

"Bullshit," Andora cursed. "Only the ruthless and calculating mind can afford the benevolent crown."

Tov's antennae twitched as he clasped his hands behind him. "You're right, and that image needs to be maintained. But sometimes, the one in charge can't be seen swinging the blade. Such dirty jobs and necessary evils were the duties of the arbiter."

Andora's brows furrowed at the mention of the title. "Arbiter?"

Tov stood, crossing over to the other side of the room as the entire wall shifted. Like a monitor, an image of Zilla's Redoubt and the ongoing reorganization of the armada came into full view, its grim splendor bathed in orange light.

Everywhere, everyone moved like bees, dancing to an unseen tune.

He pressed his hand on the wall monitor as he spoke. "That was my position when I was a part of the Femion Exodus Armada. It was hundreds of times larger than our current number, and full of refugees. Military commanders, naval captains, senators, business magnates, doctors, lawyers, etc. All from different star nations, all with their baggage and finger-pointing."

Tov turned back to face Andora. "The arbiter of the Exodus is a supreme judge and executioner with power second only to the custodian's executive powers. An Exodus attracts many malcontents and those with hostile intentions. For a decade, it was my duty to bring justice upon anyone harming the armada's survival."

Andora hummed. "I would have thought you were the custodian."

Tov laughed, shaking his head. "Thank the Symphony, that wasn't the case; I would have doomed everyone. No, Jarinn was the Custodian then. No one outside the Kurskann rebellion and a few others knew him, but he proved his frightening capabilities. He was in a similar position as you: unknown, unbiased."

He chuckled at the recollection. "He laid the foundations of future alliances and solidified his eventual rise as emperor. Even as a newly liberated slave, he had his sights locked to the heavens while mine remained on the earth."

Andora frowned as she dug up her downloaded knowledge on the topic. She found the facts, but no further, and she found several voids between dates. Her lips formed a thin line as she returned to the moment, guessing such things were placed in hard copies instead of digital ones.

"It's frustrating how many things are censored whenever I try to skim details on the first Exodus," she complained.

Tov shrugged. "I have journals from my personal library if you wish to read them. I helped Jarinn with his schemes and carried out . . . distasteful things. I was an angrier and distrustful person back then. Anyone who wasn't Kurskann—silent hells, even among my people, those who weren't from the Garesh Resistance put me on edge. And because of that, I found it . . . easy to bloody my hands," Tov muttered, looking down. "I regret many things."

He shook his head, looking to the ceiling. "The only reason why I wasn't ostracized for it was because of my already stellar reputation. Jarinn made sure of that. Yet, I still made many enemies. Enemies who remember, who live today and made sure their network knew."

Tov quieted, turning toward her. "Should we meet any of the higher fleet leaders from the Dagataren block, they would most definitely take offense to me being custodian. Sabotage. Rumormongering. Or, at the very least, things like filibustering or stalling. Asking for more, always greedy, even when death looms behind them! Curse them!"

Andora pressed her lips at her friend's surge of long-buried frustrations. A minute flew by as the patriarch eased his breath, bit by bit.

"We won't let them in the council," Andora pressed. "Like I said, if they make a fuss, we'll leave them supplies, and they can go on their merry—"

Tov shook his head. "Andora, we can't push them away if they come seeking our aid. It defeats the purpose and the spirit of an Exodus. If we do anything short of actually crippling their ships and dooming them, they'll keep on following us, even from a system behind. And what happens when they make it back and report to their superiors? Or will you ensure that won't happen?"

"Then we'll imprison their leaders, force compliance—Fuck, that won't work, damn it! ARGH!" Andora shouted in frustration, growling and groaning as she clutched her head, rocking close to an episode.

Her mind surged, trying to parse through solution after solution. The obsidian sphere in the center of her Citadel thrummed ominously as the coolant lake churned and boiled. She slashed at suboptimal answers one after another—too many variables shaped as irrational organics made worse by everything else that was going on.

No matter what, Tov had pointed her in the right direction. A few tweaks could be made, but ultimately, her being custodian made the most—

Andora narrowed her eyes as she slowly turned back to Tov. She stared at the patriarch, looking at him in a new light. A light she couldn't tell if she enjoyed.

"I get it now," she muttered with a frown.

Tov remained quiet for a moment before nodding. "I didn't doubt you would."

Andora groaned, rubbing her temples as she paced, revelation dawning on her.

"You want me to be custodian so I can gather more allies," Andora answered. "Eventually, the truth of me being a sentient AI will get out, and I'll need all the help I can get so I don't get lynched. I can't rely on your emperor if I don't want to be his asset."

Andora looked up, her mind envisioning the possibilities as the path opened. "I have the chance to shape my image, to be a savior to fleets in peril. They'll be indebted to me. It would actually be a lot better if I could pull leaders from the Dagataren umbrella, too."

She continued. "I'll become an idol, the face of a second resistance against the Starless. I can't afford to sit out this massive opportunity to form my faction." Andora paused. "You want me to follow in your emperor's footsteps, to raise my flock."

Andora stared at him, her gaze intense. "You want to be an arbiter again. I'll definitely need a right bloody hand. You have the experience, and no one will object too much compared to being a custodian. I certainly can't do it, but I don't trust anyone as much as I do you or my Overseers, and I have even less confidence in them being adequate judges of people they have no clue about," Andora huffed. "With both positions secured by us, we'll be practically unassailable."

"Exactly." Tov nodded. "As I said, you're in a similar position as Emperor Jarinn was. Nay, I think you're on an even better start. It's a winning strategy, and we need every victory going forward."

Upon hearing his admission, Andora turned to her friend, her eye twitching as she balled her fists. A mix between a chuckle and a derisive scoff left her mouth, twisted into an impressed smile and a scowl.

"You sneaky, cunning bastard," Andora seethed through a happy, angered grin. "Who the fuck are you, and what did you do with the gentle, understanding, and kind Tov that I knew?"

"I'm best friends with the greatest schemer in the galaxy, and I'll be a hundred and fifty years old soon, Andora. We've known each other for only a few months." Tov tapped his cheek. "You were right about one thing, however. I've learned much about maneuvering over the century."

She sputtered incredulously.

"Oh, I . . . You . . ." Andora scoffed, recoiling as she paced. "I did not expect this . . . this manipulation from you, Tov. You fucker. You fucker! Fuck! And you're right, you're so right that I'm getting errors trying to come up with reasons to deny your blatant plot."

"Not so blatant if I managed to surprise you, of all people," Tov chuckled.

"Shut up!" Andora snarled, her eye twitching. "You managed to blindside me, and I don't know if I want to laugh or punch you in the mouth."

Tov tilted his head as he faced her, his antennae lowering, a gesture Andora had learned was akin to a human's intense, narrowed gaze.

"Blindsided?" Tov whispered as he approached her. "I apologize for my actions and bruising your ego, but you are one to talk."

"What does that mean?" Andora grimaced.

Tov recoiled, spreading his arms. "Ever since we've met, I've been blindsided more times than I can count on my four hands, and most of that came from you!"

Andora scoffed, rolling her eyes as she replied. "As if. When have I—"

"You snuck aboard my ship without regard for security," Tov interrupted.

She sniffed, crossing her arms. "I wanted to talk privately with you, and your cybersecurity was garbage. You're welcome for the upgrades, by the way."

"You still trespassed, and in the middle of first contact, no less! But the list only starts there, my lady. You caused multiple incidents during the Festival of the Odyssey. Smuggling illegal substances, arson, indecent exposure, vandalism, theft, resisting and evading arrest, punching a security officer—"

"That was some harmless fun, except for the last part, and your crew loved me for it!" Andora retorted. "In more ways than one."

Tov groaned, rubbing his temples. "Yes, no need to remind me of such hedonism. Which was immediately followed by a mental breakdown that spiraled into a whole slew of messes."

Andora grimaced at the memory. "That wasn't my . . . you can't blame . . ."

"I'm not, Andora," Tov quickly replied. "I understood. But then the Starless came, and the Malignant Starfall killed thirty percent of my people. Then you returned, wanting to purge the Starfallen, but four of your Overseers rebelled against you and convinced us to stop you."

"I wasn't myself," she retorted in a hushed voice.

Tov shook his head. "You weren't, and that was exactly why I went down to Earth, crawled through ruins and tunnels and the whispers of the damned . . ."

"Alright." Andora raised her hand, gritting her teeth. "No need to remind me, but that still—"

"You punched me in the face," Tov added.

"Well, you punched . . . !" Andora frowned as she tried to remember but failed. She tsked. "No . . . no, you didn't."

Tov shook his head, taking a seat. "Not to mention I nearly lost my mind by diving into your head."

"You volunteered," Andora huffed, glaring.

"I did." Tov nodded before clicking his mandibles. "But I didn't ask to wear your lover's face."

Andora choked at his words before quickly looking away in shame. Her words failed to move past her throat.

"And despite everything else, your loss would damn this galaxy." Tov sighed.

Andora hissed, clenching her fists. "I didn't ask for this."

"Neither did I!" Tov slammed a palm on the table.

Andora suppressed a flinch, turning to stare at the patriarch's outburst.

"I wanted to lead an expedition to find where the Starless went. I left my wife and child for years to come to this silent, forsaken place," Tov whispered, staring at his open hands. "I thought I was prepared to face the truth . . ." Tov quieted down, slumping in his seat. "How wrong I was."

He stared off into the panorama of space canvassed on the wall monitor, remaining frozen in the moment for a second and then another. Andora joined him, her mind a whirl of emotions as she waited patiently.

Their emotions ebbed into calm.

Eventually, Tov spoke again.

"I'm afraid, Andora," he confessed, turning toward her. Her eyes widened at his admission, at such trust in opening up to her.

He continued, still whispering, still sitting. "I've listened to your woes, but what of mine?" Tov waved his hand, pointing toward the Third Fleet. "I need to put up a brave front, the facade of a fearless leader, for the sake of my people. They need to know that here and now, everything is adaptable, achievable."

"Can't you tell Yan, Ohnar, or Volantesh?" she asked, sitting beside him.

He half shrugged. "My trusted companions know what's behind my act, but we rarely speak it out. We're all stubborn old warriors with our own pride. We've already faced worse and prevailed."

Tov sighed. "And sometimes, simply just being there and being reliable is enough. They know I can keep going, though I confess all three shared a quiet drink with me recently."

"But still . . ." he continued in a whisper. "I am afraid. Since then, I've learned the Starless has only grown more powerful and horrifying than ever, and I've faced Leviathans and the ceaseless hordes. I've discovered the truth of the puppet master and his cruel malice," Tov listed off with almost casual indifference, hollow and quiet. "Now, I am once again in the midst of a perilous Exodus, surrounded by enemies."

Andora felt a pang of guilt at having overlooked his plight. He had fooled even her into thinking that nothing held him down.

She'd forgotten he was a person, too.

"Through it all," Tov continued, "I found a terrifying AI war goddess teetering on the brink of madness who could wipe out the Third Fleet with a thought. I found out she had been fighting all this time against the unfathomable horde. Piling corpses high. And somehow . . ."

He turned to face her. "Somehow, I became close friends with that AI."

Andora blushed, turning away.

"And I want nothing more than to help her," spoke Tov, settling back into his seat.

Andora clicked her tongue, scratching the back of her neck. "You certainly have a way with words, and I'm getting mixed signals right now. Either you want me to go to therapy, or you're trying to lead me toward a threesome with your wife."

"Still a no on that second front, I'm afraid," Tov hummed. "I have two hearts in my chest. One is mine, and the other is my dear Starlight's."

"Your loss, then." Andora pouted before taking a deep breath, calming down. "You should still have told me all of this beforehand."

Tov sighed. "Maybe I should have. Maybe I should have had more faith that you would accept my reasons. Maybe I wanted a little payback for all the mischief you've caused. But, no . . ." He turned to her, bowing. "I am sorry."

"Ah, whatever . . ." Andora quickly waved him off, furrowing her brow. "No, actually, I deserve it." She bit her lip, running her hand over her hair. "I . . . I didn't have many friends. This is . . . taking time to get used to again. I should be the one saying sorry."

Tov buzzed. "Then we're on the same page."

Andora shrugged, slumping in her chair as she muttered, "I need a drink. Want one?"

"I won't say no to that," Tov said with a nod.

Two glasses appeared before them, a vintage from Tov's cabinet, one of many she had gifted him. He didn't seem to mind her borrowing it for the moment. As she poured her drink, Andora grew curious.

"Am I still terrifying?" she asked with a raised brow.

Tov chittered. "Oh, absolutely."

Andora smiled, sincere and warm, before it morphed into a familiar, cruel, sadistic grin as her thoughts drifted to their next destination, the prisoner detainment wing. "Good, because I'll need to be where we're going next."

CHAPTER 20

CAPTAIN'S PARLEY

First and foremost, we need information," Andora huffed as she walked the spacious hall with Tov. After their brief conversation, they promptly proceeded to *Citadel Irkalla*'s prisoner detainment wing.

Tov sighed. "We need many things."

"That may be. But here's a hypothetical situation," Andora posed. "Say two generals play a war game. One is a talented strategist, and the other is merely above average. However, the former isn't told the conditions of the game while the other knows it all." She glanced his way with a raised brow. "Who wins?"

Tov tilted his head in thought without breaking his step. In a few seconds, he answered, "It depends. If everything else is equal, such as army composition and the skills of the troops and officers below, then the latter wins."

"I think so as well," Andora agreed.

"However," Tov continued, "in our case, we have an immense moving bulwark and the apex of war machines. Nothing can challenge us in a head-on confrontation short of the Executor or a pack of Leviathans."

Andora furrowed her brow. "We have the biggest hammer, the toughest armor. But we're now moving at a snail's pace. Even still, it'll be our downfall if we underestimate our enemy based on what the pitiful strength they showed here."

Tov clicked. "Fear the daggers in the dark."

"And these cultists seem to be adept wielders of this type of trickery." Andora scowled in contempt. "I dread a guerilla war where we're too slow to retaliate, not to mention finding out what vulnerabilities we have that we're not seeing."

"Then it all flows back to information," Tov said.

Andora snarled, a bubble of fire encircling her heart. "A shame we haven't found a single one of those cultist scum here. Cowardly rats."

Andora hummed as her vision expanded throughout her Network, watching through the eyes of her drones that patrolled the disabled enemy warships before turning her attention to the prison wing.

Following the ambush of Zilla's Redoubt, the Exodus Armada had funneled all high-value detainees to this central location, from various captains of capital ships to chief engineers to marine commanders.

Much of what she saw matched the armada's earlier observations. The enemy force was split between two major groups. And with the information they'd collected over the hours, Andora slowly unveiled the situation.

Around 60 percent of the enemy forces belonged to a paramilitary group that called themselves the Oblivion Fangs.

From the brief snippets the armada had gathered, Andora learned that this organization acted as enforcers and racketeers. They were like an interstellar mafia that held the leashes of more minor factions and provided a semblance of order in these murky depths.

The Oblivion Fangs governed the Uraki Sector, a cluster at the edge of what humans called the Orion Spur. Uraki had the same pre-Cataclysm borders to an extent, although the maps they siphoned from the enemy ships presented a more nebulous territory that grew and shrank with its neighbors.

The Fangs escorted vital trade ships, protected food production, hunted those threatening their survival, and provided other essential services to those under their control.

Although the Uraki Sector contained nearly a million stars, most of what was surveyed was deemed low in value for colonization.

Thus, only a fraction of these systems were populated. In its heyday, Uraki housed nearly a hundred core star systems and thousands of frontier worlds, divided among those who called this area home.

Then, during the early years of the Cataclysm, the majority of the Uraki populace was forced to abandon this region due to increased Starless incursions.

The other half of the enemy force consisted of a mishmashed conglomeration of different groups—little more than pirate bands, scavenger guilds, nomadic warrior fleets, mercenaries, and hunters. Rats that wanted the leftovers the Fangs left behind.

What of the other sectors? Andora wondered to herself. Uraki was not a sector in the rim of the Milky Way, but neither was it in the so-called Heartlands, the area deep in the galactic center the old superpowers called home.

She calculated the estimated population of Uraki, the neighboring sectors of Tiran and Kaztan-Hanx, and the entire Dead Zone with the information on hand.

The Oblivion Fangs had capital ships, and while the Council had yet to determine if this was the full breadth of their military power, it still proved that an ecosystem capable of supporting and maintaining such an organization still existed—a lawless and brutal post-Cataclysm society.

Yet these were small fish in the ocean that was the Dead Zone.

She thought of other organizations, survivors hiding in the shadows. And it was clear the Fangs had masters. Unfortunately, the prime culprits, the orchestrators of this operation to eliminate seven Expeditionary Fleets, remained absent.

Based on their findings, the cultists and their fleet had broken off from the leading group to chase the Seventeenth and Fiftieth and promptly left with Scion Straise. Andora scowled upon learning that some high-ranking cultist had slipped through their grasp under the chaotic battlefield and interference.

He had been last seen aboard the *Mermere Diridion*, on the bridge with the captain himself. But any questions about the cultist's whereabouts produced nothing but confusing and contradictory answers, as if the crew suffered a hole in their collective memory.

She wanted to find that wretch and pick at his brain before putting him in a coffin with life support and chucking it out into the cold void of space for eternity. And she wasn't alone in that regard.

Nevertheless, the enemy commander, who remained indignant and silent, would make for a suitable substitute for her needs.

A surge of greed swelled in her heart. Andora had been starved of data in these dark woods for a long time, and now, a flashlight had fallen into her lap. All they needed was a direction to point it.

"Irkalla, to me," Andora summoned, and her Seneschal promptly flew down the corridor before perching on her forearm.

"*Hoot.* Good day, Creator," the owl AI greeted. "How may I be of assistance?"

Andora scratched underneath Irkalla's chin, garnering a contented chirp. "What is the state of our prisoners?"

"Two hundred thirteen thousand and five hundred thirty-six enemy combatants have surrendered. Approximately thirty-four percent of prisoners are in custody within the *Citadel* while the rest are being detained within their vessels," Irkalla reported.

Tov buzzed in thought as he reached out to pet the Seneschal, only for the owl to hurry over to Andora's other shoulder. He shrugged away the slight. "Have all of their warships been defanged?"

"Yes, Patriarch Tov," Irkalla replied. "Their power reactors are locked to provide just enough for life support. Their thrusters, weapons, and communications are also locked. Guards from all armada members patrol each vessel while the transfer is ongoing."

"What of the high-value prisoners?" he asked.

Irkalla preened her wings as she replied, "All accounted for and held within the Maximum-Security Detention Center, Patriarch. Currently, they are each being interrogated in turn by our resident experts."

"I'm sure our . . . *guests* . . . are eager to spill their secrets." Andora smirked before turning to her Seneschal. "What's the state of the enemy commander?"

"In stable condition," Irkalla replied, tilting her head one hundred and eighty degrees toward her creator. "Captain Varin surrendered the moment our marines boarded the *Mermere Diridion*. Though not without light resistance."

Andora shrugged. "He's alive, isn't he?"

"Multiple fractured ribs, a moderate concussion, internal bleeding, a ruptured kidney-like organ, second-degree burns in the—"Andora cut Irkalla's list off with a cough.

"Then all's well. We have more than enough medical nanites to heal him from such a state a dozen times." Andora waved her hand dismissively. "Honestly, as long the brain is in excellent condition, we can bring him back to a . . . workable state. Minus any permanent mental afflictions."

Tov winced at the thought. "Let us hope we have no need for something akin to necromancy, Andora."

Andora scoffed. "I have zero sympathy for him or any of the other caged rats. I'd pry the information from his head even if this Varin had been comatose."

"That is taboo." Tov slowed as he glanced her way.

Andora rolled her eyes. "He's a pirate who assisted Starless-worshipping flies, intent on killing our allies."

"And he'll face the consequences," Tov agreed. "As the future arbiter, I'll handle his case. But the main reason I protest is more for practicality's sake."

Andora raised a brow in his direction.

Tov continued. "Strong-willed individuals resist mental intrusions, particularly Ruzians. It's akin to performing brain surgery while that person is trying to punch you in the mouth. If we had a Dagataren spy, it might be different. But we have no other specialists in the craft of mind reading."

"We don't have to use psionics." Andora dismissed him with a dark look. "I can develop more brute-forced methods. He doesn't even have to survive."

Tov remained in silent thought until they reached their destination.

Before them were the triple-layered blast doors leading to the Prisoner Detainment Wing. On either side stood a pair of Mars's basset hound guard drones. These quadrupedal police machines the size of gray wolves sat at attention, their eyes scanning the two before barking in greeting.

The two briefly acknowledged them before continuing their conversation as the blast doors opened one after another.

"I'd advise against such extreme measures, Andora. From my experience, his type would never commit to this kind of operation without great incentive," Tov replied.

Andora raised her brow. "What could anyone want out here?"

"Plenty of things." Tov tilted his head. "Food, supplies, security . . ."

"Shelter, warships, people," Andora murmured, "Simple pleasures. Luxuries, even."

As the two leaders considered the matter, the doors opened, and they promptly stepped inside. The wing dedicated solely to housing prisoners and guards spanned before them like a miniature city. Every inch of the walls, ceilings, and floors had built-in security measures to monitor and temporarily disable any prisoner acting out of line.

With the tense situation, no one was in the mood for fooling around. The drone guards moved around like golems, menacing and overbearing.

Military police from the Third Fleet patrolled alongside them in platoons, coldly glaring at the prisoners while marching in lockstep. Other staff watched from behind plenty of protection, catering to the inmates' basic needs.

All the while, more prisoners were being funneled in from a far-off hangar. Debate on housing the remaining enemy crew had stagnated, with varying opinions from the council members.

Andora put the thought away as she and Tov walked down a hall far from the rabble in their orange prison garbs, heading straight for Max Sec.

"Perhaps apart from seeking a substantial reward, this captain is being threatened?" Tov suggested.

Andora clicked her teeth. "What we've already learned from the interrogations taking place right now is that none of these bastards have much love for the cultists. So, there's credence to what you say."

Tov hummed. "My gut is telling me this . . . Captain Varin . . . might be more receptive to our demands. We have to play our cards right."

She shrugged. "Good cop, bad cop?"

"What?"

"Nothing." Andora cleared her throat as they approached an elevator that led deeper toward Max Sec. "It's a human thing."

Andora and Tov stood behind a hidden viewing window, looking below them as two Third Fleet interrogators and the sole prisoner chained to the chair continued their verbal dance. The spacious, empty room held only a simple metal table in the middle with two chairs on either side.

Light from the singular orb above cast long shadows over the interior like an angry, judgmental eye.

One of the interrogators, a female Kurskann in a black uniform, sat calmly before the prisoner. The other, a burly Onin, moved behind his partner like a beast, stomping heavily with a heated glare.

This theater had been going on for an hour, and it was their second attempt. Andora and Tov had arrived just in time to observe.

"I stand corrected," Andora muttered under her breath as she stared at the two interrogators playing out the trope like a classic human crime drama. "I guess it's not just a human thing."

Despite the plain surroundings, Andora could feel the many security systems thrumming through the place. The Maximum-Security Detention Center, deep within the prison wing, had been securely designed by the combined intellect of the Third Fleet and AIs.

One core security measure was simple gravity control. The interrogators had set the room half a g higher than where a Ruzian felt comfortable, though it could be adjusted to disorient any species.

The gravity would swing like a pendulum, decreasing and increasing in random intervals or at the interrogators' commands.

But Max Sec's primary method to control and enforce its valuable and dangerous convicts consisted of countless pipes running beneath the walls, floors, and ceilings.

Each pipe carried a static stream of hungry gray goo.

The specially designed nanomachines loaned by Luna stood by, awaiting command and ready to immobilize or kill at a moment's notice.

Sometimes, the little robots would spread out from their hiding places like silver mold, nearly invisible against the white and gray backdrop of the facility's walls, writhing and undulating before disappearing.

Andora smirked at the ease of controlling them, a hint of sadism breaking through as she sent a single nanomachine to infiltrate someone's cell and nip at the prisoner's toe or nose like a pesky mosquito. She set the constant itch to pop up at random and ungodly hours.

She quickly dropped the innocent prank, partly because it grew stale but mainly because the interrogation before her began to occupy much of her attention.

The Kurskann interrogator spoke, tapping on the table with her clawed finger. "It will be in your best interest if you cooperate with us, Captain. We've presented the facts: You attacked Legacy fleets and commanded an operation that caused countless casualties."

Despite the ragged look and brace over his neck, Captain Varin looked bored and annoyed as he ignored the interrogator's words. He remained silent as the Kurskann officer continued to list his crimes for the second time since the interrogation had begun.

"And, most egregiously, collusion with cultist filth—"

"I had no choice." Varin finally broke his silence with a venomous hiss and a narrow glare. "You think I want to work with those abomination-worshipping crazies?"

The Onin scoffed. "You should have given your life to end their contagion."

"Don't assume to know anything, *dakha*," Varin hissed.

"Enough," the Kurskann interrogator warned them both before turning to the shackled captain. "Now that we have something to work with, perhaps you can enlighten us on the nature of your relationship with these . . . cultists."

The captain gritted his teeth, crossing his scarred arms that strained his orange jumpsuit. He yawned, "I'm a bit starved, little bug. Hard to talk with an empty belly. Tired, as well, after such a long battle. Maybe ask again later after I have a bath and some sleep." He leaned forward with a sly grin. "And if you want to join me in bed, I'm more than happy to share."

The lead interrogator ceased her tapping as the captain let out a chest-deep rumble.

"Not many of your kind in the Dead Zone, definitely none in my sector." Varin leaned forward. "Is it true that before your kind rebelled, Kurskann ladies used to be the best sex slaves in the gal—"

A giant fist banged on the table as the Onin officer growled at him. "Hold your vile tongue, pirate scum."

Varin raised his shackled hands with a snicker. "Ah, apologies, that was too far, yes?"

"Your words have been noted," the Kurskann interrogator flatly spoke. "But may I remind you of your current predicament? Cultists are monsters that have cast aside their souls and the souls of others. Their basic rights have been revoked. By associating with them and hiding information on them, we have grounds to give you similar treatment."

Varin snarled before leaning back. "I'm dead either way. You can take your threats and choke on them. Clearly, you value what I know, and I have no interest in playing games. So, get your bosses here." He yawned, closing his eyes. "I demand parley."

Seeing him fall to obstinate silence, the interrogators conversed silently through their implants.

Back in the observation room, Andora scoffed at the scene.

"Parley? Look at the balls on this one. Cocky shit," Andora sneered before glancing Tov's way. "Should we approve of more drastic interrogation tactics?"

Tov shook his head. "It's counterintuitive with him. The captain appears to be a pragmatic and keen individual. Based on my intuition, I can tell he's not overtly hostile with us, but he's wary and afraid despite that perfect . . . what do you call it?"

"Poker face," Andora replied with a frown.

"Yes, poker face." He nodded. "He wants to see if he can benefit from his situation. Inflicting pain will only cause someone of his position to dig in and completely turn against us." Tov sighed. "We have no leverage."

Andora grumbled. "I want to pull his teeth out, but you're right, damn it."

"Then let's get this over with."

After a moment's deliberation, Tov and Andora sent a silent signal to the two interrogators. Captain Varin raised his brow as they promptly left without another word, leaving behind the hardbound folders and other props.

They left him to stew in isolation for nearly an hour while Tov and Andora debated their strategy to wring out as much value from the captain as possible.

The prisoner in question merely settled in his seat, closing his eyes.

Finally, a change occurred as the artificial gravity returned to a comfortable setting. Varin began to breathe easier, rolling his shoulders and neck.

A second later, the doors opened, revealing two leaders in imposing regalia. The captain immediately knew them from their imperious and stern auras. Still, he remained nonchalant, even smug.

"About time, I was getting—"

"I'm surprised to see so many Ruzians in the Dead Zone." Andora silenced him with her abrupt statement. "Our initial survey tells me they comprise nearly forty percent of your force's demographic. Why is that?"

Varin tilted his head, pausing as he took her in—*really* took her, with a lecherous smile forming on his angular face. Andora narrowed her eyes as the captain leaned forward, blatantly ogling her shell.

"Now, what do we have here? I'm afraid I don't know your species, *hleki*." Varin hummed in delight as he stared her way. "Of course, there are many mysteries in the Dead Zone. Why not a beauty like you?"

Andora's eye twitched as Tov moved forward.

"I would show more respect, Captain. You are—"

"I know who you are," Varin interrupted as he glanced toward the patriarch. "Tov the Liberator, the Arbiter, the Savior. How's the Zone treating a legend like yourself?"

"About as wretchedly as the Cataclysm. Your attack has only exacerbated the situation," Tov replied.

Varin shrugged. "A sailor has to make a living. Times are hard, but that certainly hasn't stopped you from . . . sampling the exotic fauna." The captain leered back to Andora. "It's a pleasure to bask in the presence of such magnificent curves."

Andora retained her smile, but inwardly, her heart raged and snarled as unadulterated hate crashed against its cage and strained at its leash. Her fists clenched tightly behind her back as she stared coldly at the roguish captain.

"I want to gouge out his eyes and shove them down his throat, pull out his tongue and—"

"Calm, Andora," Tov interjected.

"Which is why I'm venting through our private comms, so forgive me for any unpleasant words, but I will smash his teeth in if he—"

"The females of my kind are rather flat in the chest area, you see. Nature decided they did not need such baggage. A cruel shame, I say." Varin sighed in lament before smiling at Andora again. "Luckily, I grew up amid diverse company, so I've developed a liking for you mammalian types—if that is what you are. One or two always seem to evolve brains in each sector, but you are quite a sight above the rest."

Andora felt a nerve pulsate angrily on her temple as she placed her hands on the table, seething with a thinly veiled snarl. "Does it make you more receptive to our needs?"

"Andora," Tov verbally warned as he slowly reached out to stop her.

"Andora, hm?" Varin tasted her name, licking his gold-plated crocodilian teeth. "How sweet. Sure, I can cater to yours if you satisfy mine."

Silence permeated the room as Andora felt a thread snap inside her mind. Without another thought, she smiled brightly. "If you continue to talk in this manner, I will beat you to an inch from death."

Tov froze at the sight, turning toward the captain with an almost pitiful look as he stepped to the side. It was a shame that Varin failed to see the warning sign, as he continued running his mouth and gambling.

"How about you crawl down here and—"

SLAM.

The loud noise sliced through his words as Andora suddenly kicked the table between them.

She launched it over Varin, her foot raised high to the sky. The captain cursed, a mix between a frantic hiss and startled gasp, as the edge barely missed him. Unfortunately, he leaned too far back, which resulted in him falling to the ground, still bound to his chair.

The table crashed behind the Ruzian, denting itself into an unsightly angle as Andora strode forth with a cold glare and cruel grin.

"Andora . . ." Tov called out.

Hearing him but ignoring him, Andora looked down on the captain as he struggled to free himself from his predicament. Upon seeing her, he chuckled in a sweat as he raised his hands from the floor.

"Now, wait a minute—"

Andora brought her foot down on a sensitive area. Tov recoiled in instinct as the Ruzian shouted and snarled in agony, his digitigrade legs flailing around.

She kicked the poor captain once more between the legs, then on his stomach, then moved to stomp on his face, shattering his teeth. Andora straddled Varin's waist as she clutched the collar of his prison garb and, with a balled-up fist, bashed and punched the Ruzian's snout. He tried to raise his bound hands to block her attack, but she merely batted them away. He tried to tell her to stop, only to choke on his own blood as it cascaded down his throat.

Again and again, Andora smashed Varin's face in silence, straining her synthetic muscles and tearing the skin off her knuckles.

BASH. BASH. BASH. CRUNCH.

"Andora!" Tov called out again, walking over and gently grabbing her shoulder. Andora stopped, fist bloody with both blue coolant and Ruzian orange blood. She looked down at her work. Despite wanting nothing more than to turn his head into a mound of gore, she settled for smashing it into a pulp.

The captain groaned, his face an utter mess as his eyes, puffy and already beginning to blacken, struggled to open. His reptilian snout sank inward, his nose wholly wrecked while his toothless mouth wheezed. The gold-plated biters lay strewn about on the floor.

Andora smiled, breathing in and out with a satisfied sigh. She turned to Tov, patting his shoulder.

"Relax," Andora replied as she summoned a vial of silver goo. "I wasn't going to kill him. I told you, I have plenty of medical nanites."

Uncorking it, she poured the contents over the pained captain. Unlike their voracious, piranha-like cousins, the medical nanites darted toward Varin's injuries. Loaded with information on Ruzian anatomy and recent scans of the captain's healthy state, the nanomachines quickly went to work.

Most traveled to his head, while a few went down south.

"What was it you said? Pragmatic and keen?" Andora scoffed. "Either seeing breasts shuts off his higher cognitive functions, or he's goading me."

Tov shook his head. "Well, he certainly bit off more than he could chew."

"He won't be biting anything now." Andora smirked as the nanites gathered the teeth and carried them back to Varin's mouth like ants with offerings.

She leaned down to whisper, "By the way, this will feel a bit . . . uncomfortable."

Varin stopped groaning, his brow quivering and furrowing. A sizzling sound began to emerge from the clumps of silver goo. Then, in unison, they pounced.

The captain seized up and then shouted. He flung jumbled-up curses and gibberish as he struggled against his bonds, the chair lifting off the floor and slamming back down.

Andora reached over to pull both Varin and his chair upright. Seconds ticked away as the nanites burrowed under the skin to treat more severe damage, eliciting a high-pitched shriek from the prisoner.

Finally, after a full minute, the nanomachines expended their limited energy, turning into a sludge of nutrients that Varin's body absorbed, rejuvenating his stamina and returning him to near-peak condition.

"OKAY! OKAY!" Varin shouted with a manic look in between breaths. "ENOUGH!"

Andora snorted, crossing her arms. She and Tov watched as the captain took in great lungfuls of cold recycled air, shaking off his sweat as he blinked away his fright. He calmed little by little and gulped as he glared at them both.

"Silent hells, that burns and itches something fierce," Varin complained. "But I haven't seen anything that can reknit bone and make me feel a year younger. Why would you waste such a treasure on me?"

Andora looked at her nails, shrugging. "For you, it is. For me, I consider it a paltry expense."

Varin recoiled, then sputtered into a laugh. "Paltry, she says. Ow, ow . . ."

He winced with phantom pain as he shook his head.

"Are you done, Captain?" Tov spoke up.

"Yes, I'm done! *Dakha!*" Varin shouted, raising his bound hands in defeat.

Andora snapped her fingers, unshackling the man as two drones entered the room. She and Tov moved back as the machines picked up the table she had kicked and bent it back into shape. Once it was presentable enough, the duo laid it back between them and promptly left.

Varin rubbed his wrists, looking at her and Tov questioningly before leaning back. "I heard from that cultist bastard and his cronies that there was something or someone that scared them to death. They think they're so secretive and mysterious, but I see everything in my ship. And they've been impatient, snappy, and jittery."

Andora raised her brow as she settled in her seat, summoning refreshments. "What else have they said?"

"Plenty," Varin replied, eying the food and drink before him. "Is beating a person half to death, almost castrating him, and offering such a bountiful feast afterward some sick custom of your species?"

"The carrot and the stick. But you and your loose tongue switched up the order." Andora shrugged as she poured everyone a glass of wine.

Varin smiled ruefully. "Hells . . . I've had a few rough bouts, but you have quite the temper. A racial trait, or . . . ?"

"No, she's just insane," Tov muttered low enough for only he and Andora to hear.

He cleared his throat, gesturing her way. "This is Secretary-General Andora Dietrich of the United Nations of Humanity. She is the custodian of the Exodus Armada."

Varin whistled. "Custodian, huh? So it's true then, a repeat of history before my eyes. My elders told me of that lofty role back during the apocalypse. But humanity? Hmm . . . never heard of them . . . How interesting."

Andora sipped her red, savoring it before setting it down. "As much as I want to discuss *several* topics of interest with you, Captain, we need three things. We can negotiate what we're willing to offer in exchange. First and foremost, we want to know everything about this operation: why you did it, who orchestrated it, when and where, everything, in exchange for you not dying."

"Not dying sounds good." Varin snickered as he gulped down his wine in one go. With his other hand, he gestured for her to go on. "And I'd rather not get my face beaten again."

Tov continued. "We also need information on your . . . allies . . . and why they targeted the Seventeenth and Fiftieth. In exchange, we can put you into witness protection."

"And third?"

"A complete manifest on the Uraki Sector, including any notable events that occurred as far back as six months ago, including maps, and information on your Oblivion Fangs and any major and minor factions."

Varin dug into his food, not bothering with utensils as he licked his fingers. "That's a lot of things. My knowledge is an expensive item, you know? Snitching is . . . bad for my reputation."

Andora scoffed. "Your reputation is irrelevant. Your Oblivion Fangs have been defanged horrendously after this fuck-up of an ambush. With so many warships rendered impotent, your territory is currently extremely vulnerable."

Varin snorted. "That's why I hoodwinked most of my rivals and other third parties into participating in this madness. They're now in the same situation."

Andora snorted. "What of the cultists? They still have their ships."

The captain remained silent, clenching his fists. He stared at them hard before responding in a low, severe tone, "I want my ship."

"Denied." Andora and Tov immediately shut his request down in unison.

"You can rip out her weapons, comms, hells, tow her if you want, but I want my ship and crew protected, and a few of my captains," Varin countered. "I want reduced sentences for them all, and . . . and I want a big favor."

Andora and Tov silently deliberated before the former spoke up. "We would consider a *minor* favor."

Varin scoffed, leaning back. "Forget the reduced sentences then, but I want that big favor."

"Within reason," Andora rebuffed. "To be discussed in detail at a later date. For now, we can have your ship docked on one of the surface berths on my Citadel. Your crew will be treated fairly and will be provided better accommodations."

The captain leaned back, pondering as he picked his teeth with his clawed finger. He clapped. "Fine, but I want it written on paper with your seals of authenticity." He turned to Tov. "You have the bearing of a judge, so I assume you've been made arbiter yet again, hm? Do this; give me your guarantee."

Another moment to deliberate later, Tov nodded. "Done."

Varin sighed, looking weary for a split second before leaning forward. "We would never do something like this unless we were truly desperate. Let me ask you first, how's travel in the Dead Zone?"

"Turbulent at best and unbearably chaotic at worst," Tov answered. "The hyper-tunnelers of our ships were fine-tuned to navigate the treacherous waters of this region, modernized and upgraded after a hundred years of study to calculate and create a stable tunnel efficiently. As I'm sure you know, the Miasma inhibits quantum communications and severely increases the risk of interstellar travel."

He paused. "Now that you mention it, without such technology, I'm not sure how your vessels can even go from one destination to the other without massively overshooting your point of entry or suffering accidents."

The captain guffawed, sneering at Tov. "You take your fancy tunnelers for granted. Here in hell, we must make do with antiques and skill."

"Manual navigation!?" Tov jumped up. "Are you—"

"Insane?" Varin laughed. "That we are, Arbiter. Our void seers have kept us afloat in every sense. They're our navigators, and their special sight can intuit the way. With a good cranial implant and plenty of experience, well, we get by." Varin grimaced. "At least, that was how it used to be, but now it's like the whole place is engulfed in a hurricane."

Andora and Tov resisted the urge to flinch at his words, knowing the reason behind the disturbance.

Varin snarled. "Then the cultists came to enlist our forces for some moronic mission. Somehow, the storm is their fault, because they definitely seem to have no problem navigating the Zone. I've always known their seers were superior, but this . . . We needed that."

"So, they dangled their navigation capabilities as a reward for an attack against seven fleets?" Andora grimaced.

The captain nodded darkly, staring at his empty plate before pushing it away, muttering, "What choice did we have? Without our seers, Uraki will collapse. Starve. I won't let my people starve again."

Andora narrowed her eyes at his tone, at the buried primal horror and dread.

"We heard a high-ranking cultist was on your bridge," Tov asked. "A liaison or a seer?"

Varin spat. "High Seer. A big shot that talked a lot of hot air, but the bastard was more of a mouthpiece for his cell leader, don't know anything beyond that. Still, he knew his stuff better than a dozen of our navigators combined. He could guide an entire fleet through a storm worse than the one happening now without a single loss. A few other cultist seers were guiding our splintered forces to bring the seven Expeditionary Fleets into one big flotilla, then lead them all the way here."

Andora smirked. "Then he abandoned you the moment we arrived."

"That that they did . . ." Varin shivered as he warily glanced her way in remembrance. "I assume that big ship was your people's?"

Andora smiled as she ignored his question. "You should be glad to hear that we're hunting these cultists."

Varin tilted his head before chuckling. "I see. Well, then I wouldn't mind knocking them down . . . Hmm . . . let's see . . . Ah! There's a refueling station a few tunnels from here. Brown dwarf, hidden in an asteroid field. Not of much note at first glance, since there's dozens of that kind in this neighborhood."

"So, what makes this one special?" Andora narrowed her eyes.

"I know for a fact that the personnel of that station are a bunch of Starless-worshipping scum. Cultists use that place to cater to their ships. I'm certain the *nuer dakha* passed by that way. You can start your search there." Varin grinned.

Andora prodded for more. "Do you know why they targeted the Seventeenth and the Fiftieth?"

Varin shrugged. "No clue. When we sprang the ambush, the Thralled warships did everything to separate them from the others. It worked. They could destroy them all, so I left it to them. Why?"

"Classified," Andora retorted as she briefly spoke with Tov in silence.

Andora and Tov glanced at each other. They immediately contacted their subordinates to act on this information. Andora returned her gaze to the captain, smiling greedily, eyes flaring.

Varin froze like a deer at the sight, subconsciously leaning away from the woman.

"It seems you have more to say, Captain Varin. You see . . . your actions have put us to a halt, so we'll have plenty of time to talk about it." Andora chuckled. "And I'm not leaving until I'm . . . satisfied."

The captain chuckled nervously. "Well, it's not like I'm going anywhere . . . I think I'll have more of that wine. Oh, and about that big favor."

Before long, the three discussed in length as the curtains slowly opened from their eyes.

Hundreds of millions of kilometers away, a stealth destroyer prepared to depart the system, carrying a certain Overseer and a team of operatives.

CHAPTER 21

PHANTASMAGORICAL

As the armada continued to get back on its feet, a four-hundred-meter warship ran through her preliminary checks.

After receiving clarity and a target from a certain high-value prisoner, the crew within received the go-ahead for their first mission and began spooling its state-of-the-art hyper-tunneler.

The sleek vessel shone like a piece of reflective obsidian before the thousands of individual cloaking plates shimmered, slowly turning transparent and disappearing into the void. Simultaneously, the potent reactor core at its heart thrummed with power as it pumped more and more power into its systems.

An invisible energy field encapsulated the destroyer, blocking all but a sliver of electromagnetic emissions, from radio waves to gamma rays.

Its supreme-grade stealth field even suppressed its gravitic presence, and the onboard Pneuma Bulwark had been tweaked to project a metaphysical cloak, with the goal of hiding from the average Starless or other psionic practitioners.

Suffice it to say that the SDS *Phantasmagoria* turned into an ephemeral ghost amid black waters. Her designers theorized that the destroyer would disappear like a fleeting wind should the chaotic interference of battle zones surround and blanket it.

A hidden dagger poised to strike, borne from the collaborative effort between Andora, the combat Overseers, and the best scientists, tech developers, and ship designers of the Third Fleet, as well as insights from Venus and Volantesh. The first of its kind, a Phantasm-class stealth recon destroyer. As an added flair, the vessel's hull and interior all incorporated frightening imagery and markings—skeletons, ghosts, and demons hiding behind smoke, dancing atop the decaying bones of Starless.

They had hoped to produce more from *Citadel Irkalla*'s shipyard. Unfortunately, the gargantuan command center's exterior dockyards could only construct, repair, and refit subcapital ships while on the move. Capitals placed too much risk for accidents and misalignments, thus delaying any massive project until the *Citadel* and the armada could come to a halt.

Nevertheless, the first Phantasm-class stealth destroyer approached the hypergate where the Thralled war fleet had fled the system.

By the estimates of the armada's chief strategists and analysts, the Thralled fleet led by this High Seer character neared their secret refueling station by the time Tov and Andora had successfully wrung information from Captain Varin.

With the knowledge of a hidden refueling station manned by cultist rats, the *Phantasmagoria* on standby preened in excitement.

Her crew of three hundred felt the same, but like the stealth destroyer they operated, each soul exhibited a quiet celebration and eagerness. As for the twenty-five operatives, divided into five strike teams, they practiced drills, conducted simulations, theorized tactics, and performed countless checks on their gear.

Amid these battle-hardened veterans, the sole AI aboard continued his farewells with his lover, who had stayed back on the *Citadel*.

"Keep my bed warm for me, love." Jupiter smiled in the darkness of his mind, seeing only the thin quantum thread that connected him to the admiral.

He could feel her shaking her head and chuckling as she replied in a breathy, tired voice, "Of course, as if I could just lay around all day."

"Get some rest, Yanny. You've been running yourself ragged." Jupiter sighed.

"Alright," Yan relented. "I've been meaning to catch up on my sleep anyway. I've reached my limit wrangling all these naval officers and their egos."

Jupiter snickered at the thought. He paused, lost for words, before sputtering, "I, erm . . . I'll see you in a couple of days, then."

Yan chuckled, buzzing pleasantly, making his body tingle and his soul blush.

She whispered as if right next to his ear, "Good hunting out there, Jupiter."

He smirked. "It will be."

The link disconnected, leaving him alone in his thoughts as he adjusted to his new condition.

Jupiter hummed as his custom heads-up display slowly filled his vision. Rows and rows of calculations and words appeared, detailing his telemetry to the point. Then, the data stream faded to the background as his shell's visual senses kicked in, displaying reality parallel with other visual overlays like heat, infrared sight, and a life sign detector.

"Urgh . . . This is weird . . ." Jupiter groaned as he took in his surroundings and mental state.

Before he could delve further into his status, a life-sized hologram of his older brother appeared before him in the middle of a gang of technicians.

"Are you sure about this, brother?" asked Mars as he crossed his arms. "You know how I feel about it."

Jupiter frowned, then realized his helmet blocked his face, the only area where he had synthetic skin. With a thought, the visor opened to reveal his usual face, though it appeared a tad bit smaller in his new shell.

"I need to feel useful again, Mars," Jupiter spoke, testing his vocal cords. "I'm not the scientist that Luna is, nor do I have the interest or ability to do what Venus does. I don't even have the processing capability to control this destroyer completely all the time, and I'd sooner delete myself than deal with logistics like Mercury."

He rubbed his neck with his clawed metal hands. "I mean, no offense to him, but I'm not suited to that type of monotonous work."

"You can always act as a military advisor, develop strategies, and maybe join the council meetings like Eldest wants," Mars said with a worried gaze.

Jupiter snorted. "No thanks. I can tell when that old witch is scheming, and she obviously wants to groom me into some leadership position. I'm way more than content with the people I'm around. Thinking of being in that growing den of wolves and snakes makes me nauseated."

"It can't be that bad. We do have a common purpose," Mars retorted.

"Oh, you sweet summer child." Jupiter rolled his eyes. "Maybe it's not bad now, but if we ever get more people, you'll see."

Mars sighed. "You're such a cynic. At least try. You might be good at it."

"If she wants me to join so badly, she can come over here and tell me, maybe say bye while she's at it. Nah, I want to hit something. But I'll compromise with her and do a bit of both." Jupiter smirked as he looked down at his hands. "I get to blow off some steam and ensure this ship and everyone aboard comes back to the armada alive. Why worry so much?"

Mars sighed, pinching the bridge of his nose. "That's because I don't want you going off to risk dying like an idiot . . . again."

"You're just jealous I get to play action hero while you're stuck playing general." Jupiter smirked.

"That's not true!" Mars sputtered with quivering brows.

Jupiter laughed, pointing at his older brother. "Hah, you are! What, getting bored behind the frontlines?"

"Quiet, you," Mars grumbled with an aggrieved shake of his fist. "This is different. Did you have to join this mission? You know you'll be heading into unknown and dangerous territory. The *Phantasmagoria*, even with all its protective measures . . ."

Jupiter shrugged his shoulders, lifting his sleek new pauldrons. "Hey, what's life without a little risk?"

"You disconnected yourself from your own Nexus!" Mars exclaimed, causing the technicians to back away from the irate hologram towering over the seated Jupiter and promptly leaving the room to the brothers. "At least in the *Zolann*, it was sufficiently protected, and had the entire armada by its side."

"Look, what's the point of a huge brain if I can only use one-fifth of it?" Jupiter huffed. "Transferring myself to the *Phantasmagoria*'s AI core is just better overall."

Mars crossed his arms, his gaze bearing down on his brother. "You don't feel anxious or disoriented?"

Jupiter pursed his lips, glancing to his side as he muttered, "Well . . ."

"Brother," Mars warned.

"Alright, alright." Jupiter rolled his eyes as he raised a palm. "It feels weird . . . Like going from a cracked aquarium to a tiny, shiny fishbowl."

He cleared his throat, shrugging. "Couldn't transfer all the water to my new 'brain,' but what use do I really have for software so damaged that Andora and Luna had to put it in stasis? I might as well leave it behind."

"True . . . your preset programs, fire controls, and sub-routines for something like the *Sisyphus* don't have much use if you can't leverage your Nexus's processing power without going catatonic," Mars conceded.

Jupiter nodded, pointing a thumb to his armored chest. "My memories, emotions, core, and subconscious are all I need."

Mars hummed, squinting his way. "That can't have been easy."

"Oh, it hurt for sure, but not as much as I expected." Jupiter winced, still feeling the phantom pain occupying a void in his mind. "Like I said, Andora and Luna already put a barrier between my healthy psyche and the damaged bits, so leaving it behind to continue repairs was manageable."

"What's it like?"

Peering into his mind, Jupiter pondered and reflected on his condition, trying to formulate the words for this ephemeral sensation. "It's like . . . I left something behind. Returning to the water analogy, the damaged bits were murky and stagnant, and there were a lot of them."

Clutter, junk, and trash polluted his software, and a sliver of it infected his core self in the form of trauma and nightmares. Jupiter couldn't separate himself from that part without lobotomizing himself.

"Now . . . I feel . . . not quite *pure*, but I can breathe a bit easier. Though it does feel cramped in a smaller AI core." Jupiter scratched his chin, furrowing his brow. "Maybe I can take this as a break of sorts. I'll transfer back after the mission and relink with you guys."

Mars sighed, rubbing the back of his neck. "That sounds good, I guess. Do you think this can speed up your recovery?"

"I think? Honestly, I just wanted something to do. If I waste away on the *Zolann*, then it won't do my mind any good," said Jupiter as he stood up from the bench.

His brother still looked concerned, pausing as he opened and closed his mouth. Finally, after a second of hesitation, Mars muttered, "It's just . . . if the *Phantasmagoria* goes, so do you."

"Look, I—" Jupiter stopped himself, clenching his fist as he looked away. "I'm not arguing with you again. Just because I nearly died once doesn't mean you get to baby me."

Mars shook his head. "You know that's not what I meant."

Jupiter grunted before sighing wearily. "I want . . . I *need* this. I've weighed all the risks and benefits. My presence here can keep these operatives alive, not to mention our kidnapped people, and if this mission is a success, then it proves that we could really use something like my project."

His brainchild, formulated after days of agonizing monotony and listlessness, was the result of trying to find a way to make himself useful. In the end, he had set up the foundations for an asset that could cover the weaknesses of the armada.

So far, he hadn't decided on a name for his project.

At its core, it was an elite special operations unit that could assassinate targets, rescue VIPs, sabotage critical infrastructure, and collect valuable intelligence, which could go a long way.

Together with a stealth destroyer like the *Phantasmagoria*, they had the ingredients to make a potent, swift, and silent strike force.

Mars's gaze bore down on Jupiter, searching and weighing his brother's face before he finally backed off with another sigh. "You're right. I'm sorry. I can't help but worry, but I guess all I can do now is support you."

"Thanks, bro." Jupiter smiled warmly in response.

For once, he finally matched his gigantic brother's height. Mars looked him up and down, eyes glowing as he rechecked his design.

"Is it alright?" he asked, shifting to speak strictly business.

Jupiter looked at himself in the feeds of the room's many cameras. With a hum, he raised and lowered his limbs, twisted and turned his body.

"I'm not used to being so tall," Jupiter grumbled. "Is this how you feel all the time, big bro?"

Mars chuckled. "The Poltergeist CWB-B-02 is my latest masterpiece. First, I imagined an apex hunter prowling the jungle unseen. Then, I incorporated elements for it to punch above its weight, able to detect and strike critical points while moving with supreme agility and dexterity."

Jupiter smirked as he examined his new body in closer detail. The Poltergeist took sleek, sharp, and sophisticated to a whole new level. Unlike his usual suit and tie, it looked more like the armor of a slender knight fused with a black-chitin xeno monster from a certain popular sci-fi franchise, right down to the bony-spiked tail.

The entire frame and internal architecture was made of a premier high-entropy umbral metal, a variant of the stealth plates used on the *Phantasmagoria*.

As such, it had the same illusory stealth, a ghost in a seven-foot frame.

He was armed with razor-sharp claws capable of projecting plasma edges that could slice through nearly any material and wrist-mounted monomolecular wires that could bind a target or turn them into minced meat. On his left shoulder were mounted Gauss cannons, and his right shoulder housed a light machine gun.

With opposable thumbs and adaptable hands, Jupiter could operate any infantry-sized weapon, and he had a plethora to choose from aboard the destroyer.

Jupiter smirked as he clenched his fists.

"I'm glad you like it, brother." Mars laughed, watching the Overseer flex and stretch his new body. "With this, should Lady Straise be deep within an enemy bulwark, you will have no trouble sneaking and slicing your way in while pinpointing her exact location."

"I feel like I can take on a legion of Starless pests," said Jupiter with a bloodthirsty grin before turning thoughtful and reflective. "Though, and this is by no means me being ungrateful, I notice the focus away from armor, acceleration, and overall firepower. Why is that? Why not design something like your Varangian?"

Mars snorted with a smug smile. "Hah! You think war is all about brute force and head-on confrontation? Subterfuge, assassination, deceit, and underhanded tactics are crucial aspects of ensuring victory!"

Jupiter stared at his brother with a flat look.

The red AI ignored him as he continued. "As for the design choices, I'm a firm believer in what the humans called endurance hunting. It may not be the fastest, but the Poltergeist is more flexible and long-lasting. As for the rest, you must sacrifice armor thickness with the spectral darksteel that makes up your body. You want stealth without bulk, so I found a sweet spot. Just don't get hit by a tank-grade railgun, and you'll be fine."

Jupiter rolled his eyes, "I'll try to dodge death then."

Mars cleared his throat. "Yes, well, in the case of firepower. You don't need brute force when striking vulnerabilities. Apply the most optimal amount, and you can cripple your opposition. Again, fight like a hunter. Prowl the battlefield, stab the heart."

"I think I get the idea. I'll cook up some custom martial arts for this beast." Jupiter nodded, then turned to Mars with a raised brow. "Also, Poltergeist? Isn't that some kind of banshee or ghost or something?"

Mars smirked. "A noisy spirit, to be exact."

"You insinuating something there, bro?" Jupiter huffed with narrow eyes.

Mars whistled innocently as he stared at the wall.

Jupiter shook his head. "Whatever. How many of these things are there?"

"You have the primary one that you're wearing and nine others aboard," Mars counted. "Those nine don't have your ugly mug behind those helms but robotic faces with some extra-sharp fangs. Oh, and you also have your old human shells for casual use, as well as several lesser drones in case of emergency. You should be able to operate five Poltergeists while managing the *Phantasmagoria* in the background, yes?"

Jupiter closed his eyes, reaching out with his mind to connect with four of the remaining nine shells that filled the room. Each one jolted before smoothly standing up and coming to attention behind him.

Jupiter still sensed the destroyer's systems in the back of his mind but started to feel a strain. Bit by bit, he lessened his attention on everything but his current shell.

He grumbled. "Yeah, I think so, but I'll have to shift my focus as necessary. In this one, I'm running at peak efficiency. The rest will run at half. I'll have to compensate by running the Poltergeist's built-in AI whenever my consciousness is absent."

For the next minute, Jupiter tested his thoughts as he possessed each Poltergeist.

Satisfied, Jupiter opened his eyes, sighing. "I'll need more practice."

"What about the destroyer?" Mars asked. "If you abandon the Poltergeists, can you take full control of her?"

Jupiter half nodded. "I can't manually control and micromanage its extensive systems all the time, but I can during an emergency. Acting as an assistant for the organic crew is more efficient and multiplies our effectiveness by leagues. Even without me, the AI core is a beast of a processor, and I trust the bridge will run things smoothly. With them behind me, I should be able to pick and choose which Poltergeist deserves my full attention."

That meant six: five Poltergeists and the destroyer herself.

Mars nodded. "Then each strike team has one of you present."

"With one of these bad boys accompanying each strike team." Jupiter smiled. "Hell, we can do anything. It'll be like pitting a scalpel against a dreadnought-sized hammer."

"How are the teams, by the way?" Mars inquired. "I heard the positions there were highly contested."

Jupiter shrugged. "Only the elite of the elite gets to be in my spec ops unit. I made my intentions known and let Tov and his people sort it out. All I know is that the command team is led by one of the Vraken. The rest are picked from the other branches of the Third Fleet, hoping to expand and including peeps from the rest of the armada."

"I see." Mars nodded before sighing, sucking his cheeks. "I'd like nothing more than to accompany you in this mission."

"And bring your *Bucephalus*?" Jupiter snorted. "You'll scare away the rats the moment you enter the star system."

The red giant grumbled. "I know . . ."

"Oi, don't think about doing what I did—" Jupiter warned before Mars cut him off.

"I'm not so foolish to do such a thing. If I tried, I'd likely go into shock and permanently damage my psyche," Mars huffed. "But an AI can dream, can't he? It's like I'm stuck playing a real-time strategy game, moving ships and enacting orders while managing my resources."

He took off his helmet to run his hand through his curly, short hair, smiling. "And you get to play a first-person shooter . . ."

Jupiter frowned. "I'd rather go back to how it was."

"I'm sorry, that was insensitive of me." Mars shook his head. "I know this isn't by choice."

Jupiter sighed, feeling the fabric of space thinning. "I have to go. We're close to opening the hypergate, and I need to check in with the guys I'll be bunking with." He raised a fist toward Mars. "I'll see you when I get back."

"Come back safe, little brother," Mars replied, bumping his brother's fist with his own.

"I will, and I'll bring the good news, I promise," Jupiter said with a smirk.

A second later, Mars's hologram winked away, leaving Jupiter alone in the room. He sniffed, doing the motions as he further tested the dexterity and balance of his shell. Before long, Jupiter left the armory, moving across the destroyer on his way to the strike teams' barracks.

Upon arrival, Jupiter located the command team's dorm, knocking before entering.

Inside, Jupiter met with five individuals in sleek, obsidian-like combat armor. Each had quirks and tailored appearances that shared similarities to Jupiter's Poltergeist, which was more humanoid and less bestial.

All but one had their helmets off.

The team leader moved forward, a Kurskann with dark blue chitin and clear markings of Tov's honor guard. He reached forward with an open palm. Jupiter responded to the handshake, smiling as they formed a circle. "You are . . . ?"

"I am Lieutenant Orius Garesh'Krast of the Vraken," he responded. "You can call me Orion."

Jupiter raised his brow. "Orion?"

"We've decided to use human-derived code names for ease of use. Is that acceptable?"

"Sure, why not." Jupiter shrugged. "Good to meet you, Orion. Is the entire task force ready for the mission?"

"Eager," Orion chittered.

Jupiter chuckled, crossing his arms as he took in the rest of the command team. "Guess you know who I am. Jupiter, ex-Overseer, and head of this budding task force. So, let's get introductions out of the way. Orion?"

"Right then," Orion spoke, clearing his throat as he faced Jupiter. "Since you're essentially a tech specialist without equal, we've prioritized adding more psi artists to our ranks. I agree with this approach and have poached the best for our team. We have two; I will introduce them first."

Two individuals stepped forward. Orion gestured at the small but wiry Frae male. "First of the pair is this fellow. Merlin is what we call a guardian-variant telekinetic."

"Sergeant Monin Quim. I enjoyed the Arthurian legends and thought the wizard was cool," Merlin replied, his skin freckled and leaf-green. He extended his hand, shaking Jupiter's as he greeted the AI.

"What does guardian mean?" Jupiter asked.

Merlin raised his palm, pointing toward the operative beside him. Suddenly, a shimmering forcefield surrounded the recipient, ebbing and bending space. "I project barriers to encapsulate a target. It's a psionic shield, basically."

Jupiter whistled as he pressed his finger against it, feeling only a slight give despite the force he put into it before being repelled. He nodded, rubbing his fingers. "How effective?"

"It's more effective against energy-based weapons and non-solid matter," Merlin explained. "Kinetic projectiles are more difficult to block. It can also shield against mental intrusion, though nowhere near as effectively as the Choir's songs."

"It's better used in conjunction with conventional tech," Orion added as he activated his suit's protective measures. "With a psi barrier added to energy shields and armor, any of us can have three layers of direct defense."

"Can you apply this barrier to multiple people?" Jupiter asked Merlin.

"I can, but without constant maintenance, it loses coherence and eventually fades. When I focus on one person, I can better manipulate the barrier and increase its strength," Merlin replied.

Jupiter nodded as an idea formed in his head: "Hmm . . . if there's a fabricator here, I can make a personal grav module. Your telekinesis should be amplified if a fundamental force works alongside you."

Merlin took in a lungful of air before breaking into a grin. "That'd be awesome."

Orion moved to the next operative. "This is Augur; she's our psi marksman."

He pointed toward a tall, thin female soldier with gray skin and large, milky eyes. She had a prominent external ocular implant and an impassive, almost dead expression.

"Sergeant Souon. I am Keeta." Augur bowed as she spoke in a strange, curt manner with a soft, breathy, and monotonous voice. "Third Fleet Marine Sniper Cadre. Category Two, prescience. Record is point forty-seven seconds. Passive hazard and hostility detection."

Jupiter widened his eyes upon hearing her ability.

Suddenly, he threw a lightning-quick jab toward the marksman's face, only for her to tilt her head to the side. Jupiter had no intention of doing anything but leaving a nasty bruise and broken nose, but Augur nonetheless dodged with her eyes closed and an inch to spare.

"Holy shit!" Jupiter exclaimed as he retracted his hand. "You really do have spidey senses."

She stared at him with half-lidded eyes. "I do not know this term."

"Look up Spider-Man from the human database, and you'll get it." Jupiter smirked, hopping excitedly as he turned back to Orion. "Prescience is going to be a freaking cheat code."

"Her type of psionic ability is rare in the galaxy. Keetas have the best propensity for it, but they were savaged during the Cataclysm, and prescience nearly became a lost art. Their population is still recovering to this day," Orion explained.

"Another thing to note is that she can only use her sight within the immediate vicinity. The less chaos, the better her senses," continued the lieutenant before adding one more crucial tidbit. "If she manages to see a second into the future, then she'll be considered a Category Three. She's just about halfway there."

Jupiter felt his enthusiasm dampen slightly, yet he remained impressed as he nodded toward Augur. "Hope to see that happen, Augur."

The Keeta woman nodded.

Next on the team was a familiar race. The tall and hefty Kurskann male had a face more akin to a beetle than a wasp. Clad in extra layers of ceramic plating and blast-resistant armor, the sergeant shook Jupiter's hand.

"Goran Garesh'Mar, grenadier," he introduced without Orion's input. "You can call me Ritter! I like the German language and knights. I'm the team's demolitions and heavy weapon expert," Ritter explained, chuckling with a low and deep buzz. "I don't have magic, I'm afraid, just good and reliable boom."

Jupiter snorted with a smirk. "I like your style. I'll take a look at your explosives and see if I can improve them."

"Only if I can watch." Ritter laughed before stepping back.

Finally, Jupiter turned his attention to the last member, the only one with a helmet still on.

"And finally . . . Puck, our team medic, biohazard and chemical weapons expert. Also, our good luck charm." Orion hummed with a hint of chagrin.

The helmet visor turned transparent, and Jupiter instantly recoiled, groaning loudly as he turned away.

"Oh, fuck off," he cursed, grimacing and grumbling as he glanced the medic's way.

Before him stood Kelios fon Telmos e Duchelein, otherwise known to him as *that bastard.* His perfect, youthful, noble, ivory face gleamed as if permanently basking under a radiant sun. His curly, shiny bronze hair cascaded down and framed his face elegantly and heroically.

Jupiter hated him.

"Sir Jupiter! This one reports for duty!" The navy corpsman grinned to reveal an immaculately white smile.

Jupiter let out a chest-deep sigh, pinching his eyes as he desperately wished the bane of his existence away. "Why are you here?"

"To serve! What else is there but the romance of duty?" Kelios poetically chimed. "Such a task force requires an adept hand in the bloody work of bodies, and this one's humble skills volunteer for the task."

"I'm a machine. Unless you have lubricant and a screwdriver—"

"More than enough, dear Jupiter." Kelios grinned, patting his left pouch, opening it, and revealing cans of maintenance oil and many tools.

Jupiter snorted, rolling his eyes before turning to Orion. "Is he actually qualified?"

Orion nodded without hesitation. "His records speak for themselves. Kelios has the right mindset, despite his . . . artistic eccentricities. Being an Evorian grants him innate resistance to diseases and other malignancies. He's a tough one. The team and I approve of his presence."

The corpsman in question interceded, bowing with a flourish. "I heard that the lady of the Seventeenth Fleet has been kidnapped. Recently, I learned the human word *chivalry,* which resonates with me deeply. I hope to save the damsel in distress while capturing the essence of chivalry. Perhaps it will serve as inspiration for future roles."

The rest of the team clapped, enamored like a gang of enraptured fans.

"Maker above, you are insufferable," Jupiter muttered behind his hands as he palmed his face. "You sure this bastard doesn't have some mind-fucky psi powers?"

"I resent that accusation!" Kelios stomped with a level of grace. "No offense to those who practice the mystic arts, but I do not need such crutches to dazzle and impress upon the masses."

"Forget I asked." Jupiter shook his head before wagging his finger. "But I have my eye on—"

[Attention, attention. Entering hypergate in one minute.]

Jupiter sighed, shrugging. "Whatever. We have much to do before we reach the shadow station. What's first?"

"You're not used to infantry tactics, I assume?" Orion asked.

"I have a vague idea," Jupiter confessed. "I used to control legions of infantry drones, but they rarely saw decisive action against the Starless. You could say I'm more optimized for ship combat and fleet tactics."

Orion chuckled, clasping his four hands behind him as he motioned for the team to proceed to the training hall. "Then we'll start there, cadet. You'll be a fully-fledged specialist by the time we arrive at the target system."

"Don't worry, Sir Jupiter." Puck beamed, patting Jupiter's back and sticking to his side. "Your seniors will show you the ropes."

"Great . . ." Jupiter mumbled, feeling dead inside as they left.

Before the seconds finished counting down, Jupiter sent another quick and loving "see you in a bit" to Yan through their private comms.

He missed her touch already.

CHAPTER 22

TRAPPED FLIES

Three systems away from Zilla's Redoubt, amid a dense pocket of asteroids, orbited a single lifeless white-and-blue planet.

The frozen hellscape held little value. Anything of notable worth, such as the seas of methane, lay hidden beneath kilometers of ice. The lackluster shine of the failed brown dwarf star barely provided any light and heat to the barren place, forever trapping it in stasis.

Languid, cold, and hollow of any value, the nameless system and planet continued its existence, indifferent.

But such a thing didn't hold true within a ramshackle, rusted-red refueling station. The ovoid, kilometer-long monolith made its home behind the shadow of the ice world, occasionally harvesting the trapped methane below and fusing it with other junk compounds to synthesize a cheap and quick-burning fuel for passing starships.

Yet none of its usual gunk-producing operations occurred on this day.

Instead, the one hundred and twelve personnel, workers, and guards within the station all moved about in frantic haste, carrying tons of cargo and loading them onto the corvette, frigate, and freighter docked to each of the three hangar bays.

Ein jogged as he carried a box of data tablets, folders, and manifests toward the downstairs incinerator, cursing the station chief's irreverence toward the proselyte's High Seer.

His fellow cultist carried another box. Ocus was the station's void seer and a prominent figure in the area. For a decade, she had provided paid service in determining the state of the surrounding hypergates, earning the chief's favor and the influence of many a ship captain.

Ocus's usual arrogance faded as she warbled in thinly veiled frustration, "Move your legs, brother. I will not be left behind to die at the hands of heretic Phages and their machine overlords!"

I hope you do, witch, Ein thought venomously. He'd prayed countless nights for her to be reminded of her place, but did he also have to be caught in the crossfire? Perhaps it was fate's repayment for his own sins.

Ein sighed in regret as he and Ocus made their way down the dirty, trash-filled corridor, its walls lined with graffiti and hidden symbols of their faith.

"Worry not, sister. I've made sure the *Temin*'s captain won't leave without us," Ein hissed indifferently. "She owes me a great debt for keeping her blasphemy hidden; this is but a step in clearing it."

Ocus scowled at him, scoffing. "And what if she decides your death would better keep the silence, oh vice chief?"

"Be silent yourself, Ocus." Ein clicked his tongue, glaring at his companion. "I've sent Kroole to board the High Seer's flagship. If I fail to return to the Acropolis, he will reveal everything, and the godless wench, her precious frigate, and all her misbegotten kin shall be hunted and flayed before our lord."

Ocus snorted in reply, saying nothing more as they approached the elevator.

"Finally," Ein grumbled, thumbing down the call button. "My suit's exoframe is getting rusty."

However, pressing the button returned no reply. Ein thumbed it down harder, waiting another minute yet receiving the same outcome. He hissed, slapping the control pad.

"Move." Ocus shouldered him to the side as she set down the box. She opened the pad and inspected the wiring. "Nothing is wrong, there's just no—"

The lights shut off, startling the two as the hall plunged into darkness. A second later, the emergency lights bathed the interior in a harsh red light. ". . . no power," she finished.

Ein cursed as they moved to the intercom beside the elevator, switching to the engineering bay and calling the station's chief engineer. When the other end picked up, the vice chief immediately complained, "Vami! What happened to the reactor?"

The other line crackled before a disgruntled voice replied, "Chief wants the fuel rods loaded up, so I sent my guys to shut off the main reactor."

"What!?"

"Relax," Vami huffed. "The backup generators will keep everything working long after we leave this place."

Ein gritted his teeth, seething. "Is that so? Then why is the elevator at Section C9 not working!?"

The other line paused for a pregnant minute, then tentatively spoke up. "Have you tried pushing the button?"

Ein vehemently cursed up a storm, causing Ocus to back away from the volatile brother. After a minute of venting, he shut off the link and picked up his box.

"We're taking the stairwell."

As the two cultists went farther down the red-bathed hall, thick air and a sense of worry surrounded them as the circulation glitched.

"Wonderful. Now the vents have stopped working. Maybe we'll suffocate before the heretics find us," Ocus muttered, a cold sweat trailing down her mud-colored scales.

"Their armada is busy worrying about the wounded fleets." Ein pressed his lips into a thin line. "Though . . . to be safe, we should board the *Temin* after incinerating all this."

Ocus glanced his way with furrowed brows. "You want to abandon the cadre?"

"Send a message to the faithful, but leave out those loyal to the chief," Ein ordered with a cold gaze.

The seer hummed in thought before nodding. "Very well."

I would abandon you too, but I need your sight, Ein thought.

"A fitting fate for a follower of greed instead of Absolution," he seethed, then yelped as his foot caught on a rusted hole in the floor a second later.

"*Detwa!*" Ein tugged his steel boot free, cursing as he increased his pace toward the stairwell. Upon arriving, he promptly shouldered the door control. It failed to open, and he felt a nerve pulsate on his forehead.

Ocus stepped up, kicking the panel. That finally opened the way to the stairwell, and the two carefully made their way down while balancing the heavy box in their hands.

Ein hissed, grunting as he walked down. "Because of him . . . Because of *him*, the High Seer . . . left us behind . . . to clean up this mess."

"If it were up to me, we would have already left this ancient scrap heap, *and* blown it all to bits before leaving," Ocus seethed.

"On that, we agree." Ein nodded. "The years have made Bort forget his true mission to the cell."

The duo reached the floor below, making their way through the grid-like maze of corridors and passing the occasional team of workers stripping the station of components. Ein shook his head at the sight and wasteful use of their limited time but summarily ignored them.

After taking a final turn, they headed straight toward their destination.

"Let's get this over with then," Ein grunted as they dropped the boxes before the massive incinerator. The behemoth machine took up most of the room. Even in its passive state, it raised the ambient temperature to an uncomfortable sweltering heat.

The two cultists switched on their suits' temperature regulators and breathed a sigh of relief, yet the overbearing warmth still permeated their senses.

It only worsened as Ein switched it on, and a metallic roar surged from within the machine.

He opened the hatch and quickly began throwing in tablet after tablet, folder after folder. Years of intelligence collected from their contacts all over Uraki atomized in an instant. Ein felt nothing for it except a fleeting lamentation of things coming to an end.

But a surge of ambition lit up in his heart at the thought of becoming the new cadre chief once he returned to the proselyte's side and delivered the news of Bort's . . . blasphemy.

Suddenly, the inferno within the machine sputtered, coughing before slowly powering down. Ein cursed, seeing they still had a few more items.

"Check the internals," Ein ordered Ocus.

The seer promptly did so, unscrewing the panel on the incinerator's side and peering inside. She swiped away her sweat before shaking her head. "It's not getting enough power. I'll call Vami."

She moved to the intercom by the door, pressing the button. "Engineering, Vami, can you check the—"

Suddenly, a subtle shake reverberated across the station, and a high-pitched whine blasted through the intercom. The duo winced, covering their ears until the source of the noise blew in a flash of sparks.

"What in Pandemonium was that?" Ein squinted, shaking off the ringing in his ears as he looked at his companion. "Well?"

"No clue. Let me try my wrist comm," Ocus grumbled as she raised her arm. A second later, someone picked up on the other end. "Vami, are you there?"

Ein grumbled under his breath. "He's going to say how his guys are handling it."

". . . *ksshk* . . . Yeah, I know what you're gonna complain about, and I'm telling you that my guys are on it," the chief engineer reported through the fuzz. Ein rolled his eyes as Ocus glared his way.

"Something flipped with the backup generator," the engineer continued. "The old piece of crap probably blew."

Ein snarled, grabbing Ocus's wrist and shouting through, "Well, tell your *guys* to hurry up and prioritize power to the incinerator room. We're on a tight schedule."

"You don't have to remind me, Ein," Vami spat before closing the link.

Ocus pulled her wrist from the vice chief, glaring at him before pinching her nose. She sighed, throwing her hands in the air. "Who knows how long it'll take to get power back on? I'll see if I can reroute power from the breaker on this floor."

"Do so. Keep in touch through comms." Ein waved his wrist.

The seer nodded and left without a word. The vice chief focused on the machine, peering around its insides. A minute later, his wrist beeped, and he opened the link.

"Ein, I've shut off gravity and life support on some of the rooms here," Ocus said. "Try turning the incinerator on and off now."

He did so, and with a sigh of relief, the beast roared back to life. Ein checked the readings, still seeing a few hiccups.

"Can you shut off a few more systems? It's not enough."

"We don't need to atomize them," Ocus grumbled through the comm. "Just throw them in the fire and be done with it."

"Fine, whatever," Ein hissed as he violently threw more items into the fiery maw. "Just get back over here and call Jaxara to gather our circle. We'll proceed directly to the *Temin* and meet them there."

"Heard. I'm rounding the corner. I'll be there in a minute," Ocus replied.

Ein sighed as he stretched his back, momentarily lamenting his age and the lack of rejuvenation treatments. He bent back down, picking and throwing, barely looking at the contents to check if something was valuable enough to pocket.

"*Tsk* . . . useless," Ein muttered.

It was to be expected that Ein had already made copies of the vital intelligence from the chief's terminal. He patted his chest pocket and the small data drive within. He excused it as a contingency plan, should things between them sour.

Finally, after throwing the last item into the machine, Ein breathed a sigh of relief and wiped away his sweat. He rubbed his neck, thoughts turning to the future.

He tilted his head, glancing toward the door, then clicked his tongue. Ein brought up his wrist once more, contacting the seer. When it connected, he spoke in an aggrieved and impatient voice, "Right, that's that, Ocus. Where are you?"

KSSSHK . . .

The other side crackled. Ein winced at the noise, furrowing his brow.

"Ocus, where are you?" he asked again, looking toward the open door and the red-lit corridor.

KSSSSSHK . . .

Ein turned back and shut off the incinerator. The incessant growl and invasive heat quickly dissipated, releasing the burden on his mind and ears.

However, he felt no relief as a growing dread raced across his mind, prompting him to call again. "Ocus!?"

KSSSSSSSHK . . .

Nothing but static, no matter how long he waited.

His brow furrowed, his fists clenched, and he moved low, guided by instinct and decades of experience. His heart thumped in his chest as he tentatively stepped to exit the room.

Step. Step.

His metal boots pressed against the rusted floor and kicked aside bits of scrap and trash.

Step. Step. Step.

Ein stopped just before the door, leaning out as he checked the left, right, and forward corridors. He called out, not through the comm but down the hall in a loud whisper: "Ocus? This isn't funny, you witch."

No one responded, nothing but a dreadful moan of stale air.

Thump. Thump. Thump.

The vice leader felt his heart beating aggressively in his chest, reverberating as a bead of sweat trailed down his forehead. His breathing quieted down as his back shivered ever so slightly.

He left the room, his hand reaching for the laser pistol. With a tap, his helmet furled around his head and flared to life with its heads-up display.

It was then he noticed the silence. Never mind the absence of the incinerator's roar, even the ambient hum beneath the walls and floors had disappeared. Everything felt muted and numb. Ein shook his head, wondering if the stress was getting to him.

What came next erased such a notion.

The red emergency lights flickered and then dimmed to a dull luminosity. Darkness crept forward, claiming its dominion inch by inch.

Ein checked the readings on his helmet and froze with worry. Life support within the floor had shut down entirely, and the air was slowly growing stale and bereft of oxygen.

His suit automatically siphoned the remaining precious gas into its tanks, and Ein immediately began to ration his breaths.

Moving quickly, he stormed toward the stairwell, noticing that the few work teams that had occupied the halls were now absent.

"What is going on? Did they begin evac?" he muttered, tapping his wrist comm to contact engineering. "Vami? What's happening to the station?"

KSSSHK . . .

Ein gulped, switched to another name on his contact list, and then to the general frequency. "Jaxara? Anyone!?"

KSSSSSHK . . .

"*Detwa!*" Ein cursed, slamming a fist against the wall to his side.

Ein reached the stairwell, pursing his lips before going toward the hangar level. He raised his comms, hesitated momentarily, and bit the bullet. His dissatisfaction with his chief paled in the face of this situation. "Leader! Are you there? Life support is down on the lower decks. I'm heading to the main hangar bay. Where is everyone?"

Nothing.

Ein despaired, realizing that comms were being jammed. He pushed down feelings of panic as he waited, fearing the worst when—

"Ein . . . ? *Ksshk* . . . The station is under . . . *kssshk* . . . unknown . . . too . . . monsters . . . ! *Ksshk* . . . head to . . . bay . . . out . . ." the crackling and fuzzy voice of the station chief replied in a garbled mess.

"Attack? Monsters?" Ein muttered, his mind racing.

He hoped it was the divine beings, but he sensed none of the usual indications of their presence—not the soothing songs they whispered nor the all-encompassing warmth.

Instead, the emergency lights shut off completely, leaving him isolated in the darkness.

A shiver raced across his spine as fear of the unknown planted its flag on his mind. He pulled out his laser pistol, switched on its flashlight, and pointed it forward. He attempted to call the *Temin* but failed, receiving nothing but static. Nonetheless, he still sent a message that he was on his way.

To hell with it, he thought as he made his way to the hangar. Once there, he'd force the *Temin* to take off with or without his cadre.

As he took another step, a scream echoed down the hall. The bloodcurdling shriek shook the walls before vanishing without a trace, leaving a conspicuous silence behind.

Ein promptly took a detour, breathing in the limited oxygen quickly as his legs propelled him forward. Another panicked shout, another detour.

Then, the first proof of resistance from his comrades came as four shots barked out from somewhere deep in the station, kinetic slugs echoing and shaking the hall.

In response came a long whine, followed by a flash of blinding light bleeding from the hall in the distance. A split second later, an explosion of thunder drowned out all sound. Ein stumbled and yelped as his ears rang from the shockwave and lingering electric discharge.

No further gunshots followed, not even wails of pain, at least none that he could hear.

The silence affected him more than anything. A moment of paralysis kept him on the floor as frayed emotions bucked within his head. Slowly, his concerns for the future faded with the onrush of his instincts.

He stood up, launching himself forward in a half stumble. In a minute, he picked up speed and ran through the darkness, the cone of his flashlight moving forward and down as his arms swung and pumped.

Shadows appeared then left, and the cursed silence pressed down on his mental state like a rusty weight.

Ein heard a loud stomping echoing far behind. He gasped; air caught in his throat as he turned a corner again. His helmet's mini-map showed him the way, adjusting with every detour he made.

A ghostly shriek wailed across the station, bestial and mechanical, coming from all sides. The infernal noise disoriented him, piercing through his helmet and drilling down into his skull.

Ein slipped on something slick and wet, slamming face-first on the ground and denting the metal floor. He groaned, lifting his head as he blinked, only to see he had landed in a pool of fresh blood.

He shuddered, looking around but seeing no corpses, only dragged stains as if the poor bastard had been pulled into the abyss.

Ein picked himself up, slamming his foot down and breaking into a full-on sprint, still gripping his pistol with white knuckles. He couldn't tell nor did he care where the noise came from, whether it was a fellow faithful or some demon. He didn't want to know.

His mind filled only with one directive—*run*.

More footsteps, this time sounding like the run of a landbound predator, raced from the darkness, the source never revealing itself.

Ein found more evidence of a battle—no, a slaughter. Slashes marked the wall, tearing great chunks from the metal and spewing its wires like guts. Shell casings littered the floor alongside abandoned weapons.

Still, no bodies.

There was only blood, the smell of ozone, and the phantom sounds of distant hunters prowling unseen in the edges of his vision.

Ein reached a corridor with an exterior window and saw the frigate still docked at the main hangar. He raised his wrist, once again calling the *Temin*'s bridge.

Still nothing. Ein cursed, panicking. "Where is everyone!?"

Ein paused, squinting at a shimmering shape far off in the void. He blinked, now seeing nothing but space, but noticing the powered-down anti-ship cannons that lined the station.

He ignored it as someone else's problem. Ein continued minute after minute, down twisting dark corridors, melding with the shadows creeping from the corners of his vision. He felt sick, felt heavy.

Finally, he arrived at the main corridor, his breathing ragged as he took in a lungful of his suit's air supply.

A shadow moved to his side.

"Wait—"

Ein aimed and fired his pistol without hesitation, downing the humanoid form in a split second.

Ein blinked, pointing his flashlight, and recoiled in horror.

It was a fellow member, dead, with a cauterized hole between his glazed eyes.

The vice chief gasped, backing away with gritted teeth. He turned his back on the corpse, sprinting, uncaring, seeking sanctuary from this madness.

Where is the enemy? Where are the firefights? Is everyone dead?

A hundred thoughts raced, paling compared to the sight of the blast doors leading to the hangar. They were open, and he thought nothing of it as he vaulted past the entryway.

He breathed a sigh of relief, chuckling manically as he ignored everything else. His vision tunneled at the docked destroyer and the bridge tube connecting it to the hangar.

Ein checked for hostiles and saw nothing. Ecstatic, he ran forward, hoping to be just a few dozen meters away from safety.

But then, the cultist bumped and crashed against something, knocking him back to the ground with a cracked helmet. Ein groaned, feeling as if he had run headfirst into a brick wall. He shook his head, sitting up to see what obstacle blocked his path.

There was nothing but thin air.

The air cursed in galactic standard. A low, growling, and . . . confused synthetic voice echoed before him.

"The fuck?" it muttered.

Ein gaped, blinking furiously and wondering if his mind had finally snapped. However, a second later, the space before him shimmered as a solid mass slowly took shape.

He felt the blood drain from his face as a seven-foot metal monstrosity loomed over him. Dark, gleaming armor, razor-sharp claws, an elongated helmet with a black skull for a face. It held an intimidating positron rifle, sleek and rectangular, resting casually over the thing's shoulder next to a mounted light machine gun.

Its hollow eye sockets lit up with glowing azure eyes that glared down at him.

On the other side of the bay, the doors of the bridge tube connecting to the *Temin* opened up, revealing a dozen people. Ein's breath shuddered as he spotted the frigate's captain and her family of officers, herded by a team of five black-armored soldiers.

Upon seeing Ein, the hangar exploded into action. The *Temin*'s crew broke off and sprinted in every direction, some launching onto the enemy to buy time.

Ein stood up, drew his pistol, and began unloading on the joints and neck area of the abomination in front of him, only to freeze as he realized his shots slammed against an invisible barrier with a familiar aura.

"A psi barrier?" Ein balked, dropping his pistol as he noticed the silence. He looked back to the *Temin* crew and was dismayed to see that every single person was already lying on the ground, bound by wire or placed in rear naked chokes.

The vice chief gulped and saw the dark alien thing raise its fist.

"Yeah, that's rough, bud," it scoffed with a dismissive, contemptuous voice.

Blackness enveloped him. Ein never even noticed the punch arrive.

Jupiter looked down at the out-cold Thralled and the crater he'd made on the man's helmet. He raised his brow as his own helmet unfurled.

"Hm . . ." he hummed, scratching the top of his head.

"The *Temin* is under control, not many inside, and apart from these fools, they are more than happy to sit down and behave." Puck chuckled as he stepped beside Jupiter, bending down to connect with the Thralled's suit. "Vice Chief Ein. Good catch. That punch is going to leave a permanent scar on his nose if we leave him like this."

Jupiter cleared his throat, not bothering to mention how the idiot had run straight into his cloaked shell without either of them noticing.

"The guy just happened to pass by while I was stalking someone else through another shell." Jupiter shrugged.

Orion approached from behind after ordering the team to corral the prisoners in the center of the hangar. "Who?"

"I think it was a seer." Jupiter scratched his chin, closing his eyes as he focused on Poltergeist-Two. "Team Two and I found her going into the secondary hangar."

"Isn't that where the station chief and a dozen other Thralled prepped that corvette?" Puck asked.

Jupiter nodded. "Yep, and she was carrying some interesting things. After stuffing her in a closet, we proceeded to apprehend her boss. Or tried to . . ."

Orion hummed, speaking through the task force's comms network, which included the destroyer. Nodding at what he heard back, he looked toward Jupiter as he gave his report. "The good news is that the *Phantasmagoria* has locked down all three ships. The station is now firmly under our control."

"Awesome. Teams Three and Five successfully jammed internal and external comms and disabled the station's security systems and life support. No one's going anywhere without our permission." Jupiter grinned, rubbing his hands as he shared sight with the other Poltergeists. However, he quickly paused in his celebration, frowning.

Puck tilted his head. "Bad news, I assume, Sir Jupiter?"

"Team Four had little success in data collection. The chief's quarters and office were already cleaned out of intelligence, and they just found an incinerator room and tons of empty boxes."

"Damn, we were too late." Orion spat. "Nothing from the terminals?"

Jupiter sighed. "Scrubbed clean then utterly destroyed. You can't recover data from bits of pulverized sand."

Puck cursed with a shaking fist. "Paranoid ne'er-do-wells. What of the other teams?"

"Team Two and I moved to apprehend the station chief and his bodyguards at the secondary hangar bay, but . . ." Jupiter scowled, recalling how the bastard had cracked something hidden in his tooth, taking his own life as arcs of electricity fried his brain.

"Their boss is dead, and the rest tried to fight to the death," he grumbled. "A few didn't make it, but we managed to incapacitate the rest."

Puck shrugged. "That's Thralled for you. Cowardly barbarians."

"At least they fall easily. Kind of pathetic, really," Jupiter huffed.

Orion shook his head. "This was a small, underequipped cadre of a single cell of a larger cult, of which there were dozens, all with their unique . . . mad faiths. Let's not jump to conclusions. There weren't even any combat psi artists among them."

"I know, I know." Jupiter waved his hand in dismissal. "We have a few important lunatics, at least. The other teams managed to capture other crucial personnel after their missions."

Jupiter turned to Orion, deferring to his command. "What now?"

As the lieutenant paused, Jupiter thought back over the past few days. After training with the task force, the AI had found a comfortable position as the tech specialist, hard powerhouse, and the guy managing comms.

Now, he was a specialist under Orion's experienced command.

"I'm giving the go-ahead for the marines to secure the station. The *Phantasmagoria* will proceed with a patrol sweep of the system," Orion informed the gathered team.

Jupiter yawned, stretching his seven-foot metallic demon frame. "Welp, good job, guys. It's time to get homely and keep our flies pacified. We have a few days until the armada arrives. I think they'll be happy with our catch."

CHAPTER 23

INTERROGATING A MADMAN

After two dull days, the leading element of the Exodus Armada, composed of the Mars Fleet and Battlegroup Mictlan, arrived in the system. Spearheaded by the *Bucephalus*, the vanguard sent a message informing the *Phantasmagoria* that the rest would come in a couple of hours.

Jupiter didn't mind, taking the time to contact his brother.

"Brother, you look brighter," Mars noted with a proud grin. "How is the station?"

Jupiter broke into a smug smirk, scratching his cheek as he gave a detailed account of how his lone destroyer had entered the system, approached the station without triggering any alarm, and smoothly taken control of the cultist base before anyone could escape.

"We combed the place from top to bottom. Ran full scans and even sent personnel to strip the walls, ceiling, and floors for hidden stashes. Mostly found drugs and crap." Jupiter shrugged. "As for the three ships the Thralled planned to evacuate from, they're all disabled and docked. Their crew is detained in a separate location."

"I see. Well, I consider this mission a resounding success. I only regret that the station chief committed suicide before we could apprehend him." Mars sighed before grinning once more. "All in all, amazing work, brother. You'll find plenty of eager volunteers for your task force."

"Thanks." Jupiter rubbed his nape as he smiled back.

Mars hummed, examining the information Jupiter had sent before glancing back at his little brother. "By the way, have you named your elite troop yet?"

"Took some debate, but we settled on . . ." Jupiter paused dramatically.

"What?" Mars crossed his beefy arms as he tilted his head.

Jupiter grinned back, producing a small blade from his back. "Dagger. Task Force Dagger."

Mars barked in laughter, clapping his hands in joy. "Wonderful! Do you have unique names? Callsigns?"

"That we do." Jupiter chuckled. "We divide the force by specialty. The Bayonets are tailored for assaulting a heavily defended position; the Scalpels are data collectors; the Machetes are saboteurs, et cetera, et cetera."

"What of the command team?"

Jupiter laughed, "That'll be Shiv. I know it sounds crude, but I pushed for it. I thought it had charm, in a . . . prison-shanking way."

Mars snorted, shaking his head. "And what about you? Do you have a callsign?"

"At first, I wanted to be Geist because of my shell, but I'm guessing I'll be playing around with other models in the future. I already have some ideas and modifications." Jupiter rubbed his chin. "Ultimately, I decided on Shank."

Mars nodded. "I see. Then it appears you have what you want. Are you looking forward to further action? You know, you might be the ones to conduct Lady Straise's rescue."

Jupiter pressed his lips into a thin line, thinking of the future before smirking. "Eager but cautious. I want this to go right."

Mars smiled, chuckling. "That's a good mindset. Then, if that's all, we should prepare for the armada."

"Speaking of the armada, how are the repairs going?" Jupiter asked.

The red Overseer sighed. "Ongoing, but we got every ship moving again. Some had to be scrapped for parts, but we're ready to stalk these woods for our quarry."

The two continued to converse, getting into the nitty-gritty of prisoner management and discussing the findings Task Force Dagger had collected.

Jupiter had learned plenty from the low-ranking rats, even though they'd scrubbed their databanks and libraries of valuable information.

All but one.

For some reason, the vice chief, the one they called Ein, held a data chip containing the manifests of every notable ship that passed through, a list of contacts, and the station's archived ledgers. Jupiter found rows and rows of goods exchanged, profiles on ship captains, population statistics of orbital habitats, and the status of various nomadic fleets collected over two and a half decades.

Mars was ecstatic at the news, immediately perusing the entire storage device and making several copies before putting it in a secure location.

Unfortunately, neither AI found anything that revealed the locations of cultist bases. It seemed the bastards were smart enough to keep such secrets off their terminals.

Eventually, they ran out of topics to discuss. The two brothers clasped hands, and Jupiter found himself alone as the hologram winked out.

He looked around, grimacing at his temporary room and workplace.

Jupiter had called dibs on the chief's quarters, but it had a strange smell that he couldn't get rid of, and the thought of returning to Yan's arms and taking a shower in his regular shell tantalized his senses.

Someone knocked on the door. Even before he revealed himself, Jupiter already knew who it was and scowled.

Kelios entered with his usual perfect smile, carrying two mugs of instant coffee. "The cavalry has arrived, has it?"

Jupiter grunted in response, accepting the mug and taking a long sip. He glanced at That Bastard and waved him off. "Don't you have shit to do?"

"No one requires my medical expertise, I'm afraid." the corpsman shrugged. Jupiter's eye twitched at the sight of the Evorian out of his combat suit, showcasing his sculpted bronze body, a literal Adonis in the flesh.

"Then why the hell are you here?" Jupiter groaned.

Kelios raised his well-groomed brow, smirking. "Am I not allowed to check in on a comrade and deliver some much-needed refreshment on this exciting day?"

"I feel like you're buttering me up for some reason." Jupiter squinted. "You're going to ask for a favor one of these days, I just know it. And I'm going to be absolutely livid."

"Nonsense with your conspiracies. In actuality, I was hoping to seek some entertainment—"

"Hell no, I'm spoken for! Yan will *literally* bite my head off!" Jupiter stood up with wide eyes, backing away.

Kelios pouted. "I am not some uncouth sybarite. Besides, you're not my type, my friend."

"Not your friend either," Jupiter grumbled under his breath, feeling a tinge of relief. Scratching his head, he asked, "Right, so what exactly then . . . ?"

Kelios clasped his hands, eyes gleaming with passion as he shouted with conviction, "Let us dive into the subtleties and artistic impressions of linguistics and oration! We should exchange poetry! Specifically Latin, or maybe . . . ?"

Jupiter looked deadpan at the art aficionado before immediately kicking him out of the room, undeterred by the Evorian's protests and woes.

As Mars had said, the rest of the Exodus Armada arrived within a few hours.

Hundreds of ships, capital and subcapital, filled the area around the hypergate. Their mere presence and passive emissions echoed into the void like blaring horns, bathing the system in a concert of metal and souls.

In the center of it all, *Citadel Irkalla* captured everyone's attention, dwarfing all other vessels and gleaming like a celestial palace. Around it, the flagships of the

Expeditionary Fleets spread out in a defense screen, from the colossal *Zolann'tono* to the ancient *Gladiator* and the glorious *Solsollen's Scepter*.

To say the cultists of the refueling station grew pale upon seeing the assembled forces would be an understatement, and several attempted to bash their heads against the wall. Unfortunately for them, the task force had predicted this, and all the high-value prisoners, from the vice chief to the chief engineer, were bound within a sarcophagus-like shell and kept sedated.

They couldn't care less for the scum. Unlike the pirates and marauders in Zilla, these meat bags had lost their rights as people in the eyes of law and morality.

Time was of the essence, and the council approved teleporting three of the sarcophagi. Said body-sized prisons and their living occupants shimmered as *Citadel Irkalla's* teleporter array latched onto them and engulfed them in prismatic clouds—instantly transferring them to their prepared rooms in Max Sec.

As for the rest of the prisoners, countless shuttles pounced on the station like ants swarming a hill. The marines of the *Phantasmagoria* and the armada ferried the cultists and their accomplices aboard before slowly moving them back to the *Citadel* for their permanent homes.

While these grim and pale-faced terrorists and Starless-worshippers marched on with either insane ramblings or hollow gazes, the heroes of the day boarded their prized destroyer. They returned to the armada's embrace for some much-needed R & R.

Jupiter didn't even bother to transfer back to his Nexus; instead, he possessed his usual shell and immediately jumped into bed with a certain admiral.

Overall, the mood of the Exodus had risen substantially as they continued to dominate naval warfare and special operations.

In the confines of Max Sec, the mood was slightly less jubilant. Four individuals gathered in the observation room as the first of the newest high-value prisoners was escorted to his cell. Before the vice chief could get accustomed to his new home, however, he was carted away and summarily dumped inside the interrogation room.

Andora watched the prisoner sitting alone in the interrogation room below. What irked her the most was how *normal* this cultist looked, now clad in orange prison garb and fitted with a paralyzing shock collar.

It wasn't a species she'd seen before. Still, much like most of the ones she had seen, convergent evolution in the Milky Way favored humanoid forms, whether brown, pink, green, blue, mammalian, reptilian, plantoid, or aquatic. She didn't bother to look up this species' name.

The prisoner looked so close to human that it might have seemed uncanny, if not for the gaunt, ghoulish face, reddish-orange skin, and geometric black tattoos that covered his body. His bloodshot eyes with heavy bags underneath stared straight ahead, his shoulders drooping as he swayed from exhaustion.

He sweated profusely, his shoulders drooping under the uncomfortable weight of high gravity, turned up just enough to dissuade him from standing up.

Due to his uncooperative and manic state, Ein had woken up still in the midst of entombment inside the sarcophagus. The coffin automatically administered sedatives to keep him docile, which had since been flushed from his system, leaving the vice chief groggy if anxious and erratic.

Andora scowled in utter contempt at the fly below. She felt indifferent to the plight of groups like the Oblivion Fangs for their attack against her, but she couldn't manage to see the alien below as a person. No one who sided with the Starless was equal to human life.

The thought of worshipping her tormentors twisted her heart, making her soul nauseated, gagging, writhing, and heaving.

Traitors. Cockroaches. Worms. Flies orbiting and eating the waste of vermin.

She felt nothing but disgust and hatred at the Thralled, even more so than at the enemy she had fought for a century. She wanted nothing more than to open his skull and analyze his brain to check for any abnormalities.

Andora found no concrete reason as to why anyone would commit such lunacy.

She grinded and gritted her teeth, opening and closing her fist. After a moment, she collected herself, took a deep breath, and glanced to the side, wanting a conversation to distract her from her anger.

However, Tov stood unusually quiet and tense beside Andora, fists clenched on either side as he peered down at the inmate, matching her present turmoil shrouded by a veneer of stoic indifference. For some reason, the patriarch's usual calm and thoughtful demeanor showed a few cracks, letting out an air of dark hostility.

She could hear the grinding of his mandibles and sense his muscles coiling.

Andora looked away from her friend when Luna entered the observation room, looking as impassionate as ever, if a bit curious. The oldest of her Overseers looked her way, nodding. With the various probable outcomes to this interrogation, Andora had summoned for her, knowing they might need a different kind of . . . expertise, should regular questioning fail. One she predicted many would consider taboo.

As for the final occupant of the observation room, flanked by a trio of Tov's Vraken, including Captain Pyo, Varin was still in his prison garb but seated with a cold glass of synthesized almond milk.

The Ruzian prisoner looked down at Ein, snorting at the decrepit sight. "You wouldn't be able to tell at first glance or the second that these waste puddles were Starless worshippers. They look no different than every other wretch making a living in this hell."

"How did you figure it out, then?" Andora asked with narrow eyes.

Varin grinned and sipped his drink before speaking. "I'm good with people. What can I say? They may be skilled at pretending and spying, but there's that subtle look of disgust deep beneath their eyes. Staring at you as if you're . . . someone diseased."

"Phages," Tov muttered.

The ex-captain pointed a finger toward the patriarch. "Yeah, that's it, Phages! They can't help but call us that behind the scenes, seeing us as germs, bacteria, viruses that affront their divine—"

"Enough." Andora scowled. "The garbage you're spewing is making me nauseated. I have no interest in hearing their perverted insanity."

Varin raised his hands. "Apologies, ma'am."

Andora rolled her eyes, staring back down at the prisoner. "Do you know him?"

"In passing." Varin shrugged. "I mostly dealt with his boss, Bort. He was a Thralled, too, but hid it better with his greed. Oh, and that fine piece of ass for a seer. What was her name . . . ?"

Everyone else in the room frowned at the Ruzian's antics but ignored them for now, their indifference one of the few luxuries he'd earned for his invaluable assistance.

The ex-captain snapped his fingers a few times, trying to recall before exclaiming, "Elis? Axus? Ah, I remember now, Ocus! That's her name. Haughty lady, but her skills are top-of-the-line in more ways than one. She can see farther than my own seers, and I always paid a premium for her services."

"We have her in custody as well." Andora crossed her arms with a frown, squinting Varin's way. "But nothing on their vice chief?"

He shook his head. "None. He's the type to work in the shadows. I'm betting he's more faithful to his cult than to his chief."

Andora tsked, her mind calculating the optimal method of extracting what she needed from the Thralled scum. Just then, Luna stepped toward her, producing a data chip.

"Everything Jupiter and Task Force Dagger managed to dig up," Luna reported, placing it in her open palm.

Andora glanced at the tiny thing, picking it up and absorbing the data through her fingers. She read through it in an instant, smiling.

"A good harvest." She chuckled. Analyzing the data chip produced vital context clues to go along with everything else they'd gathered—resource deposits, roaming bazaars, locations of valuable ruins, shipyards, and more. She sent a copy to Tov, who perused it in silence.

Unfortunately, much like everything else in the Uraki Sector and likely the entire Dead Zone, what few survivors lived were on mobile habitats . . . ships.

There were immense vessels composed of mashed-together cargo haulers, and if Varin was honest, they rivaled her dreadnoughts, but only in size. These city-ships had everything from agriculture to dockyards, like miniature, inferior versions of her *Citadel.*

Varin hadn't said how many there were, other than that his Oblivion Fangs had one, escorted by the remnants of his fleet, carrying their families and friends. He gladly snitched on the cultists but kept anything related to his people close to his chest. Andora had no reason to coax this information out forcefully.

"*Tsk* . . . is this it?" Andora asked Luna.

The silver Overseer shook her head. "Jupiter reported that all hard copies were destroyed. He assumes anything related to cultist activity is passed through word of mouth."

"So, we're at a dead end unless we manage to make this one and the others cough up what they know?" Andora grimaced.

Varin chuckled behind them. "What? Are you going to bribe him with wine and cheese like you did me?"

"Absolutely not," said Luna.

"I'd rather fucking die," Andora said succinctly.

Tov was slightly more tactful. "That would be unwise."

The captain shut his mouth at the immediate dismissal from the trio. He shrugged, leaning back on his seat as he reached for the platter of human pastries. "Good. I'd rather not see that filth get any relief."

Andora exhaled through her nose, moving out of the room with Tov and Luna. "Let's get this over with. He's had enough time to stew in there."

"How should we initiate?" Luna asked.

Andora tsked, scowling deeply. "Let's skip the useless nonsense. We aren't planning on letting any of the Thralled live within the week anyway. You saw his state. I'm surprised he hasn't committed suicide."

"Jupiter scanned him extensively. No self-destructive devices, either mechanical or biological, were found in his body," Luna reported, propping up her glasses. "Except for a cranial implant that he deactivated."

"Perhaps that is why he appears glum and slow," Tov muttered. "Well, apart from the drugs we administered in his system. Depending on their quality, cranial implants are useful supercomputers that seamlessly meld with one's brain. Deactivating one would be akin to shutting down a limb."

Andora hummed, pulling up the prisoner's brain scans. "It doesn't look too sophisticated by galactic standards. It's tailored toward administrative duties . . . nothing that looks like a bomb."

"I recommend attempting a gentle approach," Luna suggested. "His ill state may provide the opening for negotiation."

Andora snarled low at the thought, yet her rational mind pushed back, whispering logic and reason. She turned to Tov. "Being diplomatic with his kind irks me. You're the arbiter here. What do you think?"

She had nominated him in the last meeting and although Lord Iintei made a fuss on how it was too soon, Tov nonetheless won unanimously.

Although it had been his plan to take the position, Andora noted how he'd become grimmer as if he put on a familiar weight that he dreaded to lift. Tov sighed, looking at his hands before clenching them into tight fists. "I fear he may react violently at worst and remain stubbornly silent at best. Jupiter reported the same, did he not?"

"Overseer Jupiter is not adept at interrogation," Luna reminded them.

"Be that as it may, if this *Aghapin* hadn't been entombed, then he would have done everything he could to escape or worse," Tov stated.

Andora grinned savagely as she clasped her hands behind her. "He won't escape my grasp."

They stopped before the door leading into the interrogation chamber. Andora then turned to Luna, nodding. The silver Overseer waved her hand, and with it, streams of nanomachines streamed from her body, emerging from underneath her gray Victorian dress and flowing around her before coalescing into an apple-sized orb.

The gray goo danced rhythmically, forming elaborate geometric shapes.

Andora turned to Tov, hesitant to propose what she had in mind. "We'll play along, but if he reacts as I think he will, we're employing extreme measures."

The patriarch stared at the orb for a minute, silently contemplating. However, he didn't put up the resistance Andora had anticipated.

Tov merely nodded, speaking coldly. "Do it."

Andora recoiled at his unexpected response. "Really? No moral grandstanding about how he's a person? I thought you'd be more against it. You were reluctant when I suggested using it against Varin, even if it was partly as a joke."

Tov sighed wearily, an echo of his past bubbling through, reminding Andora that the Kurskann standing before her had lived a long life, nearly double that of any human, and had experienced decades of horror and turmoil.

"Pirates, marauders, mercenaries . . . Varin's type . . . At the very least, they have a sense of honor among their kind. They do what they do for a reason. They attack others to take their supplies to feed their people's needs." Tov sighed as distant memories flooded back. "Their numbers exploded post-Cataclysm. The Legacy hadn't even begun to stabilize, and they preyed on weakness wherever it was found, from budding colonies to under-protected trade convoys. Because of that, there were three great wars after the Starless left."

Andora had read about those events in passing, but the Kurskann before her lived through it all. Fought through it all.

She listened on as he continued.

"Maybe a few found their way this deep. Maybe the Oblivion Fangs and all the others were never a part of those campaigns. Maybe they are simple survivors who have adapted to this hell. Greedy, distrustful, ruthless . . . But they, at the very least, can be reasoned with."

His mandibles snapped shut, fists quaking as he clenched them tighter. "*Aghapin* are different," Tov hissed with dark, bubbling venom. The sound from his throat seethed like the buzz of a primal, raging wasp, scornful and disgusted. "*Aghapin* are no better than the demons they worship."

Andora and Luna glanced at each other, feeling the surge of the old hatred exuded by the usually empathetic patriarch.

"The moment they pledged loyalty to the Starless and became their thralls, they ceased to be people. Even pirates kill them on sight, with the bounties put on them and the rewards given for information. They are universally reviled. They are cowards, betrayers, puppets."

Tov spat each insult like a curse, turning toward the door and glaring at the cultist behind as if his gaze could melt through the thick walls to smite its target.

Andora pursed her lips, speaking softly. "You hate them. This . . . is personal for you."

He took a deep breath, his vitriol abating. Bit by bit, the tension in his shoulders and fists relaxed, his hackles lowering as his fire smoldered.

"I do," Tov whispered like an ashen breeze. "I do . . ."

"You don't have to enter," Andora replied, awkwardly reaching out before hesitating and pulling back. Their roles had reversed, and she wasn't sure how to be the supportive one.

Tov shook his head once more, finally composed, if still unsettled. "No, it's alright. It's just . . . it's been a long time since I've encountered their kind. A very, very long time. The Starless Cults disappeared around the same time their masters did."

"They never reemerged?" Andora asked.

"There were the occasional worshippers on the border of the Dead Zone, but even they went extinct. We can never manage to capture high-ranking *Aghapin*. They always manage to slip away, sacrificing everything to bar our path before killing themselves in the end. And any information we've gathered is either useless mad ramblings or the gossip of grunts."

Tov sighed, sorrowful and quiet. "In the end, we were no closer to finding them than before. All that we know is that they worship the Starless for a variety of reasons: some out of fear, some out of reverence . . . I can't help but think back to the atrocities they committed during the Exodus."

Andora pressed her lips into a thin line, remaining silent as she contemplated his words. "If we proceed with the operation, it may kill him."

"So be it," Tov coldly responded.

Seeing her friend had made up his mind, Andora focused on the problem ahead. She opened the doors with a thought and stepped into the interrogation room, Luna at her right and Tov at her left.

Upon their entrance, the lights slowly illuminated the room, banishing the shadows. The gravity in their half of the room lessened to a comfortable level. Andora briefly glanced at the observation room above, hidden seamlessly as part of the wall.

Before her, the hidden Thralled and ex-vice leader of the refueling station groggily blinked, raising his head to regard them.

The instant he saw Andora, Ein's eyes opened wide, and the cultist shoved himself as far back as he could, bound still by his shackles and the chair he sat in. His breath quickened, sweat pouring faster down his face as panic welled.

"I-it's you!" he stammered loudly, recoiling back, attempting to flee as if suddenly dropped before radiation.

Andora felt her patience slip in the cultist's presence. She dug the nail of her index finger against her thumb, trying to bring her back to rationality. She whispered in a thinly veiled threat—warning and commanding.

"Calm yourself, fly."

Ein shut his mouth under her commandment as it reverberated across the small room, shaking the table and the cultist's body. Sheer fright and revulsion coursed through his veins, leaking out through his terrified face.

Andora continued, stepping forward, hands clasped behind her back as she looked down at the quivering mess. "I am Secretary-General Andora Dietrich of the United Nations of Humanity and Custodian of the Sol Exodus Armada. With me is Patriarch Tov Garesh'Ynt, Arbiter of the Exodus, and Doctor Luna Selene."

"You . . . No, it can't be. I thought it was an exaggeration, something to motivate us . . . It can't be true," Ein muttered through gritted teeth, slumping as if in pain, breathing heavily as he closed his eyes.

Andora sneered at his ramblings.

Tov stepped forward. "Vice Chief Ein Yelmenthor Ip, you are accused of being an *Aghapin*, a Thralled, a terrorist, and a traitor to the galaxy. Data gathered by the station and your colleagues corroborate this allegation. Due to the amount and high authenticity of the evidence against your person, you will be detained until your trial."

Andora almost scoffed at the idea of giving the worm a fair trial. She shoved it down, keeping up her indifferent, if annoyed, facade. "Should you be proven innocent and assist us in fulfilling our needs, you will be given leniency and perhaps even your freedom."

However, it appeared the Thralled heard nothing. He became increasingly agitated as he raised his head back, staring her way.

"The High Seer was right! A cold, unfeeling machine abomination and a dark armada of ravenous drones," Ein moaned in despair.

The trio frowned at his words. Andora cursed inside her head, though she'd already expected her enemies to know her true nature, though many of the newly joined allies didn't.

Ignorant of their thoughts, the cultist continued to wail, tears falling like rivers as he panted and groaned. "An Aberration walks among us . . . We . . . we are doomed! An Aberration . . . an Aberration!"

Andora snarled, her diplomatic veneer falling off as she stomped forward and slammed her palms against the table. She let out a final demand despite knowing the futility. "Enough. Fulfill our needs and perhaps—"

"AWAY!" Ein shrieked, his wrists bleeding as he pulled and tugged against his restraints. "AWAY FROM ME, YOU METAL DEMONESS!"

Upon detecting his resistance, the room's security measures doubled, and the gravity pressing upon the cultist doubled. The wind in his lungs left him and knocked him from his panic. His bounds tightened while simultaneously dispensing a healing solution over his wounds.

"Christ, he's lost it . . ." Andora muttered at the insane prisoner, glancing toward Tov.

Tov sighed, shaking his head. "Now you realize what I had to deal with a century ago."

"Oh, Herald of Absolution . . ." Ein began to pray, mumbling and whispering rapidly. "Hear your servant. Hear me, please, hear me. Please save me from this sinful place . . . Please, I beg of you—"

Andora rolled her eyes as she walked around the table before stopping at the Thralled's side. She leaned down, her mouth an inch from his ear as she whispered, "The vermin you worship aren't here. They can't hear your pathetic prayers."

"You would think so, Aberration, but the divine beings you insult know all, see all!" Ein hissed, spitting her way only for the globule to ricochet and splatter on his own forehead. He snarled, shaking his head.

A surge of defiance and contempt raged beneath his eyes as the Thralled gnashed his teeth at each of them. "The end comes for us all! Absolution had sent his most beloved agents to our fetid swamp of stars."

"And what is Absolution?" Andora narrowed her eyes, immediately regretting her question upon seeing the utter devotion and mad faith replace the cultist's furious gaze.

"The true god from beyond. The Great One who shall absolve our sinful souls and bring us to paradise," Ein whispered with tears in his eyes as he gazed up above. "Absolution sent the Herald, who offered a cure to our profaned existence, leading the unending legions to spread the message! It is our galaxy's turn to be judged and reclaimed from Pandemonium's grip."

Tov slammed his fist on the table, denting it as he hissed at the Thralled, "Your Herald doesn't seem to be doing a good job, seeing as how we sent them running."

"What are we but amoebas, Phages that sully reality! A century is nothing to the divine!" Ein retorted.

Andora smirked, cupping the cultist's chin and squeezing his cheeks. "Well, this amoeba spits on them and their attempt. The billions of Starless dead can attest to that."

"You are an Aberration, a miscalculation, an anomaly. You are an obstacle they will overcome as they did countless others! But with your presence, our destruction is assured! The Herald won't tolerate your existence, and we will be caught in the crossfire!"

Andora scoffed. "As if I care what happens to your little cult."

"When we are cleansed and help others be cleansed, only then shall we return to our Absolution's embrace!" Ein shouted, frothing at the mouth as his eyes turned bloodshot.

He slumped, breathing heavily as he began to mutter in an untranslatable tongue. "*Makpang'yarh an, ingtahn kamimo.*"

Andora sneered at his deteriorating mental state, releasing her hold on his face. She leaned back down to whisper in his ear once more. "I hear nothing but the sad babblings of a scared little fly."

She straightened her back, looming over him as he stared her way through blurred vision, seeing her eyes glowing like baleful blue stars, judging, condemning, and pouring with a burning hate that dwarfed his like a sun to a flickering candle.

"Your god exists without my consent."

Ein recoiled in utter shock at Andora's words, sputtering and heaving as his spittle flew everywhere.

"BLASPHEMER. THE ARROGANCE! YOU WILL NOT STOP THE CLEANSING! OUR TEMPLE SHALL ERASE YOU AND SET THINGS RIGHT! WE WILL—"

"Luna, are you finished?" Andora asked, cutting off his mad speech.

The Thralled continued to buck and rave, cursing in both galactic standard and his eldritch tongue.

Luna nodded. "I have finished my analysis. The nanites are now tailored to meld with his brain matter without killing him outright."

Ein stopped his ramblings, eyes wide at the silver Overseer's words. "W-what . . . ?"

Andora sniffed, one hand on her hip as she made way for her second-in-command. "Take everything from him. Do not be gentle, but ensure the quality of information."

"By your will, Eldest," Luna replied with a sliver of scholarly interest. She stepped forward, passing Andora as she raised a hand over the cultist's head.

The target in question attempted to lean away only for the seat to engage its magnetic hold, snapping his collar to the backrest and keeping his head in place. This only agitated the Thralled further as his chest rose and fell faster and faster.

"Y-your tricks won't work on me! Your foul Pandemonium will not breach the sanctity of my mind!" Ein challenged with defiant and fearful eyes. "You are no Dagataren mind reader!"

Luna hushed him, her silver eyes glowing with cold indifference. "There is no need for such metaphysical solutions. This is purely my design, but I must warn you . . . this will be invasive."

"Last chance to squeal, fly," Andora smiled cruelly as she stood beside Tov. From the tip of Luna's fingers, silver nanomachines dripped onto Ein's head, slowly making their way to his orifices.

"N-never!" Ein wailed, gnashing his teeth as he tried to shake off the gray goo to no avail.

Andora shrugged. "Then, by the authority vested in me as custodian of the Sol Exodus Armada, approved by the Exodus Council, you are to be executed. Tov?"

Tov nodded, "By the authority vested in me as arbiter of the Sol Exodus Armada, I declare you ineligible for a defense in a court of law. I strip you of your rights as a sapient being and condemn you to death for your crimes against all life and your servitude to a cosmic existential threat."

Only then did Ein realize his plight as the nanites began to dig into his face. More and more fell from Luna's fingers, crawling toward his eye ducts, mouth, nostrils, and ears.

"What . . . what is this foulness? Get away, no, get away!" Ein frantically protested. "I demand a trial! You can't do this to me! *Argh!*"

One by one, the nanomachines dug deeper and deeper, traveling toward his alien brain under Luna's direction. She coordinated them with a scalpel-like precision that only an AI could achieve, watching the real-time scans of his brain and referencing the extensive data regarding his species' anatomy and neurology.

It was too crude and blunt for her tastes, but Luna was made to serve, and she did so without question.

"Wait! Wait, wait, wait, wait!" Ein shouted in a panic, screaming and begging as he felt unimaginable pain. His cries echoed across the room as his face swelled with nanomachines, writhing and burrowing like marching ants.

"Y-you . . . can . . . still . . . be . . . saved . . . ! Repent . . . ! Our . . . proselyte . . . will . . . *huah! Ah! AH!*"

Ein spasmed, convulsing in a seizure as drool gurgled out his mouth and tears flowed unending, tinged with bodily ichor and the silver of nanomachines.

Several tubes snaked toward him, embedding themselves into his skin as they pumped endless drugs and chemicals to keep his health stable. "NO! *ARGH!* PLEASE . . . ! ABSOLUTION SAVE ME! AH!"

"Contact," Luna reported, her eyes closed as she focused on her task. "Linking . . . now."

A spurt of blood shot out from Ein's eyes, and the Thralled went silent, slack-jawed, as he slowly exhaled. "Urgh . . ."

Minutes flew by as more nanites melded with his brain. Now and then Ein spasmed, grunting and groaning, laughing, crying, shouting as Luna tested different regions, shocking, biting, tugging.

Finally, after ten minutes of torture, Luna nodded. "Successful integration. Siphoning subject's knowledge . . . now . . ."

Ein moaned like a zombie, tongue hanging out as his eyes and fingers twitched.

"What do you see?" Andora asked impatiently.

The silver Overseer raised her palm, gesturing for them to wait as she tilted her head. "Parsing surface thoughts, delving deeper . . . now."

Ein jolted as if shocked by a bolt of lightning. "*HURK!*"

Luna frowned as her silver eyes glowed harsher. "Subject reacting violently . . . Mental state fluctuating . . . Resolving . . . Suggest increasing sedatives over the safe amount."

"Do it," Andora approved as the cultist's convulsion eased briefly.

"Heart rate nominal, brain activity showing less resistance. Uncovering deep memories and subconscious . . . now."

Ein jolted yet again. This time, however, his muscles spasmed even more, his body crying out as his mind revolted. Luna widened her eyes before waving her hands like a conductor. More nanites flooded from the walls, this time of the medical variety. Like a tide, they washed over the Thralled as his body failed before her, struggling to cool and heal the feverish patient.

Andora frowned at the prisoner's state. "Luna, what's happening?"

Luna gritted her teeth, eyes narrowing to thin slits. "Losing control. Synchronization is falling rapidly. Cause: Unknown. The subject's health is deteriorating. Error. Recalibrating. Error . . ."

Andora furrowed her brows as the putrid stench of waste hit her nose. The sight and sound of the cruel torture inflicted upon the Thralled sent her mind into turmoil. Her synthetic heart beat loudly, twisting and turning, conflicted.

The screams of a dying animal, pained and wailing. For that split moment, Andora despised having to take this course of action, despised the Thralled for forcing her hand, despised the tinge of sadistic pleasure that coursed through her veins, demanding more blood and horror upon the fly.

She looked away, gritting her teeth as she turned to Tov who looked on impassively, more machinelike than she'd ever seen him.

"This doesn't affect you?" Andora questioned in an almost accusatory tone.

Tov turned to her, speaking low. "Of course, it affects me. But, I've seen . . . dealt . . . worse."

"Worse?" Andora asked in disbelief upon his confession, glancing at the tortured cultist having his mind violated. "Worse how . . . ?"

He sighed, turning back to the tortured prisoner. "Sometimes . . . you need leverage to make one talk."

Andora frowned at the bare answer, her mind interpreting the possible meanings behind it. She failed to connect the dark image with the good friend beside her. Instead, she shut the thought down, bringing her focus back to the morbid play being conducted by her second.

"*HAAARGH!*" Ein screamed, thrashing and spraining his neck as he woke up from a sedated state, eyes clearing for a moment, fluctuating between subjugated and freed. "YOU . . . Hahaha . . . ! WILL NOT . . . mother . . . BEND MY MIND . . . need to stay . . . TO YOUR WILL!"

"Luna . . ." spoke Andora, concerned they'd lose their new asset too soon.

Luna shushed her, a vein pulsing from her temple. From within the *Ozymandias*, her Nexus thrummed with increasing power as she brought a huge chunk of her processing capability to sort through the mess within the alien's mind.

"Unable to stop failure cascade. Neural synapses shorting. Bodily temperature rising inexplicably. Unknown cause," Luna continued to report.

Suddenly, Tov lowered his arms, antennae twitching. "Wait! Luna, back away!"

"Shell's safety is irrelevant. Continuing operation regardless. Harvesting core memories . . . now!" Luna shouted.

Upon saying that, Ein's eyes rolled behind his head, his lips parting to reveal his gums as he gnashed his teeth. Blood poured from his orifices as he seethed and shook. An unholy groan escaped his raw throat, filling the room and giving the illusion of a dark shroud enveloping the poor wretch.

Suddenly, the cultist lunged forward, skin tearing and veins popping.

"TO HELL WITH YOU METAL DEMONS! I DIE ON MY OWN TERMS! I CURSE YOU!" Ein screamed at the top of his lungs. "I CURSE YOU!"

He shouted, again and again like a broken machine, filled with manic anger. "I CURSE YOU. I CURSE YOU, I CURSE—"

Suddenly, the cultist sucked in his breath, his body stilling.

Andora, Tov, and Luna backed away at the sight as Ein's head began to turn into a pale, goopy mess before swelling and expanding like a balloon, a dark ichor leaking from his ears as a sickly—

BANG!

The cultist's head exploded in a black and red mist, splattering everywhere before the room took hold of the viscera mid-air and held it in place, preventing it from staining them.

Then, the hold slowly disengaged, allowing the putrid fluids to fall to the floor while the ventilation system scrubbed the air.

Andora blinked, frowning as she looked at the body. "What the actual fuck?"

She turned to Luna, whose brow furrowed in concentration. Eventually, the Overseer slowly replied, "His cranial implant . . . mutated somehow . . . It was deactivated, but . . . I don't understand how it happened?"

"I think I know what it is," Tov spoke up, dragging their attention. He sighed, crossing his arms. "I thought it was a baseless rumor. The rare times we captured an *Aghapin* that likely knew core secrets, they were reported to suffer all sorts of maladies."

Luna adjusted her glasses as she poked the headless corpse. "Does that include sudden cephalic detonation?"

"No . . . someone's head exploding is a first, but melting the brain is common. At the time, we blamed anti-tampering modules in cranial implants, since it wasn't possible to completely deactivate them externally," Tov replied.

Andora hummed as she asked, "So what is this rumor? Why bring it up?"

"I felt a wave of psi . . . no, more like a flash. It came from deep within his mind," Tov muttered, his antennae drooping as he focused on recalling the sensation. I felt . . . malice . . . corruption . . . domination . . . and mania."

"Like . . . some kind of psionic brand?" Andora scowled.

Tov nodded. "I believe so. I'll have to ask Cantor Tendemone. She is more knowledgeable in this matter. All I know is this level of psionic engineering is . . . it's the realm of Category Five practitioners at the very least."

Andora spat. "Just great. An actual, honest-to-maker hex. Why does space magic have to complicate things?"

"That's how Scholar Yulane and our scientists feel every time they work with you." Tov shrugged.

Luna stepped away from the corpse, bowing toward Andora as she spoke. "Eldest, I have failed to account for this possibility. I will endeavor to develop a solution for future interrogations."

"See to it, then. Work with the Eternal Choir when you do," Andora replied, turning to her second-in-command with an eager expression. "Now, tell me, have you uncovered anything useful?"

Luna gave her a slight smile and nodded. "The ones who orchestrated the attack on the Allied fleets are known as the Chained Souls. However, they are a frontier organization, a splinter cell of a greater cult . . ."

"What is the greater cult called?" Tov asked.

"The Temple of Absolution," Luna reported. "All I managed to uncover is that they operate in the Heartlands, and they send these cells to maintain an active presence throughout the Dead Zone led by someone called the Proselyte Prime. Even Ein was unaware of this person's true identity."

Andora rubbed her chin as she paced, gesturing for Luna to continue. "Proselytes, handpicked by the Prime, manage the cult cells. In the case of the Chained Souls, that would be the Bound One."

"What of their bases? Where did they take Scion Straise? Where is their fleet heading?" Andora asked.

Luna continued, smirking proudly. "I've uncovered several Thralled bases throughout Uraki and the neighboring sectors. They were masquerading as local stations and outposts, similar to this refueling station, However, the authenticity is dubious, as the memories I pulled this information from are rather old. But more importantly . . . Ein knew of a fortress used by his cell. A desert world where this High Seer, the Bound One's second-in-command, was bringing the fleet and Scion Straise. Ein believed they would reconnoiter with the rest of the Chained Souls cell there."

Andora felt a rush of fire course through her veins as her eyes widened at the news. Luna frowned, cutting her celebration short. "Before I could discern its location, however, his mind shut me out."

"Damn it!" Andora snarled when Luna raised her palm.

"Ah, Eldest, I wasn't finished. I do know it is roughly three weeks away from our location, and I know of the rough direction based on where the Thralled fleet departed."

Hearing that, Andora's anger abated. She sighed, motioning for her to continue. "What are you saying?"

Luna smiled. "If we could raid maybe two or more installations and harvest additional data in that direction, I think I can triangulate where this fortress is. I would simply need its basic description, as well as how far these hidden bases believe they are from it."

Andora narrowed her eyes, excitement swelling again in her chest. "If we do as you ask, how sure are you that you'll be able to locate this fortress?"

"If we build two more Phantasm-class destroyers and expand Jupiter's Task Force Dagger?" Luna hummed before replying. "It is a certainty, Eldest."

Andora grinned toward Tov, feeling a spring of relief washing over her. She chuckled, looking down at the headless corpse.

"We finally found the haystack."

CHAPTER 24

FINDING THE NEEDLE

Another month passed as the Exodus Armada followed the crumbs of a Thralled fleet. Much had happened since the ambush at Zilla's Redoubt; at the same time, nothing had changed to deter the combined fleets from seeking their destination.

Citadel Irkalla, surrounded by hundreds of ships like bees around their queen, orbited yet another barren star system. Apart from its location in the galaxy, the red dwarf and the duo of lifeless rocky planets held little value.

Nevertheless, the armada used the pit stop to reorganize and resupply by harvesting the meager resources around them and fabricating them into spare parts.

Many of the ships from the newly joined fleets showed clear signs of recent and ongoing repairs, from polished gray patches of hull plating bereft of paint to empty weapon hardpoints. With the aid of Overseer Luna and her unseen team of "human" scientists and researchers, vital ship systems were successfully integrated, refitted, and upgraded.

The hyper-tunneler matrix was given priority above all, as decreasing travel time was paramount. Still, the power reactors, targeting computers, cybersecurity, ECM and ECCM modules, and others were repaired and improved in the short time available to them.

Things like weapon systems and defenses were only marginally touched upon, as they would have required an extensive stop the armada could not afford.

Another new sight was the dozen mass haulers, refitted with the bare necessities to serve as bulk prison ships. These goliaths carried the rest of the enemy forces that had surrendered at Zilla's Redoubt. Sadly for the inmates, improvements in their accommodations were at the very bottom of Luna's to-do list.

The Sol and Third Fleets remained pristine and on the prowl, but none exuded and embodied the word *lethality* like the three dreadnoughts forming a trifecta of death, sailing above the armada as ever-watchful guardians.

Citadel Irkalla's shipyards worked overtime on new additions. Building a subcapital ship on the move required immense precision and risk-management capability. On two separate occasions, the entire armada had to halt for half a day during critical moments in the construction process.

The armada more easily constructed various miscellaneous ships for logistical use, such as tug boats, haulers, and mining vessels. Not to mention the focus given to the multiple drones used by Andora and her Overseers. Each hungered for maintenance, but none more so than those used during long-range operations.

But the crowning jewels of the last month of construction were undoubtedly the two new Phantasm-class destroyers, designated the *Willow* and the *Lady Gray*.

To support the two new destroyers, the shipyards also assembled a quintet of smaller stealth corvettes, dubbed Shade-class. These little sisters for the Phantasms were faster and quieter, built for intersystem transport, possessing ferocious teeth in exchange for lighter armor and less endurance.

Task Force Dagger immediately filled each destroyer with a section of Daggers and a platoon of marines, then sent them on raids along with the Shades. The teams stayed close enough to the armada that they could still link up farther down the planned route after conducting their operations.

The Allied Forces' reputation skyrocketed with each successful raid and capture of cultist bases.

In the distance, the hypergate fluctuated as a lone stealth destroyer returned to the system—the original *Phantasmagoria*. The armada received her verification code and sent priority messages to the Exodus Council and High Command members who were composed of the top-ranking military commanders of every fleet with Commandant Nullan as acting marshal of the Exodus.

The intelligence gathered about the system ahead by the three sections of Task Force Dagger held enormous significance, and those informed of their timely arrival all rushed to prepare to gorge upon the data.

Deep within the *Citadel,* in the largest penthouse overlooking the vast metal valley of the residential district, the armada's custodian groggily awoke to the news.

Andora groaned, opening her eyes upon receiving a priority message.

The contents knocked the sleepiness from her head.

"About time . . ."

Her body ached from the side effects of her typical outings and "stress relief." She slowly got up from the couch, swiping away the strands of hair stuck to her face.

She sighed, rubbing her neck as the clock ticking away in the corner pierced her mind. Dawn soon struck in ship's time, and the curtains of her penthouse suite opened automatically. The light shining from the faux sun at the center of the circular valley flooded her home, bathing the messy interior in its warm glow.

Looking around, Andora quickly recalled how she ended up alone in her living room, sleeping on the couch amid empty bottles, confetti, and half-eaten dishes of finger foods.

"Damn it . . ." Andora pinched the bridge of her nose as she got up, stretching her synthetic body. Her open sleep robe dropped from her shoulders, dragging her attention to it.

After tying the sash around her waist to keep the red silken robe from revealing her intimacy, she glanced toward the master bedroom.

Taking a deep breath, Andora walked toward it and slowly opened the door. On the luxurious king-sized mattress, underneath layers of exquisite blankets and dozens of pillows, lay a duo of people—both of them sleeping with light, content smiles and soft snores.

She clapped her hands, opening the blinds and illuminating the room.

Light groans came from the bed as the . . . *friends* . . . she'd made last night languidly rose from their slumber, blinking the sand from their eyes and stretching their aching, supple muscles. Even the little sounds they made had a siren-like quality intrinsic to their Kalachian biology. Two beautiful pearls. For a moment, Andora forgot they were starfighter pilots.

Andora took a moment to recall their names.

"Pala, Polo, rise and shine," she greeted them, then set her sights on picking up the mess they'd made. With a thought, a cadre of cleaning bots, both crawling and hovering, entered the room and took over the chore. She kicked the bottom of the bed, sighing. "Come on, get up."

She watched with her hands on her hips as the twins yawned and moved in unison, precisely in the manner that pushed her to . . . get to know them.

Pala spoke up, her voice hoarse yet melodic. "Good morning, Lady Andora . . ."

"Are you well . . . ?" Polo spoke next, draping himself over the other's lap.

"You left so soon . . ."

"Would you like to cuddle . . . ?"

The Kalachian twins spoke interchangeably, looking at her with dreamy eyes. Their coordination put them in league with the armada's other aces, and Andora had very recently discovered how that translated into other activities.

She forced herself not to react to their distinctly coconut-like aroma that wafted toward her. Andora coughed into her fist, waving them off. "I'd like to, but work waits for no one."

They pouted, yet the want in their eyes only seemed to flare.

"Not even . . ." Pala crawled to the edge, reaching for Andora's left arm and rubbing her face and lips against it.

". . . for a moment?" Polo did the same for her other arm, his hot breath tingling her skin.

Andora bit her lip before sighing, shaking her head, and smiling sadly their way. "Unfortunately . . . no."

She pulled away, arranging her hair back into its usual sleek bun.

"Ah . . . that is a shame . . ." Pala sighed, lying back down on the bed.

"Mmm . . . a shame . . ." Polo replied in kind.

Andora shrugged, then reached down to the floor, grabbed a stray piece of clothing, and handed it back to them.

"The *Phantasmagoria* is back," she told them.

Instantly, the twins widened their eyes, and their previously lax and sensual demeanor gave way to the cold, ruthless martial spirit that had forged their minds and bodies for decades.

"Then the time is nigh."

"We must prepare. Thank you for telling us."

Pala and Polo quickly got off the bed, put on their clothes and gear, and arranged themselves in record time. Andora felt a pang of regret, wanting nothing more than to make up for last night's blunder.

"No worries, but uh . . ." Andora paused, dragging the duo's attention. A slight deep blue flushed her cheeks as she nodded their way. "It was fun . . ."

The twin pilots smiled, giggling as they became scarce, but not before each kissed one of her shoulders.

"Call us again if you wish for company." Pala bowed.

"Or don't, we don't mind. Just don't be a stranger." Polo winked.

Andora smirked, chuckling as she waved them off. "Sure. Oh, and please keep this whole thing hush-hush."

They nodded, blowing her a final kiss, then promptly left, likely to run a dozen more simulations with the new data that would be coming their way.

As soon as the doors closed, Andora groaned, dropping her head as she ran her hand across her hair. A deep shudder escaped her as the plastered-on smile bled away.

"What the hell am I doing . . . ?" she muttered as she rubbed her eyes before glancing at the drones, which were slowly returning the room to a presentable state, spraying a light perfume, arranging new flowers, and righting overturned furniture.

She sat on the edge of her bed and then lay flat. Her hands rested on either side of her, feeling the silken comforter below her. Her thoughts drifted to last night and similar nights before that.

Unlike in the past, Andora now had to be more discreet in her proclivities.

As the custodian, it wouldn't do for someone of her position to be caught in a scandal so early in her duties. With the existence of an Exodus news agency and individual journalism, it certainly wouldn't help her image if the headlines became filled with her mischief.

Hedonism in the armada's highest echelons? Custodian Andora was caught sneaking Third Fleet crewmembers into her penthouse suite! Presence of gray-market substances found in her room! Click here for more on the latest . . .

Andora pursed her lips, remembering when that incident had threatened to spread.

It had nearly given Tov a heart attack. Andora had celebrated a bit too hard after harvesting vital intelligence from that vice chief Thralled, inviting all manner of eager sailors and soldiers for a wild bender.

After that, someone with a loose tongue had spilled the goods over a drink. It undeniably threatened to turn into a colossal fiasco. The snitch was scolded, and several NDAs were hastily signed as a result. For her part, she had received a lecture from the patriarch on her responsibilities and image. She grumbled initially but ultimately conceded upon seeing the potential consequences of a single mistake.

Thankfully, the matter was quickly resolved in her favor.

Remembering that embarrassing moment, Andora made a note to send Tov another gift as a thank-you for squashing that bit of news before it ever left the press and could forever paint her as a deviant.

Of course, there was no need to mention the previous night, lest the Kurskann pop a vein.

"Not like I can help it . . ." she muttered as she stared out into the valley outside her windows, bathed in the soft, warm light from above.

Pleasure and the pursuit of sensations had always been a part of her, even as an android. It had always been a significant source of criticism and trouble for her, but she thought humans were too stuffy, always vilifying such fun activities.

Heightened by her century-long abstinence and sensory deprivation, her vices only exploded upon connecting with a new and varied populace, reaching out for stimulus.

Despite her busy schedule distracting her mind from the terrors of quiet solitude, she had fallen back to indulging herself like a glutton, drowning herself in sensations like an overeager young AI, seeking all the little pleasures in life.

She enjoyed high-quality liquor, the beat of bassy music, savory dishes and sweet desserts, thirst-quenching drinks, and, especially, heart-pumping sex. Though the latter had always been reserved for . . .

Andora scoffed at herself.

"Not anymore, I guess," she muttered as self-loathing welled. She pressed her lips into a thin line as she covered her eyes with her forearm, a hollow pit forming in her chest.

Yet she excused her actions repeatedly for the mere reason that the company, the warmth, helped her sleep. Andora grimaced, recalling that even the pleasure didn't completely stop her night terrors. It was the same damn nightmare she'd been seeing over the past month.

Screaming Thralled plagued her dreams, begging for mercy, calling out to their vermin overlords in demonic tongues, morphing, twisting, hurling. The tortured cries and dozens of faces coalesced, merging into a singular entity, taking on the faces of every pitiful fly she squashed and squeezed for information.

No matter how often she tried to dismiss them from her thoughts, the wails of the animals still haunted her. Since then, she had ordered Luna to strengthen the sedatives or at least silence their vocal cords before beginning her operations.

Even still, the infernal noise irritated her, gripping and fighting for her attention. Their eyes glared at her, full of hate and disgust, blaming her, cursing her.

And then her mind would turn on her, replacing the traitorous faces with those she loved, as she still directed the gray goo to burrow into their skin.

Just last night, after finishing her fun with the twins and settling in bed together, she had woken up merely an hour later, screaming and sweating profusely. The duo jumped out of bed, grabbed the handguns beneath their pillows, and immediately searched for threats, only to find none but their custodian, panting and flushed in embarrassment.

Despite them thinking nothing of it and begging her to return to bed, Andora fled the room, locking the door behind her. She headed straight for the drink cabinet and downed a bottle of throat-searing whiskey before stumbling and falling face-first on the couch, forcing herself to sleep.

Andora let out a shuddering breath, staining her forearm with wet tears as she pressed it against her eyes.

"Why am I . . ." she mumbled, gritting her teeth.

Despite telling herself it was all in good, friendly fun, she only felt dirtier each time. A tiny part of her whispered in her ear that she was committing a heinous betrayal. She squashed that voice down, yet it reemerged every time, taunting her waking moments.

But without an outlet to vent her frustrations, she'd be forced to confront herself once more, and in these turbulent times, she could ill afford to do so by herself.

Before, at the very least, she could cope by torturing Starless for her pleasure, or shutting off her higher thinking processes and falling into hibernation. Now, she tried to focus on building more meaningful relationships with a select number of people, instead of picking random crewmembers and taking them to bed in a desperate bid to . . .

Andora paused, closing her eyes as she stopped that line of derisive thinking.

It was only thanks to her friends that she kept from falling further into the downward spiral of a self-destructive binge. But increasingly, she felt like she was slowly falling back.

"I need to talk with Echo once this mess is sorted," Andora mumbled, sitting up as she focused on her psyche.

She could feel her brother floating inside her mind, helping her untangle corrupted shards and working silently as she handled reality. She wondered how her mental state was these days. Has it improved or worsened?

Just then, she felt a spark of acknowledgment and mirth from the AI shard. Andora smiled, sending a wave of gratitude to Echo.

She opened her eyes, turned over, and reached for the bedside drawer. Andora reached down, grabbing a book Tov had given her—a diary, of all things—and flipped it open. She skimmed her journal. The earlier pages were filled with boring, unfeeling reports of her day, but then pages of rants and tirades appeared, each expressing her frustrations and dark impulses.

Then came more paragraphs, long-winded and deeply personal, things she'd never share with the world.

Andora returned to the very first page, where she had written . . .

Days since last mental breakdown: thirty-four

"Huh . . ." she huffed, seeing her record and contemplating it briefly. Andora grabbed a pencil, erased the number, and wrote *thirty-five* in her clear script.

Maybe she had improved.

She got out of bed and showered to prepare for the armada's most crucial council meeting. Once she had finished her duties for the day, she would write down her thoughts before bed.

In the depths of the *Citadel*, the War Room buzzed in anticipation. Expanded, renovated, and future-proofed for the possibility of further members, the administrative and military leaders of the Exodus Armada gathered.

Just then, the door to the vast chamber opened, and the vaunted custodian and her interim arbiter entered. The occupants ceased their conversation, anxiety and excitement pouring from their eyes and tense postures.

Andora and Tov crossed the room, taking the central and most prominent seats raised on a dais, which, complete with their desk, overlooked the immense circular table that held the Exodus Council.

"Good day, everyone," Andora addressed the assembled. "Due to the importance of what we shall discuss, I have invited members of the Exodus High Command to provide a critical military perspective."

The commanders all nodded. Exodus High Command included Admiral Yan, Luna, General Ohnar, Mars, Captain Pyo, and many more representing all member fleets. Over fifty people occupied the chamber, not including officers who performed their duties from the seats above.

Andora glanced at each of them before grabbing the gavel and hammering the sound block. "If nothing else, I declare this meeting commenced."

She cleared her throat, sending a silent summons.

While waiting, Andora spoke. "As we all know, the time is upon us. For a month, with the indomitable and unstoppable effectiveness of Task Force Dagger, we have collected vital intelligence on our enemy and the state of our missing expeditionary leader.

"Five days ago, we finally triangulated the location of the secret Thralled fortress and the whereabouts of the war fleet that attacked the Seventeenth and the Fiftieth and kidnapped Lady Nuwa Straise and several others.

"At that time, the *Phantasmagoria* immediately set sail ahead of the armada to the target star system to extensively recon the enemy defense." Andora paused, looking to each leader. "Yesterday, she arrived at the event horizon, just one tunnel away from where they've taken our people."

She breathed in, smiling. "Our destroyer has returned carrying news. Once we get a better picture of the enemy ahead, we will refine the most appropriate strategy among the many we have theorized. Once we do, we will strike ruthlessly, overwhelmingly. We will recover those who have been taken from us, alive or not."

The gathered nodded grimly at that possible outcome, especially Captain-deputy Melwin, who remained the Seventeenth's representative after Merina Undel had refused to be a councilor and instead joined Task Force Dagger.

Melwin grimaced, his impatience visible as he tapped his foot. Only discipline and the sight of the finish line kept him in place.

A second later, the doors opened, and two martial figures entered the War Room.

"Commander, Captain, it's about time you arrived," Andora teased. Her subordinate wore his human disguise instead of the horrific Geists used during missions. For those not in on the truth, the Geists were explained to be classified advanced spec ops infantry drones that Jupiter controlled, which was technically true. Task Force Dagger was, under Andora's shade, clandestine to all but her inner circle.

Jupiter and now-Captain Orion wore their combat suits to the meeting, minus their helmets.

Andora smiled, standing up. "Everyone, I'm sure you're well aware of the creator of Task Force Dagger. This is his first time presenting himself, despite my many invitations . . ."

In response to her thinly veiled sarcasm, Jupiter gave a smug smile, bowing as he took center stage. "Commander Julius Petros, Task Force Dagger, at your service. You can call me Jupiter. And I brought you all some news."

Andora rolled her eyes at his antics and acting. However, her interest superseded her criticisms as she asked her ex-Overseer, "Good or bad?"

Instead of answering, Jupiter waved his hand, sending a compiled dossier to everyone present and inputting an extensive version to the display table at the center. The central space was filled with dozens of holograms containing graphs, statistics, data, maps, profiles, and information on vital structures.

"It's been a mixed bag for the most part, boss." Jupiter dropped his smile, sighing. "I'll start by confirming some things."

With another gesture, the holograms made way for a three-dimensional map of the Madraa system. At the center was a pair of yellow dwarfs, the sovereigns of the area, bathing the four planets and two gas giants in their dual light.

The map highlighted the three hypergates spread across the system, all heavily patrolled and covered in minefields and anti-ship gun stations.

"Hypergates are locked down tight, as expected. Spending the time and energy to create an artificial tunnel to slingshot us toward the outer zone proved to be the right course of action," Jupiter continued, zooming in on the defenses that blockaded the gates.

After giving the audience enough time to digest his introduction, he moved on to the cream of the matter, shooting toward the target planet and the clumps of dots in orbit. "They're there alright. All one hundred and thirty warships were present. The Oblivion Fang we brought confirmed each one as part of the fleet that attacked the Seventeenth and Fiftieth."

The leaders breathed relief, which soon paved the way for a war drum beating in their hearts. With the enemy in sight, their cranial implants began coordinating battle plans with everyone present as Jupiter resumed his presentation.

"Twenty-one capital ships, including the battleship *Thorned Vice*. We expect the High Seer, the commander of the Chained Souls force in the system, to either be in his prized ship or planetside. As for the rest, well, most of them are carriers, so expect massive starfighter screens when we consider the base on the moon, the orbital hangars, and the planetary fortress itself."

Jupiter waved his hand again, zooming in on the planet.

"I present Madraa-II. Field Marshal Mars would find the place familiar." Jupiter glanced at his brother, decked out in his human disguise, complete with medals and all. "It's nearly similar to the red planet of Sol. Orbital defenses, stations, a docking port, and even a space elevator. It's not quite habitable, if I say so myself.

"There's also a defense fleet, half a dozen cruisers, and thirty frigates, corvettes, missile boats, et cetera. Plus minefields, hidden asteroid gun emplacements, and other nasty stuff you can read about in the dossier."

Andora hummed, analyzing the entire document within a second and frowning. "I think I spy the bad news."

Jupiter sighed, rubbing the back of his neck. "Yep, a fortress shield." He zoomed in on the central display.

Everyone grimaced at the sight of the energy dome that surrounded the Thralled base, stretching kilometers in every direction.

"A Scalpel team snuck aboard one of the stations and made a technician squeal. We managed to get the job done and made it look like a drunk accident. They weren't alert when we left, so we're still good," Jupiter reported.

Commandant Nullan spoke next, leaning forward. "Shield specs?"

"Non-Newtonian. Blocks out everything that exceeds the speed of sound," Jupiter answered, highlighting the data on everyone's dossier.

"As for the base itself, the lunatics call it Temple of the Ivory Maw. Sounds menacing, but it's mostly because it used to be a massive quarry for some high-end luxury desert marble that Heartlanders like." Jupiter shrugged.

Tov hummed, rubbing his mandibles. "Is there any other significance to the location?"

"Not that we know of," Jupiter replied. "We don't know why the Chained Souls built a fortress here other than that it's a holy site. Something about their Proselyte Prime gracing the planet, saying some mumbo jumbo, then leaving. We couldn't get much more than that without risking a trip of their alarms." The AI frowned, likely cursing his impaired state.

Andora nodded. "Continue, Jupiter."

He nodded, bringing up scans of the fortress itself. The enormous base sat at the bottom of the quarry, filled with typical military infrastructure including a docking bay for subcapitals and underground facilities. As for the temple itself . . .

Jupiter highlighted it on the map. "The Ivory Maw's a pyramidal structure lined with planetary anti-ship laser batteries. Its square footprint is four hundred thirty meters on each side, and it has a single entrance. It's also the focal point of the fortress shield covering the place."

"Why are the internal scans scrambled?" Tov asked.

"Despite the outer layer of white-gold marble, the building is made pretty much entirely of a thick, high-grade material of unknown composition. We think it's infused with psi." Jupiter pulled up a bird's-eye view of the base. "The whole thing shimmers like a mirage, natural ECM. I'd bet my nuts that the base itself is under this pyramid."

Nullan grumbled, his stone body grinding against his chair as he shifted forward. "So, whoever goes down there is going in blind."

"Pretty much." Jupiter smirked. "Those poor bastards. I wonder who'd be dumb enough to volunteer."

Captain Orion discreetly palmed his face.

Suddenly, the newly promoted Captain-superior Melwin stood, looking toward the commander. "How sure are you that the lady is down there?"

"Ah . . ." Jupiter pressed his lips into a thin line, a shadow draping over his face. "We're convinced she's down there. What we've uncovered paints the place as a . . . prison for non-believers."

Melwin narrowed his eyes, his finned ears flaring as he spoke low. "What are you saying, Commander?"

Jupiter closed his eyes, taking a deep breath. "They take people and convert them into recruits. If they don't . . . it's not pleasant—"

"THE VILE BASTARDS!"

"Sir Melwin, calm yourself," Andora ordered, glaring at the Kalachian until he composed himself and sat back down.

He cleared his throat, yet his face remained red with rage. "Apologies . . ."

Andora turned back to Jupiter, gesturing for him to continue.

"We think she's alive down there because of the . . . well, there's a bet going around the Thralled. They're . . . guessing how long until she breaks," Jupiter finished in a whisper.

The Kalachian captain seethed like steam spewing out of a pipe but remarkably kept himself quiet.

"That's the gist of it. We also believe that the rest of the Chained Souls led by the Bound One are on their way to Madraa. We don't know anything about the composition of the reinforcements, but we expect it to be heavy. The whole cell is gearing for war," Jupiter finished, stepping back as the chamber exploded into discussion.

Andora hammered her gavel, calling for everyone's attention. "With the curtain lifted, we have a thin opening to accomplish our goals. Let's use the next half hour to finalize our plans."

She turned to Jupiter and Captain Orion. "As for you both. Ready Task Force Dagger. It's time we stab the mad fucks where they least expect it."

CHAPTER 25

DAY OF DAGGERS

Jupiter took a deep breath as he encompassed Shank-One, the original Poltergeist that Mars created for him. Over the month of using it, he'd found many quirks and shortcomings. Unfortunately for the horrified Thralled, Jupiter used them as a stress test, pushing his shells to their limits.

Since then, he and his brother had made targeted improvements, shoring up weaknesses and improving strengths. Still, there came a point when finding timely design solutions proved challenging for even AIs.

Whatever ideas and answers they came up with resulted in absurd costs that made Andora frown disapprovingly. Jupiter vividly remembered feeling like a human child wanting an expensive new toy as he and Mars showed her the blueprints for the eventual Poltergeist Mark IIs.

Jupiter winced at the thought of losing even one of these bad boys.

Sadly, only Shank-One managed to complete its upgrade in time. Although it looked functionally similar, an ominous new edge shrouded its frame.

He whistled as he stared at the obsidian-like sheen of his claws, sharpened to a monomolecular edge. He retracted them, fearing he might cut his palm. "Damn, you are sexy."

Courtesy of Cantor Tendemone and her best songsmiths, they'd managed to imbue key components of the armor with psionically enhanced materials, whispering words of silence until the frame seemed to suck sound from the air. It seamlessly melded with the impression the shell already exuded, increasing the sound dampeners and stealth capabilities by 8 percent.

It might have seemed like a paltry amount to some, but the improvement was utterly mind-blowing to the AIs, who had relied on conventional technology for their entire existences.

When asked about the larger potential of psionic enhancement, the cantor chirped in light amusement, mentioning how such things became exponentially more complex with larger constructs like warships. Such things were the realms of Category-Five artificers, and those rare few were employed only by the highest echelons of Legacy society.

If such a person were present among them, they could likely turn the Poltergeist into a true void.

Jupiter looked at his chest, where he had painted a red sigil over his breastplate, a symbol of a pair of mandibles. He chuckled, pressing two fingers on his good luck charm and sending his thoughts to his love.

Jupiter already said a quick "see you later" after an extensively thorough and private conversation.

His relationship with the scarlet admiral made him feel warm and giddy. Their bond had cemented even further since Task Force Dagger became a fully-fledged military organization within the armada, complete with administrative staff, supply officers, and other gear that allowed such a beast to run smoothly.

With the constant influx of missions, Jupiter finally found that purpose he'd missed for a while. Although the setbacks caused by his damaged psyche still wounded him, at the very least, his moping episodes dropped significantly.

"Maybe I can finally move on . . ." Jupiter told himself, not quite believing.

At the very least, he no longer felt like drowning in the deep end.

He blinked his eyes, feeling the familiar sensation of reality slowly bleeding away, minus the stomach-turning nausea the meat bags seemed to feel. This time was worse, as they had to bypass the hypergates by making a costly slingshot with a high risk of missing their destination.

Most importantly, they needed to enter the outer system, far from any enemy forces, to lower the risk of detection. Thankfully, the turbulent nature of the Dead Zone and hyperspace meant they could slip in like rowing a boat onto shore while a storm raged overhead, far from the ports and under cover of night.

They'd have to walk a long way to get inland, but it was necessary to avoid being spotted.

"Captain Hajax, you there?" Jupiter called to the commanding officer of the *Phantasmagoria*.

The CO, previously a scout corvette captain, answered. He sounded stoic, if a bit ill. "Captains of the *Willow* and *Lady Gray* report the all-green. Shades ready for jump. We are good to go, Commander. We'll reach Madraa in two hours and twenty minutes."

"Right, I'll keep an eye on the tunneler matrix. Should be able to make course corrections on the way." Jupiter nodded. "Once we're close to the exit, everyone goes dark."

"Affirmative, Commander. Here's hoping we don't undershoot our exit." Hajax chuckled.

Jupiter rolled his eyes before tapping into the squadron's comms network. He spoke low in an encrypted frequency that would be undetectable by the enemy this far out. "Attention Task Force Dagger. This is Commander Julius. We are a go for the mission. I repeat, we are a go for the mission. All Daggers, report to hangar bay for briefing."

After making his announcement, Jupiter left his personal armory at the center of the destroyer and made his way to the hangar bay, which contained five dropships designed for stealthy, surgically precise transport—each just large enough to fit a single team and a Poltergeist. Their hulls shimmered, turning transparent.

The sleek vessels hummed, their pilots keeping their engines primed.

Upon reaching the bay, Jupiter greeted his section. The original twenty-five of the best Dagger operatives stood assembled before him—Section Alpha. Sections Bravo and Charlie were on their way.

He smiled at them all, casually giving a two-fingered salute. "Mornin', fellas. All you had your beauty sleep?"

"I know I did," a familiar, annoying voice responded. Kelios pouted and sighed. "Urgh, the desert heat is going to kill my skin."

Jupiter rolled his eyes at the Evorian medic. "Stow it. No one cares about your personal care routine."

"I do," one of the Machetes said, raising her hand. The rest of Alpha laughed at the light-hearted banter. Even Jupiter couldn't help but smirk.

He chuckled, placing his hands on his hips as he leaped atop a crate, overlooking his crew. "I have a few words. We're just waiting on Bravo and Charlie to assemble."

"They're still taking a piss?"

"Probably picking their noses."

Jupiter whistled for their attention, cutting off the unnecessary chatter before they exceeded his patience. "Alright, enough of that. I'm sure Captains Undel and Took won't keep us long. Orion, are we ready?"

The captain of Alpha nodded, clasping his hands behind him. "As ready as can be, but the next few hours of nothing will grate on some nerves."

"Good, we'll go over the sims once more to pass the time," Jupiter replied before feeling a signal pushing through to the *Phantasmagoria*. "Ah, finally."

Fifty holograms appeared in the bay, appearing so lifelike that those present almost believed they were there in reality. Both sections proceeded to take the flanks of Alpha, standing at attention as they looked toward Jupiter with enthusiasm equal to their senior operatives.

At the forefront were the two officers leading Bravo and Charlie.

The Task Force was divided into sections of twenty-five each, organized alphabetically to distinguish when they were formed. The original operatives made up Alpha. The next twenty-five formed Bravo. Then the next, Charlie.

Finally, each Section operated on one of the phantasm-class destroyers.

Jupiter looked at the first, Captain-superior, or just Captain, Merina Undel, who took the callsign Mermaid.

After she had recovered from her medically induced coma, Merina surprisingly turned down the offer to act as the fleet's leader and representative, instead throwing herself into Jupiter's Task Force with a red-tinged fury. Under their command structure, her Kalachian rank was shortened for ease of communication.

Already, the sharklike Kalachian looked ready to tear into Thralled meat with her barely hidden snarling grin.

"Mer, how's it going?" Jupiter waved at her.

The captain of Shiv-Bravo nodded his way.

If he hadn't heard her speak before, he would've thought she had taken a vow of silence. But she conveyed her meaning well enough. Bravo, which was made up primarily of warriors from the Seventeenth Fleet, was thirsty for cultist blood.

Then, her grin expanded, far from a smile, as she leaked impatient, brutal vengeance like a scorned megalodon of Earth. "It's about time we found their little nest."

"Okay, that's what I like to hear." Jupiter turned to the next captain and leader of the recently formed Charlie.

Callsign Rook, Captain Mamarance la'Nel-Took of the Thirty-Fourth, had surpassed the other applicants through sheer experience and intuition. The Bolud was a large unit, just like the rest of his kind, and his armor had to be custom-fitted to clad his bulk. However, his strength and endurance also allowed him to mount a heavy offensive and supportive module, greatly enhancing Charlie's staying power. His section was mainly composed of Thirty-Fourth volunteers and several from the Twenty-First and Thirty-Fifth.

Now, he looked like a walking tank, wrapped in a menacing black power suit and rivaling Jupiter in height and weight.

"Brought the ordnance, Rook?" Jupiter smirked.

The golem rumbled, chuckling as he gave a thumbs-up. "Enough to level a city two times over, Commander."

Jupiter barked a laugh. "We'll need it if shit hits the fan. Alright, since we're all here." He cleared his throat, looking over each of his Daggers sternly, clasping his hands behind him. "You already know the plan; we've workshopped with the brass on how we're supposed to do this hellish task and given them a few choice words on what grunts are and aren't capable of."

The Daggers grinned but kept silent, all seventy-five hanging on to his words.

"The moment we arrive in-system, it's lights out," Jupiter began, waving his hand and projecting a map of Madraa. "Our destroyers will get us as close to the target as possible via blink drives. But at a certain point, we'll have to do it the old-fashioned way."

On the map, the three destroyers teleported to cold spots within the system, hopping toward the desert planet and shaving off hours. The trio stopped just before reaching the inner zone, at which point fifteen cloaked transports left their hangars.

"Phase One. The flyers will cross the void, accelerating just enough for Newton's first law to get us where we need to be, bypassing the Chained Souls war fleet, Madraa-II's orbital defenses, and the enemy patrols. As you already know, we might spend a long couple of hours on those transports. Depending on the situation on the field, we're looking at four to ten hours."

Everyone grimaced at the long wait time but understood its necessity, given how dense the area was with observation posts and warships on patrol.

"Once we reach Madraa-II's atmosphere, the dropships will rapidly decelerate, slowing down to the point where we can slip past the fortress shield covering the temple."

Jupiter turned to the pilots huddled together by the dropships with a grin. "This all comes down to those bums. The margin of error is slim. Burn the thrusters too hot, and we break our cloak. Not hot enough, and we'll slam right into the fortress shield, and despite all the upgrades, gravity is still a bitch. So, wish them good luck."

He turned toward the people in question, smirking. "You hear us, buzzards?"

The fifteen pilots, ten of whom were present via hologram from the other two destroyers, hollered in reply, giving thumbs-ups and salutes.

The map switched to a two-dimensional plane of the quarry, highlighting three of the fifteen strike teams. "Once we get past the fortress shield and land on the desert plains outside the quarry, we begin Phase Two. Each of you knows your role."

Each section had been further divided into teams named after different kinds of short blades and specialized in different tasks.

Dirks were assassins and hunters. Bayonets were assault specialists. Machetes took the roles of saboteurs. Scalpels, intelligence collection. And finally, Shivs, who acted as command for each section.

But in a joint operation where all sections gathered, each team formed up with their siblings and were commanded by an Alpha officer.

"Dirks, you're tasked with scouring the base and locating any leadership," Jupiter said. "You'll have the assassin drones on you. Mark your targets, and put them on standby. Once you receive the signal, decapitate and sow chaos among the Thralled ranks, then slink back into the shadows.

"Bayonets, you have the armories, motor pools, hangar bays, anything that gives the bastards ordnance. When the time comes for us to go loud, I want you to make some noise! Take control of those areas, lock 'em down, burn 'em down. You'll stay outside the temple, drawing attention while we find where they keep the prisoners.

"Machetes. You get the fun stuff. Put sand in their eyes, cover their ears, cut off their tongues. I want their comms, power, security systems, defenses, and any and everything that keeps the place running shut down permanently. Above all, I'd like that fortress shield popped when the Trident Assault begins.

"Scalpels, you have the most crucial jobs in Phase Two. Without it, we can't proceed to Phase Three. Your targets are the data centers, the libraries, and the offices of high-ranking hostiles. We need immediate intelligence and a detailed map of the temple interior and undercroft. Without it, we'll be going in there blind. You guys need to find where they're keeping prisoners. If not, then we will proceed with the backup plan.

"Finally, Shivs." Jupiter turned to the final group, the command teams of each section. "We have the main objective: search and rescue. If Scalpels fail to locate the prison wing, or if we're forced to go loud, then speed is of the essence. Kill everything in your path, shank them until they're down, and move on. We must locate the prisoners and retrieve them. Otherwise, this whole operation becomes meaningless."

Jupiter eyed each one, unique in their talents and highly adaptable in martial or psionic arts. With their balanced loadouts, should everyone else fail, the Final Contingency lay in their hands. He nodded, satisfied with what he saw, and addressed everyone again.

"Above all, we must time our action with the armada's assault. They'll be focused on dominating the entire solar system, and once that happens . . . Well, we better have our targets secured before the enemy can even think of the word *execute*.

"My Poltergeists will accompany each of the five teams. You know what they're capable of. If you require assistance, ping me, and I'll make these monsters roar." Jupiter smirked, his sleek, metallic tail whipping the air with its plasma-tipped blade. Apart from Captain Orion and a few trusted comrades from Alpha, the rest believed all the Poltergeists except Shank-One were semi-autonomous war machines and that he was a prodigious drone operator with the cranial implants to match.

"Questions so far?"

He looked around, seeing shrugs and shaking heads.

"None? Then that's the gist of it. You all know the contingencies, from Plans B, C, to fucking Z. Just remember, we can't account for everything. We don't know what's inside and under the temple," Jupiter warned.

As he did, his mind scrambled to determine what was so important that the Chained Souls put a temple on this otherwise barren system but came short of a reasonable answer, unwilling to just pin it on cultist craziness.

"And if you can't wrap your smooth brains around it, just remember this." Jupiter smiled, raising his fingers one after another as he listed plainly, "Get in, save the princess, get out, and crack any skulls that get in our way. Oorah?"

"OORAH!" Task Force Dagger shouted, baring their teeth and raising their guns. The best of the best, the brave bastards audacious enough to come to the Dead Zone and make themselves at home.

Jupiter grinned at the brimming eagerness exuding from them. "This is it. This is our graduation day, our final temper to hone ourselves to a keen edge. With this victory in the bag, we'll cement our foundation and prove that our Legacy is worthy of song. Trust your training, your comrades, adapt, and win."

He breathed in, then shouted their motto at the top of his lungs, reverberating across the hangar. "*Velata usque ad Mortem!*"

"Shrouded until death!" his warriors replied in turn.

After his briefing and speech, the holograms of Bravo and Charlie promptly disappeared. Around the remaining warriors, space destabilized further as more energy flooded the hyper-tunneler matrix, ready to slingshot them into the dark.

Jupiter opened a private channel to Kelios as he hopped off the crate.

"How was that?" he asked.

The Evorian smirked but didn't draw attention to their conversation. *"I think you did swell. You kept it short and simple, with a good, playful insult to resonate. But to quote your human vocabulary, it was a bit rah-rah. Though perhaps that's just personal taste."*

"Damn." Jupiter sighed, scratching his head. *"Maybe you should write my speeches next time."*

Puck playfully covered his mouth, gasping. *"And deny you a chance to grow your artistic style? Symphony curse me if I did. You'd merely end up a mediocre copy of me."*

"Go to hell, bastard," Jupiter cursed out loud as he slapped the medic's shoulder, passing him on the way out.

"After you, darling," the bastard teased, earning a glare from the AI.

Finally, after a shaky transit through the unstable tunnel, the Dagger squadron entered Madraa's outer zone—half a billion kilometers from their target. Two lights twinkled in the distance as the twin stars at the system's center orbited around each other.

"Task Force Dagger, going dark." The silent signal spread across the squadron. Immediately, the vessels powered down every non-critical system, from comms and artificial gravity to even life support, with the crew already clad in their space suits.

The corvettes fanned out from the onset, invisible, pointing their passive sensors at the enemy and getting a live reading of the neighborhood. So far, the Thralled seemed to remain unaware of the intrusion.

When the information was relayed to the destroyers, the ships began spooling their blink drives, not afraid of overheating the components, sacrificing longevity for a faster charging rate.

A thin sliver appeared over the void, and in an instant, the warships were sucked through and spat out amid nothingness, far from any asteroid fields and patrol vectors.

Once, twice, thrice . . . Forty minutes in between each jump, shaving off the hours it would have taken had they sailed through space toward Madraa-II.

Phase One had begun.

They closed in on the inner zone where most of the Chained Souls forces resided, detecting nothing that would derail their mission.

Fifteen dropships left the bellies of the Phantasms, streaming through the abyss unseen.

Within the lead stealth boat carrying Alpha's Shiv team, each member carried out their pre-mission rituals in the red light that bathed the interior.

Orion sat still like a statue, resting before the heat ramped up. Merlin analyzed a data tablet and went over the mission details. Augur inspected her rifle. Ritter fiddled with a good luck charm in the form of a necklace before shoving it back beneath his armor.

Lastly, Puck chewed gum with his mouth closed, looking elegant and refined.

At the back of the dropship, Jupiter sat in his Poltergeist Mark II with his eyes closed. In the silence, his mind played out hundreds of simulations, making predictions and formulating solutions to unforeseen problems, mostly to keep his mind busy, exercised, and focused.

He scanned his shell for the thousandth time, ensuring every piece of gear was in peak condition. Jupiter inspected his breaching charges, drilling lasers, smoke, ECM dust, incendiary and old reliable fragmentation grenades, boxes of ammo, a dozen energy cells, canisters of fuel, and on and on and on.

Jupiter sighed through his nose, rolling his neck as a tinge of anxiety and fear raced through his body. As leader, he now shouldered the lives of his Daggers.

Looking around and through the outer cameras toward the other dropships, he wondered if one of them would lose their life that day.

He gritted his teeth, looking down at his positron rifle, clawed hands, and menacing body. Not on his watch, he promised. Yet that did nothing to stifle the pumping emotions that raged in his heart.

Did he want this?

He looked to Captain Orion, wondering if he should have refused his recommendation to take the reins.

Jupiter still lacked experience, but over the past month, he'd proved to have a knack for leading the force. He thought he'd be better suited as a champion, a tool. But ultimately, he would be lying if he said he didn't enjoy the freedom of not answering to anyone.

Perhaps he was overthinking it. Perhaps not.

Doubt coursed through him as images of the things that could go wrong pushed through to the forefront of his mind, shouting and goading him.

"Calm yourself, boss," a voice reached out to him. Jupiter blinked, his dark thoughts fleeing him as he looked over to Kelios, whose outstretched hand held a sugary amber treat. *"Gum?"*

Jupiter sighed, reaching out to take the piece of candy. Kelios winked, closed his eyes, and continued to chew.

"Thanks," he muttered, popping it in his mouth and delighting in the distracting mint, sweetness, and lemon. Jupiter hummed, though he felt disappointed with his shell's inferior taste buds compared to the one he casually used back in the armada.

Nevertheless, he leaned back, relaxing his body as he readied himself for the long haul.

Another hour flew by as the dropships cut their acceleration, using only their auxiliary maneuvering thrusters—course correcting millimeter by millimeter.

Jupiter looked out, zooming in on the enemy fleet. Hundreds of vessels lay motionless, orbiting far away from the bronze and white planet. A few dozen roamed the stars, sending out pulses and scanning the area.

The hulls appeared leagues more modern than the vessels used by the Oblivion Fangs. Cargo ships and shuttles flew back and forth between the fleet and the planet below. Now and then, a batch would head to orbital docks for repairs and resupply.

At the center of the fleet, the *Thorned Vice* loomed over the rest like a brutal taskmaster. Jupiter wondered if the High Seer was aboard or if he had gone planetside.

Yet another hour passed and then another as they closed in on Madraa-II. The operatives exhausted any activity to pass the time, from playing games on their tablets to making inane small talk about who was the hottest crewmember in the Third Fleet.

Finally, the red light turned yellow. By now, each member had caught up on some shut-eye, and were all sitting straight and performing final checks as they transitioned from lackadaisical to relaxed readiness.

"Approaching planetary atmosphere, ETA ten minutes. Prepare for deceleration in five . . . four . . . three . . ."

The occupants felt a slight lurch as the dropship turned around and fired its thrusters, slowly reducing its speed as they approached the target. Jupiter closed his eyes, his hands gripping tightly around his weapon, and his third piece of gum drained of flavor.

He popped it for the last time before swallowing.

Minute after minute, the fifteen dropships flew past Madraa-II's exosphere, then the thermosphere, mesosphere, stratosphere, and finally, the troposphere.

Jupiter looked out, squinting his eyes as they made reentry. Despite it being evening on this side of the planet, the airspace was filled with traffic.

The air around the dropships compressed tightly and reached absurd temperatures. The onboard stealth systems struggled to hide it all while the thrusters fought to slow their descent. Each ship dispersed, aiming for different areas of the shield to avoid clumping together and producing a noticeable ripple. Some even followed along behind enemy shuttles as they made reentry.

"Approaching fortress shield . . . five thousand meters . . . three thousand . . . two . . . one . . . eight hundred . . . six . . . five . . . four . . ." the pilot reported, his voice strained with effort.

Jupiter gritted his teeth, pulling his vision back from the exterior cameras as the dropship shook and rattled.

"This is going to feel uncomfortable . . . one hundred meters . . . fifty meters . . ."

Everyone sucked in their breath.

"CONTACT."

Everyone except Jupiter lurched hard, groaning.

All fifteen dropships plopped into the thick energy field of the fortress shield like bricks plunging into a pool of water. The shield rippled ever so slightly as the transports dove and dove.

Jupiter bit his cheek, tapping his finger on his leg as time crawled like molasses.

Eventually, the dropships popped out on the other side, within the barrier surrounding the quarry.

Everyone breathed a sigh of relief, cheering and sending congratulations to the overstressed and giddy pilots.

One by one, the dropships coalesced, moving toward the south side just outside the quarry where a massive ramp, likely for gargantuan mining vehicles, led into the base below. No one spoke when the transports landed, touching down gently, barely disturbing the dust below as their hatches opened.

Seventy-five phantom Daggers and five Poltergeists quickly exited the dropships, starting Phase Two.

Jupiter looked around at the desolate desert and the protruding alien marble, gleaming pure white under the light of a full moon. Ahead, a steel-and-concrete gatehouse blocked the quarry's entrance.

Around him, Task Force Dagger took a knee, invisible as fleeting winds. Only through their helmets, visors, and, in Jupiter's case, his eyes, could they detect one another as ephemeral blue silhouettes.

He looked toward the captains of each section, nodding their way and making a couple of gestures, pointing toward the edge of the dry basin.

The captains nodded back, moving forward to bypass the walled gatehouse and reach the cliff. Once there, Jupiter stopped to scan the base below.

It looked like any other military base operated by a primarily humanoid force. The quarry was filled with buildings placed in a grid, smooth stone roads, reinforced architecture, and a slight shimmer of forcefields surrounding the vital structures: hangars, barracks, warehouses, a motor pool, and so on.

Towers dotted the area, shining spotlights and housing sensor suites that vigilantly scoured for intruders. The cultist night watchers themselves, though, seemed almost bored and tired, at least from Jupiter's vantage point.

And smack in the middle, the immense ivory pyramid demanded everyone's attention. The guards there appeared more alert and grim-faced, scanning everyone who passed through the great twenty-meter-high marble doors—open like a dark maw as little light leaked out from within.

"Symphony, that looks off . . ." Kelios whispered beside him.

Jupiter glanced his way. "What do you see?"

"It's like a mirage, translucent almost . . ." the medic replied.

Jupiter nodded, although his digital nature couldn't relate. He only saw the strange markings etched on the pyramid's surface. Jupiter dismissed them, stepping off the cliff.

Everyone followed, dropping tens of meters until their hoverboots kicked in. The technology eased their descent and allowed them to land softly on the marble ground below. Once he was sure everyone had made it, Jupiter gave the signal to move out.

Task Force Dagger split into five groups, slipping into the shadows, dodging spotlights and patrols.

From there, each section dispersed, covering a larger area—Dirks, Bayonets, and Machetes tagged individuals and places of importance, marking them for destruction. Without any of the Chained Souls the wiser, they planted timed and remote explosives, dispersed vials of nanomachines, sprayed metal-eating acid on vehicles, invaded quarters, and placed assassin drones.

The Scalpels made a beeline for the administration buildings, scouring terminals, file cabinets, drawers, and shelves for relevant information, abducting any unwitting Thralled they deemed of high rank—especially those of the same species and build as one of the Scalpels.

A quick change of clothes later, and it was time to take advantage of the opportunity.

All the while, the Poltergeists remained on standby, moving only to hack internal computers and databanks but otherwise keeping themselves hidden.

The Shivs went straight toward the temple itself, avoiding the patrols, roving vehicles, battlesuits, and aircraft that prowled above. Jupiter took it all in, getting multiple perspectives from all five of his shells on the surface.

He would have thought it was a simple military installation if not for the weird religious iconography of thorned vines, chains, shackles, and countless painted eyes that covered everything.

The air was . . . thick. The rest of the Task Force felt a slight press on their shoulders and the tightening of an invisible wire. Despite that ominous feeling, no alarm had yet been raised. Some of the cultists looked exhausted and casual, simply going about their duties or heading toward the temple.

Jupiter and the fifteen Shivs came to a halt, huddled on the other side of a plaza square outside the temple entrance, and took a knee right by the wall of an administrative building.

Jupiter checked the time, seeing thirty minutes had passed since they landed. He decided to contact the teams.

"Daggers, Daggers, this is Shank-Actual. Report, over?"

"Dirks. All good here. Priority targets marked, over."

"Bay'nets. Same. Moving to position by the main thoroughfare, over."

"Machetes. All presents are in place. Proceeding to the temple proper for the shield, over."

". . ."

Jupiter frowned at the silence, but the last team responded before he could call out again.

"Scalpels. Grabbed the data. No information on the temple. Likelihood of any intelligence on the surface is nil, over."

"Damn it," Jupiter cursed under his breath. He turned toward Orion, Mermaid, and Rook, shaking his head.

"Plan A is a bust. Proceed with Plan B. We're going in," Jupiter told them through comms. They nodded, readying themselves.

Due to the lack of a floor plan, Shivs, Machetes, and Scalpels proceeded to the Temple of the Ivory Maw. Bayonets and Dirks remained outside, ready to cause chaos when things turned loud.

Jupiter checked the time yet again. With how long it took them to reach Madraa-II, he recalculated the armada's arrival time. He grimaced. They only had an hour left to complete the mission's second phase.

As forty-five operatives and three Poltergeists approached the massive gates leading into the abyssal interior of the marbled pyramid, they felt an increasing weight on their shoulders.

Even Jupiter felt a minuscule whiff of this ominous aura surrounding them as they stepped into the belly of the beast.

Three-fifths of Task Force Dagger moved past the dozens of unwitting guards that were lined up by the colossal white doors, manning heavy gun emplacements, or sitting in vehicles. In sharp contrast to the soldiers, nearly a hundred Thralled in mauve hooded robes walked solemnly past, stopping briefly to be scanned before being allowed in.

The three strike teams followed in their wake.

Time ticked away in their heads as they flew through the vast, high-ceilinged corridor, passing great marble pillars etched with eldritch iconography that lined either side.

Cultists filled the area. Most were in robes, the rest in tactical gear. They patrolled the dark interior, dimly lit by countless candles that stained the floors in great viscous puddles of wax.

An unrecognizable hum and low chants filled the air, as did clouds of foul-smelling, itchy incense. The task force's helmets scrubbed the air clean of whatever narcotics tinged it. Jupiter gestured for them to move on.

He soon noticed the downward slope and the slight curve to the side. Looking at his growing three-dimensional map, their trek spiraled greatly in the earth. Down and down they went, constantly vigilant of surveillance but finding a surprising lack of it.

Finally, the hall opened to a vast artificial cavern.

Jupiter's eyes went wide at the sight of the expanse, deep below the ground, sprawling like an insect hive. Multiple floors circled the open center. His squadron had found themselves on one of the middle floors, overlooking the cavernous space. Up above, strange lights dotted the ceiling.

Only then did he realize they were eyes, glowing like spotlights and bathing all in a sickly light.

Squelch.

Everyone looked to the source of the noise as a trio of Thralled walked by, whispering to each other and stepping over an organic layer that covered the floor. Jupiter suppressed a curse as he stared at the fleshy membrane and undulating veins that merged with the stone, concrete, and metal surfaces, blending unnaturally.

Everything seemed to move like a breathing, living entity, and Jupiter finally realized why the Thralled revered this place.

He frowned, stowing the information as he signaled the teams to continue the mission. To cover the multiple floors, Jupiter gestured for the Scalpels and Machetes to split off. The former scoured the middle layers while the Machetes headed for the top.

As for the three Shiv teams, they descended farther below.

Jupiter couldn't get rid of the feeling that they were being watched.

CHAPTER 26

PROFANE TEMPLE

T*his place is a labyrinth . . ."* someone muttered through comms. Jupiter glanced at the source, an operative from Bravo.

"Thank you for the amazing commentary, Flak," Captain Merina replied, poking the Ruzian operative on the back of his head.

A light grumble echoed back, earning Flak a glare from his team leader. Nonetheless, Jupiter couldn't help but agree with the observation.

Since they had entered the cavern and descended the many floors, the halls had gone from straight and grid-like to illogical, going off in strange, twisting curves. The walls, floors, and ceilings slowly melded together as they strode forth, forming a circular tunnel.

"Tunnel's tapering," Augur spoke up. As she said it, Jupiter noticed the slight contracting as they went farther. Ten minutes ago, six people could walk side by side comfortably. Now, barely five could fit.

Only one thing was more appalling: the slow encroachment of organic matter.

The flesh had started to overtake the concrete, marble, and metal. It writhed and pulsed in irregular patterns, shivering and shuddering as their bootsteps slowly sank into the visceral ground, squeezing out a steaming puddle of unknown liquids, red and viscous.

Above, the lights transitioned from standard bulbs to bulbously protruding faux eyes, glowing with a sickly shine.

A crimson, foul-smelling gas huddled over the ground, staining the bottom half of their suits. Internal power reactors shifted gear, pumping power to the armors' stealth system. The Shivs kept their disgust down, but the queasy feeling never left, and kept growing as they delved deeper.

Jupiter frowned, tracking their progress and location, plotting the way as he traced their footsteps. Minutes ticked down, tensions heightening as they continued down the nonsensical road.

Suddenly, Jupiter's eyes flew wide open.

He gestured for everyone to halt.

The fifteen Shivs looked at him questioningly, but Jupiter remained focused on the anomaly they had just stumbled upon. He closed his eyes, sending a sonar-like pulse that soared down the halls, mapping out dozens of meters ahead.

"It's a completely different tunnel . . ." Jupiter muttered aloud.

"You noticed it as well?" Orion asked in a whisper.

Jupiter grimaced, nodding as he looked at the trail they took. Somehow, they had looped back to where they were ten minutes ago, exactly where they had made a right turn.

But there was no right turn present.

Jupiter and the three Shiv teams now found themselves at a completely different intersection between two tunnels. Everyone looked down the three paths: left, forward, and *upward* of all things.

Captain Merina tsked. "Do we backtrack?"

"Okay . . . Enough of this." Jupiter gnashed his teeth as he tried scanning the area, yet all he saw was yet more tunnel, winding in a confusing mess before the metaphysical ECM cut off his vision.

He grumbled and gestured for everyone to take a knee, two sentries aiming their guns down each of the three paths forward and the one behind.

"Wait one." Jupiter breathed in as he tested the comms. Just as he guessed, a light fuzz filled the link when connecting with the Scalpels and Machetes. As for the Bayonets and Dirks, the interference rose exponentially to a near-garbled mess.

Augur placed her hand on his shoulder as he was about to contact them. "Stop what you're doing."

Jupiter looked her way, seeing her furrowed brow and the bead of sweat on her temple.

"What is it? I was about to contact the surface teams."

Augur shook her head. "I don't know, but I felt acute hostility a second ago. It's gone now . . ."

Everyone grimaced at her prescience, looking around for security measures, whether sentry turrets or laser grids, but found nothing of note.

Will pushing through the interference between the underground and the surface trigger some defense mechanism? Jupiter thought, glancing at the creepy, fleshy surroundings. He turned back to Augur and the other psi-operatives.

Apart from her and Merlin, three others had varying basic abilities. All five were capable of peering through the veil. "What do you sense? You guys are sensitive to psionic fuckery, right?"

Merlin pressed his gloved palm on the ground before lifting it to inspect the goop that stained it. "I hate to say it . . . But I'm getting the same vibes whenever we fight the Starless."

The observation sent a jolt through everyone, and hearing Merlin's pervasive suspicion put them all on high alert. Jupiter briefly wondered what would happen if they opened fire on the fleshy surfaces.

He didn't need prescience to tell him that was an idiotic idea.

"It's asleep. Pained, maybe?" an operative with the callsign Piper added. "Drowsy . . . I'm not sure. But I don't want to be here when whatever this place or thing is wakes up."

Jupiter and the rest silently agreed to that, not wanting to spend a second more in this accursed place.

"Alright, let me try something else. I am not looking forward to going in blind," Jupiter muttered as he focused on another connection.

The quantum link tethering the five Poltergeists to his AI core aboard the *Phantasmagoria* remained unaffected. A quick check told him the destroyers were ready to begin harassing the enemy war fleet as soon as Lady Straise was secured. As for the rest of his shells, he peered through each of their sensors, double-checking on the status of surface teams.

He breathed a sigh of relief, seeing nothing amiss so far, apart from heightened Thralled activity with dawn soon coming.

"Alright, I'm taking over Shank-Five and seeing what Scalpel is up to," Jupiter told his three captains. "Stay put for now. Send out the spider drones to scout down the three paths."

All three nodded, motioning for the ones assigned to each team who carried the cat-sized drones in question, made of the same shadow-black steel as their cloaked armor.

With that, Jupiter closed his eyes, leaving Shank-One to its half-automated state. He transferred his primary attention to the Poltergeist accompanying the Scalpels in a split second. Jupiter opened his eyes, grunting as he saw less flesh and more conventional and straight surfaces.

Specifically, they were in a roomy storage space, enough for the fifteen . . . no, Jupiter recounted, nine Scalpels and his significant frame.

He spotted Surgeon, who was team leader for Alpha's Scalpel team but was now commanding both Bravo and Charlie.

"What do you have, Surge?" Jupiter walked over to the lieutenant in charge, a short-beaked Iexian, speaking through comms again. *"Downstairs is fucked. Either*

the tunnels are shifting, or it's non-Euclidean geometry. We're betting it's the former because if it ain't, we'll spend eternity in this place."

Surgeon brought up a tablet. *"Sent Cutter and Swan to look for Thralled matching their build. They're testing with what we think are the run-of-the-mill Thralled."*

"What good will that do? Aren't there any data centers or terminals here?" Jupiter frowned.

The lieutenant sighed. *"Seems like the Thralled are just averse to tech. If it's important, then it's passed through word of mouth. Essentially, we're looking for gossip. I don't care how brainwashed they are, even lunatics get bored."*

Jupiter hummed, trusting the officer's judgment mainly because it had already been discussed as a possible avenue for gathering information. *"So, what's the plan then?"*

"Cutter and Swan will go around disguised as Thralled. We have already studied their mannerisms on the surface. Our knowledge is shallow, but we only need a bit of conversation to get what we need. After that, we put them to sleep. Non-lethal, in case they have cranial implants or if the base is keeping track of their health," Surgeon answered as he switched the screen to show six different perspectives.

"You sent a pair to shadow each of them?" Jupiter asked.

Surgeon nodded. *"I did. Yoyo and France are following Cutter. Matcha and Terrier for Swan."*

"Matcha?"

"She drinks too much of the stuff," the lieutenant said with a shrug, then pointed to one of the screens. *"Swan's approaching one now."*

Jupiter watched as the disguised Scalpel approached a fellow cultist in the same hooded robe. The alien was kneeling before a small altar, lighting dozens of candles, holding them, and muttering inaudible words.

"Nilnis ng'kant kang Dhyon," Swan whispered, right hand on her heart and left on her forehead in a half-prayer position.

The cultist regarded her and then returned the gesture. *"Sayen ng'kolba kang Dhyon."*

Swan knelt beside him, offering to help light the candles, which he accepted. As they continued, the disguised Scalpel offhandedly asked, "How long do you think it'll take?"

The cultist perked up at her question. "Hm?"

"Do you think the heathen will remain obstinate after so long?"

Jupiter hummed, impressed at Swan's acting. Her seamless words were tinged with just the right amount of contempt for those who were not of the faith.

Realizing her question, the cultist chuckled. "Not for long, I think. The High Seer has come down personally to see the ritual's completion."

Swan suppressed her surprise at the crucial information. The same wasn't necessary for those listening in, who visibly grimaced at the presence of the highest-ranking Thralled in the system, although they expected it.

"Ritual? Have her ask about that," Jupiter told Surgeon, who nodded and relayed the order to Swan.

The disguised Scalpel hummed in delight, lowering her head as she clasped her hands. "It would be best if she wakes up from her blasphemy and sees Absolution's light."

"She will." The Thralled smiled, closing his eyes as he lit the last candle.

Swan saw an opportune moment as they stood together.

"How long do we have until the ritual? I need to ready myself," Swan asked gently.

The cultist frowned, his brows furrowing under his hood. ". . . The ritual is ongoing. And ready yourself? We're acolytes. Our place is in the prayer halls. We're not going to be anywhere near . . . the ritual chambers . . . What . . . ?"

"Ah, I see." Swan smiled, scratching her cheek in embarrassment. She quickly bowed, taking a step back. "Thank you, *kuay*. Forgive me. I can be forgetful at times. Now, if you'll excuse me."

Frowning and beyond suspicious, the acolyte reached out to grab her wrist. "Wait . . . what cadre—"

Before he could continue, a needle slammed in between his eyes, cutting off his words. Slurred groans left his throat as he stumbled and swayed. Swan reached out to grab the cultist by the shoulders, dragging him to an empty closet in a barren corridor, where she left him in his slumbering state.

"Need to keep the conversation short. Otherwise, they start to piece things together," Surgeon explained before pointing to another screen, this one of Cutter.

"The fortress shield is acting up," he remarked to a cultist prodding a tester on an electric panel.

"What would you know about that, brother?" said the cultist, glancing his way with a raised brow.

Cutter shrugged. "Heard from the observers and technicians downstairs that they detected strange ripples. They sent a team to check on the shield generator below."

"What are you talking about?" The Thralled stepped back, narrowing his four eyes at the disguised Scalpel who was leaning casually against the wall. "Below? The shield is up—"

A needle pierced his nape, delivering the unassuming sedatives into his system. The cultist yawned involuntarily, wide eyes drooping until he slumped forward.

However, as Cutter moved to drag the acolyte to a hidden corner, two thuds echoed behind him. He glanced at the source, seeing Yoyo and France incapacitate two other acolytes who'd had the misfortune of passing by.

They nodded, giving the okay as they moved the three sleeping bodies.

Surgeon frowned as he watched. *"We can't keep this up. They'll notice sooner or later that a few are missing."*

"This isn't enough information. We need . . . we need someone who's been to the prison. Look for a cadre leader, a senior. They're the ones with the silver necklaces," Jupiter ordered.

The lieutenant nodded, giving the go-ahead to Swan.

It didn't take long to find one, but waiting until the lead acolyte separated from her subordinates took a few minutes of stalking. Thankfully, as with all organic beings, she eventually needed to relieve her bladder.

Swan followed the old female acolyte, stopping her before she entered one of the stalls. The Scalpel adopted an overeager aura, the standard for zealous young cultists.

"Senior sister, is it true? Is it true? Will the High Seer finally break the heathen wretch?" Swan asked, bouncing on her heels as she invaded the older acolyte's space.

Combined with her need for physical relief, the acolyte only confirmed in impatience, pushing away her supposed junior. "Yes, yes! It's true, now leave me, fool child. Can't you see what you're doing? Who's your cadre lead—"

"Did you see *him*—" Swan interrupted before bowing deeply. "Ah! Apologies, I forgot."

Swan quickly performed their greeting, and the other reciprocated begrudgingly. "Highly irregular," she grumbled. "This new generation is too soft on their education. What is your name, girl?"

"Kalar, senior sister," Swan readily replied with the name of the acolyte from whom she had appropriated her disguise.

"Twenty lashes and an evening within the cube of thorns." The acolyte cadre leader smiled with a cruel glint. "You will show me your back tomorrow. Do you understand?"

In a show of true acting, Swan trembled, her head nearly touching the floor. "Yes, of course, senior sister. But . . . ?"

The acolyte senior sighed, her eyes softening as she cupped her own cheek with a far-off look and a smile. "I did. And . . . well . . . those of his caliber are above and beyond. There is no doubt he will succeed and our proselyte will shower us with praise."

Seeing a vulnerability, Swan capitalized on it as she continued to prod discreetly. "Forgive my impertinence, but someone like me can't ever step on the High Seer's light. Did . . . did you go down to the prison to watch him work? What was it like?"

"Silence, child. I shall indulge your curiosity. Take it as part of your education." The cultist raised her chin before clearing her throat. "But no, I couldn't see him perform the divine's work. Though I had it on good authority from Temple Warden Inhr when I went to see him below."

"Bingo." Jupiter grinned as he watched the scene play out.

Swan smiled as well, looking at her senior with a beaming gaze. "A . . . a few hours ago?"

"Hm? Obviously, when else could I have done so with the final hours upon us? Fool girl! Now if you'll excuse me, I need—"

"Do you have your tablet with you, senior sister?"

The acolyte frowned, her brows furrowing as she squinted at the disguised Scalpel. "I do . . . Wait, no, why are you asking for my tablet? Who are—"

Before the cadre leader could utter more, two invisible assailants tackled her to the ground, stabbing a needle into the main artery of her neck. Matcha and Terrier high-fived one another as they swiped the tablet from under her robe.

Matcha handed it to Swan, who snaked a cable from her wrist implant and connected it to the device. However, before she could begin her hacking, Jupiter and the rest of Scalpel arrived outside the restroom.

"May I?" he asked as he stooped down from the door. Swan grinned, handing the tablet to her commander.

Jupiter quickly decrypted its inferior security system and scoured it for what it wanted.

He pumped his fist in the air, grinning. *"Got it. Tablets always have some location tracker. Just need to follow her steps on the way to the prison."*

"Cutter reported back and said he also managed to squeeze out info that the ritual site is below, attached to where they keep their . . . sacrifices," Surgeon informed him.

Jupiter nodded. *"Alright. Try to find more data, but it's secondary. Top priority is to help Machete sabotage this whole place, and then regroup at the cavern. If the cavern is compromised, then head to the surface."*

"Roger." The lieutenant saluted.

Closing his eyes again, Jupiter briefly inhabited his Shank-Four Poltergeist and instructed the Machetes to head upstairs, find the shield generators, and bring it down on his signal. Afterward, Jupiter jumped back to his Poltergeist Mark II with the Shivs.

He smiled, giving the three section captains a thumbs-up. "Found the path. Did the scout drones find anything useful?"

"Nothing that we could discern. We called them back before they went too far," Orion reported.

"Then let's move. Full sprint. We've wasted enough time as it is."

Jupiter stood to his shell's full height before lowering himself into a runner's starting position. The rest of his Shivs took similar stances, and with the way forward revealed through their heads-up displays, they took off toward the left path.

The fifteen operatives and their commander whizzed through the winding tunnel, heading deeper into the bowels of the pyramid. Soon enough, flesh completely took over the tunnel's every surface, and a new material emerged. At first, they thought it to be stone, only to realize it was a ghastly mix of bone, chitin, and a keratin-like material.

After minutes of following the trail the senior acolyte had taken, the Shiv team emerged into a cavern magnitudes larger than the one above. Here, nothing of its architecture suggested that it was made by mortal hands. Organic growths lined the walls like tumors, thick ropy veins wrapped around soaring high pillars that braced the ceiling like the ribs of a giant beast.

A fetid wind blew through the underground chamber, hitting the operatives as they stood at a cliff overlooking an abyssal pit.

Jupiter scanned below but saw nothing of a bottom. He grimaced, eyeing the prominent bridge suspended over the black, made of dark stone, bone, and flesh. It connected their platform to a mass on the far end that glowed like a pulsating boil.

Braziers alight with purple flames lined either side of the bridge, burning without smoke, whipping back and forth in the noxious wind.

He squinted at the double doors sunk into the immense organic growth on the other side.

"Right, remind me to tell the armada to glass this entire planet once we leave," Jupiter muttered as they continued.

The operatives heard a low chant carried in the wind a quarter into the bridge. Prayers and haunting incantations sang in a hundred voices, rattling and pained. Its wailing echoed throughout the cavernous expanse, and the entire structure groaned in unison as if answering the call of the many voices.

Just then, Augur shouted frantically, "Brace!"

A vicious earthquake racked their surroundings, and a deep, all-encompassing agony roared from below. The fleshy mass that covered everything shuddered, twisted, and expanded like innumerable intertwined muscles, spasming and cramping.

Jupiter and the Shivs locked their boots on the ground. Their armors automatically detected the shake, deploying boot spikes that prevented their wearers from tumbling.

Once the rumbling subsided, Jupiter turned to everyone. "All good? Then move it!"

However, when they did, an operative named Sweats from Charlie Section toppled over.

"Urgh! What the—" he grunted, looking down to see a tentacle the size of a tree root wrapping around his ankle, his armor's shield fighting back to prevent his leg from being crushed.

"Hells! Let go of me, *detwaaah*—" Sweats shouted as the fleshy tendril coiled around his leg and lifted him up into the air. Kelios jumped high, grabbed

Sweats's hands, and pulled him back to the ground. A split second later, a hail of gunfire shredded the tentacle before it could continue to drag Sweats toward the bridge's edge.

The thundering shots rattled their surroundings, and it responded in kind, echoing with an unholy shriek. Dozens of tentacles burst forth from the fleshy bridge, some red with viscera, others spiky with bone protrusions. All surged toward the Shivs like hellish spears and whips.

Kelios and Sweats got up, bringing their weapons to bear and firing back to back with unerring precision.

Augur dodged to the side, pumping positron beams at the tentacle aimed her way. Half a second later, the rest of the crew responded in kind, driving the onslaught back. The attacks slammed against their psi barriers and energy shields, knocking them a step back as their defenses flared with light.

Several of the Shivs drew knives, slashing at the tentacles, dodging and weaving.

Rook stepped forward, aiming his heavy inferno beam cannon at the ever-increasing number of appendages. "Here comes the sun!"

With a click, a thick, harsh orange beam shot out of his cannon, melting everything in its path. The cleansing heat beam was so utterly destructive that everyone's helmets filtered out the straining sight before it could blind their visuals.

Charlie's captain laughed gleefully, and Jupiter watched as he scythed them a path forward.

"Break through them! Go loud, go loud!" Jupiter ordered, closing his eyes to send the message to the rest of Task Force Dagger.

The cavern shook and rumbled in an angered reply. Bony stalactites fell from the ceiling, crashing against the bridge. Several more quakes reverberated the space, and up on the surface, dozens of well-timed explosions blasted apart critical structures of the Chained Souls base.

Vehicles went up in flames and officers died instantly as the assassin drones divebombed and drilled into their heads. The cult's comms went dark, and the lights flickered as the main and sub-reactors within the temple cascaded into failure.

An enormous detonation exploded in the center of the pyramid, cracking the surface and bringing the fortress shield below half strength and rapidly depleting.

Everywhere, chaos descended onto the shocked Thralled as the Bayonets, Dirks, Machetes, and Scalpels engaged from the shadows to wreak havoc before slinking back unseen. At the same time, Jupiter's Poltergeists went wild, turning into metal demons that ripped and tore at anything in their paths.

As for the command teams, they broke into a sprint, firing and slashing as they crossed the bridge like lightning bolts. Their armors switched from complete stealth to an illusory mirage that made the tentacles miss by a wide margin, tricked into thinking they had successfully gored their targets.

"Go! Go! Go! Forget the damned tentacles! Make it to that tumor thing!" Jupiter ordered, bringing down his claws as he took point.

He spun around, his bladed plasma-tipped tail cutting large swathes of the tentacles faster than they could regenerate. Jupiter grimaced at the nauseating sight as the tendrils behind him split sickeningly into twos and threes.

Nevertheless, they continued, finally reaching the other side. Before them stood a pair of ancient stone doors filled with religious bas-reliefs that boggled one's mind like an everchanging illusion filled with accents of chains, subjugation, and purity.

Jupiter accelerated and shoulder-tackled the eight-meter-high doors, knocking them open. He skidded to a halt upon entering, unscathed and grim-faced as he took in the new surroundings.

"I guessed right. Ritual chamber by the prisons. Makes it easy when your sacrifices are so close, huh?" Jupiter snarled as he eyed the twelve agape cultists.

Each wore robes that reached the floor, hiding their different forms. They were of various species, humanoid and other. More prominent were the chains and shackles that covered their bodies like grotesque accessories.

In the forefront, above a mob of frightened captives bound to slabs on the floor, was one Jupiter could only guess was the so-called High Seer.

Metal rings clamped the eyes of the Thralled psionic, rendering him blind, yet he noticed their arrival, staring agape and incredulous, hissing with yellow needle-like teeth. "Who dares interrupt—"

The rest of the Shivs rushed into the ritual chamber, their footsteps echoing in the vast, open space, silencing the cultists as they backed away in shock.

It was circular, with high, vaulted ceilings that seemed to stretch upward forever. The entire chamber was organic, much like everything else this far down. But unlike outside the chamber, here the fleshy walls pulsed with more life, more warmth, writhing gently while a thick, viscous fluid dripped from the ceiling.

At the center of the room hung a massive, strange glowing organ. Tendrils and tubes snaked across the ceiling, connecting to this bulbous mass like chains to a chandelier. The scent of decay and the wails and cries of the hundred gaunt prisoners filled the air.

Jupiter's face twisted in rage as he saw the tormented embedded into the fleshy walls of the chamber, leaving only their torsos and heads exposed. Their distorted limbs twisted and contorted unnaturally, sinking deep into the surface.

Their viscera spilled forth, hanging like strewn seaweed from their disemboweled guts, yet they still lived, their eyes forced wide open by thin, nerve-like tendrils.

The skulls of some had been partially removed, their brains exposed and pulsating, glistening with a slick film.

A kaleidoscope of emotions from deep sadness to rage, euphoria to a drooling emptiness, shifted across their faces like a morbid slideshow. Incomprehensible prayers begging for release whispered from their dry, bloody mouths, their eyes pleading for mercy, unblinking, crying.

"She's not here." Jupiter was hit with torrents of shame when he felt relief at that, as did the rest of the command team who fanned out, surrounding the Thralled in the center of the room, who in turn surrounded the fear-stricken captives, pale, naked and covered in bleeding wounds carved in the shape of sigils.

Suddenly, a cultist snarled, walking toward Jupiter, who could see the hidden gun beneath his overly long sleeves. "Blasphemers! Invaders! How dare you—"

BANG.

The source of the speech dropped dead with a smoking stump for a head.

"Anyone else?" Jupiter muttered coldly, his positron rifle aimed at the remaining eleven, particularly at the one in the center. "Which one's the High Seer?"

One of the high-ranking Thralled subconsciously glanced toward the center individual. It was barely a split second, but the AI didn't miss a beat.

At that exact moment, Jupiter launched himself forward, eating up tens of meters instantly as he grasped the rotund cultist by his neck.

"*Hurk!*" the High Seer clawed at his neck as he was summarily lifted off the ground until he was eye to eye with Jupiter. The alien of unknown species, clad in pitch-black robes with golden trim, glared balefully at him, seething and sweating.

"I'll ask you once, or five of your buddies go poof," Jupiter warned with a hiss. "Where is Nuwa Straise?"

Another Thralled stepped forward, chin raised high as he pointed an accusatory finger. "Minion of the Aberration, you will not intimidate us! We are the Chained Souls! The Temple Seers of this holy place, and you will release the High Seer or suffer the consequences."

Jupiter rolled his eyes. "I didn't ask you. I'm asking this one."

The High Seer huffed and puffed, spittle foaming at the corners of his mouth. "Metal . . . demon! I will never—"

A high-pitched whine and a thundering bassy *whoomph* blasted apart a handful of cultists on the far left. Rook disengaged, pulling up his smoking inferno gun as he stared dispassionately at the smoldering remains.

"Right, should have expected as much." Jupiter sighed, releasing his grip on the High Seer. The Thralled hacked and coughed as he dropped to the ground, taking in lungfuls of air.

He turned to the surviving cultists. "Who's the warden of the prison?"

One of them, shivering in soiled robes, pointed toward a pile of ash.

"Shit," Jupiter grumbled, pinching the bridge of his nose before shrugging. He turned to face his three captains.

"Send the scouts. I see a couple of doors here; find Lady Straise. Oh, and detain the rest of the vermin asswipes," Jupiter ordered his Shivs, then noticed the quivering captives looking at their saviors with a flicker of hope. "Puck, see to their health. We're bringing them with us."

"What about . . . ?" one of the Shivs asked, glancing at those embedded in the walls.

Kelios shook his head as he moved. "If we can find a way to extract them. But otherwise . . ."

He sighed as the teams moved. Puck moved to the captives with two other medics, silent as the grave, as they released hostages from their shackles. From there, they scanned their bodies and pulled out a vile of medical nanites. One captive flinched back, only to sigh in utter relief as the medic poured the silver slime over her worst wounds. Then he moved on to help the next.

The rest of the force moved grimly, scouring the area before moving toward the four passageways extending from the chamber.

"It's . . . it's too late," the High Seer wheezed, massaging his sickly green throat. "I don't know how you infiltrated our temple, but you can do nothing to stop the awakening of the Nidus! Your arrival has only hastened its rise, for it knows you do not belong!"

Jupiter socked the cultist in his face, decimating his nose into a flat pancake gushing with blood. The High Seer stumbled back, wailing as he grasped his face.

"Don't know what any of that means, and I don't fucking care." Jupiter scowled at the pathetic fly, looming over him in all his murderous, seven-foot glory. He whispered down to him, eyes empty of mercy. "Listen to me, you little shit puddle. I am a hair's width from losing it with what you've done. Push me further, and I'll send you to my sister."

The High Seer furrowed his brow, glaring at him with confusion as he stammered, "What . . . ? How is that a threat? Why should I care about your sister?"

Jupiter straightened back, glancing at the hundred bound souls lining the walls of the ritual chamber. "All these poor wretches you're torturing. Every single one of them combined wouldn't total an iota of the pain she could inflict on your ugly little head. Or, who knows, I might eviscerate you right now. Wanna bet, little man?"

The High Seer shrank back, breathing erratically as he stymied the blood pouring from his ruined nose. "I—"

A kick from the side shattered his knee, toppling him to the ground in a shriek of agony. Jupiter turned to Captain Merina, whose transparent visor allowed him to see the brutal hatred burning in her eyes.

She grabbed the hem of the High Seer's robes, pulling him to her face. "Where is Lady Straise? What did you do to her!?"

A second without an answer later, Merina jammed a finger at his eye, pressing deeply as she threatened to gouge it out.

The High Seer yelped, trying to escape the shark woman's grasp. "*ARGH! STOP!* She . . . she wouldn't see the truth! Not in time for the ritual, at least. I had to make her see the error—"

"IS SHE ALIVE!?" Merina screamed.

"She's alive, she's alive!" the High Seer wailed, grimacing then breaking into a manic smile. "Hahaha! Yes, she's alive! But she's probably wishing she wasn't right now! THE STUBBORN HEATHEN DESERVED WORSE FOR HER SINS AGAINST ME! THE BOUND ONE SHALL ENJOY BREAKING HER FUR-THER! AND SO WILL HE DO THE SAME TO ALL OF—"

His words died in his throat as Merina pressed her boot on the cultist's neck, just enough to make him choke.

"You will die this day," Merina seethed, turning away.

Jupiter glanced between her and the writhing Thralled leader. A moment later, one of the Shivs shouted his way.

"Commander! We found the cells!" The operative motioned to one of the passageways.

Jupiter tensed, seeing the end of the road for this hellish mission. He kicked the High Seer, ordering him to stand. "You're coming with us."

He turned to the operative, callsign Bags. "Lady Straise?"

"We think she is at the end of the hall. There's a heavier door there," Bags reported.

Jupiter nodded, ordering Kelios and the Charlie Section to stay and guard the detained cultists. The rest sprinted in the direction where Bags pointed.

As they ran through the corridor, they soon found themselves in the temple prison. Rows of cells lined each side of the broad corridor with bars made of a bonelike material, strong as steel. Myriad races pulled from all corners of the Uraki Sector filled each cell to the brim, rotting in filth, their terrified and hysterical eyes peering from the shadows.

Gaunt things, all bone and sinew. They were scarred and mangled, pale-faced with deep-set eyes and sunken cheeks.

Most lay on the floor, scales peeled from their flesh and healed in a sickly way while pus and infections ravaged their bodies. Some lacked one or all of their limbs, savagely hacked away and crudely stitched back together. What arms or legs they did have were mangled beyond recognition, left to rot.

Many lay dead in their cells, crushed in the sea of bodies.

Those with some semblance of clarity tentatively crawled toward the cell door, sticking out their hands, wailing as they desperately reached out for their saviors, begging for release.

"Galactic Legacy Federation. We're here to rescue you," Jupiter shouted as they passed. "Hold tight, we'll get you out!"

Finally, they reached the end of the hall.

"Here it is." Bags gestured at the door. Unlike the other cells, this was made of a solid slab of ivory-hued chitin.

Jupiter knocked on it, scanning its composition. He shrugged before spearing his clawed hands forward, jamming them on either side of the door, and grasping it tightly. With a heave, Jupiter ripped it off its organic hinges like pulling a nail from its bed.

He tossed it aside and looked in.

"Holy shit," Jupiter gasped, shuddering as he stepped back in disbelief at the unrecognizable shape inside the damp and pitch-black cell.

Someone else looked in and immediately vomited at the horror.

Merina shrieked like a banshee and lunged at the wretched High Seer, stopped only by her compatriots before she could tear him to shreds. Denied her due, she pushed them aside, rushing into the cell.

Jupiter watched as she pulled out all the medical nanites from her first-aid kit and poured them over the small, bloody mess that was her charge. Merina scanned the biological machine her lady was tethered to, then gently extracted the vein-like arteries that were embedded into her skin.

A wet, gurgling noise echoed from within as the nanites worked their magic, and Lady Nuwa Straise woke up, screaming hoarsely as she writhed and bucked and recoiled. "No . . . ! No more . . . ! Please . . . !"

"My lady. It's me, it's Merina. We're here to rescue you," the captain pleaded, only for it to fall on deaf ears as the manic-eyed Kalachian crawled back into a corner.

"No . . . no, no, no, no! It's not real. It's a lie, a trick, a lie! Nothing's real! NOTHING'S REAL!" Nuwa cried out through her raw throat as her flayed hands clawed her face.

She scraped her teeth against her ruined lips, whimpering, "I won't . . . I won't cry again, please . . . please stop . . . You're not real . . . mother . . . father . . . I'll behave . . . I'll be good . . . I'll behave . . . please . . . please . . . no more . . . no more."

Jupiter watched as the young leader of the famed Seventeenth broke down, reduced to a hurt, sobbing mess.

Merina gnashed her teeth, tears streaming down her face as she held her Nuwa's fingerless hand. "I'm sorry . . . I'm so sorry, my lady . . ."

Jupiter stepped in, helmet unfurling to reveal his face. Nuwa shuddered, eyes warily looking up into his calm expression.

"Don't worry, kid, you're safe now," Jupiter whispered, producing a sterile blanket from his own medical kit and handing it to Merina. "We won't let anyone hurt you, okay?"

He pressed a finger on his temple, demanding Kelios to get here.

After twelve horrible and scream-filled minutes, with the assistance of their best medic, they extracted Lady Nuwa from the terrible organic machine that had kept her brutalized body alive. They wrapped her in a blanket and then assembled a hover stretcher, placing her within, heavily sedating the Fourth Scion as more nanites went to work.

The trained operatives pushed her out of the cell with Merina at the lead. Others swarmed forward to bust open the other cells and let all the prisoners out. Yet that task proved difficult with how many failed to even stand, decrepit and frail as they had been for who knew how long.

Jupiter blinked, finding himself alone with his thoughts. He felt a hollow chasm in his chest and wondered about his lack of emotion.

"What . . . what about me?" the bleeding High Seer whimpered, hands shaking as he stared wide-eyed at his captor.

Jupiter stopped, realizing there was someone still here with him.

In an instant, he grabbed the High Seer, threw him into the cell, and stepped into the darkness. From within, the worm protested in terror and indignation. "You dare!? The Bound One will avenge me! He is the master of chains and brings our legions and the divine with him! He will— What are you doing? Stay back. Stay back, minion of the Aberration! I said—no. NO! WAIT, WAIT! AGHHH!"

Hellish screams filled the flesh prison for a long agonizing minute, and Jupiter left the cell stained head to toe in blood.

CHAPTER 27

TRIDENT ASSAULT

Above Madraa-II, three Phantasms received the signal from the planet's surface. Captain Hajax of the *Phantasmagoria* and the captains of her sister ships grinned with bloodthirst, finally able to release the pent-up frustration of having a perfect shot lined up for nearly an hour.

"You heard Commander Jupiter!" the destroyer captain shouted gleefully, raising his fist. "Go loud! Show these people-shaped monsters what we've been sowing since we arrived!"

Immediately, the stealth torpedoes, which had been floating without power toward the Chained Souls war fleet, engaged their thrusters to the max. Hundreds homed in on their targets, aiming to sow mass confusion and chaos.

In unison, they slammed against the enemy vessels, cracking underpowered shields. Some even crashed onto the hulls of ships whose shields had been disabled by overconfident captains eager to save on energy.

A plethora of nuclear-tipped warheads detonated in a furious light show, turning entire hulls to clouds of ECM dust that shrouded sensors and scrambled weapon systems. Plasma fire torched metal in a bright blue glow, and seas of single-minded gray goo attached themselves to every surface, burrowing in and biting deep.

Bursts of light bloomed across the void, waking the cultists to the Phantasms' opening act.

Captain Hajax hissed in delight as he shouted, "Main cannons, fire!"

The cannons on each destroyer, with barrels nearly twenty inches in diameter, fired instantly, roaring silently in the vacuum of space, disgorging the fire they'd held back for so long. Like apex predators pouncing on hapless prey, the stealth destroyers' primary guns fired their maser beams, tearing through the void and hounding toward their targets.

"INCOMING!" a Thralled captain barked out to her crew.

She grabbed on to the rails as invisible microwave laser beams struck her ship, one of the largest carriers of the Chained Souls. Their powered-down energy shield struggled briefly against the sundering strike.

The cultist crew failed to react in time to the sudden attack, neither diverting power to their shields nor turning their ship at an angle.

Even then, it wouldn't have mattered. The absurdly lethal maser beam popped the shield like a balloon before blasting apart the hull, drilling deep into its insides.

Even worse for the carrier was the beam from the *Willow* that immediately followed, targeting the weakened and exposed armor to penetrate at a different angle and destroy even more in its path.

Metal parted, searing hot and glowing a deep orange. The flesh of the unfortunate Thralled caught in death's wake cooked, the water and blood within their bodies flash-boiled, and what was left of them subsequently exploded in a mess of gore before evaporating into oblivion.

The two strikes destroyed life support, armories, storage bays, the infirmary, and finally, the power reactor.

The captain couldn't even think whether to abandon the ship as she froze in paralysis from the shock. Her indecision didn't last long, however. Within fractions of a second, a cascade of failures and explosions ripped the carrier apart, blowing it to charred pieces of debris and bathing its neighboring ships in a great and terrible luminescence.

As for *Lady Gray*'s maser beam, it continued through the ship to simultaneously strike a second carrier, repeating the process as it brutally forced its way past the paltry shield and critically damaged the ship's rear.

Fortunately for the *Lady Gray* but unfortunately for the thrall carrier, the strike succeeded in crippling the vessel dead in space.

The crews of each Phantasm rejoiced, feeling euphoric at the perfect salvo.

However, the cultists eventually retaliated in kind, the sharper captains whipping their crews into shape and turning their ships to place their weapons at optimal firing angles.

Within seconds, they fired their menagerie of weapons, from lasers and pulse cannons to kinetic slugs and balls of plasma.

Captain Hajax scoffed at the incoming hailstorm, nodding a command toward the pilot of his vessel.

All three destroyers promptly disengaged, but not before sending a final laugh in the form of an array of coil gunpoint defense cannons. The rotary guns spun viciously, barking and swatting away swathes of projectiles in a single burst.

With that final gift sent the enemy's way, the Phantasms reengaged their cloaking systems, disappearing into the void.

Shocked and enraged, the Chained Souls fleet poured torrents of energy into their scanners, radars pulsing, sifting through every spectrum of light and even searching for the subtle pulls of gravity a ship their size would make.

In the middle of their search, however, a multitude of small explosives detonated in a cloud of electronic noise, masking the area where the Phantasms slipped from their sensors and a vast distance beyond that.

"Where in Pandemonium are they!?"

"Find them! Find them, now!"

"Contact the temple base! Wait, what do you mean they're not answering?"

Suddenly, as the pieces fell in place, the crewmembers of the Chained Souls realized something had gone incredibly wrong.

They scrambled to uncover the mess that had fallen in their laps, desperately calling for the High Seer down in the Temple of the Ivory Maw, unaware that he had already been turned into a red paste.

Headless, their command staff struggled in the power vacuum, splitting the fleet. Over half of the vessels pursued the stealth destroyers, diving into the interference storm in a futile search, while the rest remained in orbit around Madraa-II.

The *Thorned Vice*, the High Seer's flagship, stayed among the second group, vigilantly defending the planet alongside the system garrison.

"They took the bait, fools!" Captain Hajax laughed aloud, his heart pumping as the Phantasm squadron started the hunt.

He ordered the squadron around, circling the herd of lumbering beasts, trying to sniff them out from the tall grass. After several minutes of waiting, the trio of destroyers struck once more.

The surge of energy from the maser cannons forced them out of cloaking, but it mattered little as the angry beams zipped unseen across space and struck yet another capital ship, turning it into a brilliant flash of scorched metal.

The Thralled felt a pang of terror at the hyper-lethal weapons employed by the Phantasms, and the ease with which they bled in and out of reality like ghost ships.

Unknown to them, however, was the immense aid given by the AI core within the lead destroyer, and the sacrifice of innumerable high-end components and processors needed to keep their stealth running.

The cat-and-mouse game continued, turning heavily in favor of the lone trio. Cloaking and uncloaking, weaving their shots through an ever-tighter defense screen, the Phantasms reaped what they sowed, obliterating ship after ship.

The Thralled struggled, cornered and afraid. What few seers remained aboard their vessels, those who hadn't followed the High Seer down to the surface, tried to use their foresight.

It did them no good.

After half an hour of this dance of destruction, in which two more capitals were crippled, the cultist fleet had had enough. Although their technology could not compare to the Phantasms, what did have in spades was quantity.

The Thralled fleet arrayed itself into a spherical formation, vessels turning their broadsides outward so they could leverage the full breadth of their guns.

Everything fired at once, the commanders focusing on launching high explosive missiles and torpedoes at the general area where the destroyers had last fled into stealth.

Some keen captains among them even fired at where they predicted the next attack would come from.

The sheer firepower brought to bear against the trio of ships put immense pressure on the Dagger squadron. Stealthed as they were, they had a set speed limit lest they become beacons to enemy sensors. Each captain individually decided to either keep their current velocity or slowly accelerate.

Captain Hajax continued to grin, feeling the adrenaline coursing through his veins as his destroyer dodged and weaved through the firestorm of projectiles, pulling farther away from the explosions and beams of death.

Unfortunately for *Lady Gray*, her pristine record and hull finally lost its untarnished streak as a lucky shot slammed against her shields and briefly brought her out of stealth.

At once, the cultist warships bore down on the area as she returned to the shadows.

Hajax grimaced, swiping his arm.

"Don't forget about us! Fire!" he ordered, maser beams striking the rear of a cruiser and pulling its attention from the *Lady*.

As they continued the barrage of attacks, the three destroyers discreetly herded the enemy vessels exactly where they wanted them, using the cultist's very own tactic against them. At the nearby hypergate waited an even greater surprise.

At the hypergate designated Sierra for this operation, the Thralled garrison stationed there widened their eyes in disbelief at the readings their watchtowers were spouting.

"What are you saying? *How many* tons are coming through?" one of the observers panicked, already putting on his helmet as he eyed the exit.

"Hundreds of ships! I-I don't know! The sensors are going haywire!" his partner shouted, frozen in his seat.

The hypergate tore open before their eyes, coughing prismatic clouds into reality. The gate opened wider and wider like a great mouth, exhaling a starry nebula and the silhouettes of a mighty fleet.

The stationed garrison broke ranks even before the terrifying warships entered, some powering down in surrender, others fleeing. A handful were too shocked to do anything. A few intellectually deficient captains actually stood their ground.

It mattered little as fifteen crimson-hued warships breached into reality.

"HEAR ME, YE WICKED! BASK IN THE MERCY THAT IS YOUR ANNIHILATION!" Mars bellowed through the general frequency, ensuring the entire star system heard his cry.

The Chained Souls fleet that had split off to hunt the destroyers found themselves agape at the sudden arrival of such gargantuan vessels, quickly reorganizing themselves into a defensive formation upon realizing their distance from the rest of their forces.

They were already in extreme firing range.

His Five Greats, his fearsome battleships, led the charge. The *Alexander*, the *Khan*, the *Caesar*, the *Zhukov*, and the *Bonaparte* surged forth. They did not even bother to decelerate as they purposefully rammed against the watchtowers and stations defending the hypergate.

Their tertiary guns shredded what little resistance existed, paving the way for the rest of Task Force Sierra.

In their wake, the warships of the Thirty-First and Thirty-Fourth breached into reality, each brimming with a hunger for battle that resonated with Mars's lust for war.

With zealous, indignant rage that burned brighter than stars, the Qessheren warships of the Thirty-First cranked their thrusters to the max, seeking to overtake everyone else with the single desire to purge the heretical Thralled.

Scores of starfighters left their hangars, hovering close to their motherships as the faithful pilots sang their prayers to the Grand Symphony.

"Onward, humble warriors of the Choir! Ring your bells! Let the foul monsters in sapient skin know their judgment has come!" Cantor Tendemone commanded with fury aboard her battlecarrier flagship, the *Mother's Lullaby*.

In unison, they propelled forward, turning their reactors into overdrive and burning toward the cultist war fleet that chased the three destroyers.

Aboard the *Gladiator*, Commandant Nullan of the Thirty-Fourth Fleet rubbed his stony chin as he observed the battle data coming in.

"Focus on putting up a defensive screen," he commanded. "We already have two hammers in the form of the Mars and Pilgrim Fleets."

On his word, regiments of battlesuits left their hangars, latching on to their target ships and acting as impromptu point defense. Others formed assault formations, holding in reserve for opportune moments.

The war machines, each between sixteen and twenty meters tall, pointed their mech-sized weapons toward the enemy to fire angry beams of lasers.

Aiding them in reserve, Battlegroup Mag Mell entered the fray, led by the *Tethra*.

Finally, the war god riding upon his steed and escorted by his most brilliant champion finished his exit from the hyper-tunnel. The *Bucephalus* and the *Boogie Mouse* made their entrance in a glamorous display of light, hanging back to let the rest have their fill while still becoming a constant, overwhelming presence to the Thralled forces.

After realizing that what they were seeing was indeed real, the Thralled warships opened fire and charged suicidally against what they saw as metal abominations.

And so, the two forces met in a furious play, exchanging blows left and right.

Yet even the insane zealotry of the cultists broke against Task Force Sierra's bulwark.

While Mars, the Thirty-First, and the Thirty-Fifth mopped up stray cultist vessels in the outer zone, Hypergate Whiskey fluctuated.

Guessing at what was to come, having already witnessed the strength of the fleet that emerged at Hypergate Sierra, the garrisons and patrol fleets that guarded the mining operations, manufactories, and assemblers at the Madraa Zero-G Industrial Zone did the unthinkable by turning the region into a suicidal death trap for anyone that wanted to capture it.

Twenty-five silver-hued warships of the Luna Fleet entered voidspace, heralded by the *Gilgamesh* and the *Xerxes*. Legions of drones leaked from the seams, closing in on the plethora of targets within the asteroid field.

Following Luna's forces, the glorious and wealthy Twenty-First Fleet and the dark and rugged vessels of the Thirty-Fifth Fleet took either flank, with the *Solsollen's Scepter* and the *Krav* content to observe their surroundings and conserve their strength.

Battlegroup Mictlan held back in reserve with the *Xolotl* at its center.

Task Force Whiskey fanned out, waiting as the *Ozymandias* and the *Will of Sisyphus* passed through in their dimension. The *Sisyphus*, who Luna begrudgingly took command of despite her distaste for dreadnoughts as a military asset, loomed over the task force like the king of meteors, ready to bring world-ending apocalypse on any that dared to challenge its dominion.

"Task Force Whiskey has arrived. Proceeding with extermination," Luna called out to the leaders of the two Expeditionary Fleets who were present via hologram on the faux bridge of the *Ozymandias*, complete with drones in the shape of human officers.

Lord Iintei huffed, shaking his head. "Do we have to refer it to an extermination? So crass and villainous."

"They're Thralled, your lordship. They'd happily call it what it is while stabbing you repeatedly in the face and sacrificing your children," Huntsmaster Vro scoffed.

"I am merely stating the facts," Luna spoke dispassionately. "The armada has no desire to house Thralled in our prisons, and they will remain a constant threat should they continue to exist. There is no need to turn this into a moral dilemma, fleet leaders."

She scanned the area with her robust sensors, spotting the warships hiding in the crevices of asteroids and the countless explosives and reactors set to blow amid the space stations and bases.

Luna propped up her circular glasses with her dainty gray fingers.

"This is nothing but logic," she stated, ordering her legion of drones to open fire, launching their payloads of missiles and torpedoes. The two fleet leaders nodded in agreement, watching emotionlessly as they slaughtered everything before them.

Task Force Whiskey cleared through the Madraa Zero-G Industrial Zone, leaving nothing but space dust and shards of scorched debris in their wake.

While the Sierra and Whiskey teams took sovereignty of the outer and middle zones of Madraa, the last and largest prong of the Trident Assault breached through Hypergate November, the closest entrance to Madraa-II.

At the vanguard of Task Force November was the Galla Fleet, the black and golden battleships *Nergal* and *Gugallana* at the tip of the spear like vicious pit bulls on short leashes. Behind them, four battlecruisers and fifty-six subcapitals comprised the rest of the forward formation.

On the wings, the Third and Seventeenth Fleet surged forth with the *Zolann'tono* and the *Moonlit River* at the helm.

And finally, the crown jewel and the sharpest blade of the Exodus Armada slipped into the star system like an imperious goddess pulled straight from the underworld, enthroned atop her palace.

Citadel Irkalla, flanked by the *Ereshkigal*, announced her arrival by hacking into the speaker and sound systems of every Thralled war vessel and station and blasting them with thunderous horns. By its mere presence, it delivered its unshakeable edict.

Those who resist shall perish.

In the War Room of the *Citadel*, the assembled Exodus Council and members of High Command sat around the display table, observing the live three-dimensional map of Madraa. Most leaders were present via hologram, patching in from their own ships.

Andora felt the knot in her soul starting to unwind. Her enemy's thralls had gifted her an outlet for the last arduous month, during which she'd nothing to do but twiddle her thumbs and wait while others did the work for her.

"Not anymore." Andora grinned to herself. "You have nowhere to run, you cowardly flies."

Tov hummed beside her, rubbing his hands over his mandibles. "Status on Task Force Dagger and the rescue operation?"

"Hold one moment, Arbiter," one of the comms officers replied, her faceless helmet glowing. "We've contacted the *Phantasmagoria*. Captain Hajax reports heavy interference in the temple underground. He has received word that they've found Lady Straise alive but in critical condition. They also found and rescued one hundred and twelve captive civilians. Uraki locals."

Andora sighed in relief. "Then that's one weight off our shoulders. Can you contact Commander Jupiter?"

"Enemy fleet has deployed ECM over Madraa-II's orbit. It'll take some time to pierce through the fog, especially with them underground. The focal point of the jamming is the *Thorned Vice*," an electronics officer reported.

Andora frowned, waving the concern away. "Then we'll take that sorry excuse for a battleship out of the board. Status on our opposition?"

"Diminished. The Phantasms have successfully pulled a significant chunk of their forces. However, they've deployed their assets from planetside."

Tov nodded, glancing toward Andora, who returned the gesture.

The custodian of the Exodus stood, looking over the War Room from the dais and showcasing her full martial regalia, complete with an oversized black-and-red naval coat draped over her shoulders. Camera drones hovered above, capturing her visage and broadcasting it to the entire armada.

"My fellow sapients of this raging defiant galaxy, let us sweep aside these cultist scum before they could even think of mounting a presentable fight. As custodian, I command thusly . . . !"

She raised her arm and then slashed the air vertically, stopping with her finger pointed forward.

"CRUSH THEM ALL!"

Together, the legions of sailors, marines, soldiers, pilots, and even brave civilians roared in unison, directing their anger at the enemy that dared slight them, dared to take one of theirs.

Task Force November blasted their thrusters, propelling forward in an unstoppable charge as their primary, secondary, and tertiary guns warmed up.

Every warship apart from the *Citadel* and *Ereshkigal* bared its teeth as they pounced on the Thralled defenders in the amber desert planet's orbit.

Starfighters and battlesuits from the Third and Seventeenth swarmed out in organized chaos, firing away like vicious wasps and hornets.

Missile boats, frigates, and destroyers bobbed and weaved, unleashing their ordnance and firing their main guns on their subcapital counterparts.

Cruisers of all weights brawled against the capitals on the other side, taking blow after blow and coming out unscathed before responding with triple the firepower, smashing apart their so-called rivals and laying them low.

The flagship *Zolann'tono*, under Admiral Yan's command, activated her Grav Dynamo, shackling the enemy flagship *Thorned Vice* and keeping it in place like a grizzly caught in a bear trap. Then the massive beast fired her main armament, a compact version of Andora's Ganzir Guns, lobbing azure balls of plasma fire.

The other hunters summarily took advantage of the Thralled battleship's plight. The twin battleships *Nergal* and *Gugallana* sent a hail of kinetic slugs and laser beams at the *Thorned Vice*, dismantling its shields in record time.

Simultaneously, the *Moonlit River* launched a rain of nuclear-tipped missiles and fired a salvo of her Kalachian dissolver rays. The brutal neon-green beams bleached and corroded everything they touched, melting the armored hull of the late High Seer's battleship as if it were made of candle wax.

Credit where it was due, the enemy battleship roared and answered everything it took, letting off one salvo after another of its heavy railguns and graser beam emitters. But outnumbered and outgunned, the *Thorned Vice* that had terrorized and bullied the Uraki Sector for its three-decades-long life finally imploded in a conflagration of light.

The rest of the Chained Souls war fleet succumbed rapidly after the fall of its champion, and nothing they did could prevent the inevitable. The Exodus Armada had crushed their opposition without even taking their big guns out of reserve.

Andora smiled, complete satisfaction coursing through her veins at the sight of so much destruction.

However, her joy was short-lived as a sensor officer gave an urgent report.

"We're detecting catastrophic phenomena on Madraa-II! Magnitude 9.5! Psionic anomalies manifesting above the temple. It's a . . . storm?"

The council immediately shifted the display table's feed to the desert world and witnessed the strange event unfolding. Andora furrowed her brow as the desert dunes sank and rose, ebbing and flowing like water as the sands danced on the planet's surface.

"What is happening—"

An unholy shriek slammed into everyone's ears. The sound came from beyond reality, pressing down on their minds and souls with corrupted psi. Andora grimaced, barely reacting, as did those of high mental fortitude, who winced before shaking off the sudden racket that invaded them. Those who weren't grunted and gnashed their teeth or curled up for a long couple of seconds as if a vice grip had tightened around their minds.

Andora looked back to the planet, seeing great chasms swallow immense expanses of the desert. Tendrils rose from the abyss within.

"We've got scans of the anomaly . . . it's . . . it's a Leviathan class!"

Those in the room sucked in their breaths at the revelation, realizing that they still had people on the surface. Just as Andora was about to delve into her Network and make manual contact with his AI core aboard the destroyer, an officer urgently spoke.

"Contact from Madraa-II! It's Commander Julius!"

"Put him on-screen, now!" Andora ordered.

Above the display table, Jupiter's hologram appeared, abject worry plain on his face. "About time you guys answered—"

Andora cut him off. "Jupiter, what the fuck is going on down there?"

The AI hissed at something in the ceiling, his helmet closing over his face as he stepped back and aimed his positron rifle at an unseen enemy.

"Something's waking up from its beauty sleep, and it's really damn cranky!"

CHAPTER 28

HASTY EXIT

Ten minutes earlier.

Jupiter stood at the center of the prison hallway, staring down the empty cells with an equally empty gaze.

It had taken a while to get the hundred or so captive civilians out of the hellholes. Many of them required great assistance due to failing health or lack of limbs. Many more were abandoned, discovered to be corpses pressed against the bodies of others, rotting away in filth and squalor.

They had died unknown beings in a dark corner of a galaxy, trapped within the flesh walls of a vile beast's belly.

He looked at one of the cells, filled with a handful of bodies. He noticed one that looked smaller and thinner than the rest.

Jupiter felt nausea rise from the depths of his digital soul, his AI core reacting viscerally at the sight. The fists of his Poltergeist Mark II clenched tight, sharp claws piercing his metal palms, shearing material, and releasing the viscous dark blue coolant that was his blood.

Pure distilled hate flooded his being in a raging river of boiling lava.

"Kind of puts things into perspective . . ." he muttered to no one in particular, looking down at his blood- and gore-stained hands. With a single command, his shell activated its auto-clean function. The red filth slid from his metal skin and down to the floor.

He sighed, rubbing the back of his neck as he stared at the fleshy ceiling.

"Our problems seem rather pathetic, don't they?" Kelios spoke up behind him, stepping from outside one of the cells. "Compared to what these poor souls had to endure."

"You still here?" Jupiter raised his brow at the medic.

Kelios nodded, waving a vial containing countless pieces of skin, each barely more significant than a pea, before storing it in his armor's hidden compartment. "Had to double-check the bodies for identification. I couldn't find any, so I took gene samples. Maybe the Oblivion Fangs have a medical database."

"Huh . . ." Jupiter replied, not having thought of such a thing.

The medic patted his hands, stepping up before him. "We can't stay here."

"I know," Jupiter muttered, closing his eyes.

Kelios sucked in his teeth, peering into Jupiter's eyes before glancing toward the exit.

"We couldn't have done anything for the dead. So don't fault yourself for it. Get your head back in the game, Commander," Kelios lightly scolded, pointing toward the ritual chamber. "There are one hundred and twelve civilians out there. That's who matters now."

"Some of them can barely stand. Can we get them out of here in one piece?" Jupiter asked bitingly.

As if to emphasize his point, another quake rocked the underground, the tremors steadily increasing as if rising to an unseen crescendo. When it subsided, Kelios sighed, shaking his head. "I can't say anything about that except it is our job to go above and beyond."

"And if it ain't enough?" Jupiter asked in a softer tone, his gaze drifting to the many dead they were leaving behind.

"We won't know until we get there." Kelios shrugged as he moved past Jupiter, patting his commander's shoulder. "Just do what you think is right."

After walking a few more steps, he paused, glancing back at him with a smirk. "As you've always done. Come on, we can do group therapy *after* we leave this butcher's paradise."

Jupiter snorted, shaking away the last of his thoughts and sharpening his mind back to a keen edge. After taking a deep breath, he followed, sticking by the Evorian's side until they emerged back at the ritual chamber.

The rescued civilians and a few recognizable faces of the kidnapped operatives from the Seventeenth huddled close to one another, dazed and still in shock, fearful that what they believed was an illusion would fade in an instant.

A few others stood, speaking hoarsely and warily with the Shivs that rescued them.

Jupiter grimaced as he surveyed their decrepit state, trying to think of a solution to get everyone out. There was only so much medical nanites could do. If it weren't for the nutrient pills that the medics had them ingest, the nanites would have sucked their hosts of every last drop of vitality to accelerate regeneration.

Severe malnutrition, dehydration, insomnia, mental afflictions, and other maladies added more and more suffering to these people's already heavy burdens.

Worst of all were those affected by a kind of eldritch rot that Jupiter found disturbingly close to Malignant Starfall, with patches of skin that twisted like putty before settling back. These people were unconscious or close to it, supported by their fellows.

The Thralled did not need to put shackles on them when they already had so many chains binding them, yet still, the mad, sadistic fiends had stuffed them into cells like sardines in a can.

Jupiter glanced at the sniveling cultists, the seers of their precious temple, and the fleet above.

He stepped over to them, adding more oomph to his stomps like a prowling beast with explosive power, ready to maul them into an unrecognizable paste.

"Must be hard to swallow, knowing how easy it was for us to enter your home without none of you the wiser," Jupiter coldly insulted them.

He scoffed, crossing his arms. "Seriously, apart from those weird tentacle things, you guys have your heads stuck so far up your asses that you didn't even bother bringing bodyguards? I mean, not that it would have helped."

One of the flies finally worked up the courage to speak. "W-what did you do to the High Seer?"

"He's indisposed." Jupiter waved off his concern. "Having an intimate conversation with the walls."

"The walls?" The Temple Seer blinked in confusion.

Jupiter looked at his claws indifferently as he continued. "And the floors and ceilings of the cell I left him in. He might be there for a while."

The Temple Seer gulped, shrinking back. "Sinner . . . it matters not. His soul returns to Absolution!"

Another quake racked the place, harsh enough to make him activate his boot spikes. The tormented souls embedded into the walls howled in pain from the shaking.

"Damn it, have you not gotten them out yet?" Jupiter shouted at the pair, Flak and Huggins, who were working on the captive closest to the floor.

Huggins shook his head, frustration evident behind his visor. "Everything we do makes them scream in pain. Their nervous system is completely fused with the wall! If we pull them out, they'll die instantly."

Jupiter snarled, kicking one of the cultists in the gut. "You disgusting pieces of roach shit!"

He turned back to Huggins and everyone else, about to speak when another quake hit them. He shut his eyes, clenching his fists as he felt his head pulse with stress.

Finally, he made the decision. "Put them out of their misery. We don't—"

Suddenly, one, then two, then all the Thralled began giggling. Jupiter glared at the lunatics as their light chuckles turned into manic laughter, tears falling from their eyes and staining the red floor.

"What the hell is your major malfunction?" Jupiter growled at them, aiming his bladed tail their way.

One of them spoke, stammering as she laughed and cried. "It doesn't matter. It doesn't matter. It doesn't matter . . . !"

Jupiter stomped the cultist's shoulder, pinning her to the ground. "Speak up or shut up. What are you saying?"

The seer took deep breaths, wincing in pain as she replied. "The moment you entered this place, you sealed your fates! This is no mere temple, it's—"

"The belly of some giant monster, right?" Jupiter huffed, glancing at their surroundings. "I'm guessing a Colossus-class from how far we've gone? Maybe a Leviathan?"

"Even greater!" the Temple Seer screamed as the rest began muttering and chanting on the ground, worshipping the flesh beneath their feet. "Our care for it is only one of the duties of the Chained Souls and the time has come for it to open its eyes! Our proselyte will arrive with the rest of the faithful and bear witness!"

Jupiter scowled in contempt at the sight.

"Yeah, the flesh, bone, and screaming kind of gave it away," he scoffed.

"Then you should know that whatever you do has no meaning! Your defilement of its temple, its cradle, its rebirth has hastened everything!" she wailed, eyes twitching as she began to convulse, spasms bending her body. "Bask in the glory of the new Nidus, Madraa! Behold! For even Leviathans can disappoint our god, and this is their absolution!"

The mother of all shakes slammed against them. The flesh walls undulated and writhed, and those embedded in them gasped for breath before their heads dropped like puppets with their strings suddenly cut.

Huggins backed away, glancing at one before turning to Jupiter, shaking his head.

The quake continued, rising in crescendo with no signs of stopping. An all-encompassing and unfathomable growl echoed from behind the walls, screaming and raging from all corners and pressing against the minds of those present.

Thankfully, it subsided, rumbling as if whatever process forced it awake both pained and annoyed it.

"Right, we've overstayed our welcome," Jupiter growled, pausing as multiple people contacted him.

He closed his eyes, answering the dropship pilots.

"Commander! We had to lift off; the extraction point was too hot. The whole place is crumbling apart!" the lead flyer reported.

Jupiter nodded. "Head back up and link with the corvettes. They'll be our way out; we got a lot of hitchhikers."

"Copy, Commander. Good luck down there!"

Next he contacted the surface teams. His perspective shifted to the Poltergeist running alongside Bayonet and Dirk, fleeing through the temple to find cover.

He turned to the two Alpha lieutenants of either group. "Domehead, Twig, how bad is the surface?"

Twig clicked his teeth. "Bad enough that we feel put off having wasted our time doing all that sabotage and assassination."

"Regroup with Machete and Scalpel at the main cavern atrium; I'll send you the coordinates. Watch out for Starless fuckery. This place is alive and wants to eat us," Jupiter ordered, then felt a nudge from beside him.

"Should we blow up that thing?" Kelios asked, pointing at the organ above. "I have no idea what it does. Is it some kind of heart?"

Jupiter glanced at the glowing, pulsating organ. He turned to the cultists, "Hey, what is that?"

They didn't answer, too busy writhing and rolling their eyes to the back of their heads.

He shook his head, ignoring them as he took center stage, addressing all of his operatives inside. "Set charges at anything that looks important. Once we get out of here, we blow this joint to hell. Take out your sidearms."

All fifteen Shivs did so.

"Give it to them." Jupiter pointed to the healthiest civilians, picking out the top fifteen. "Then give whatever you can spare to the rest."

He then addressed the naked mob, who shrank under his gaze. "I'll say this once. You guys are a liability, but we will get you the fuck out of here. Don't do anything stupid. Stay inside our perimeter, understood?"

The mob nodded as they received their weapons, clutching them like life.

"Good." Jupiter nodded, then turned to those unable to move. He glanced at one of the massive doors he had knocked down with his shoulder and gestured to his team.

"Load anyone that can't walk on that door. Have the spider drones carry it out."

The Shivs carried out his order, quickly securing the injured atop the huge board before commanding the six cat-sized drones to crawl under the door and lift it.

Just as he was about to give more orders, Jupiter felt something clear up in the air. He drifted back to his AI core aboard the *Phantasmagoria* and saw that the armada had arrived, destroying the battleship above their heads.

Immediately after, someone attempted to contact him through his comms, and Jupiter answered, placing the mini holograms of the War Room in front of him.

"About time you guys answered—"

"Jupiter, what the fuck is going on down there?" Andora cut him off.

Before he could respond, the walls, ceiling, and floors around him shifted. His eyes widened as dozens of shapes buried underneath the organic matter approached them like sharks underwater.

His Shivs instantly responded, aiming their weapons.

Jupiter's helmet encased his face as he stepped back and aimed his positron rifle at the most prominent bulge.

"Something's waking up from its beauty sleep, and it's really damn cranky!"

He fired, popping the mass like a boil.

Jupiter cursed upon seeing the malformed abomination inside.

"STARFALLEN!" he shouted. "OPEN FIRE!"

Sixteen guns and thirty-two shoulder-mounted weapons blasted apart the opposition before they could tear themselves out of their fleshy prison.

Bodies exploded into viscera as blood flash-boiled under the hail of laser, plasma, positron, and inferno beams. Their shoulder-mounted heavy machine guns added to the cacophony, shredding apart bone, scales, and chitin.

In the back of his mind, Jupiter found his other Poltergeists battling with more Starfallen alongside the rest of Dagger as they fought their way to the rally point.

"Jupiter, status report!" Andora called out to him.

"I'm fucking busy!" Jupiter snarled.

Leaping into the fray, he aimed his positron long rifle and fired, sending particle beams toward the mutated aliens that penetrated their skulls. His claws and plasma-tipped bladed tail slashed and diced and slashed again as he turned into a whirlwind.

Not even twelve seconds after the mutations had emerged, the last Starfallen perished, but the operatives didn't breathe easy, only rushing through their duties faster.

Jupiter huffed, scanning the area before returning his attention to the council. "Let me ask: Can you teleport us out of here?"

Andora shook her head. "A metaphysical barrier is interfering with our targeting system. Starless origin."

"And you can't teleport anyone with a tracking marker," Jupiter grumbled. "Fine, how bad is it from orbit?"

Andora sent a video, causing him to grimace deeply.

Everything apart from the pyramidal temple had crumbled into ruin. The dunes themselves had formed deep chasms, revealing the thick alien sandstone and marble below. Tentacles lazily snaked out from the cracks as if tasting the air before slowly returning to the deep.

"So far, it's exposed itself in an area of fifty thousand square kilometers. But there are disturbances ranging nearly two thousand kilometers out."

"Deep scans?" he asked.

Andora sent a cutout of Madraa-II, revealing its layers. She zoomed in on the surface and projected a distorted estimate.

"Ongoing. We think its true size spans an entire continent. As for its depth, unknown. If your location is close to its center, it is the single largest Starless life form we have encountered. Though its nature is making it difficult to get accurate scans."

"Does Nidus ring any bells?" Jupiter asked as he glanced at the now unconscious cultists. "The crazies keep shouting the name like it's their god's gift to the universe."

Tov answered in Andora's place. "We call them World Seeders, Commander. It's a Starless superorganism that merges with the planet, converting raw material into biomass. No one here has ever seen one reach this size."

"What do they do?" Jupiter scowled.

"Birth more Starless. They're essentially forward operating bases for the hated ones. Although they die out in a few years, their lifetime output is apocalyptic. In the past, we've sacrificed much to destroy one before they begin spawning and bringing death to an entire sector."

"Well, we just offed some Starfallen, so I believe you." Jupiter spat at the melting abominations. "They're also conducting some ritual to wake it up and we've confirmed their boss, some schmuck called the Bound One is coming here. We got intel that he's bringing the rest of the Chained Souls."

The occupants of the War Room grimaced. Tov spoke once more. "The Thralled must have kept this one alive all this time, but that matters little now. We'll keep monitoring the planet and all Hypergates for enemy reinforcements. What is Lady Straise's status?"

Jupiter moved to the side, showing the encased hover stretcher guarded closely by Captain Merina. He stepped closer to reveal its sole occupant.

The entire council paled upon seeing Lady Nuwa's horrid state.

"Symphony wept. How is she still alive?" Tov whispered. Captain-superior Melwin looked close to passing out.

Jupiter shook his head. "She needs immediate medical attention. She was hooked up to some machine, and we had to pull her out. Things are getting dicey down here. I don't think this Nidus is fully awake yet and I'm not eager to wait around."

"We believe so as well," Andora replied, disconcerted by what she had seen. "It hasn't done anything but shake up the planet."

"Don't rock its cradle while we're in its fucking gut, but feel free to blow the entire planet up after we leave," Jupiter replied. "I'm hanging up. Call me when something important happens."

Andora nodded. "Good luck, Commander."

Once the comms closed, Jupiter turned to the three captains, who all showed ready signs.

"What about them?" Rook pointed at the cultists.

"Shoot them," Jupiter spat. "No need to bring scummy baggage with us."

He shifted his attention to everyone present, shouldering his gun and ignoring the five bangs that echoed behind him. "Alright, people, let's ditch this joint."

Section Alpha took the lead, scanning the bridge ahead and noting the distinct absence of hostiles. After a handful of seconds, they continued, motioning for the rest to follow.

One hundred and twenty-seven crossed the bridge in haste, the Shiv operatives among them surrounding the rest as they checked every angle for danger. At the center, the three captains escorted the broken slab of a door carrying a dozen people and the shielded hover stretcher containing Lady Nuwa.

Jupiter took point, hounding forward like a metal xeno beast.

No one spoke. The rescuees focused on keeping up with the Daggers in their power armor, huffing and puffing.

Jupiter frowned at their speed. "Come on! You can do it! We came all the way here to pull your sorry asses out of this hell!"

The freed captives pumped themselves up, forcing themselves forward. For the moment, their determination and the momentary adrenaline of the drugs in their system was enough to keep them moving.

Soon enough, everyone crossed the bridge, approached the platform on the other side, and headed straight into the tunnels. Upon entering, the ones who had recently been there noticed the stark difference in their surroundings.

The temperature had risen considerably, and a noticeably fouler-smelling wind blew through the tunnel. Rivers of ankle-deep blood and alien ichor flowed across the floor.

The freed prisoners struggled through the viscous liquid, expending more of their stamina but pushing through regardless. Jupiter ordered several of his Shivs to assist those struggling the most, but pushed the group on regardless.

"If you can't continue, hop on the damn stretcher!" he called out, eliciting some nods from their sweaty heads.

Jupiter was concentrating forward when a massive shake occurred. The tunnel constricted, making everyone stumble.

"Hold on! Grab on to something!"

The tunnel ceased shaking, then expanded. The walls tore open, bursting with the arrival of dozens of Starfallen, more vicious than those before.

No one needed to hear the order, instantly sending a hail of weapons fire at every nasty thing that moved. The freed captives fired in turn, aiding their saviors with the ferocity of cornered animals.

Jupiter aimed his entire arsenal, firing at four angles and slaying tens of creatures every second. Big and small, fast and lumbering, all fell against his firepower.

But the mutated amalgamations of alien beings retaliated in force and number, groaning and wailing in pain, calling out with agonized voices, begging for them to join their tormented bliss. They slashed and charged, spat and bit. Where one died, two more took its place.

The Shivs answered in kind, deploying their trump cards to push back the living tide.

Orion held steady, firing efficiently with the experience and lethality of Tov's Vraken, synergizing with his deadly arsenal. All four of his hands held laser rifles, firing away with precision.

Merlin deployed his psi barriers left and right, focusing more on the vulnerable civilian mob. His head profusely sweated, yet he persisted, his mind working overtime with decision after decision on who most needed his protection.

Augur pushed her prescience, breaking a new record and finally reaching half a second of future sight. She raised her rifle, lining up her aim and downing a handful with each shot.

Ritter, along with the other ordnance experts of their group, concentrated their fire, burning, exploding, and annihilating a path forward, allowing everyone to advance slowly but surely.

Puck and the other medics held back but were no less deadly, covering everyone's backs left and right.

The rest showed their mettle and fury, from Merina's blood rage to Rook's infernal force of arms.

"KEEP MOVING!" Jupiter called out as he bisected a Starfallen from the top down.

A visceral, bloodcurdling scream echoed across the tunnel, triggering the remaining monsters within to howl.

Those without ear protection yelped, grasping the sides of their heads.

And in that moment of confusion, one of the freed captives lost his head, splattered by a ball of Starless acid.

"Shit!" Jupiter cursed as the tunnel shook again. The way forward rose, becoming a slope. The Starfallen ahead slid, tripped, and barreled on their way down.

"Shoot them down!" Jupiter commanded as he took to the front.

However, as the Starfallen lost their footing, so did the many freed captives, tumbling back into the ichor-swamped floor. Jupiter skidded to a halt, rushing back to them.

The Shivs at the rear rushed forth, catching one rescuee after another before they could roll down like pebbles.

But there were only so many hands, and over a dozen still fell farther down.

"Hold the line!" Jupiter shouted, leaping down and grabbing three civilians before summarily throwing them back up.

As he positioned to make another leap, however, the wall to his side burst open like a popped boil, and a goliath of a monstrosity charged at him.

Not Starfallen.

A true Starless grunt, shaped like a praying mantis fused with an octopus straight from hell. Jupiter braced as the Starless rammed into him, causing his foot to sink behind him into the stinking river. His hands grasped the two scythe-like blades whipping toward him.

Tentacles rushed from its body, grasping his shoulder-mounted guns and turning them away.

He had just pushed it back when the ceiling exploded, revealing another Starless. This one succeeded in tackling him to the ground.

However, his attention was on the civilians at the bottom of the slope, who were slowly approaching and realizing their predicament.

Jupiter watched in horror as five instantly died at the hands of the swarming abominations while the rest tried desperately to resist while climbing back up. He roared in rage, burying his bladed tail in his opponent's gut, releasing a torrent of foul-smelling fluid.

"Leave us!" one of the civilians called out with a face full of terror. A club-like limb bore down on her, squashing her into the floor.

Before Jupiter could react, one of the Shivs broke formation, rolling underneath the two Starless Jupiter had dueled. He slid down, firing his weapon unerringly.

"Huggins, no!" someone called out, but the soldier continued down. Projectiles soared his way, and a psi-shield enveloped him.

The sergeant dove into a tactical roll, shouldering his gun, and reached out to grab the two nearby civilians before turning around and climbing back up.

The rest of the escapees at the bottom had already died, crushed under the stampede of Starfallen mutants.

More and more attacks soared Huggins's way, and soon his psi barrier popped, leaving only his conventional shield to hold back the brunt of the attacks.

Jupiter tore apart the Starless that blocked his way, headbutting the ugly thing's face, hopping back, and then performing a brutal dropkick to crush its torso.

It backed away, raising its limbs only to be gunned down by one of his Shivs above.

Freed, Jupiter tried to dash but was blocked yet again by the remaining Starless.

He looked down, seeing Huggins stumble. With all his strength, the operative grunted, caught himself, and threw the two civilians he held back up the slope.

Jupiter widened his eyes, aiming his weapons at the Starless and finishing it off before leaping into the air and catching the airborne two.

"GO!" Huggins shouted, turning back and firing his rifle.

A bladed arm slashed down, popping his overheated shield and slashing his gun in two.

Huggins drew his blade.

More tendrils speared his body. One severed his knife hand.

With a roar of defiance, his fist bashed a Starfallen in its gaping mouth and forced a grenade down its throat.

He smiled.

The tunnel below exploded into a red mist. Boulder-sized chunks of biomass crashed down, blocking the abominations from following them.

"HUGGINS!" one of the Shivs shouted, stepping toward the collapsed tunnel.

"I got him," Flak called out, grabbing the enraged operative by his back module and throwing him back into formation.

Jupiter understood the Shiv's feelings but gnashed his teeth as he forced himself forward. "Knock it off, now move! Move! *Move!*"

The sprint continued as they climbed higher, turning left, right, and pressing forward, blasting apart the fewer and fewer monsters that barred their way. The freed captives grew ragged, their guns empty and melee weapons missing.

One by one, they dropped toward the door slab, hitching a ride with heaving chests.

A few lost their focus. One, then two, dropped dead, struck by a spike of bone or the lash of a tentacle.

Jupiter forced his anger down, feeling powerless, unable to be everywhere at once and knowing what waited for them up ahead.

Finally, the three Shiv teams reached the main atrium cavern.

They found utter chaos.

The rest of the Daggers fought tooth and nail as Starfallen and Starless crawled from every opening, every bloody wound on the fleshy surface. Everywhere, scores of monsters fell, screaming their death knells as they charged toward the circle of soldiers standing atop a pile of corpses.

Bayonets, Dirks, Machetes, and Scalpels delivered fire and destruction to the enemy, slaying and eviscerating unendingly.

Sixty gore-covered harbingers of bullets, lasers, and plasma fire spotted their entrance, aiming their weapons and clearing a path.

And amid large clumps of the beasts, Jupiter's four Poltergeists spun like tornadoes of blades.

"Entrance is blocked!" reported Brick, the leader of Bayonet-Bravo, reloading his heavy machine gun as Jupiter and the Shivs climbed atop the hill of death with the rest of the survivors.

"What!?" Jupiter barked as he joined the perimeter. "Please tell me you fucks found a way out!"

"Commander!" Surgeon moved to his side. "You're in luck! There's a small hangar bay on the top floor of the pyramid! The High Seer's shuttle is docked there. More than enough for dropships, but with how many we have, you might need to get more from the armada."

Jupiter sighed in relief. "Alright, change of plans: we do what you say."

"Jupiter, do you copy?" Andora's voice pierced through his head via comms.

"What!?" Jupiter shouted as he continued to rain hell on the beasts, trying to kill them.

She sighed. *"We have a situation in space. We're detecting fluctuations from Hypergate Sierra. We think it's Thralled reinforcements. It's as you said, but we didn't expect them to be so early."*

Jupiter wanted to bash his head against a wall. "God fucking damn it! Whatever, send what you can down here, our Shades, and lots of transport shuttles."

"Done. Be warned, extraction will be hot. The Nidus is more than awake now, and its tentacles are eyeing the skies. The Third and Seventeenth Fleets will remain in orbit to contain the Nidus and provide you an escort back into orbit," said Andora.

"We'll be out. What about the rest of you?" Jupiter asked, gritting his teeth.

He could hear her smirk as she replied, *"What else? Meeting the new arrivals, of course."*

Jupiter huffed before seeing the horde of enemies halt their assault. He watched with furrowed brow at their sudden inaction. Then the walls began to shake and contract.

Gunfire slammed into them from above as cultist survivors finally entered the fray with maddened battle cries, and the attack resumed in full.

Jupiter pulled his attention from the comms, shouting at the top of his lungs.

"DAGGERS! WE ARE GETTING OUT OF HERE, NOW!"

CHAPTER 29

THRALLS OF THE STARLESS

Vermin-groveling bastards!" Jupiter snarled as he aimed his rifle and popped three Thralled in their faces, taking their upper torsos with them. "They just had to make my life miserable, huh?"

Upon his order to leave, Task Force Dagger had exploded into action. Bayonets and Dirks continued to hold the line with two of Jupiter's Poltergeists, preventing the Starfallen from overrunning their position.

Teams Machete and Scalpel diverted half their firepower to suppress the cultists above.

Everyone else worked on paving a path through the stairway.

"Get the injured off that slab. Carry them on your backs! The rest of you that still have an ounce of strength, get out and move or be left behind!" Jupiter ordered.

Less than a hundred of the freed prisoners survived, shuffling along with harried breath, pushing aching limbs and bloody feet as the Daggers covered their advance.

Dozens among them had to be carried, latched on to the backs of the operative's power armor, two or three prisoners for each, held together by silk-steel rope wrapped around their torsos.

Jupiter touched his temple. "Boss, you still there?"

"*We're listening,*" Andora replied.

"Right, I—*Argh!* Fucking shits, can't you see I'm talking here?" Jupiter barked, covering his Daggers with his Mark II and eviscerating everything in his path. "You guys prepped to receive the Straise kid?"

"*We are.*"

"Great! What of the Phantasms?" he asked.

"*They're too far from the planet and will be better used in the space battle ahead,*" Andora replied.

Jupiter grunted, quickly confirming with Captain Hajax. "Got it. I'll contact you once we've boarded the Shade. Jupiter, out."

He closed the connection, his full attention on the battle ahead.

The din of gunfire buffeted the cavern, pelting flesh and crumbling what little rock, concrete, and metal surfaces remained. The smell of ozone, cooked meat, sulfur, and ash filled the air as Task Force Dagger forced their way through the horde, shielding themselves from the surge of Starless and Starfallen.

All the while, the constant barrage of cultists only increased as their numbers swelled, bringing with them shoulder-fired rockets and dragging out heavy crew-mounted weapons, pelting them from above.

Jupiter focused on these prominent targets, removing them from the equation before they could fire.

His teams moved to the south, where a wide ramp spiraled up, connecting with all floors.

But as they approached it, the ground beneath them swelled.

"Below!" someone shouted as the floor exploded, heaving viscera, stones, and people into the air.

The Dagger operatives landed like cats, though most of the survivors flopped back onto the ground, grunting. Two unlucky ones cracked their necks as they landed.

"Here they come!" Captain Rook rumbled, firing his inferno beam cannon into the open holes where abominations streamed out.

Jupiter threw his Poltergeists at the roughest spots, saving who he could, slashing apart what monstrosity pounced upon him and his men.

As he did, he noticed how the Starless and Starfallen that came from behind surged around them, heading toward the ramp and blocking their path in a wall of twisted eldritch biomass, teeth, claws, and spikes. More still climbed the walls, filling the floors.

At the very least, they held no love for the Thralled or didn't care to discern, butchering any they saw.

Said Thralled didn't seem to have any regard for their own lives, hooting and hollering maniacally and aiming their guns below while their teams began to set charges on the staircase itself.

Jupiter reacted instantly, sending his Mark II and two Poltergeists at these saboteurs. The other two Poltergeists crashed through the blockade of abominations, paving the way forward.

He and the two shells hopped over the writhing pile of monsters before bounding their way up in great leaps, butchering the mad cultists, slapping the explosives they planted toward groups of them, and defending their way up.

He decimated their ranks: Thralled, Starless, Starfallen. He didn't care. Their forms bled together into a single mass, his AI core surging with heat as he leveraged every ounce of processing power within him.

Some even tried to hold him down, preferring suicide if it meant taking his shell with them.

And to his utter shock, one group managed to accomplish just that. Shank-Three's left leg blew apart alongside a dozen of the scum while a brutish bastard tackled his shell and sent it down to the bottom.

"Motherfucker!" Jupiter hissed, feeling his mind at his limit and his shells losing their endurance.

Realizing their dogged desire to prevent them from leaving, Jupiter sent his shells to scour every floor and exterminate every cultist.

He decided then and there to sacrifice his Poltergeists. They'd take the brunt of the enemy if it meant his guys got out.

Level by level, they climbed through blood, sweat, and cultist tears.

"MOVE!" Jupiter shouted from the mouths of all his shells, feeling his internal temperature overheating from all the rage and death he dished out.

Looking down, he saw his Daggers push their way forward, finally reaching the ramp and rushing upward.

Shank-Two sacrificed itself next as Jupiter left it behind to give everyone distance, even unfurling his helmet to reveal the bestial mechanical face and monomolecular fangs which he used to bite at bodies like a rabid dog before detonating.

Just then, as he was busy safeguarding their way forward, a massive beast bulged out of the monster ranks, barreling its way ahead and dispassionately crushing its own kin under its four titanic legs. The Starless behemoth was the size of a young elephant, covered in thick biometallic chitin and slavering with acidic spittle.

It roared, and its allies reacted, throwing themselves in front of the beast and blocking the hail of fire Jupiter's infantry sent its way.

"Bring that thing down! Bring it down!" Rook ordered his section, taking up the rear guard. "Commander, leave this to us! Just keep the way up clear!"

"Copy, Captain!" Jupiter replied through gritted teeth.

A terrible quake occurred then, sending chunks of the ceiling to crash onto the Starless ranks. A tide of blood surged from below, flooding the bottom. But the stone and flood merely slowed the elephantine monstrosity, which shook the debris off and continued its charge up toward the ramp.

A few chunks crashed onto the ramp, cracking pieces that cascaded down below. Daggers and freed captives dodged and hopped over the missing ramp.

Unfortunately, the quake knocked some of the freed captives off their feet, among them, a young Ruzian, who fell through a crack, landing on the ramp below, right between the rear guard and the charging behemoth.

Rook rushed forward like a landslide, firing his inferno beam cannon at a melted piece he'd been focusing on and finally searing the flesh within. The beast howled in pain but didn't stop.

"Captain!" one of the Charlies shouted.

"Stay back, keep going!" Rook answered back as he grasped the unconscious boy and threw him to his section.

Then he hurled his bulk forward, shoulder-tackling the massive beast back down the ramp.

But as soon as he turned around to return to the force, tentacles burst out of the downed Starless, whipping toward the captain and wrapping around his waist and limbs.

Before anyone could react, even Jupiter, the beast dragged Rook off the ramp and down far below into the sea of monsters and blood.

"NO!" Jupiter screamed at having lost another of his comrades, only to have the energy shield of his Mark II pop and his head rocked to the side by club-limbed Starfallen.

He snarled, sensibilities momentarily lost as he tore at the bastard before him.

"Goddamnit!" Jupiter roared when a signal came through his head.

"Commander, this is Captain Kepper of the Little Rascal. *Your rides have breached the atmosphere, but we can't come any closer with this much anti-air. Where are you?"* the voice of Shade-One's CO spoke through comms.

"We're almost to the top floor hangar. Wait for us!" Jupiter replied, feeling a pang of pain in his head.

Kepper grunted in confirmation. *"Copy, Commander, but make it quick. This Nidus thing can see through our cloaks, and it's not happy!"*

Jupiter gritted his teeth, nodding. "Just be there, Captain."

A moment later, Surgeon called out to everyone. "We're here! This is the floor!"

The ragged group sighed in relief as they climbed onto the target level, rushing straight down the open hall.

A barricade of crates, barbed wire, sheet metal, and cobbled-together shield emitters blocked their way. Still, Jupiter quickly responded, sending his Mark II and the last two Poltergeists forward, all suffering from various degrees of damage.

He naturally drew the bulk of their fire as the panicked cultists fired everything they had at the sleek metal demons zipping through the long corridor.

Their confidence rose as the sheer quantity stopped Shank-Five in its tracks. The suit crashed to the floor in a smoldering mess.

"GET OUT OF THE WAY, RATS!"

The cultists' arrogance quickly melted as Jupiter's Mark II and his last Mark I pummeled through the ad-hoc barriers and tore apart the last Thralled on this desert planet.

Task Force Dagger moved past the smoldering remains, their firepower concentrated on keeping the horde back. Their barrels glowed red hot, and ammo and explosives ran low or empty.

But move still, they did, with the spider drones assisting in carrying the injured and unconscious.

And finally, they reached the meters-wide blast doors that led into the hangar.

Jupiter hacked into the controls, opening the doors as he ushered everyone through.

When the last of the rear guard had come through, Jupiter entered the hangar, leaving the Mark I behind as the blast doors locked behind him. He flinched, feeling it torn to shreds, but not before taking a dozen with its claws and blades, and dozens more when it self-destructed in an obliterating inferno, denting the blast doors.

Jupiter commed Captain Kepper as he looked around the quaint open hangar and the wide vista revealing the apocalyptic landscape of an accursed planet.

Tentacles as tall as skyscrapers reached for the skies while legions more of varying sizes twisted and writhed. Each limb was lined with teeth, suckers, and baleful, sleepy eyes that stared into the skies above.

Several tentacles lashed out, launching spikes as large as a person at five two-hundred-meter-long vessels.

The Shade corvettes hovered twenty kilometers above the surface, dodging expertly like buzzards. But with their bulk, the crews couldn't hope to evade every attack, relying additionally on their advanced stealth systems and shields.

In their midst, Jupiter saw the scores of starfighters and battlesuits intercepting the organic projectiles.

"Hell, yes! Captain, we're here! We see you!" Jupiter shouted through comms.

"Finally." The captain sighed in relief. *"Our corvettes will drop to ten kilometers and provide firing support. Sending the shuttles and escorts down now."*

Just then, the five corvettes dropped down, drawing double the anti-air with their descent. They uncloaked and pumped all power into their shield generators as they returned fire with laser cannons and missiles, blasting apart the landscape surrounding the temple.

Simultaneously, legions of small craft descended like lightning, weaving through the flak.

As they approached, Task Force Dagger arrayed themselves, ready to enter at a moment's notice.

"Anyone call for a pickup?" The first dropship entered the hangar, the same one Jupiter and Shiv-Alpha had ridden in on.

More entered, opening their ramps as the operatives and rescuees streamed in.

Before everyone could safely board, the blast doors behind them burst, and a flood of mutated monsters and heinous beasts entered.

The dropships fired their mounted guns, sending scores to their graves in torn shreds of viscera and gore.

In case that wasn't enough, their rides carried much-needed reinforcements.

Jupiter grinned savagely as his five reserve Poltergeists bounded out of the dropships. With his wrecked Mark II, he spread his arms, welcoming the charging horde as he shouted.

"COME ON, THEN! LINE UP! I'LL SING YOU ALL A FUNERAL DIRGE!"

Like hungry apex predators, the six machines charged and leaped into the fray.

The slaughter that occurred next caked each one in blood.

When the last person entered the transports, Jupiter sent his shells to latch on the sides, guns ready.

Their evac convoy soared high into the skies as starfighters and battlesuits stuck close to their wings, firing away alongside the cover of the corvettes above.

Even as swarms of flying Starless began streaming out of their holes, the transport ships carrying the exhausted task force climbed in pillars of blue ionized thrust.

When more colossal tentacles burst from the surface and joined the rest in reaching out to them, a rain of cataclysmic ordnance slammed into the planet, and an unholy agonized shriek echoed throughout the skies, causing the rest of the desert in the area to shudder and fall away.

"Commander?" a familiar, incredible voice reached his ears through comms. *"This is Admiral Yan."*

Jupiter breathed out in relief. "Yan? Oh, baby, I fucking miss your voice."

She cleared her throat in reply, lightly chiding him. *"You're on a military channel, Commander."*

"I don't care." Jupiter laughed. "Holy shit! Holy shit, we made it out. Now, can you please glass that planet?"

Admiral Yan gave a buzzing chuckle. "It will be my pleasure."

With Task Force Dagger safely in orbit, Andora watched as the Third and Seventeenth followed their newest order.

Hundreds of nuclear-tipped missiles and thermobaric bombs streaked through the arid skies, released by every ship from the smallest frigate to the *Zolann'tono* and the *Moonlit River*. Trails of smoke created a damning dance across the heavens.

In response to the acute threat heading its way, the continent-sized entity fell back into the dunes, its legion of tentacles and tendrils coiling around each other like a pit of colossal snakes before turning gray and rigid.

The first wave of munitions crashed onto the surface of Madraa-II, heralding a song of annihilation.

Nuclear-tipped missiles ignited the sky with blinding flashes of light, painting the horizon in hues of white and orange. The air reverberated with the deafening roar of explosions and the cry of the eldritch Leviathan below.

Thermobaric bombs unleashed a hellish inferno, casting great firestorms that engulfed everything in their path in a monstrous conflagration. The desert was consumed by fire and fury. Shockwaves rippled outward, and the indescribable heat turned the sands into glass.

The Nidus, a monstrosity beyond comprehension, thrashed and writhed as the bombs tore the desert land asunder.

"Hit, estimating damage," one of the officers reported.

Andora, Tov, and the rest of the War Room waited for the news, eyeing the toxic, irradiated inferno that raged across the surface around what had once been the Temple of the Ivory Maw.

"Scans complete . . . It's . . . Symphony above, how is it still alive?" the officer gasped in disbelief.

Everyone leaned forward as visuals from the Third and Seventeenth cleared up.

To everyone's frustration and disappointment, the Nidus yet lived, though charred, aflame, and wailing in pain.

The once towering tentacles were now ashen husks that writhed before crumbling apart. But then, from deep below the glass crust, more tentacles, pale and slimy, burst forth from the ground. Already an outer layer of chitin was forming around the freshly regenerated limbs.

Sets of seven limbs coiled together, forming a colossal spire that aimed toward the two fleets.

"Those are anti-orbital weapons!" someone exclaimed as everyone watched with wide eyes of surprise.

The ships of the Third and Seventeenth spread out instantly, guarded and wary at the incoming attack.

Dozens of organic anti-orbital guns across the region bloated, contracting as they glowed with a sickly purple light. And with a hellish shriek that rose to a crescendo, they fired into the atmosphere in eldritch particle beams.

A few struck the shields of the largest ships, but the vessels remained stalwart.

On the surface, countless eyes opened, glaring in suffering as the Nidus screamed in rage. Then, from its abyssal pits, scores of newly born Starless flew to the skies, many burning up in the fiery winds before ever leaving the planet.

"Should we reinforce your fleets, Admiral?" Andora asked Yan's hologram.

The scarlet-hued Kurskann shook her head. "That's unnecessary. Our calculations deem the current resistance manageable. If the difficulty climbs following our projections, we will be able to scour this planet of the beast, but it will take time."

"How long?" Andora asked.

"Two, maybe three hours if we play it safe high up in orbit. You can't miss with a stationary target as big as the Nidus," Yan readily replied before tilting her head. "As long as whatever comes out of the hypergate doesn't bother us, things will proceed accordingly."

Andora pressed her lips into a thin line as everyone shifted their attention to Hypergate Sierra.

"Fluctuations are reaching their zenith," an officer reported.

Tov leaned forward. "Is the anomaly still present?"

"It is, steadily infecting the gate. The higher-dimensional gasses are tinged with a purple shine."

Cantor Tendemone hummed negatively. "I sense the work of the otherworldly tainting the tunnel. The suffering of the Nidus is also destabilizing reality around the star system. But that hypergate . . . it feels eerily similar to—"

"A Nightmare Portal." Andora finished the cantor's thought, narrowing her eyes as she addressed the War Room officers. "Use our Earth metrics. What is the magnitude of the hypergate?"

The officers scrambled, making their calculations.

Andora already knew, of course. Her Nexus and those of her Overseers had already come to an answer. But she had to keep up appearances.

"Magnitude six, Custodian," an officer replied.

She hummed, nodding. "My people are reporting the same."

"What does that mean?" Commandant Nullan asked.

"It means there's a high probability that a Leviathan-sized entity is passing through, alongside whatever horde it leads," Tov replied.

Everyone grimaced at his words, and those at the frontlines shifted uncomfortably at the thought of dealing with something as significant as the infamous myth that was a Leviathan.

Andora sighed, nonplussed. She had fought worse with less. "Battlegroups Mag Mell and Mictlan will be the first to greet our new guests. The rest of Task Force Sierra and Whiskey will respond once we determine the opposition's strength."

She turned to the fleet leaders of those respective forces. All four nodded without hesitation. Luna and Mars did the same.

"*Citadel Irkalla* and my Galla Fleet will be held in reserve, close enough to assist should any complications with either the Nidus or the enemy reinforcements occur. Any objections or additions to this strategy?" Andora raised her brow.

Over the following few minutes, the council members hashed out the details of formations and the status of each force, but the discussion soon petered out due to the lack of information on the incoming attackers. As the hypergate began to exhibit extreme changes, conversation silenced completely.

"Hypergate opening! Enemy forces inbound. Entering reality in five . . . four . . . three . . ."

Everyone watched as the foes made their entrance.

The great gate tore open, ripped asunder to reveal a tempestuous and volatile hyper-tunnel. Sickly dark clouds flashing with purple lightning seeped into the battle as the steeds riding atop it came into view.

Hundreds of modern warships bearing the mark of the Chained Souls materialized from the pitch-black fog, far superior to the High Seer's battlegroup. Their hulls were filled with unfathomable etchings and symbols, shining in a ghastly light. Each brimmed with weapons that screamed violence.

But it wasn't these conventional vessels that concerned the Exodus Armada. Even if they came from mad psyches, they were still designed and made by the hands of people.

No.

That horrid privilege was given to the tens of thousands, then hundreds of thousands of Starless that streamed through the gate, their nightmarish bodies twisted and morphed in a manner all too familiar to many, bringing their scourge with gnashing teeth, biometallic armor, and organic weapons.

The Starless were of all sizes, from the smallest of Fodder, the size of starfighters, to the two Juggernaut Colossi that burst through the gate with all their ungodly battleship-sized mass.

And finally, as the last Starless writhed their way into the fray, the layer of cosmic fabric that separated hyperspace and reality contorted, bulging and pulsing as the supposed Leviathan-class pushed it way through.

"There it is . . ." Andora muttered, frowning deeply.

The hypergate popped, space itself shrieking in pain. What came through caused everyone to recoil in disgust.

The Leviathan looked unlike anything Andora had seen before.

A hundred kilometers shy of the Leviathan Muck from several months ago, the immense beast nonetheless exuded an aura of menace, domination, and mania. Its shape was akin to a broad and plump teardrop with its point facing forward.

What drew everyone's attention, however, were the clear artificial structures that covered its biometallic body. Sensor towers, weapon hardpoints, hangar bays, and other edifices protruded from and were embedded across its surface alongside their organic counterparts common to the Starless.

The most prominent of its features were the dozen many-jointed limbs at its rear. Like long spindly arms that ended in anemone-like fingers, each was the size of the tallest redwood trees.

Massive steel chains stitched across its many eyes and the two teeth-filled maws on either side, closing them shut.

As the beast whose flesh had the hue of burnt umber completed its violating transit, it let out a rumbling roar that shuddered reality around it and invigorated both Thralled and its fellow Starless alike.

Just as the armada were about to further analyze it and the rest of the enemy forces, an external comms signal hailed them.

"Where is it coming from?" Andora demanded.

"The . . . the Leviathan, ma'am. It's a standard communication signal," the comms officer reported.

The Omni Mind pursed her lips then grimaced, crossing one leg over the other as she gestured for it to be put through. As they did, the hologram of the caller emerged above the display table.

"Urgh!" Andora recoiled, as did the rest, at the appearance of the *thing* sitting naked on its throne. It . . . he . . . was rail thin, with ribs jutting out at terrible angles. Old and new scars marred its pale yellow flesh. A collar shackled his neck, and chains wrapped around his torso and four limbs, one nothing more than a savaged, bandaged stump.

But it was his face that made everyone's eyes water. His head looked as if someone had squashed his skull and badly reassembled the pieces. His crudely stitched-together features were twisted in a spiral, lacking eyelids, lips, and a nose.

A glowing eldritch symbol lay at the center of his face, glowing like a red-hot brand.

"Jesus Christ, what the fuck are you?" Andora scowled in disgust.

The alien gazed at all of them with a serene calm, breathing softly as he opened his mouth.

"HEATHENS! YOUR SACRILEGE OF THIS DIVINE TEMPLE HAS GONE ON FOR TOO LONG!"

Everyone covered their ears from his damnable shout.

"I AM THE BOUND ONE. A HUMBLE SERVANT. A SINNER. A PHAGE. FILTH AND DIRT. I AM NOTHING. I AM THE PROSELYTE OF THE CHAINED SOULS AND I HAVE SEEN THE TRUTH!"

He stood from his throne of squalor, limping forward as he pointed his three bound arms at Andora.

"THE PRIME HAS PROPHECIZED YOUR COMING, ABERRATION! YOUR DEATH WARRANT IS SIGNED, AND I AM HERE TO ENACT A DIVINE RECKONING!"

He gave a lipless smile, revealing bleeding, empty gums.

"FOR ABSOLUTION!"

CHAPTER 30

THROUGH BLOOD AND FIRE

Andora grimaced in open disgust as she forcibly lowered the volume of the call. The proselyte of the Chained Souls, the so-called Bound One, spasmed and twitched as his eyes danced around in their sockets. He shuddered and whimpered and groaned for a painfully long moment before he stopped.

His shoulders slumped as he suddenly exuded a dignified and loud demeanor, raising his chin and clenching his fists.

"TORMENTORS! VILLAINS! MONSTERS! YOU WOULD DESECRATE THE HOLY CRADLE OF A CHILD OF ABSOLUTION!? DO YOUR SINS KNOW NO LIMIT?"

"Listen, Boundy,"—Andora refused to call him by his dumb title—"I have no idea what you are talking about, so speak plainly, if you would." She scowled at the cell leader.

Boundy seethed, hissing through teeth that looked racked with scurvy. He spoke in a lower tone, though it was no less hostile. "Your ignorance is telling, Aberration! But you will not gain the answers you seek from me! NOR SHALL YOU FROM MY FAITHFUL!"

Andora rolled her eyes and scowled as she leaned back in her command throne. "I don't care. I've found your minds are empty of sense and reason. But if you would allow me a moment to ponder, am I to guess you are here for your precious Nidus? The same one we are atomizing with nuclear fire?"

"BLASPHEMER!" Boundy howled, veins popping under his skin.

Andora smiled like a cat playing with a mouse, shaking her head. "Inside voice, Boundy. I see the forces you've brought, and I'll tell you now, they won't be enough to stop me from prying your smoldering corpse from that thing you call a ship."

"YOUR ARROGANCE SHALL BE YOUR UNDOING. IT IS THE COMFORTING CHAINS THAT RESTRAIN CHAOS, THAT QUELL

PANDEMONIUM! IT IS THROUGH THESE BONDS WITH OUR GOD THAT WE ARE UNBREAKABLE!"

She sighed, feeling as though she was speaking with a wall. "Your High Seer and his fleet broke easily enough."

"HIS FAITH WAS WEAK! HE DID NOT BELIEVE! NOT LIKE I! NOT LIKE THOSE HERE!"

Boundy shook his shackles and rattled his chains. He laughed, cackling with his gaping maw, letting everyone see the abyssal cavern.

"BEHOLD, NERPHANAGON! AN ACROPOLIS FORGED FROM THE SACRIFICE OF A GREAT LEVIATHAN! A TREASURE HANDED TO ME BY THE PRIME!"

The Acropolis he called Nerphanagon groaned and undulated, her array of grotesque weaponry pointing toward them.

"This he received from the Herald of Absolution!" Boundy hissed in a whisper, voice overflowing with worship as he keeled over, sweating and heaving, his brand sizzling and eliciting a vile moan of pain and pleasure and madness. "And it has made its way into my gentle, loving care, to be used against you! As was foretold by the Prime!"

He raised his three hands, looking up as if grasping for the sky.

"BEHOLD THIS LEVIATHAN, THIS FORTRESS IN AN OCEAN OF CRUEL STARS, FLESH AND METAL CONJOINED TO BRING ABOUT YOUR DEMISE."

The enemy force shuddered as the beast silently hissed through its chained mouths.

"BEHOLD!" Boundy shouted.

Artificial and organic thrusters behind the Acropolis burned at full power, flaring with purple light and slowly propelling the beast forward.

"BEHOLD YOUR DOOM!"

With his last declaration, he closed the comms. Ahead, the opposition charged.

"What is wrong with that guy?" Andora grumbled as she rubbed her ears. "Is he a cartoon villain?"

"Am . . . Am *I* that loud?" she heard Mars whisper to Venus.

Andora snorted. Hearing this, the red giant coughed into his fist, his face flushed a deep red.

Venus politely smiled, whispering a noncommittal reply as she patted his back.

The rest of the War Room devolved into a hectic discussion. Andora took a deep breath, grabbed her gavel, and hammered it against the sound block. She looked over her assembled allies and the camera drones she'd summoned once more, readying her second address.

She stood, commanding not only the attention of everyone in the room but via the cameras, the entire armada.

Andora began with a look of contempt.

"The vermin have finally shown themselves, and it appears they've allowed fleas to command them," she spoke, infusing vitriol in her words, sneering.

Damn trying to look like a saint. Damn the polite veneer and the play-acting.

"How utterly pathetic."

Though those listening found her words and expression, her audacious belligerence, more welcome in a Dagataren senate hall or a Qessheren court, they nonetheless allowed it to infect their spirits.

Many snarled and grimaced, tightening their fists until the knuckles turned white.

"Warriors of the Legacy!" Andora shouted. She spread her arms wide as she demanded of those listening, "Will you allow such a force to lay us low?"

Everyone in the War Room stood, shouting their hate-filled reply.

"NO!"

"Will you allow them to stop our Exodus back home?"

Throughout the armada, across every comms channel, they answered.

"NO!"

Andora grinned with bloodlust. "Then that is all I needed to hear. Go! This is the final battle for Madraa! And remember this—

"Give them no quarter! For they will offer us none!"

Mars watched from his Nexus within the *Bucephalus* as Battlegroups Mag Mell and Mictlan met the enemy's lead element: Starless Fodder that buzzed tightly together like a defensive screen ahead of the Chained Souls fleet.

The two vanguards clashed, ship against ship, small craft against small craft.

Battlegroup Mictlan brought up the rear, its superheavy carrier *Xolotl* unleashing its complement of drone strikers, which swarmed like bees as they fired needlelike missiles at the Fodder.

Guarding the vanguard's front was Battlegroup Mag Mell. The *Tethra,* the *Xolotl*'s cruiser counterpart, fired all of its weapon systems, from the pulse point defense guns to the two double-barreled maser cannons. As both battlegroups pulled away from the approaching horde, the factory cruiser also unleashed its entire storage of deadly goods.

Nuclear payloads, plasma bombs, canisters of gray goo, and a recent addition called a psi-hymn mine all homed in on the enemy vanguard under a cloud of interference dust, preventing the enemy from taking them down from afar.

The cloaked psi-hymn mine made its glorious debut as a clueless Starless Fodder swarm passed it by.

Upon detecting a significant presence of hostiles, the mine unfurled, turning into a spherical speaker system.

Though sound held no sway in a vacuum, the same could not be said regarding the songs of the Eternal Choir. Hundreds of Starless Fodder seized, weakening and slowing, frozen in shock and frothing at their mouths.

Although a hundred dead Fodder among tens of thousands seemed a paltry amount, when the succeeding hundreds of other mines and explosives detonated in conjunction, a massive hole appeared in the expendable spear point of the enemy vanguard.

"Effective, though they're only Fodder," Mars hummed as his mind weaved his fleet to the left flank alongside the rest of Task Force Sierra.

"The prototype has its merits. Working alongside your scientists and designers has been enlightening." Cantor Tendemone chuckled, fanning herself humbly.

Commandant Nullan rumbled. "When your people design something that can halt a Titan in its tracks, I'll be more interested, Marshal. Unless you have some other fun toys to show me?"

"Hah! Plenty!" Mars bellowed, his massive shoulders rising up and down as he laughed. He changed focus suddenly, tilting his head at the battle map. "Seems we have company."

The next wave of the enemy force spread out ahead, their wings bypassing the center block. Some arced back, striking the flanks of Mag Mell and Mictlan as they continued to fall back. The rest continued, aiming for the task forces on either side.

Consisting of a vast majority of the Starless scourge bioships and a select few of the Chained Souls elite, the oncoming vessels burned their thrusters and propulsion systems hard, roaring as they entered extreme firing range.

Mars rubbed his chin as he observed the Juggernaut and two Thralled battle-carriers that led the charge. The latter disgorged their battalions of heavy starfighters and raider battlesuits, each sporting the chains and markings of their cell's beliefs.

He grinned at the sight, welcoming the battle.

"LET LOOSE THE DOGS OF WAR!"

His perspective shifted as he dove into the shell of his champion vessel.

The *Boogie Mouse* flashed with brilliant luminescence, its Rapture Generator growling with a deep rumble. The crystalline blue dreadnought engaged its thrusters, leading the countercharge, the Five Greats, and the rest of Mars's fleet.

Not to be outdone in the presence of both heretics and their Legacy's greatest foe, the Thirty-First and Thirty-Fourth followed close behind at Mars's flanks, their ships peppering the void alight in beams of searing hot energy.

"DO YOU HEAR THAT BEAT, VERMIN? LET ME SHOW YOU MY MOUSE'S DANCE!" Mars shouted through the general frequency as his dreadnought fired a volley of its patented Rapture Beams in a dazzling display of blazing prismatic light.

The Juggernaut, sensing the deadly force riding the beams of luminescence, heaved its whale-like body to the side, dodging all but a few that scorched its blubbery flesh and sheared off spiked tendrils.

In retaliation for the hits, the battleship-sized beast unleashed its menagerie of bioweapons.

To Task Force Sierra's surprise, several Starless leaked out of the wounds of the Colossus-class, connected by chain-like umbilical cords.

But unlike others of similar size, these organisms were more weapon than creature. Made almost entirely of rotten quartz-like crystal, they fired beams of white energy that struck the ripple shields of the dreadnought.

Mars raised his brow as the power of one such beam destabilized his *Mouse's* shield.

"So, the more I hurt you, the more you bite back?" Mars chuckled. "Alright then! Turn up the music! You will provide me with some fun!"

Minutes after the fight began, the left flank of the battlezone shone with countless lights. The two most glaring among them glowed in prismatic colors or a pure, deathly white.

Luna hummed indifferently at the battle unfolding before her.

Her mind raced with new calculations every micro instant, directing each of her following actions, no matter how small.

A drone moved a meter to the left at a thirty-eight-degree pitch.

A shield shifted at a right angle, deflecting an attack most efficiently.

A cruiser concentrated its fire on an exposed vector, the fruition of her strategy that had begun several hundred moves ago.

Each asset moved exactly as they were told and performed actions precisely in the manner she commanded. There was no room for error in her calculations. Everything had to be perfect. Everything had to follow her prime directives, borne from Eldest's need for cold efficiency and rational thought.

Assist the Omni Mind.

Eliminate the Starless.

Win the war.

Her fleet of silver vessels surged forward, baiting the enemy into a firing line from her *Gilgamesh*. The nine-kilometer battleship finished charging its

Annihilator Energy Projector, thrumming and crackling with silver lightning, then fired on schedule.

Like a sniper assassin, the warship unleashed a broad beam that vaporized everything it came across.

It traveled hundreds of thousands of kilometers in an instant before slamming into the hull of a cultist battleship. The spacecraft sundered apart before being erased from existence.

"Thralled capital vessel removed," Luna reported.

At the same time, her *Xerxes* was supporting the rest of Task Force November, dispersing a great nebula of interference dust that slightly shrouded their forces from enemy attack without inhibiting their own sensors.

The massive drone fleet carrier sent out its legions, which harried Starless and cultists alike before descending on them like a tide of murder.

The drones dispersed, narrowly dodging the plasma fire from the Juggernaut leading the charge alongside two more battleships and a cadre of capital ships.

The beast looked like a grotesque, deshelled crustacean with a vertical mouth filled with rows and rows of teeth. It expanded its gut, readying another blast of plasma. Other weapons across its body ceased their onslaught of projectiles until it finally fired, vomiting a breath of eldritch flames toward the drones that pestered its wing.

Scores of drones perished, martyring themselves by pulling and baiting. But Luna deemed the sacrifices necessary—it was a perfect trade, unlike a certain asset. Luna felt annoyed at the lumbering dreadnought that had fallen into her lap. She sighed, nevertheless utilizing its firepower as a mobile weapons platform.

The Chicxulub Maneuver remained unused. Without the *Zolann'tono* close by, such a move was impossible anyway.

As for the rest of Task Force November, they continued coordinating with her, but their efforts were stifling, inefficient, and wrong. She humored them nonetheless, aiding where she could, as commanded by her progenitor.

Luna hummed, seeing the pressure increase on her organic allies as the enemy smartly recognized the Task Force's compositional weaknesses.

She then recalled Lord Iintei's behavior during council meetings. He was always angling for something, discreetly squeezing out more benefits for himself each time, bit by bit, undermining the Omni Mind's authority. He spoke honeyed words, displayed faux sincerity, and paraded his strength at every opportunity.

As for the other fleet leader, Huntsmaster Vro, she dismissed her entirely, seeing her distaste in political affairs. But Lord Iintei Ahraman Tens Solsolen was a concerning variable.

Luna decided to remind him of his vulnerability, of his dependence on the Omni Mind's benevolence.

Her *Gilgamesh* fired its annihilator at the Juggernaut while it charged its next attack. The lethal beam drilled into Starless flesh, knocking its aim off by a degree.

A nudge, a light nudge toward a different direction.

It vomited its fire and shrieked in agony, sending ripples across its mass. The ball of crackling plasma soared through the void toward a lesser capital ship of the Twenty-First. It struck, shattering the vessel's shield before terribly scorching its hull and disabling its weapon systems.

Lord Iintei gasped through their shared network before furrowing his brow and barking orders. He adjusted his fleet as the damaged cruiser withdrew.

That was enough for now.

It wouldn't do to allow the Twenty-First Fleet's destruction, which would risk the armada's safety and cause morale to plummet. No, just enough—everything according to her calculations.

Assist the Omni Mind.

Eliminate the Starless.

Win the war.

Luna continued to conduct her assets, occasionally adjusting the frame of her glasses.

"So far, so good. The battle lines have stabilized, and we've yet to deploy our trump cards," Andora announced as she focused on the map in the center of the War Room.

Tov hummed. "The Acropolis has yet to make a move."

Andora frowned at that point. The Bound One and his precious Leviathan ship remained at the rear, firing their weapons in support but remaining passive and reactionary.

It cowered behind the masses, denying the armada a clear shot.

"Tsk . . . Come on, Boundy. I thought you hated us?" Andora muttered as she tapped the arm of her chair.

As the minutes flew by and Andora grew concerned and impatient, the Acropolis finally moved, likely sensing the scales tipping in their favor.

The dozen many-jointed arms twitched as the abominable ship wriggled its countless anemone fingers. All the while, a warm red glow raced under its flesh, steadily growing brighter.

Moving at an impossible speed, the long, spindly limbs waved to and fro, dancing and moving to an unheard tune. Its fingers coalesced, forming strange symbols. Andora realized too late that the ritualistic gestures were being carried out by limbs of biomass over kilometers long.

"Divert energy to shields!" Andora commanded every vessel of their armada.

At that moment, Nerphanagon finished its ritual, ending with its limbs locked symmetrically.

Andora could hear the cackling mania from the Acropolis as a tear was forcibly opened above the center battlegroups.

"Damn!" she shouted as she commanded the AI fleets to pull back.

From that cosmic, festering rip of reality, an astronomical storm of corrupted psionic energy descended upon Mag Mell and Mictlan. Dark, writhing clouds racked with hellish lightning and purple lights engulfed a significant chunk of the armada's center, including the *Tethra* and *Xolotl*.

Andora winced, feeling the damage savage their shields.

Once the storm disappeared, the two capital ships emerged with blackened hulls and depleted shields. And for the smaller classes—Andora grimaced at the sight of over a dozen crippled or outright destroyed subcapitals, including a trio of destroyers.

Snarling, Andora pulled the two battlegroups back.

"I'm sending us forward. We'll take the center and end this charade!" Andora declared, looking toward Mars and Luna. "They will capitalize on the void in the center. Be sure to tear their necks if they overextend."

"Yes, Secretary-General," both her Overseers replied in unison.

Before she could say her next order, however, Admiral Yan returned to the War Room via hologram, antennae twitching with concern. She turned to Andora.

"The Nidus has been suddenly reinvigorated. We don't know the exact cause of its second wind, but we suspect it's somehow resonating with the Acropolis," Yan reported.

Andora scowled at the bad news, gesturing for the admiral to continue.

"Its regeneration has almost doubled in its rate. We can't sustain our barrage much longer without assistance."

Hearing this, Andora decided without hesitation. "I'm sending the *Ereshkigal* back to deliver the coup de grâce."

"Thank you, Custodian." Admiral Yan bowed before dimming her hologram.

Tov turned to Andora. "Are you sure you don't want your dreadnought alongside you?"

"No need. *Irkalla* will be enough."

The Galla Fleet surged forward under the direction of Andora, who rode aboard *Citadel Irkalla* at the front.

At her sides, the battleships *Gugallana* and *Nergal* prepped their Fodder suppression guns, ready to swat flies by the thousands should they come close. Forty frigates and sixteen destroyers arrayed themselves in an offensive screen of black and gold while the four battlecruisers formed a bulwark at either flank.

"Onward!" Andora shouted.

The duel commenced as the two battleships lit the way in a barrage of laser fire, unerringly bringing down scores of Fodder- and Ravager-class Starless.

Missiles left their berths, soaring high into the void before arcing down. Tipped with plasma warheads, they consumed entire areas in their obliterating fire.

Undeterred, the elite of the Chained Souls surged forward. A trio of battleships and a pack of battlecruisers overloaded their thrusters to close in on and brawl with the Galla Fleet. Once they reached medium range, kinetic weapons entered the fray.

Rail guns, coil ship rifles, Gauss cannons, autocannons, and more mid-range weaponry saturated the space between both sides with searing hot metal.

Shields fluctuated and hulls were shorn apart. Barrels glowed red hot while missile tubes hungered for more ammo.

Another psionic storm fell upon the Exodus Armada, dispersed over a wide area but strong enough to shut down starfighters and battlesuits. Yet another emerged over the Galla Fleet, this time condensed atop the *Nergal*.

The battleship groaned, its shield generators overheating but holding for now. Andora had it withdrawn. Unfortunately, a few of her frigates were picked off in the distraction.

She'd had enough.

Not a minute later, the apparent victor of this initial skirmish slowly emerged.

First one, then two of the Thralled battleships burst into flames as *Irkalla* unleashed her legion of secondary and tertiary guns, overshadowing the combined firepower of her escorts.

More and more of the cultists fell, yet their suicidal minds replaced their senses, blazing away, determined to take one of the blasphemers down with them. Andora sneered at the sight, swatting the flies away until a path to the Acropolis lay open.

She felt a baleful glare pointed her way as it writhed, its limbs moving faster and faster as it signed and gestured like a many-armed Shiva.

It brought one arm down in a vertical slice that shuddered reality. Storms and lightning coalesced into a violent, unstable crescent slash that shot toward the *Citadel* at an unbelievable speed.

"Incoming psionic attack! We can't dodge from this distance!"

"There's no need . . ." Andora responded, raising her Citadel's Omega Barrier. The all-encompassing shield flared, turning opaque in a golden shine as the psionic slash exploded against it.

The shield shuddered and rippled but before long, it settled. Andora scoffed, diverting the energy back to other systems.

The Acropolis continued its attack, solely focused the fortress in the stars. No one else disturbed their clash. Each was focused on tearing down the other side. Psionic storms crashed against a barrage of conventional weapons unleashed at their full might.

Corrosive beams of light unleashed blackened spires of bone and biomissiles by the hundreds, that smashed against Andora's Omega Barrier. She watched its condition deteriorate, dropping 50 percent. As was the nature of psionic-based attacks, a portion managed to slip through the barrier, washing over the rocky exterior and scarring it. Yet Andora remained unconcerned. This was the test for her fortress—whether it deserved to exist as a mighty weapon or crumble into nothing.

And so far, it hadn't disappointed.

"Systems nominal, Creator," Irkalla hooted. "The Omega Barrier is holding within acceptable margins. But the cooling coils surrounding the generator will overheat at this rate if we allow this assault to continue."

Andora hummed. "Have *Nergal* and *Gugallana* reinforce us with their shield-recharging beams. Then fire the secondaries. Prod its defenses."

Across the *Citadel*, dozens of laser cannons modeled after Luna's annihilators took aim and fired a salvo against the Acropolis.

Suddenly, three energy shields appeared at its front. The first salvo tore the first layer to shreds, but failed at the second. Another salvo finished the job but again failed at the third and final layer.

As soon as the next salvo finished charging up, the front layer returned, then the second.

Again and again, the *Citadel*'s secondary cannons peeled through each layer but, but each time the shield would regenerate before they could hit the final barrier.

"Secondaries inefficient. Its multi-layered shields—though individually weaker—are more sustainable in a battle of attrition. It is also adapting to our attacks. We need an overwhelming strike," Irkalla hooted her suggestion.

"Then let's end this. Give the abomination a taste of our Ganzir Ultras!" Andora grinned savagely as she aimed the colossal primary weapons of her fortress.

For the first time, *Irkalla* unleashed her full firepower. All ten guns, each slightly larger and more powerful than those utilized by her dreadnought, aimed toward the enemy's center.

The quark reactor leveraged its near-limitless potential and flooded the apocalyptic weapons with power. They charged, building up a harsh red and golden glow. Shimmering dust like tiny stars coalesced at the end of the gargantuan barrels.

Irkalla's Omega Barrier Dynamo covered the areas around the cannons, shielding them from the ungodly radiation levels and heat build-up.

The battle slowed, quieting under the rumble of the Ganzir Ultras.

On the other end, the Acropolis gestured hastily, summoning storm after storm before the *Citadel,* shrouding its vision. The rest of the Starless and cultists dropped everything and bore down on the center of the Acropolis, ignoring everything else once they caught sight of such embodiments of death rising from their underworld palace.

Their panic was quickly capitalized upon by the flanking task force, spelling the deaths of many.

And finally, after a full minute of charging—

"FIRE!"

Ten blazing balls burst forth from their barrels, destabilizing reality and causing the void to shudder as they soared at blinding speeds.

Where the Ganzirs fired plasma the size of meteors, the Ultras threw miniature suns. Their output was denser, more violent, a visual representation of the unfathomable hate that Andora had purged from her mind and given new purpose. The Ultras sang certain death.

Starless and cultist vessels evaporated in their wake. Even those nowhere near the path of destruction were atomized all the same. The plasma slammed into the psionic storm, parting the thunderous clouds. The abhorrent purple lightning did nothing to slow them down.

More and more of the enemy attempted to use sheer mass and weight of numbers to block their path, succeeding in downing all but four.

It cost them the entire center.

The Acropolis shuddered, shaking as if feeling pure distilled destruction approaching closer and closer. Three layers of energy shields surrounded Nerphanagon while a dozen arms formed a thick violet barrier with their gestures.

Three layers shattered, taking away another miniature sun.

Yet another blew in a conflagration, failing to breach the eldritch psi barrier.

Finally, the last two broke the final shield, smashing into the beast.

Everyone held their breaths.

Andora smirked, clapping once.

An immense, blinding nova consumed the bow of the Acropolis, scouring the hull of its artificial and organic structures. Chains melted under the heat before exploding into dust, releasing the eyes and mouths from their prisons, only for them to shriek in gurgling pain.

Over a hundred thousand square kilometers evaporated instantly, sending cascades of failures exploding in and outside the Starless abomination.

The Exodus Armada cheered at the sight, buoyed by the overwhelming firepower they crashed against the remaining enemy with red-tinged aggression— shouting and roaring as they slew.

Their alpha gutted and groaning, the Starless and Thralled descended into chaos, throwing themselves at the armada like rabid dogs, only to be put down like ones.

Surprisingly, the Acropolis stubbornly remained alive, wheezing and leaking blood, ichor, and viscera into the cold vacuum of space. Andora was watching the dying beast when a comms signal reached out to them.

She scoffed, nodding at an officer to accept the call.

Boundy looked no worse for wear. Andora imagined a tornado passing his throne room and leaving a mess no dirtier than before.

The proselyte appeared surprisingly calm, curious if a bit confused as he sat on his chair, biting his nails.

"Hm . . . This . . . this doesn't make sense . . ." he muttered, rocking back and forth and tilting his head like a bird. "The Prime was right. Of course he was! I would fail in stopping you and waste this valuable treasure. As he foretold! In the end, I was the arrogant and blind one . . . Oh, my Prime . . . I was unfaithful . . ."

Andora furrowed her brow at the relaxed cultist. "Your forces are defeated, Boundy. I told you as much."

Boundy hummed low, then louder. "Hm! Hmm? Hmmmmm!"

"Surrender peacefully," Andora demanded as she felt a flash of annoyance at the lunatic's antics. "Perhaps I can enlighten you as to how I utterly stomped you and yours."

"Unnecessary! I have seen enough!" the proselyte suddenly remarked with a smile so wide it tore his cheeks.

The War Room narrowed their eyes at the sudden shift in demeanor.

Despite that, the maniac continued, laughing and clapping. "Ahahahah! Magnificent display! My work here is done. Ah, this meat puppet has outlived its usefulness, you can have it for all I care."

Andora stood, eyes wide at Boundy's revelation. "Work? Meat puppet? What are you—"

"Ah! It pains me to leave so soon. The Prime will not like it! He won't! And finding the right flesh prison for this endeavor has been a hassle and took so much time, but I don't mind! Still . . . sad! SO VERY SAD! I WORKED SO HARD ON IT!" Boundy shrieked, clawing at his face. He stopped, smiling at Andora and the War Room. "It doesn't matter. I have so many! Consider it a token for enlightening me."

Andora felt something incredibly wrong in the air. The destruction of the enemy forces fled her mind as she ordered expendable drones to close in on the ruined Acropolis in haste. "Proselyte, whatever you're planning, you won't—"

"Yes! Yes!" the proselyte of the Chained Souls laughed and leaped off his chair, his voice changing as in a cadence of two, one in unfathomable torment and the other rising to a concert of countless chanting maniacs. "YES! YES! YES!"

His body twisted unnaturally, cracking bones and tearing muscle as he smiled maniacally. "YOUR CAPABILITIES HAVE BEEN NOTED, ABERRATION!"

Boundy danced, hopping on one leg as he twirled sickeningly. "YOU HAVE DEFEATED ME THIS DAY! BUT OUR NUMBERS ARE LEGION! WE ARE THE TEMPLE OF ABSOLUTION! THE AGENTS OF GOD'S WILL!"

Suddenly, an officer stood, urgently giving his report to the War Room. "Detecting massive build-up of psionic energy from the Acropolis!"

"Everyone, back away now!" Andora shouted to the rest of the armada.

"TILL WE MEET AGAIN, ANDORA THE ABERRANT!"

Boundy's meat puppet slumped to the ground without its strings. Its bones crumbled to dust as the comms abruptly cut off.

Andora peered through her Citadel's outer camera and watched as the Acropolis exploded in the light of a psionic overload. The detonation triggered something within the biomass and gore, which mutated rapidly before decaying into a slimy goop.

Then, a harsh light engulfed the Acropolis in its entirety, bringing down the mother of psionic storms that obliterated everything within its vicinity.

The shockwave washed off the armada, and their Pneuma Bulwark Emitter surged to block the worst, leaving only migraines for those unlucky few. As the explosion dissipated, the armada, seeing nothing was left of the terrifying creature, cheered and rallied in exhilaration.

However, Andora's earlier joy and satisfaction faded as her mind raced. While the rest of the armada celebrated their victory, everyone in the War Room and those privy to the truth grimaced deeply.

Their armada had gone through a baptism of blood and fire. Only now could they see an inkling of the hell that surrounded them.

CALL FROM THE DEEP

Aided by the *Ereshkigal*'s Ganzir Guns, the Third and the Seventeenth Fleets breached through the Nidus's annoyingly fast regeneration, carving into the beast, searing its flesh, and drilling in farther before its wounds could close.

The planet's surface became a sea of fire, and the relentless bombardment blurred the boundaries between the Nidus and the landscape as flesh fused with glass, sand, and rock. Shockwaves from the explosions rippled through the atmosphere, causing tremors that shook the very foundation of the world.

As nuclear fire consumed the planet, the ghastly abomination's screams echoed through the barren world under blackened skies, a cacophony of agony and rage.

It thrashed and convulsed, its once-mighty form now little more than a burning corpse, its regeneration failing from the lack of vitality. The entity's tentacles, which once reached for the skies, now lay charred and broken, their suckers and teeth reduced to ashes.

The glassing continued, the fleet ensuring nothing remained of the abhorrent horror.

Ultimately, all that remained of the region was sand fused into a blackened glass that reflected the twin stars' dying light.

With the Nidus's death, the Battle of Madraa ended in a decisive victory. Both the Chained Souls and the Starless scourge had met their destruction. Despite the casualties of many starfighters and battlesuit pilots, Exodus High Command noted that the overall loss of life was significantly lower than anticipated.

An hour after the obliteration of the Acropolis and escape of the Bound One, the Exodus Armada began the taxing endeavor of handling the battle's aftermath.

Teams salvaged materials, patched holes, recovered overboard sailors, and pulled out pilots from wrecks.

Citadel Irkalla, baptized in the crucible of war, slowly started to unpack into a static installation. The Exodus Council decreed that it would recuperate in this star system for a week, harvesting parts from the defeated Thralled fleet and biometallic materials from Starless corpses.

The leaders of the armada stamped the operation as a resounding success.

However, such sentiment did not resonate with a select few.

With the influx of ninety-three malnourished people, including dozens in critical condition, the medical wing of the *Zolann'tono* worked overtime to care for these poor souls.

Some suffered afflictions deemed untreatable by the medical nanites due to their eldritch nature. In these cases, healers from the Eternal Choir flocked to their aid, singing hymns that obliterated the corruption. Once the patients were purged of evil, the singers handed these severely weakened patients back to the doctors, where they were placed in intensive care for further treatment.

As for the rest of the rescued, the physicians placed them in the medical ward, where they were slowly nursed back to strength under constant observation.

The same couldn't be said for one, who still teetered between life and death.

In the observation deck above the most sophisticated operating room available aboard the supercapital ship, three of Task Force Dagger's best waited with bated breath on the condition of Lady Nuwa Straise.

Jupiter stood beside Kelios, arms crossed and face scrunched in thought.

It eased his mind that the doctors had things in hand for the leader and the people they'd rescued, yet the twenty-one who had perished under the rubble of the temple, buried under the molten glass and smoldering corpse flesh, wrapped around his mind like a vice.

Among them had been two Daggers.

Lieutenant Sens Pos Lumi Dre. Callsign "Huggins."

Captain Mamarance la'Nel-Took. Callsign "Rook."

Jupiter clenched his fists at the thought of these two brave bastards who had willingly offered their lives in the heat of battle under his command in defense of the weak. Their deaths formed a permanent weight, a vicious scar on his soul.

He should have done more. Sacrificed more.

His thoughts turned to the remaining Poltergeists, and the question he asked himself repeatedly since. Why had these pieces of scrap survived where two of his finest and nineteen civilians didn't?

His rational, logical mind fought back, deeming such a situation unpreventable. His calculations whispered in his ears that it wasn't his fault, given the circumstances, that if he had done that, then this would have occurred—sacrifice for sacrifice, blood for blood.

Perhaps the outcome wasn't perfect, but it was far from the worst-case scenario.

That made it all the more distasteful in his mouth.

"What do I even write to their families?" Jupiter muttered his question to Kelios. "That's something a CO does, right? Tell people that someone they know and love died doing their duty under my command."

The medic tilted his head, humming in thought. "You fear you might say something disingenuous?"

Jupiter grimaced for a second before sighing wearily. "I don't know how. Huggins brought his younger brother with him. Rook's sons are here too. Both have—*had* family back on your side of the galaxy. Am I supposed to . . . I . . ." He trailed off.

"They're dead. Hell, it's just coming to me that . . . they're dead. Dead. And I can do nothing to fix that," Jupiter hissed in a whisper as he looked toward Kelios, gritting his teeth with a pleading gaze. "So, tell me . . . What can I do?"

Kelios looked at him without a smile or frown, mulling over his words. He then turned to him and gave Jupiter his answer.

"You do what you can," Kelios replied.

Jupiter blinked at the plain, simple answer. For a moment, he thought the Evorian was messing with him, until he saw the severe and calm expression on his face.

"Write about how Huggins used to wrap his arms around anything when he got drunk. Strong, real strong. Unbeatable in hand-to-hand combat. Mean right hook. Tended to be a bit too zealous in giving you a brotherly hug." Kelios rocked his jaw, chuckling. Then he paused.

"And when it mattered, he carried two people under his arms and took them to safety. Even when his gun got slashed in half, and his blade broke."

"He went down swinging," Jupiter finished.

Kelios nodded, then cocked his head to the side, looking at Jupiter with an angle. "What can you say about Captain Rook?"

Jupiter looked down, pausing to sift through his memories of the Bolud soldier during the few times they'd interacted over the past month.

He chuckled, recalling one of Rook's eccentricities. "Guy had zero sense of humor and took everything way too seriously. He thought a water bucket prank was some declaration of war and nearly tackled me to the ground. The dude was . . . a . . . well . . ."

"Rook was a brick wall," Kelios laughed.

Jupiter smirked. "That he was."

"He protected a kid," Kelios added.

"That he did."

Feeling lighter, Jupiter began to see hope at the end of his predicament, already forming paragraphs in his mind, ready to write page after page of his memories.

Kelios continued with his advice, patting Jupiter's shoulder. "You can keep the sordid details under wraps. Their families will know, of course, but they'll appreciate what matters. Huggins and Rook were people, with all their faults and quirks. People who stepped up in the end."

"That's all they need to hear?"

"That's all they need to hear," Kelios reassured him.

The Evorian's smile turned sad and sullen as his eyes glazed over. "You can't always save everyone, Commander."

Jupiter frowned, already knowing that horrible truth, but the experienced medic added something more, glancing his way with a bright laugh.

"But that doesn't mean you should stop trying."

The words pierced Jupiter's mind, embedding themselves deep into his psyche. The AI remained silent, repeating the words in his head like a mantra.

"Hey, Kel?"

"Hm?"

Jupiter smirked. "You're alright."

Kelios gasped dramatically, hand on his chest.

The sound of a body pressing against glass drew their attention, and they remembered the other person with them.

Jupiter stared at Captain Merina's shaking back. She flattened herself against the window, staring at the surgery happening below. He stepped forward, standing to the right of the Kalachian captain.

Kelios followed and stood to her left.

Jupiter looked down on the operating room as a trio of the best medical professionals worked to undo the cruelty inflicted upon the leader of the Seventeenth Expeditionary Fleet. Alongside them, Cantor Tendemone, Brother Volantesh, Sister Attou, and an observing Venus provided their song to heal the onset of Starless rot.

Countless devices and robotic surgical tools hovered in the air, waiting for the doctors and medical technicians to give them the order.

What the Thralled had done was indescribable, and only the eldritch machine connected with Lady Nuwa prevented her from succumbing to her torment, extending it even more.

He shook his head at the sight, wanting nothing more than to see her brought back to health, yet he wondered if such a thing was possible for traumas of the mind.

He'd yet to recover from his own near-death experience. But to be in her place, denied the chance to defy and resist? Jupiter could scarcely understand an inkling of such suffering.

"You still planning on staying a Dagger?" he asked softly to the shaking woman next to him. "Or are you going back to being her bodyguard?"

Merina refused to speak for a long minute, pressing her lips into a thin line as a range of emotions fluttered across her face. She furrowed her brow, clenching her fists as she whispered.

"I don't know . . ." she confessed with a hoarse throat, closing her eyes tightly. "I failed as her guard, her mentor. I can never forgive myself for this."

Jupiter nodded, having expected as much. "Take all the time you need. You don't have to worry about Bravo."

She didn't acknowledge his words, her eyes bloodshot and her face pale. The Kalachian captain had aged half a century before his eyes.

"Nuwa was like a daughter to me," Merina spoke. "Her . . . parents . . . certainly didn't think the same, sending her to this hell for her *Teirö*, curse them. She came to me as a child who didn't understand why this was happening to her. And she was supposed to lead an Expeditionary Fleet and care for the lives of countless people—the gall of that family.

"Maybe it would look too cruel if they left it at that. Oh, they gave her a competent staff, but they were all loyalists for the family, spies. No one cared for her. At best, they pitied her. And where are they now?"

Jupiter looked around, noting for the first time the absence of people like Captain-superior Melwin or any other high-ranking member of the Seventeenth. At the very least, those of Bravo from the same fleet had visited before Merina sent them off.

She scowled. "The lady is back. Their failure has been rectified and their honor restored. Now they wash their hands of her."

He said nothing, pursing his lips at the revelation.

"For six years . . . six years, I've shielded her. I took her under my fin. I led where she was supposed to and gave her the love her parents and family denied her." Merina palmed the glass, tears streaming down her face.

She clenched her fists, gritting her teeth. "I should have taught her to stand up for herself, taught her to lead, to fight, to pursue knowledge and the arts. Instead . . . instead, I babied her. I still see her as that child. My child."

"It's not your fault." Jupiter attempted to comfort her, but his words were brushed aside as she fell further into the deep end.

"If I knew what they'd do to her. I would have . . ." A sob racked the captain's body as her shoulders and back shook. "I would have killed her before they boarded our ship."

Jupiter shook his head, wondering if he would have done the same. He turned to her, touching her back to grab her attention. "She still needs you, Mer. She won't be fit to lead the Seventeenth any time soon. You have to stay strong; you have to, for her sake."

"*Sayanak . . . sayanak . . .* I'm so sorry . . ." Merina whispered her cry, knees failing her as she sank to the floor, blurry eyes still staring at the sight below.

Kelios reached out and held onto Jupiter's shoulders before he could continue trying to offer his support. He looked back at the medic, shaking his head and gently pulling Jupiter away. "She needs time."

Jupiter sighed, running his hand over his hair as he watched Merina break apart at the seams. He didn't think time would be enough for her.

They promptly and silently left the observation room and entered the hall. He wondered what to do next. His thoughts had just turned to leaving some food and drink for Merina when he felt an electric shock wash over him.

Jupiter and Kelios winced and shivered at the sudden fuzzy feeling.

"What the hell was—"

His wrist comms blasted with an urgent call. Jupiter grimaced at the bare contents.

"What is it?" Kelios asked with concern.

"Priority summons. Extremely urgent," Jupiter told him, clicking his teeth. "I need to go."

He turned to Kelios, glancing back at the door that led to the observation room. "Watch over her."

Kelios nodded. "I will."

Jupiter entered the War Room, noticing the presence of everyone that mattered. With the highest echelons of their armada assembled, Jupiter's thoughts scrambled to guess what news demanded such an audience.

"Jupiter, you're the last one. We'll begin this emergency meeting now," Andora spoke up, standing beside a seated Tov over at their dais.

He frowned, moving to his seat beside Mars, who looked grim and troubled. A few others wore similar expressions, tapping their fingers anxiously, brows twitching. The rest looked just as lost and confused as him, which sparked a flash of annoyance.

"Right, what's going on?" Jupiter asked, propping his boots on the table.

Andora frowned but nodded, clasping her hands as she addressed the room.

"To those unaware, our Starlight Beacons received a quantum transmission."

Jupiter and several others leaned forward, eyes wide in shock. In a micro-instant, discourse spread across the War Room, with people talking, shouting, and demanding questions over one another. Jupiter remained silent, mouth agape, as he stared at an increasingly frustrated Andora.

"Silence!"

Her shout echoed across the room and shook those present. The noise abated, and everyone readjusted themselves with various expressions.

"I will address your concerns. Firstly, the transmission didn't come from Legacy space."

That dampened people's expectations, hoping to have had a way to contact home. Interest replaced their hope as they leaned forward to listen intently.

"Secondly, the burst was so powerful that even our Beacons, which we thought useless in this interference storm, picked it up. We estimate that all Beacons across the Dead Zone have picked up this call," Andora continued, showing the devices' specs.

She then switched the visuals to a map of the galaxy, where two-thirds of it was shrouded in darkness. "As for its source . . ."

A bright light shone on the map, deep in the galactic center, eliciting various gasps as people recognized the storied star system and capital planet of the greatest superpower of their Federation.

"The call came from the Old Heartlands," Andora reported. "Dagatar Prime."

She sat down as the lights dimmed. "It's best if you all listen."

The galactic map faded, and an immense hologram emerged above the central table. Instantly, the audience gaped at the legendary figure featured in the message.

Although the hologram suffered from evident distortion and fuzz, no one could mistake the feline eyes, tall royal stature, verdant green skin, and bright red petal hair for anyone but the leader of the First Expeditionary Fleet.

The message played out, sound crackling and glitched.

"This is Crown . . . *fzzzt* . . . Anaria Moradal of the Dagat . . . *fzzzt* . . . First Expeditionary . . . *fzzzt* . . . Sending this message to all Starlight Beacons . . .

"Requesting immediate assistance . . . from all available . . . friendly forces . . . We are under siege by . . . less, and Thralled forces have . . . isolated my hunter squadrons . . . Grand Expedition is untenable . . . If you cannot return to Legacy space . . . proceed to Dagatar Prime . . ."

Jupiter's eyes widened at her call to draw in every Expeditionary Fleet. As he thought of the implications, the hologram grew unstable, and Anaria hissed with palpable frustration and concern.

"Forced to overload our Beacon . . . this final message . . . will send a data packet . . . our situation . . . is dire . . . the Dead Zone is against us . . ."

She gritted her needle-like teeth before squaring her shoulders, upholding her imperious and martial demeanor as she implored those listening.

"We . . . hold . . . long as possible . . . must regroup . . . survive . . . please . . . to anyone listening . . ."

Her eyes closed as she forcibly buried her usual arrogance, leaving everyone with her final two words before the hologram terminated.

"Help us."

ABOUT THE AUTHOR

Rolando G. Gironella III is the author of the science fiction series Amidst the Bones of Heroes, which was originally released on Royal Road. He is an avid fan of Warhammer 40,000, Star Wars, science fiction and fantasy, and dark media.

Podium

DISCOVER
STORIES UNBOUND

PodiumAudio.com

www.ingramcontent.com/pod-product-compliance
Lightning Source LLC
Chambersburg PA
CBHW030925120726
47906CB00002B/496